The Exemplary Novels of Cervantes

Miguel de Cervantes Saavedra

ISBN-13: 978-1523604319

ISBN-10: 152360431X

BOHN'S STANDARD LIBRARY.
THE EXEMPLARY NOVELS
OF
CERVANTES.
THE
EXEMPLARY NOVELS
OF
MIGUEL DE CERVANTES SAAVEDRA.

TRANSLATED FROM THE SPANISH
BY
WALTER K. KELLY.
LONDON: GEORGE BELL AND SONS, YORK STREET,
COVENT GARDEN.
1881.
LONDON:
PRINTED BY WILLIAM CLOWES AND SONS, LIMITED,
STAMFORD STREET AND CHARING CROSS.

PREFACE.

It seems to be generally admitted that in rendering the title of a book from one language into another, the form of the original should be retained, even at the cost of some deviation from ordinary usage. Cicero's work De Officiis is never spoken of as a treatise on Moral Duties, but as Cicero's Offices. Upon the same principle we have not entitled the following collection of tales, Instructive or Moral; though it is in this sense that the author applied to them the epithet exemplares, as he states distinctly in his preface. The Spanish word exemplo, from the time of the archpriest of Hita and Don Juan Manuel, has had the meaning of instruction, or instructive story.

The "Novelas Exemplares" were first published in 1613, three years before the death of Cervantes. They are all original, and have the air of being drawn from his personal experience and observation. Ticknor, in his "History of Spanish Literature," says of them, and of the "Impertinent Curiosity," inserted in the first part of Don Quixote:—

"Their value is different, for they are written with different views, and in a variety of style greater than he has elsewhere shown; but most of them contain touches of what is peculiar in his talent, and are full of that rich eloquence and of those pleasing descriptions of natural scenery which always flow so easily from his pen. They have little in common with the graceful story-telling spirit of Boccaccio and his followers, and still less with the strictly practical tone of Don Juan Manuel's tales; nor, on the other hand, do they approach, except in the case of the 'Impertinent Curiosity,' the class of short novels which have been frequent in other countries within the last century. The more, therefore, we examine them, the more we shall find that they are original in their composition and general tone, and that they are strongly marked with the original genius of their author, as well as with the more peculiar traits of the national character,—the ground, no doubt, on which they have always been favourites at home, and less valued than they deserve to be abroad. As works of invention, they rank, among their author's productions, next after Don Quixote; in correctness and grace of style they stand before it.... They are all fresh from the racy soil of the national character, as that character is found in Andalusia, and are written with an idiomatic richness, a spirit, and a grace, which, though they are the oldest tales of their class in Spain, have left them ever since without successful rivals."

The first three tales in this volume have merely undergone the revision of the editor, having been translated by another before he was engaged on the work. For the rest he alone is responsible.

W.K.K.

DEDICATION

TO DON PEDRO FERNANDEZ DE CASTRO, COUNT OF LEMOS, ANDRADE, AND VILLALBA, &c.

Those who dedicate their works to some prince commonly fall into two errors. The first is, that in their dedicatory epistle, which ought to be brief and succinct, they dilate very complacently, whether moved by truth or flattery, on the deeds not only of their fathers and forefathers, but also of all their relations, friends, and benefactors. The second is, that they tell their patron they place their works under his protection and safeguard, in order that malicious and captious tongues may not presume to cavil and carp at them. For myself, shunning these two faults, I here pass over in silence the grandeur and titles of your excellency's ancient and royal house, and your infinite virtues both natural and acquired, leaving it to some new Phidias and Lysippus to engrave and sculpture them in marble and bronze, that they may rival time in duration. Neither do I supplicate your Excellency to take this book under your protection, for I know, that if it is not a good one, though I should put it under the wings of Astolfo's hippogrif, or beneath the club of Hercules, the Zoili, the cynics, the Aretinos, and the bores, will not abstain from abusing it, out of respect for anyone. I only beg your Excellency to observe that I present to you, without more words, thirteen tales,[1] which, had they not been wrought in the laboratory of my own brains, might presume to stand beside the best. Such as they are, there they go, leaving me here rejoiced at the thought of manifesting, in some degree, the desire I feel to serve your Excellency as my true lord and benefactor. Our Lord preserve, &c.

Your Excellency's servant,
MIGUEL DE CERVANTES SAAVEDRA.
MADRID, 13th of July, 1613.

[1] There are but twelve of them. Possibly when Cervantes wrote this dedication he intended to include "El Curioso Impertinente," which occurs in chapters xxxiii.-xxxv. of the first part of "Don Quixote."

AUTHOR'S PREFACE.

I wish it were possible, dear reader, to dispense with writing this preface; for that which I put at the beginning of my "Don Quixote" did not turn out so well for me as to give me any inclination to write another. The fault lies with a friend of mine—one of the many I have made in the course of my life with my heart rather than my head. This friend might well have caused my portrait, which the famous Don Juan de Jauregui would have given him, to be engraved and put in the first page of this book, according to custom. By that means he would have gratified my ambition and the wishes of several persons, who would like to know what sort of face and figure has he who makes bold to come before the world with so many works of his own invention. My friend might have written under the portrait—"This person whom you see here, with an oval visage, chestnut hair, smooth open forehead, lively eyes, a hooked but well-proportioned nose, & silvery beard that twenty years ago was golden, large moustaches, a small mouth, teeth not much to speak of, for he has but six, in bad condition and worse placed, no two of them corresponding to each other, a figure midway between the two extremes, neither tall nor short, a vivid complexion, rather fair than dark, somewhat stooped in the shoulders, and not very lightfooted: this, I say, is the author of 'Galatea,' 'Don Quixote de la Mancha,' 'The Journey to Parnassus,' which he wrote in imitation of Cesare Caporali Perusino, and other works which are current among the public, and perhaps without the author's name. He is commonly called MIGUEL DE CERVANTES SAAVEDRA. He was for many years a soldier, and for five years and a half in captivity, where he learned to have patience in adversity. He lost his left hand by a musket-shot in the battle of Lepanto: and ugly as this wound may appear, he regards it as beautiful, having received it on the most memorable and sublime occasion which past times have over seen, or future times can hope to equal, fighting under the victorious banners of the son of that thunderbolt of war, Charles V., of blessed memory." Should the friend of whom I complain have had nothing more to say of me than this, I would myself have composed a couple of dozen of eulogiums, and communicated them to him in secret, thereby to extend my fame and exalt the credit of my genius; for it would be absurd to expect the exact truth in such matters. We know well that neither praise nor abuse is meted out with strict accuracy.

However, since this opportunity is lost, and I am left in the lurch without a portrait, I must have recourse to my own tongue, which, for all its stammering, may do well enough to state some truths that are tolerably self-evident. I assure you then, dear reader, that you can by no means make a fricassee of these tales which I here present to you, for they have neither legs, head, bowels, nor anything of the sort; I mean that the amorous intrigues you will find in some of them, are so decorous, so measured, and so conformable to reason and Christian propriety, that they are incapable of exciting any impure thoughts in him who reads them with or without caution.

I have called them exemplary, because if you rightly consider them, there is not one of them from which you may not draw some useful example; and were I not afraid of being too prolix, I might show you what savoury and wholesome fruit might be extracted from them, collectively and severally.

My intention has been to set up, in the midst of our community, a billiard-table, at which every one may amuse himself without hurt to body and soul; for innocent recreations do good rather than harm. One cannot be always at church, or always saying one's prayers, or always engaged in one's business, however important it may be; there are hours for recreation when the wearied mind should take repose. It is to this end that alleys of trees are planted to walk in, waters are conveyed from remote fountains, hills are levelled, and gardens are cultivated with such care. One thing I boldly declare: could I by any means suppose that these novels could excite any bad thought or desire in those who read them, I would rather cut off the hand with which I write them, than give them to the public. I am at an age when it does not become me to trifle with the life to come, for I am upwards of sixty-four.

My genius and my inclination prompt me to this kind of writing; the more so as I consider (and with truth) that I am the first who has written novels in the Spanish language, though many have hitherto appeared among us, all of them translated from foreign authors. But these are my own, neither imitated nor stolen from anyone; my genius has engendered them, my pen has brought them forth, and they are growing up in the arms of the press. After them, should my life be spared, I will present to you the Adventures of Persiles, a book which ventures to compete with Heliodorus. But previously you shall see, and that before long, the continuation of the exploits of Don Quixote and the humours of Sancho Panza; and then the Weeks of the Garden. This is promising largely for one of my feeble powers; but who can curb his desires? I only beg you to remark that since I have had the boldness to address these novels to the great Count of Lemos, they must contain some hidden mystery which exalts their merit.

I have no more to say, so pray God to keep you, and give me patience to bear all the ill that will be spoken of me by more than one subtle and starched critic. Vale.

Don Antonio de Isunza and Don Juan de Gamboa, gentlemen of high birth and excellent sense, both of the same age, and very intimate friends, being students together at Salamanca, determined to abandon their studies and proceed to Flanders. To this resolution they were incited by the fervour of youth, their desire to see the world, and their conviction that the profession of arms, so becoming to all, is more particularly suitable to men of illustrious race.

But they did not reach Flanders until peace was restored, or at least on the point of being concluded; and at Antwerp they received letters from their parents, wherein the latter expressed the great displeasure caused them by their sons having left their studies without informing them of their intention, which if they had done, the proper measures might have been taken for their making the journey in a manner befitting their birth and station.

Unwilling to give further dissatisfaction to their parents, the young men resolved to return to Spain, the rather as there was now nothing to be done in Flanders. But before doing so they determined to visit all the most renowned cities of Italy; and having seen the greater part of them, they were so much attracted by the noble university of Bologna, that they resolved to remain there and complete the studies abandoned at Salamanca.

They imparted their intentions to their parents, who testified their entire approbation by the magnificence with which they provided their sons with every thing proper to their rank, to the end that, in their manner of living, they might show who they were, and of what house they were born. From the first day, therefore, that the young men visited the schools, all perceived them to be gallant, sensible, and well-bred gentlemen.

Don Antonio was at this time in his twenty-fourth year, and Don Juan had not passed his twenty-sixth. This fair period of life they adorned by various good qualities; they were handsome, brave, of good address, and well versed in music and poetry; in a word, they were endowed with such advantages as caused them to be much sought and greatly beloved by all who knew them. They soon had numerous friends, not only among the many Spaniards belonging to the university,[2] but also among people of the city, and of other nations, to all of whom they proved themselves courteous, liberal, and wholly free from that arrogance which is said to be too often exhibited by Spaniards.

Being young, and of joyous temperament, Don Juan and Don Antonio did not fail to give their attention to the beauties of the city. Many there were indeed in Bologna, both married and unmarried, remarkable as well for their virtues as their charms; but among them all there was none who surpassed the Signora Cornelia Bentivoglia, of that old and illustrious family of the Bentivogli, who were at one time lords of Bologna.

Cornelia was beautiful to a marvel; she had been left under the guardianship of her brother Lorenzo Bentivoglio, a brave and honourable gentleman. They were orphans, but inheritors of considerable wealth—and wealth is a great alleviation of the evils of the orphan state. Cornelia lived in complete seclusion, and her brother guarded her with unwearied solicitude. The lady neither showed herself on any occasion, nor would her brother consent that any one should see her; but this very fact inspired Don Juan and Don Antonio with the most lively desire to behold her face, were it only at church. Yet all the pains they took for that purpose proved vain, and the wishes they had felt on the subject gradually diminished, as the attempt appeared more and more hopeless. Thus, devoted to their studies, and varying these with such amusements as are permitted to their age, the young men passed a life as cheerful as it was honourable, rarely going out at night, but when they did so, it was always together and well armed.

One evening, however, when Don Juan was preparing to go out, Don Antonio expressed his desire to remain at home for a short time, to repeat certain orisons: but he requested Don Juan to go without him, and promised to follow him.

"Why should I go out to wait for you?" said Don Juan. "I will stay; if you do not go out at all to-night, it will be of very little consequence." "By no means shall you stay," returned Don Antonio: "go and take the air; I will be with you almost immediately, if you take the usual way."

"Well, do as you please," said Don Juan: "if you come you will find me on our usual beat." With these words Don Juan left the house.

The night was dark, and the hour about eleven. Don Juan passed through two or three streets, but finding himself alone, and with no one to speak to, he determined to return home. He began to retrace his steps accordingly; and was passing through a street, the houses of which had marble porticoes, when he heard some one call out, "Hist! hist!" from one of the doors. The darkness of the night, and the shadow cast by the colonnade, did not permit him to see the whisperer; but he stopped at once, and listened attentively. He saw a door partially opened, approached it, and heard these words uttered in a low voice, "Is it you, Fabio?" Don Juan, on the spur of the moment, replied, "Yes!" "Take it, then," returned the voice, "take it, and place it in security; but return instantly, for the matter presses." Don Juan put out his hand in the dark, and encountered a packet. Proceeding to take hold of it, he found that it required both hands; instinctively he extended the second, but had scarcely done so before the portal was closed, and he found himself again alone in the street, loaded with, he knew not what.

Presently the cry of an infant, and, as it seemed, but newly born, smote his ears, filling him with confusion and amazement, for he knew not what next to do, or how to proceed in so strange a case. If he knocked at the door he was almost certain to endanger the mother of the infant; and if he left his burthen there, he must imperil the life of the babe itself. But if he took it home he should as little know what to do with it, nor was he acquainted with any one in the city to whom he could entrust the care of the child; yet remembering that he had been required to come back quickly, after placing his charge in safety, he determined to take the infant home, leave it in the hands of his old housekeeper, and return to see if his aid was needed in any way, since he perceived clearly that the person who had been expected to come for the child had not arrived, and the latter had been given to himself in mistake. With this determination, Don Juan soon reached his home; but found that Antonio had already left it. He then went to his chamber, and calling the housekeeper, uncovered the infant, which was one of the most beautiful ever seen; whilst, as the good woman remarked, the elegance of the clothes in which the little creature was wrapped, proved him—for it was a boy—to be the son of rich parents.

"You must, now," said Don Juan to his housekeeper, "find some one to nurse this infant; but first of all take away these rich coverings, and put on him others of the plainest kind. Having done that, you must carry the babe, without a moment's delay, to the house of a midwife, for there it is that you will be most likely to find all that is requisite in such a case. Take money to pay what may be needful, and give the child such parents as you please, for I desire to hide the truth, and not let the manner in which I became possessed of it be known." The woman promised that she would obey him in every point; and Don Juan returned in all haste to the street, to see whether he should receive another mysterious call. But just before he arrived at the house whence the infant had been delivered to him, the clash of swords struck his ear, the sound being as that of several persons engaged in strife. He listened carefully, but could hear no word; the combat was carried on in total silence; but the sparks cast up by the swords as they struck against the stones, enabled him to perceive that one man was defending himself against several assailants; and he was confirmed in this belief by an exclamation which proceeded at length from the last person attacked. "Ah, traitors! you are many and I am but one, yet your baseness shall not avail you."

Hearing and seeing this, Don Juan, listening only to the impulses of his brave heart, sprang to the side of the person assailed, and opposing the buckler he carried on his arm to the swords of the adversaries, drew his own, and speaking in Italian that he might not be known as a Spaniard, he said— "Fear not, Signor, help has arrived that will not fail you while life holds; lay on well, for traitors are worth but little however many there may be." To this, one of the assailants made answer—"You lie; there are no traitors here. He who seeks to recover his lost honour is no traitor, and is permitted to avail himself of every advantage."

No more was said on either side, for the impetuosity of the assailants, who, as Don Juan thought, amounted to not less than six, left no opportunity for further words. They pressed his companion, meanwhile, very closely; and two of them giving him each a thrust at the same time with the point of their swords, he fell to the earth. Don Juan believed they had killed him; he threw himself upon the adversaries, nevertheless, and with a shower of cuts and thrusts, dealt with extraordinary rapidity, caused them to give way for several paces. But all his efforts must needs have been vain for the defence of the fallen man, had not Fortune aided him, by making the neighbours come with lights to their windows and shout for the watch, whereupon the assailants ran off and left the street clear.

The fallen man was meanwhile beginning to move; for the strokes he had received, having encountered a breastplate as hard as adamant, had only stunned, but not wounded him.

Now, Don Juan's hat had been knocked off in the fray, and thinking he had picked it up, he had in fact put on that of another person, without perceiving it to be other than his own. The gentleman whom he had assisted now approached Don Juan, and accosted him as follows:—"Signor Cavalier, whoever you may be, I confess that I owe you my life, and I am bound to employ it, with all I have or can command, in your service: do me the favour to tell me who you are, that I may know to whom my gratitude is due."

"Signor," replied Don Juan, "that I may not seem discourteous, and in compliance with your request, although I am wholly disinterested in what I have done, you shall know that I am a Spanish gentleman, and a student in this city; if you desire to hear my name I will tell you, rather lest you should have some future occasion for my services than for any other motive, that I am called Don Juan de Gamboa."

"You have done me a singular service, Signor Don Juan de Gamboa," replied the gentleman who had fallen, "but I will not tell you who I am, nor my name, which I desire that you should learn from others rather than from myself; yet I will take care that you be soon informed respecting these things."

Don Juan then inquired of the stranger if he were wounded, observing, that he had seen him receive two furious lunges in the breast; but the other replied that he was unhurt; adding, that next to God, a famous plastron that he wore had defended him against the blows he had received, though his enemies would certainly have finished him had Don Juan not come to his aid.

While thus discoursing, they beheld a body of men advancing towards them; and Don Juan exclaimed—"If these are enemies, Signor, let us hasten to put ourselves on our guard, and use our hands as men of our condition should do."

"They are not enemies, so far as I can judge," replied the stranger. "The men who are now coming towards us are friends."

And this was the truth; the persons approaching, of whom there were eight, surrounded the unknown cavalier, with whom they exchanged a few words, but in so low a tone that Don Juan could not hear the purport. The gentleman then turned to Don Juan and said—"If these friends had not arrived I should certainly not have left your company, Signor Don Juan, until you had seen me in some place of safety; but as things are, I beg you now, with all kindness, to retire and leave me in this place, where it is of great importance that I should remain." Speaking thus, the stranger carried his hand to his head, but finding that he was without a hat, he turned towards the persons who had joined him, desiring them to give him one, and saying that his own had fallen. He had no sooner spoken than Don Juan presented him with that which he had himself just picked up, and which he had discovered to be not his own. The stranger having felt the hat, returned it to Don Juan, saying that it was not his, and adding, "On your life, Signor Don Juan, keep this hat as a trophy of this affray, for I believe it to be one that is not unknown."

The persons around then gave the stranger another hat, and Don Juan, after exchanging a few brief compliments with his companion, left him, in compliance with his desire, without knowing who he was: he then returned home, not daring at that moment to approach the door whence he had received the newly-born infant, because the whole neighbourhood had been aroused, and was in movement.

Now it chanced that as Don Juan was returning to his abode, he met his comrade Don Antonio de Isunza; and the latter no sooner recognised him in the darkness, than he exclaimed, "Turn about, Don Juan, and walk with me to the end of the street; I have something to tell you, and as we go along will relate a story such as you have never heard before in your life."

"I also have one of the same kind to tell you," returned Don Juan, "but let us go up the street as you say, and do you first relate your story." Don Antonio thereupon walked forward, and began as follows:—"You must know that in little less than an hour after you had left the house, I left it also, to go in search of you, but I had not gone thirty paces from this place when I saw before me a black mass, which I soon perceived to be a person advancing in great haste. As the figure approached nearer, I perceived it to be that of a woman, wrapped in a very wide mantle, and who, in a voice interrupted by sobs and sighs, addressed me thus, 'Are you, sir, a stranger, or one of the city?' 'I am a stranger,' I replied, 'and a Spaniard.' 'Thanks be to God!' she exclaimed, 'he will not have me die without the sacraments.' 'Are you then wounded, madam?' continued I, 'or attacked by some mortal malady?' 'It may well happen that the malady from which I suffer may prove mortal, if I do not soon receive aid,' returned the lady, 'wherefore, by the courtesy which is ever found among those of your nation, I entreat you, Signor Spaniard, take me from these streets, and lead me to your dwelling with all the speed you may; there, if you wish it, you shall know the cause of my sufferings, and who I am, even though it should cost me my reputation to make myself known.'

"Hearing this," continued Don Antonio, "and seeing that the lady was in a strait which permitted no delay, I said nothing more, but offering her my hand, I conducted her by the by-streets to our house. Our page, Santisteban, opened the door, but, commanding him to retire, I led the lady in without permitting him to see her, and took her into my room, where she had no sooner entered than she fell fainting on my bed. Approaching to assist her, I removed the mantle which had hitherto concealed her face, and discovered the most astonishing loveliness that human eyes ever beheld. She may be about eighteen years old, as I should suppose, but rather less than more. Bewildered for a moment at the sight of so much beauty, I remained as one stupified, but recollecting myself, I hastened to throw water on her face, and, with a pitiable sigh, she recovered consciousness.

"The first word she uttered was the question, 'Do you know me, Signor?' I replied, 'No, lady! I have not been so fortunate as ever before to have seen so much beauty.' 'Unhappy is she,' returned the lady, 'to whom heaven has given it for her misfortune. But, Signor, this is not the time to praise my beauty, but to mourn my distress. By all that you most revere, I entreat you to leave me shut up here, and let no one behold me, while you return in all haste to the place where you found me, and see if there be any persons fighting there. Yet do not take part either with one side or the other. Only separate the combatants, for whatever injury may happen to either, must needs be to the increase of my own misfortunes.' I then left her as she desired," continued Don Antonio, "and am now going to put an end to any quarrel which may arise, as the lady has commanded me."

"Have you anything more to say?" inquired Don Juan.

"Do you think I have not said enough," answered Don Antonio, "since I have told you that I have now in my chamber, and hold under my key, the most wonderful beauty that human eyes have ever beheld."

"The adventure is a strange one, without doubt," replied Don Juan, "but listen to mine;" and he instantly related to his friend all that had happened to him. He told how the newly-born infant was then in their house, and in the care of their housekeeper, with the orders he had given as to changing its rich habits for others less remarkable, and for procuring a nurse from the nearest midwife, to meet the present necessity. "As to the combat you come in quest of," he added, "that is already ended, and peace is made." Don Juan further related that he had himself taken part in the strife; and concluded by remarking, that he believed those whom he had found engaged were all persons of high quality, as well as great courage.

Each of the Spaniards was much surprised at the adventure of the other, and they instantly returned to the house to see what the lady shut up there might require. On the way, Don Antonio told Don Juan that he had promised the unknown not to suffer any one to see her; assuring her that he only would enter the room, until she should herself permit the approach of others.

"I shall nevertheless do my best to see her," replied Don Juan; "after what you have said of her beauty, I cannot but desire to do so, and shall contrive some means for effecting it."

Saying this they arrived at their house, when one of their three pages, bringing lights, Don Antonio cast his eyes on the hat worn by Don Juan, and perceived that it was glittering with diamonds. Don Juan took it off, and then saw that the lustre of which his companion spoke, proceeded from a very rich band formed of large brilliants. In great surprise, the friends examined the ornament, and concluded that if all the diamonds were as precious as they appeared to be, the hat must be worth more than two thousand ducats. They thus became confirmed in the conviction entertained by Don Juan, that the persons engaged in the combat were of high quality, especially the gentleman whose part he had taken, and who, as he now recollected, when bidding him take the hat, and keep it, had remarked that it was not unknown.

The young men then commanded their pages to retire, and Don Antonio, opening the door of his room, found the lady seated on his bed, leaning her cheek on her hand, and weeping piteously. Don Juan also having approached the door, the splendour of the diamonds caught the eye of the weeping lady, and she exclaimed, "Enter, my lord duke, enter! Why afford me in such scanty measure the happiness of seeing you; enter at once, I beseech you."

"Signora," replied Don Antonio, "there is no duke here who is declining to see you."

"How, no duke!" she exclaimed. "He whom I have just seen is the Duke of Ferrara; the rich decoration of his hat does not permit him to conceal himself."

"Of a truth, Signora, he who wears the hat you speak of is no duke; and if you please to undeceive yourself by seeing that person, you have but to give your permission, and he shall enter."

"Let him do so," said the lady; "although, if he be not the duke, my misfortune will be all the greater."

Don Juan had heard all this, and now finding that he was invited to enter, he walked into the apartment with his hat in his hand; but he had no sooner placed himself before the lady than she, seeing he was not the person she had supposed, began to exclaim, in a troubled voice and with broken words, "Ah! miserable creature that I am, tell me, Signor—tell me at once, without keeping me in suspense, what do you know of him who owned that sombrero? How is it that he no longer has it, and how did it come into your possession? Does he still live, or is this the token that he sends me of his death? Oh! my beloved, what misery is this! I see the jewels that were thine. I see myself shut up here without the light of thy presence. I am in the power of strangers; and if I did not know that they were Spaniards and gentlemen, the fear of that disgrace by which I am threatened would already have finished my life."

"Calm yourself, madam," replied Don Juan, "for the master of this sombrero is not dead, nor are you in a place where any increase to your misfortunes is to be dreaded. We think only of serving you, so far as our means will permit, even to the exposing our lives for your defence and succour. It would ill become us to suffer that the trust you have in the faith of Spaniards should be vain; and since we are Spaniards, and of good quality—for here that assertion, which might otherwise appear arrogant, becomes needful—be assured that you will receive all the respect which is your due."

"I believe you," replied the lady; "but, nevertheless, tell me, I pray you, how this rich sombrero came into your possession, and where is its owner? who is no less a personage than Alfonso d'Este, Duke of Ferrara."

Then Don Juan, that he might not keep the lady longer in suspense, related to her how he had found the hat in the midst of a combat, in which he had taken the part of a gentleman, who, from what she had said, he could not now doubt to be the Duke of Ferrara. He further told her how, having lost his own hat in the strife, the gentleman had bidden him keep the one he had picked up, and which belonged, as he said, to a person not unknown; that neither the cavalier nor himself had received any wound; and that, finally, certain friends or servants of the former had arrived, when he who was now believed to be the duke had requested Don Juan to leave him in that place, where he desired for certain reasons to remain.

"This, madam," concluded Don Juan, "is the whole history of the manner in which the hat came into my possession; and for its master, whom you suppose to be the Duke of Ferrara, it is not an hour since I left him in perfect safety. Let this true narration suffice to console you, since you are anxious to be assured that the Duke is unhurt."

To this the lady made answer, "That you, gentlemen, may know how much reason I have to inquire for the duke, and whether I need be anxious for his safety, listen in your turn with attention, and I will relate what I know not yet if I must call my unhappy history."

While these things were passing, the housekeeper of Don Antonio and Don Juan was occupied with the infant, whose mouth she had moistened with honey, and whose rich habits she was changing for clothes of a very humble character. When that was done, she was about to carry the babe to the house of the midwife, as Don Juan had recommended, but as she was passing with it before the door of the room wherein the lady was about to commence her history, the little creature began to cry aloud, insomuch that the lady heard it. She instantly rose to her feet, and set herself to listen, when the plaints of the infant arrived more distinctly to her ear.

"What child is this, gentlemen?" said she, "for it appears to be but just born."

Don Juan replied, "It is a little fellow who has been laid at the door of our house to-night, and our servant is about to seek some one who will nurse it."

"Let them bring it to me, for the love of God!" exclaimed the lady, "for I will offer that charity to the child of others, since it has not pleased Heaven that I should be permitted to nourish my own."

Don Juan then called the housekeeper, and taking the infant from her arms he placed it in those of the lady, saying, "Behold, madam, this is the present that has been made to us to-night, and it is not the first of the kind that we have received, since but few months pass wherein we do not find such God-sends hooked on to the hinges of our doors."

The lady had meanwhile taken the infant into her arms, and looked attentively at its face, but remarking the poverty of its clothing, which was, nevertheless, extremely clean, she could not restrain her tears. She cast the kerchief which she had worn around her head over her bosom, that she might succour the infant with decency, and bending her face over that of the child, she remained long without raising her head, while her eyes rained torrents of tears on the little creature she was nursing.

The babe was eager to be fed, but finding that it could not obtain the nourishment it sought, the lady returned the babe to Don Juan, saying, "I have vainly desired to be charitable to this deserted infant, and have but shown that I am new to such matters. Let your servants put a little honey on the lips of the child, but do not suffer them to carry it through the streets at such an hour; bid them wait until the day breaks, and let the babe be once more brought to me before they take it away, for I find a great consolation in the sight of it."

Don Juan then restored the infant to the housekeeper, bidding her take the best care she could of it until daybreak, commanding that the rich clothes it had first worn should be put on it again, and directing her not to take it from the house until he had seen it once more. That done, he returned to the room; and the two friends being again alone with the beautiful lady, she said, "If you desire that I should relate my story, you must first give me something that may restore my strength, for I feel in much need of it." Don Antonio flew to the beaufet for some conserves, of which the lady ate a little; and having drunk a glass of water, and feeling somewhat refreshed, she said, "Sit down, Signors, and listen to my story."

The gentlemen seated themselves accordingly, and she, arranging herself on the bed, and covering her person with the folds of her mantle, suffered the veil which she had kept about her head to fall on her shoulders, thus giving her face to view, and exhibiting in it a lustre equal to that of the moon, rather of the sun itself, when displayed in all its splendour. Liquid pearls fell from her eyes, which she endeavoured to dry with a kerchief of extraordinary delicacy, and with hands so white that he must have had much judgment in colour who could have found a difference between them and the cambric. Finally, after many a sigh and many an effort to calm herself, with a feeble and trembling voice, she said—

"I, Signors, am she of whom you have doubtless heard mention in this city, since, such as it is, there are few tongues that do not publish the fame of my beauty. I am Cornelia Bentivoglio, sister of Lorenzo Bentivoglio; and, in saying this, I have perhaps affirmed two acknowledged truths,—the one my nobility, and the other my beauty. At a very early age I was left an orphan to the care of my brother, who was most sedulous in watching over me, even from my childhood, although he reposed more confidence in my sentiments of honour than in the guards he had placed around me. In short, kept thus between walls and in perfect solitude, having no other company than that of my attendants, I grew to womanhood, and with me grew the reputation of my loveliness, bruited abroad by the servants of my house, and by such as had been admitted to my privacy, as also by a portrait which my brother had caused to be taken by a famous painter, to the end, as he said, that the world might not be wholly deprived of my features, in the event of my being early summoned by Heaven to a better life.

"All this might have ended well, had it not chanced that the Duke of Ferrara consented to act as sponsor at the nuptials of one of my cousins; when my brother permitted me to be present at the ceremony, that we might do the greater honour to our kinswoman. There I saw and was seen; there, as I believe, hearts were subjugated, and the will of the beholders rendered subservient; there I felt the pleasure received from praise, even when bestowed by flattering tongues; and, finally, I there beheld the duke, and was seen by him; in a word, it is in consequence of this meeting that you see me here.

"I will not relate to you, Signors (for that would needlessly protract my story), the various stratagems and contrivances by which the duke and myself, at the end of two years, were at length enabled to bring about that union, our desire for which had received birth at those nuptials. Neither guards, nor seclusion, nor remonstrances, nor human diligence of any kind, sufficed to prevent it, and we were finally made one; for without the sanction due to my honour, Alfonso would certainly not have prevailed. I would fain have had him publicly demand my hand from my brother, who would not have refused it; nor would the duke have had to excuse himself before the world as to any inequality in our marriage, since the race of the Bentivogli is in no manner inferior to that of Este; but the reasons which he gave for not doing as I wished appeared to me sufficient, and I suffered them to prevail.

"The visits of the duke were made through the intervention of a servant, over whom his gifts had more influence than was consistent with the confidence reposed in her by my brother. After a time I perceived that I was about to become a mother, and feigning illness and low spirits, I prevailed on Lorenzo to permit me to visit the cousin at whose marriage it was that I first saw the duke; I then apprised the latter of my situation, letting him also know the danger in which my life was placed from that suspicion of the truth which I could not but fear that Lorenzo must eventually entertain.

"It was then agreed between us, that when the time for my travail drew near, the duke should come, with certain of his friends, and take me to Ferrara, where our marriage should be publicly celebrated. This was the night on which I was to have departed, and I was waiting the arrival of Alfonso, when I heard my brother pass the door with several other persons, all armed, as I could hear, by the noise of their weapons. The terror caused by this event was such as to occasion the premature birth of my infant, a son, whom the waiting-woman, my confidant, who had made all ready for his reception, wrapped at once in the clothes we had provided, and gave at the street-door, as she told me, to a servant of the duke. Soon afterwards, taking such measures as I could under circumstances so pressing, and hastened by the fear of my brother, I also left the house, hoping to find the duke awaiting me in the street. I ought not to have gone forth until he had come to the door; but the armed band of my brother, whose sword I felt at my throat, had caused me such terror that I was not in a state to reflect. Almost out of my senses I came forth, as you behold me; and what has since happened you know. I am here, it is true, without my husband, and without my son; yet I return thanks to Heaven which has led me into your hands—for from you I promise myself all that may be expected from Spanish courtesy, reinforced, as it cannot but be in your persons, by the nobility of your race."

Having said this, the lady fell back on the bed, and the two friends hastened to her assistance, fearing she had again fainted. But they found this not to be the case; she was only weeping bitterly. Wherefore Don Juan said to her, "If up to the present moment, beautiful lady, my companion Don Antonio, and I, have felt pity and regret for you as being a woman, still more shall we now do so, knowing your quality; since compassion and grief are changed into the positive obligation and duty of serving and aiding you. Take courage, and do not be dismayed; for little as you are formed to endure such trials, so much the more will you prove yourself to be the exalted person you are, as your patience and fortitude enable you to rise above your sorrows. Believe me, Signora, I am persuaded that these extraordinary events are about to have a fortunate conclusion; for Heaven can never permit so much beauty to endure permanent sorrow, nor suffer your chaste purposes to be frustrated. Go now to bed, Signora, and take that care of your health of which you have so much need; there shall presently come to wait on you a servant of ours, in whom you may confide as in ourselves, for she will maintain silence respecting your misfortunes with no less discretion than she will attend to all your necessities."

"The condition in which I find myself," replied the lady, "might compel me to the adoption of more difficult measures than those you advise. Let this woman come, Signors; presented to me by you, she cannot fail to be good and serviceable; but I beseech you let no other living being see me."

"So shall it be," replied Don Antonio; and the two friends withdrew, leaving Cornelia alone.

Don Juan then commanded the housekeeper to enter the room, taking with her the infant, whose rich habits she had already replaced. The woman did as she was ordered, having been previously told what she should reply to the questions of the Signora respecting the infant she bore in her arms Seeing her come in, Cornelia instantly said, "You come in good time, my friend; give me that infant, and place the light near me."

The servant obeyed; and, taking the babe in her arms, Cornelia instantly began to tremble, gazed at him intently, and cried out in haste, "Tell me, good woman, is this child the same that you brought me a short time since?" "It is the same, Signora," replied the woman. "How is it, then, that his clothing is so different? Certainly, dame housekeeper, either these are other wrappings, or the infant is not the same." "It may all be as you say," began the old woman. "All as I say!" interrupted Cornelia, "how and what is this? I conjure you, friend, by all you most value, to tell me whence you received these rich clothes; for my heart seems to be bursting in my bosom! Tell me the cause of this change; for you must know that these things belong to me, if my sight do not deceive me, and my memory have not failed. In these robes, or some like them, I entrusted to a servant of mine the treasured jewel of my soul! Who has taken them from him? Ah, miserable creature that I am! who has brought these things here? Oh, unhappy and woeful day!"

Don Juan and Don Antonio, who were listening to all this, could not suffer the matter to go further, nor would they permit the exchange of the infant's dress to trouble the poor lady any longer. They therefore entered the room, and Don Juan said, "This infant and its wrappings are yours, Signora;" and immediately he related from point to point how the matter had happened. He told Cornelia that he was himself the person to whom the waiting woman had given the child, and how he had brought it home, with the orders he had given to the housekeeper respecting its change of clothes, and his motives for doing so. He added that, from the moment when she had spoken of her own infant, he had felt certain that this was no other than her son; and if he had not told her so at once, that was because he feared the effects of too much gladness, coming immediately after the heavy grief which her trials had caused her.

The tears of joy then shed by Cornelia were many and long-continued; infinite were the acknowledgments she offered to Heaven, innumerable the kisses she lavished on her son, and profuse the thanks which she offered from her heart to the two friends, whom she called her guardian angels on earth, with other names, which gave abundant proof of her gratitude. They soon afterwards left the lady with their housekeeper, whom they enjoined to attend her well, and do her all the service possible—having made known to the woman the position in which Cornelia found herself, to the end that she might take all necessary precautions, the nature of which, she, being a woman, would know much better than they could do. They then went to rest for the little that remained of the night, intending to enter Cornelia's apartment no more, unless summoned by herself, or called thither by some pressing need.

The day having dawned, the housekeeper went to fetch a woman, who agreed to nurse the infant in silence and secrecy. Some hours later the friends inquired for Cornelia, and their servant told them that she had rested a little. Don Juan and Don Antonio then went to the Schools. As they passed by the street where the combat had taken place, and near the house whence Cornelia had fled, they took care to observe whether any signs of disorder were apparent, and whether the matter seemed to be talked of in the neighbourhood: but they could hear not a word respecting the affray of the previous night, or the absence of Cornelia. So, having duly attended the various lectures, they returned to their dwelling.

The lady then caused them to be summoned to her chamber; but finding that, from respect to her presence, they hesitated to appear, she replied to the message they sent her, with tears in her eyes, begging them to come and see her, which she declared to be now the best proof of their respect as well as interest; since, if they could not remedy, they might at least console her misfortunes.

Thus exhorted, the gentlemen obeyed, and Cornelia received them with a smiling face and great cordiality. She then entreated that they would do her the kindness to walk about the city, and ascertain if anything had transpired concerning her affairs. They replied, that they had already done so, with all possible care, but that not a word had been said reacting the matter.

At this moment, one of the three pages who served the gentlemen approached the door of the room telling his masters from without, that there was then at the street door, attended by two servants, a gentleman, who called himself Lorenzo Bentivoglio, and inquired for the Signor Don Juan de Gamboa. Hearing this message, Cornelia clasped her hands, and placing them on her mouth, she exclaimed, in a low and trembling voice, while her words came with difficulty through those clenched fingers, "It is my brother, Signors! it is my brother! Without doubt he has learned that I am here, and has come to take my life. Help and aid, Signors! help and aid!"

"Calm yourself, lady," replied Don Antonio; "you are in a place of safety, and with people who will not suffer the smallest injury to be offered you. The Signor Don Juan will go to inquire what this gentleman demands, and I will remain to defend you, if need be, from all disturbance."

Don Juan prepared to descend accordingly, and Don Antonio, taking his loaded pistols, bade the pages belt on their swords, and hold themselves in readiness for whatever might happen. The housekeeper, seeing these preparations began to tremble,—Cornelia, dreading some fearful result was in grievous terror,—Don Juan and Don Antonio alone preserved their coolness.

Arrived at the door of the house, Don Juan found Don Lorenzo, who, coming towards him, said, "I entreat your Lordship"—for such is the form of address among Italians—"I entreat your Lordship to do me the kindness to accompany me to the neighbouring church; I have to speak to you respecting an affair which concerns my life and honour."

"Very willingly," replied Don Juan. "Let us go, Signor, wherever you please."

They walked side by side to the church, where they seated themselves on a retired bench, so as not to be overheard. Don Lorenzo was the first to break silence.

"Signor Spaniard," he said, "I am Lorenzo Bentivoglio; if not of the richest, yet of one of the most important families belonging to this city; and if this seem like boasting of myself, the notoriety of the fact may serve as my excuse for naming it. I was left an orphan many years since, and to my guardianship was left a sister, so beautiful, that if she were not nearly connected with me, I might perhaps describe her in terms that, while they might seem exaggerated, would yet not by any means do justice to her attractions. My honour being very dear to me, and she being very young, as well as beautiful, I took all possible care to guard her at all points; but my best precautions have proved vain; the self-will of Cornelia, for that is her name, has rendered all useless. In a word, and not to weary you—for this story might become a long one,—I will but tell you, that the Duke of Ferrara, Alfonso d'Este, vanquishing the eyes of Argus by those of a lynx, has rendered all my cares vain, by carrying off my sister last night from the house of one of our kindred; and it is even said that she has already become a mother.

"The misfortune of our house was made known to me last night, and I instantly placed myself on the watch; nay, I met and even attacked Alfonso, sword in hand; but he was succoured in good time by some angel, who would not permit me to efface in his blood the stain he has put upon me. My relation has told me, (and it is from her I have heard all,) that the duke deluded my sister, under a promise to make her his wife; but this I do not believe, for, in respect to present station and wealth, the marriage would not be equal, although, in point of blood, all the world knows how noble are the Bentivogli of Bologna. What I fear is, that the duke has done, what is but too easy when a great and powerful Prince desires to win a timid and retiring girl: he has merely called her by the tender name of wife, and made her believe that certain considerations have prevented him from marrying her at once,—a plausible pretence, but false and perfidious.

"Be that as it may, I see myself at once deprived of my sister and my honour. Up to this moment I have kept the matter secret, purposing not to make known the outrage to any one, until I see whether there may not be some remedy, or means of satisfaction to be obtained. It is better that a disgrace of this kind be supposed and suspected, than certainly and distinctly known—seeing that between the yes and the no of a doubt, each inclines to the opinion that most attracts him, and both sides of the question find defenders. Considering all these things, I have determined to repair to Ferrara, and there demand satisfaction from the duke himself. If he refuse it, I will then offer him defiance. Yet my defiance cannot be made with armed bands, for I could neither get them together nor maintain them but as from man to man. For this it is, then, that I desire your aid. I hope you will accompany me in the journey; nay, I am confident that you will do so, being a Spaniard and a gentleman, as I am told you are.

"I cannot entrust my purpose to any relation or friend of my family, knowing well that from them I should have nothing more than objections and remonstrances, while from you I may hope for sensible and honourable counsels, even though there should be peril in pursuing them. You must do me the favour to go with me, Signor. Having a Spaniard, and such as you appear to be, at my side, I shall account myself to have the armies of Xerxes. I am asking much at your hands; but the duty of answering worthily to what fame publishes of your nation, would oblige you to do still more than I ask."

"No more, Signor Lorenzo," exclaimed Don Juan, who had not before interrupted the brother of Cornelia; "no more. From this moment I accept the office you propose to me, and will be your defender and counsellor. I take upon myself the satisfaction of your honour, or due vengeance for the affront you have received, not only because I am a Spaniard, but because I am a gentleman, and you another, so noble, as you have said, as I know you to be, and as, indeed, all the world reputes you. When shall we set out? It would be better that we did so immediately, for a man does ever well to strike while the iron is hot. The warmth of anger increases courage, and a recent affront more effectually awakens vengeance."

Hearing this, Don Lorenzo rose and embraced Don Juan, saying to him, "A person so generous as yourself, Signor Don Juan, needs no other incentive than that of the honour to be gained in such a cause: this honour you have assured to yourself to-day, if we come out happily from our adventure; but I offer you in addition all I can do, or am worth. Our departure I would have to be to-morrow, since I can provide all things needful to-day."

"This appears to me well decided," replied Don Juan, "but I must beg you, Signor Don Lorenzo, to permit me to make all known to a gentleman who is my friend, and of whose honour and silence I can assure you even more certainly than of my own, if that were possible."

"Since you, Signor Don Juan," replied Lorenzo, "have taken charge, as you say, of my honour, dispose of this matter as you please; and make it known to whom and in what manner it shall seem best to you; how much more, then, to a companion of your own, for what can he be but everything that is best."

This said, the gentlemen embraced each other and took leave, after having agreed that on the following morning Lorenzo should send to summon Don Juan at an hour fixed on when they should mount their horses and pursue their journey in the disguise that Don Lorenzo had selected.

Don Juan then returned, and gave an account of all that had passed to Don Antonio and Cornelia, not omitting the engagement into which he had entered for the morrow.

"Good heavens, Signor!" exclaimed Cornelia; "what courtesy! what confidence! to think of your committing yourself without hesitation to an undertaking so replete with difficulties! How can you know whether Lorenzo will take you to Ferrara, or to what place indeed he may conduct you? But go with him whither you may, be certain that the very soul of honour and good faith will stand beside you. For myself, unhappy creature that I am, I shall be terrified at the very atoms that dance in the sunbeams, and tremble at every shadow; but how can it be otherwise, since on the answer of Duke Alfonso depends my life or death. How do I know that he will reply with sufficient courtesy to prevent the anger of my brother from passing the limits of discretion? and if Lorenzo should draw the sword, think ye he will have a despicable enemy to encounter? Must not I remain through all the days of your absence in a state of mortal suspense and terror, awaiting the favourable or grievous intelligence that you shall bring me! Do I love either my brother or the duke so little as not to tremble for both, and not feel the injury of either to my soul?"

"Your fears affect your judgment, Signora Cornelia," replied Don Juan; "and they go too far. Amidst so many terrors, you should give some place to hope, and trust in God. Put some faith also in my care, and in the earnest desire I feel to see your affairs attain to a happy conclusion. Your brother cannot avoid making this journey to Ferrara, nor can I excuse myself from accompanying him thither. For the present we do not know the intentions of the duke, nor even whether he be or be not acquainted with your elopement. All this we must learn from his own mouth; and there is no one who can better make the inquiry than myself. Be certain, Signora, that the welfare and satisfaction of both your brother and the Signor Duke are to me as the apples of my eyes, and that I will care for the safety of the one as of the other."

"Ah Signor Don Juan," replied Cornelia, "if Heaven grant you as much power to remedy, as grace to console misfortune, I must consider myself exceedingly fortunate in the midst of my sorrows; and now would I fain see you gone and returned; for the whole time of your absence I must pass suspended between hope and fear."

The determination of Don Juan was approved by Don Antonio, who commended him for the justification which he had thereby given to the confidence of Lorenzo Bentivoglio. He furthermore told his friend that he would gladly accompany him, to be ready for whatever might happen, but Don Juan replied—"Not so; first, because you must remain for the better security of the lady Cornelia, whom it will not be well to leave alone; and secondly, because I would not have Signor Lorenzo suppose that I desire to avail myself of the arm of another." "But my arm is your own," returned Don Antonio, "wherefore, if I must even disguise myself, and can but follow you at a distance, I will go with you; and as to Signora Cornelia, I know well that she will prefer to have me accompany you, seeing that she will not here want people who can serve and guard her." "Indeed," said Cornelia, "it will be a great consolation to me to know that you are together, Signors, or at least so near as to be able to assist each other in case of necessity; and since the undertaking you are going on appears to be dangerous, do me the favour, gentlemen, to take these Relics with you." Saying this, Cornelia drew from her bosom a diamond cross, of great value, with an Agnus of gold equally rich and costly. The two gentlemen looked at the magnificent jewels, which they esteemed to be of still greater value than the decoration of the hat; but they returned them to the lady, each saying that he carried Relics of his own, which, though less richly decorated, were at least equally efficacious. Cornelia regretted much that they would not accept those she offered, but she was compelled to submit.

The housekeeper was now informed of the departure of her masters, though not of their destination, or of the purpose for which they went. She promised to take the utmost care of the lady, whose name she did not know, and assured her masters that she would be so watchful as to prevent her suffering in any manner from their absence.

Early the following morning Lorenzo was at the door, where he found Don Juan ready. The latter had assumed a travelling dress, with the rich sombrero presented by the duke, and which he had adorned with black and yellow plumes, placing a black covering over the band of brilliants. He went to take leave of Cornelia, who, knowing that her brother was near, fell into an agony of terror, and could not say one word to the two friends who were bidding her adieu. Don Juan went out the first, and accompanied Lorenzo beyond the walls of the city, where they found their servants waiting with the horses in a retired garden. They mounted, rode on before, and the servants guided their masters in the direction of Ferrara by ways but little known. Don Antonio followed on a low pony, and with such a change of apparel as sufficed to disguise him; but fancying that they regarded him with suspicion, especially Lorenzo, he determined to pursue the highway, and rejoin his friend in Ferrara, where he was certain to find him with but little difficulty.

The Spaniards had scarcely got clear of the city before Cornelia had confided her whole history to the housekeeper, informing her that the infant belonged to herself and to the Duke of Ferrara, and making her acquainted with all that has been related, not concealing from her that the journey made by her masters was to Ferrara, or that they went accompanied by her brother, who was going to challenge the Duke Alfonso.

Hearing all this, the housekeeper, as though the devil had sent her to complicate the difficulties and defer the restoration of Cornelia, began to exclaim—"Alas! lady of my soul! all these things have happened to you, and you remain carelessly there with your limbs stretched out, and doing nothing! Either you have no soul at all, or you have one so poor and weak that you do not feel it! And do you really suppose that your brother has gone to Ferrara? Believe nothing of the kind, but rather be sure that he has carried off my masters, and wiled them from the house, that he may return and take your life, for he can now do it as one would drink a cup of water. Consider only under what kind of guard and protection we are left—that of three pages, who have enough to do with their own pranks, and are little likely to put their hands to any thing good. I, for my part, shall certainly not have courage to await what must follow, and the destruction that cannot but come upon this house. The Signor Lorenzo, an Italian, to put his trust in Spaniards, and ask help and favour from them! By the light of my eyes. I will believe none of that!" So saying, she made a fig[3] at herself. "But if you, my daughter, will take good advice, I will give you such as shall truly enlighten your way."

Cornelia was thrown into a pitiable state of alarm and confusion by these declarations of the housekeeper, who spoke with so much heat, and gave so many evidences of terror, that all she said appeared to be the very truth. The lady pictured to herself Don Antonio and Don Juan as perhaps already dead; she fancied her brother even then coming in at the door, and felt herself already pierced by the blows of his poniard. She therefore replied, "What advice do you then give me, good friend, that may prevent the catastrophe which threatens us?"

"I will give you counsel so good," rejoined the housekeeper, "that better could not be. I, Signora, was formerly in the service of a priest, who has his abode in a village not more than two miles from Ferrara. He is a good and holy man, who will do whatever I require from him, since he is under more obligations to me than merely those of a master to a faithful servant. Let us go to him. I will seek some one who shall conduct us thither instantly; and the woman who comes to nurse the infant is a poor creature, who will go with us to the end of the world. And, now make ready, Signora; for supposing you are to be discovered, it would be much better that you should be found under the care of a good priest, old and respected, than in the hands of two young students, bachelors and Spaniards, who, as I can myself bear witness, are but little disposed to lose occasions for amusing themselves. Now that you are unwell, they treat you with respect; but if you get well and remain in their clutches, Heaven alone will be able to help you; for truly, if my cold disdain and repulses had not been my safeguard, they would long since have torn my honour to rags. All is not gold that glitters. Men say one thing, but think another: happily, it is with me that they have to do; and I am not to be deceived, but know well when the shoe pinches my foot. Above all, I am well born, for I belong to the Crivellis of Milan, and I carry the point of honour ten thousand feet above the clouds; by this you may judge, Signora, through what troubles I have had to pass, since, being what I am, I have been brought to serve as the housekeeper of Spaniards, or as, what they call, their gouvernante. Not that I have, in truth, any complaint to make of my masters, who are a couple of half-saints[4] when they are not put into a rage. And, in this respect, they would seem to be Biscayans, as, indeed, they say they are. But, after all, they may be Galicians, which is another nation, and much less exact than the Biscayans; neither are they so much to be depended on as the people of the Bay."

By all this verbiage, and more beside, the bewildered lady was induced to follow the advice of the old woman, insomuch that, in less than four hours after the departure of the friends, their housekeeper making all arrangements, and Cornelia consenting, the latter was seated in a carriage with the nurse of the babe, and without being heard by the pages they set off on their way to the curate's village. All this was done not only by the advice of the housekeeper, but also with her money; for her masters had just before paid her a year's wages, and therefore it was not needful that she should take a jewel which Cornelia had offered her for the purposes of their journey.

Having heard Don Juan say that her brother and himself would not follow the highway to Ferrara, but proceed thither by retired paths, Cornelia thought it best to take the high road. She bade the driver, go slowly, that they might not overtake the gentlemen in any case; and the master of the carriage was well content to do as they liked, since they had paid him as he liked.

We will leave them on their way, which they take with as much boldness as good direction, and let us see what happened to Don Juan de Gamboa and Signor Lorenzo Bentivoglio. On their way they heard that the duke had not gone to Ferrara, but was still at Bologna, wherefore, abandoning the round they were making, they regained the high road, considering that it was by this the duke would travel on his return to Ferrara. Nor had they long entered thereon before they perceived a troop of men on horseback coming as it seemed from Bologna.

Don Juan then begged Lorenzo to withdraw to a little distance, since, if the duke should chance to be of the company approaching, it would be desirable that he should speak to him before he could enter Ferrara, which was but a short distance from them. Lorenzo complied, and as soon as he had withdrawn, Don Juan removed the covering by which he had concealed the rich ornament of his hat;

but this was not done without some little indiscretion, as he was himself the first to admit some time after.

Meanwhile the travellers approached; among them came a woman on a pied-horse, dressed in a travelling habit, and her face covered with a silk mask, either to conceal her features, or to shelter them from the effects of the sun and air.

Don Juan pulled up his horse in the middle of the road, and remained with his face uncovered, awaiting the arrival of the cavalcade. As they approached him, the height, good looks, and spirited attitude of the Spaniard, the beauty of his horse, his peculiar dress, and, above all, the lustre of the diamonds on his hat, attracted the eyes of the whole party but especially those of the Duke of Ferrara, the principal personage of the group, who no sooner beheld the band of brilliants than he understood the cavalier before him to be Don Juan de Gamboa, his deliverer in the combat frequently alluded to. So well convinced did he feel of this, that, without further question, he rode up to Don Juan, saying, "I shall certainly not deceive myself, Signor Cavalier, if I call you Don Juan de Gamboa, for your spirited looks, and the decoration you wear on your hat, alike assure me of the fact."

"It is true that I am the person you say," replied Don Juan. "I have never yet desired to conceal my name; but tell me, Signor, who you are yourself, that I may not be surprised into any discourtesy."

"Discourtesy from you, Signor, would be impossible," rejoined the duke. "I feel sure that you could not be discourteous in any case; but I hasten to tell you, nevertheless, that I am the Duke of Ferrara, and a man who will be bound to do you service all the days of his life, since it is but a few nights since you gave him that life which must else have been lost."

Alfonzo had not finished speaking, when Don Juan, springing lightly from his horse, hastened to kiss the feet of the duke; but, with all his agility, the latter was already out of the saddle, and alighted in the arms of the Spaniard.

Seeing this, Signor Lorenzo, who could but observe these ceremonies from a distance, believed that what he beheld was the effect of anger rather than courtesy; he therefore put his horse to its speed, but pulled up midway on perceiving that the duke and Don Juan were of a verity clasped in each other's arms. It then chanced that Alfonso, looking over the shoulders of Don Juan, perceived Lorenzo, whom he instantly recognised; and somewhat disconcerted at his appearance, while still holding Don Juan embraced, he inquired if Lorenzo Bentivoglio, whom he there beheld, had come with him or not. Don Juan replied, "Let us move somewhat apart from this place, and I will relate to your excellency some very singular circumstances."

The duke having done as he was requested, Don Juan said to him, "My Lord Duke, I must tell you that Lorenzo Bentivoglio, whom you there see, has a cause of complaint against you, and not a light one; he avers that some nights since you took his sister, the Lady Cornelia, from the house of a lady, her cousin, and that you have deceived her, and dishonoured his house; he desires therefore to know what satisfaction you propose to make for this, that he may then see what it behoves him to do. He has begged me to be his aid and mediator in the matter, and I have consented with a good will, since, from certain indications which he gave me, I perceived that the person of whom he complained, and yourself, to whose liberal courtesy I owe this rich ornament, were one and the same. Thus, seeing that none could more effectually mediate between you than myself, I offered to undertake that office willingly, as I have said; and now I would have you tell me, Signor, if you know aught of this matter, and whether what Lorenzo has told me be true."

"Alas, my friend, it is so true," replied the duke, "that I durst not deny it, even if I would. Yet I have not deceived or carried off Cornelia, although I know that she has disappeared from the house of which you speak. I have not deceived her, because I have taken her for my wife; and I have not carried her off, since I do not know what has become of her. If I have not publicly celebrated my nuptials with her, it is because I waited until my mother, who is now at the last extremity, should have passed to another life, she desiring greatly that I should espouse the Signora Livia, daughter of the Duke of Mantua. There are, besides, other reasons, even more important than this, but which it is not convenient that I should now make known.

"What has in fact happened is this:—on the night when you came to my assistance, I was to have taken Cornelia to Ferrara, she being then in the last month of her pregnancy, and about to present me with that pledge of our love with which it has pleased God to bless us; but whether she was alarmed by our combat or by my delay, I know not; all I can tell you is, that when I arrived at the house, I met the confidante of our affection just coming out. From her I learned that her mistress had that moment left the house, after having given birth to a son, the most beautiful that ever had been seen, and whom she had given to one Fabio, my servant. The woman is she whom you see here. Fabio is also in this company; but of Cornelia and her child I can learn nothing. These two days I have passed at Bologna, in ceaseless endeavours to discover her, or to obtain some clue to her retreat, but I have not been able to learn anything."

"In that case," interrupted Don Juan, "if Cornelia and her child were now to appear, you would not refuse to admit that the first is your wife, and the second your son?"

"Certainly not," replied the duke; "for if I value myself on being a gentleman, still more highly do I prize the title of Christian. Cornelia, besides, is one who well deserves to be mistress of a kingdom. Let her but come, and whether my mother live or die, the world shall know that I maintain my faith, and that my word, given in private, shall be publicly redeemed."

"And what you have now said to me you are willing to repeat to your brother, Signor Lorenzo?" inquired Don Juan.

"My only regret is," exclaimed the duke, "that he has not long before been acquainted with the truth."

Hearing this, Don Juan made sign to Lorenzo that he should join them, which he did, alighting from his horse and proceeding towards the place where his friends stood, but far from hoping for the good news that awaited him.

The duke advanced to receive him with open arms, and the first word he uttered was to call him brother. Lorenzo scarcely knew how to reply to a reception so courteous and a salutation so affectionate. He stood amazed, and before he could utter a word, Don Juan said to him, "The duke, Signor Lorenzo, is but too happy to admit his affection for your sister, the Lady Cornelia; and, at the same time, he assures you, that she is his legitimate consort. This, as he now says it to you, he will affirm publicly before all the world, when the moment for doing so has arrived. He confesses, moreover, that he did propose to remove her from the house of her cousin some nights since, intending to take her to Ferrara, there to await the proper time for their public espousals, which he has only delayed for just causes, which he has declared to me. He describes the conflict he had to maintain against yourself; and adds, that when he went to seek Cornelia, he found only her waiting-woman, Sulpicia, who is the woman you see yonder: from her he has learned that her lady had just given birth to a son, whom she entrusted to a servant of the duke, and then left the house in terror, because she feared that you, Signor Lorenzo, had been made aware of her secret marriage: the lady hoped, moreover, to find the duke awaiting her in the street. But it seems that Sulpicia did not give the babe to Fabio, but to some other person instead of him, and the child does not appear, neither is the Lady Cornelia to be found, in spite of the duke's researches. He admits, that all these things have happened by his fault; but declares, that whenever your sister shall appear, he is ready to receive her as his legitimate wife. Judge, then, Signor Lorenzo, if there be any more to say or to desire beyond the discovery of those two dear but unfortunate ones—the lady and her infant."

To this Lorenzo replied by throwing himself at the feet of the duke, who raised him instantly. "From your greatness and Christian uprightness, most noble lord and dear brother," said Lorenzo, "my sister and I had certainly nothing less than this high honour to expect." Saying this, tears came to his eyes, and the duke felt his own becoming moist, for both were equally affected,—the one with the fear of having lost his wife, the other by the generous candour of his brother-in-law; but at once perceiving the weakness of thus displaying their feelings, they both restrained themselves, and drove back those witnesses to their source; while the eyes of Don Juan, shining with gladness, seemed almost to demand from them the albricias[5] of good news, seeing that he believed himself to have both Cornelia and her son in his own house.

Things were at this point when Don Antonio de Isunza, whom Don Juan recognised at a considerable distance by his horse, was perceived approaching. He also recognised Don Juan and Lorenzo, but not the duke, and did not know what he was to do, or whether he ought to rejoin his friend or not. He therefore inquired of the duke's servants who the gentleman was, then standing with Lorenzo and Don Juan. They replied that it was the Duke of Ferrara; and Don Antonio, knowing less than ever what it was best for him to do, remained in some confusion, until he was relieved from it by Don Juan, who called him by his name. Seeing that all were on foot, Don Antonio also dismounted, and, approaching the group, was received with infinite courtesy by the duke, to whom Don Juan had already named him as his friend; finally, Don Antonio was made acquainted with all that had taken place before his arrival.

Rejoicing greatly at what he heard, Don Antonio then said to his comrade, "Why, Signor Don Juan, do you not finish your work, and raise the joy of these Signors to its acmè, by requiring from them the albricias for discovering the Lady Cornelia and her son?"

"Had you not arrived, I might have taken those albricias you speak of," replied Don Juan; "but now they are yours, Don Antonio, for I am certain that the duke and Signor Lorenzo will give them to you most joyfully."

The duke and Lorenzo hearing of Cornelia being found, and of albricias, inquired the meaning of those words.

"What can it be," replied Don Antonio, "if not that I also design to become one of the personages in this happily terminating drama, being he who is to demand the albricias for the discovery of the Lady Cornelia and her son, who are both in my house." He then at once related to the brothers, point by point, what has been already told, intelligence which gave the duke and Lorenzo so much pleasure, that each embraced one of the friends with all his heart, Lorenzo throwing himself into the arms of Don Juan, and the duke into those of Don Antonio—the latter promising his whole dukedom for albricias, and Lorenzo his life, soul, and estates. They then called the woman who had given the child to Don Juan, and she having perceived her master, Lorenzo Bentivoglio, came forward, trembling. Being asked if she could recognise the man to whom she had given the infant, she replied that she could not; but that when she had asked if he were Fabio, he had answered "yes," and that she had entrusted the babe to his care in the faith of that reply.

"All this is true," returned Don Juan; "and you furthermore bade me deposit the child in a place of security, and instantly return."

"I did so," replied the waiting-woman, weeping. But the duke exclaimed, "We will have no more tears; all is gladness and joy. I will not now enter Ferrara, but return at once to Bologna; for this happiness is but in shadow until made perfect by the sight of Cornelia herself." Then, without more words, the whole company wheeled round, and took their way to Bologna.

Don Antonio now rode forward to prepare the Lady Cornelia, lest the sudden appearance of her brother and the duke might cause too violent a revulsion; but not finding her as he expected, and the pages being unable to give him any intelligence respecting her, he suddenly found himself the saddest and most embarrassed man in the world. Learning that the gouvernante had departed, he was not long in conjecturing that the lady had disappeared by her means. The pages informed him that the housekeeper had gone on the same day with himself and Don Juan, but as to that Lady Cornelia, respecting whom he inquired, they had never seen her. Don Antonio was almost out of his senses at this unexpected occurrence, which, he feared, must make the duke consider himself and Don Juan to be mere liars and boasters. He was plunged in these sad thoughts when Alfonso entered with Lorenzo and Don Juan, who had spurred on before the attendants by retired and unfrequented streets. They found Don Antonio seated with his head on his hand, and as pale as a man who has been long dead, and when Don Juan inquired what ailed him, and where was the Lady Cornelia, he replied, "Rather ask me what do I not ail, since the Lady Cornelia is not to be found. She quitted the house, on the same day as ourselves, with the gouvernante we left to keep her company."

This sad news seemed as though it would deprive the duke of life, and Lorenzo of his senses. The whole party remained in the utmost consternation and dismay; when one of the pages said to Don Antonio in a whisper, "Signor, Santisteban, Signor Don Juan's page, has had locked up in his chamber, from the day when your worships left, a very pretty woman, whose name is certainly Cornelia, for I have heard him call her so." Plunged into a new embarrassment, Don Antonio would rather not have found the lady at all—for he could not but suppose it was she whom the page had shut up in his room—than have discovered her in such a place. Nevertheless, without saying a word, he ascended to the page's chamber, but found the door fast, for the young man had gone out, and taken away the key. Don Antonio therefore put his lips to the keyhole, and said in a low voice, "Open the door, Signora Cornelia, and come down to receive your brother, and the duke, your husband, who are waiting to take you hence."

A voice from within replied, "Are you making fun of me? It is certain that I am neither so ugly nor so old but that dukes and counts may very well be looking for me: but this comes of condescending to visit pages." These words quite satisfied Don Antonio that it was not the Lady Cornelia who had replied.

At that moment Santisteban returned and went up to his chamber, where he found Don Antonio, who had just commanded that all the keys of the house should be brought, to see if any one of them would open the door. The page fell on his knees, and held up the key, exclaiming, "Have mercy on me, your worship: your absence, or rather my own villainy, made me bring this woman to my room; but I entreat your grace, Don Antonio, as you would have good news from Spain, that you suffer the fault I have committed to remain unknown to my master, Don Juan, if he be not yet informed of it; I will turn her out this instant."

"What is the name of this woman?" inquired Don Antonio. "Cornelia," replied Santisteban. Down stairs at once went the page who had discovered the hidden woman, and who was not much of a friend to Santisteban, and entered the room where sat the duke, Don Juan, and Lorenzo, and, either from simplicity or malice, began to talk to himself, saying, "Well caught, brother page! by Heaven they have made you give up your Lady Cornelia! She was well hidden, to be sure; and no doubt my gentleman would have liked to see the masters remain away that he might enjoy himself some three or four days longer."

"What is that you are saying?" cried Lorenzo, who had caught a part of these words. "Where is the Lady Cornelia?" "She is above," replied the page; and the duke, who supposed that his consort had just made her appearance, had scarcely heard the words before he rushed from the apartment like a flash of lightning, and, ascending the staircase at a bound, gained the chamber into which Don Antonio was entering.

"Where is Cornelia? where is the life of my life?" he exclaimed, as he hurried into the room.

"Cornelia is here," replied a woman who was wrapped in a quilt taken from the bed with which she had concealed her face. "Lord bless us!" she continued, "one would think an ox had been stolen! Is it a new thing for a woman to visit a page, that you make such a fuss about it?"

Lorenzo, who had now entered the room, angrily snatched off the sheet and exposed to view a woman still young and not ill-looking, who hid her face in her hands for shame, while her dress, which served her instead of a pillow, sufficiently proved her to be some poor castaway.

The duke asked her, was it true her name was Cornelia? It was, she replied—adding, that she had very decent parents in the city, but that no one could venture to say, "Of this water I will never drink."

The duke was so confounded by all he beheld, that he was almost inclined to think the Spaniards were making a fool of him; but, not to encourage so grievous a suspicion, he turned away without saying a word. Lorenzo followed him; they mounted their horses and rode off, leaving Don Juan and Don Antonio even more astonished and dismayed than himself.

The two friends now determined to leave no means untried, possible or impossible, to discover the retreat of the Lady Cornelia, and convince the duke of their sincerity and uprightness. They dismissed Santisteban for his misconduct, and turned the worthless Cornelia out of the house. Don Juan then remembered that they had neglected to describe to the duke those rich jewels wherein Cornelia carried her relics, with the agnus she had offered to them; and they went out proposing to mention that circumstance, so as to prove to Alfonso that the lady had, indeed, been in their care, and that if she had now disappeared, it was not by any fault of theirs.

They expected to find the duke in Lorenzo's house; but the latter informed them that Alfonso had been compelled to leave Bologna, and had returned to Ferrara, having committed the search for Cornelia to his care. The friends having told him what had brought them, Lorenzo assured them that the duke was perfectly convinced of their rectitude in the matter, adding, that they both attributed the flight of Cornelia to her great fear, but hoped, and did not doubt, that Heaven would permit her re-appearance before long, since it was certain that the earth had not swallowed the housekeeper, the child, and herself.

With these considerations they all consoled themselves, determining not to make search by any public announcement, but secretly, since, with the exception of her cousin, no person was yet acquainted with the disappearance of Cornelia; and Lorenzo judged that a public search might prove injurious to his sister's name among such as did not know the whole circumstances of the case, since the labour of effacing such suspicions as might arise would be infinite, and by no means certain of success.

The duke meanwhile continued his journey to Ferrara, and favouring Fortune, which was now preparing his happiness, led him to the village where dwelt that priest in whose house Cornelia, her infant, and the housekeeper, were concealed. The good Father was acquainted with the whole history, and Cornelia had begged his advice as to what it would be best for her to do. Now this priest had been the preceptor of the duke; and to his dwelling, which was furnished in a manner befitting that of a rich and learned clerk, the duke was in the habit of occasionally repairing from Ferrara, and would thence go to the chase, or amuse himself with the pleasant conversation of his host, and with the knowledge and excellence of which the good priest gave evidence in all he did or said.

The priest was not surprised to receive a visit from the duke, because, as we have said, it was not the first by many; but he was grieved to see him sad and dejected, and instantly perceived that his whole soul was absorbed in some painful thought. As to Cornelia, having been told that the duke was there, she was seized with renewed terror, not knowing how her misfortunes were to terminate. She wrung her hands, and hurried from one side of her apartment to the other, like a person who had lost her senses. Fain would the troubled lady have spoken to the priest, but he was in conversation with the Duke, and could not be approached. Alfonso was meanwhile saying to him, "I come to you, my father, full of sadness, and will not go to Ferrara to-day, but remain your guest; give orders for all my attendants to proceed to the city, and let none remain with me but Fabio."

The priest went to give directions accordingly, as also to see that his own servants made due preparations; and Cornelia then found an opportunity for speaking to him. She took his two hands and said, "Ah, my father, and dear sir, what has the duke come for? for the love of God see what can be

17

done to save me! I pray you, seek to discover what he proposes. As a friend, do for me whatever shall seem best to your prudence and great wisdom."

The priest replied, "Duke Alfonso has come to me in deep sadness, but up to this moment he has not told me the cause. What I would have you now do is to dress this infant with great care, put on it all the jewels you have with you, more especially such as you may have received from the duke himself; leave the rest to me, and I have hope that Heaven is about to grant us a happy day." Cornelia embraced the good man, and kissed his hand, and then retired to dress and adorn the babe, as he had desired.

The priest, meanwhile, returned to entertain the duke with conversation while his people were preparing their meal; and in the course of their colloquy he inquired if he might venture to ask him the cause of his grief, since it was easy to see at the distance of a league that, something gave him sorrow.

"Father," replied the duke, "it is true that the sadness of the heart rises to the face, and in the eyes may be read the history of that which passes in the soul; but for the present I cannot confide the cause of my sorrow to any one."

"Then we will not speak of it further, my lord duke," replied the priest; "but if you were in a condition permitting you to examine a curious and beautiful thing, I have one to show you which I cannot but think would afford you great pleasure."

"He would be very unwise," returned Alfonso, "who, when offered a solace for his suffering, refuses to accept it. Wherefore show me what you speak of, father; the object is doubtless an addition to one of your curious collections, and they have all great interest in my eyes."

The priest then rose, and repaired to the apartment where Cornelia was awaiting him with her son, whom she had adorned as he had suggested, having placed on him the relics and agnus, with other rich jewels, all gifts of the duke to the babe's mother. Taking the infant from her hands, the good priest then went to the duke, and telling him that he must rise and come to the light of the window, he transferred the babe from his own arms into those of Alfonso, who could not but instantly remark the jewels; and perceiving that they were those which he had himself given to Cornelia, he remained in great surprise. Looking earnestly at the infant, meanwhile, he fancied he beheld his own portrait; and full of admiration, he asked the priest to whom the child belonged, remarking, that from its decorations and appearance one might take it to be the son of some princess.

"I do not know," replied the priest, "to whom it belongs; all I can tell you is, that it was brought to me some nights since by a cavalier of Bologna, who charged me to take good care of the babe and bring it up heedfully, since it was the son of a noble and valiant father, and of a mother highly born as well as beautiful. With the cavalier there came also a woman to suckle the infant, and of her I have inquired if she knew anything of the parents, but she tells me that she knows nothing whatever; yet of a truth, if the mother possess but half the beauty of the nurse, she must be the most lovely woman in Italy."

"Could I not see her?" asked the Duke. "Yes, certainly you may see her," returned the priest. "You have only to come with me; and if the beauty and decorations of the child surprise you, I think the sight of the nurse cannot fail to produce an equal effect."

The priest would then have taken the infant from the duke, but Alfonso would not let it go; he pressed it in his arms, and gave it repeated kisses; the good father, meanwhile, hastened forward, and bade Cornelia approach to receive the duke. The lady obeyed; her emotion giving so rich a colour to her face that the beauty she displayed seemed something more than human. The duke, on seeing her, remained as if struck by a thunderbolt, while she, throwing herself at his feet, sought to kiss them. The duke said not a word, but gave the infant to the priest, and hurried out of the apartment.

Shocked at this, Cornelia said to the priest, "Alas, dear father, have I terrified the duke with the sight of my face? am I become hateful to him? Has he forgot the ties by which he has bound himself to me? Will he not speak one word to me? Was his child such a burden to him that he has thus rejected him from his arm's?"

To all these questions the good priest could give no reply, for he too was utterly confounded by the duke's hasty departure, which seemed more like a flight than anything else.

Meanwhile Alfonso had but gone out to summon Fabio. "Ride Fabio, my friend," he cried, "ride for your life to Bologna, and tell Lorenzo Bentivoglio that he must come with all speed to this place; let him make no excuse, and bid him bring with him the two Spanish gentlemen, Don Juan de Gamboa and Don Antonio de Isunza. Return instantly, Fabio, but not without them, for it concerns my life to see them here."

Fabio required no further pressing, but instantly carried his master's commands into effect. The duke returned at once to Cornelia, caught her in his arms, mingled his tears with hers, and kissed her a thousand times; and long did the fond pair remain thus silently locked in each other's embrace, both speechless from excess of joy. The nurse of the infant and the dame, who proclaimed herself a Crivella, beheld all this from the door of the adjoining apartment, and fell into such ecstasies of delight that they knocked their heads against the wall, and seemed all at once to have gone out of their wits. The priest bestowed a thousand kisses on the infant, whom he held on one arm, while with his right hand he showered no end of benedictions on the noble pair. At length his reverence's housekeeper, who had been occupied with her culinary preparations, and knew nothing of what had occurred, entered to notify to her master that dinner was on the table, and so put an end to this scene of rapture.

The duke then took his babe from the arms of the priest, and kept it in his own during the repast, which was more remarkable for neatness and good taste than for splendour. While they were at table, Cornelia related to the duke all that had occurred until she had taken refuge with the priest, by the advice of the housekeeper of those two Spanish gentlemen, who had protected and guarded her with such assiduous and respectful kindness. In return the duke related to her all that had befallen himself during the same interval; and the two housekeepers, who were present, received from him the most encouraging promises. All was joy and satisfaction, and nothing more was required for the general happiness, save the arrival of Lorenzo, Don Antonio, and Don Juan.

They came on the third day, all intensely anxious to know if the duke had received intelligence of Cornelia, seeing that Fabio, who did not know what had happened, could tell them nothing on that subject.

The duke received them alone in the antechamber, but gave no sign of gladness in his face, to their great grief and disappointment. Bidding them be seated, Alfonso himself sat down, and thus addressed Lorenzo:—

"You well know, Signor Lorenzo Bentivoglio, that I never deceived your sister, as my conscience and Heaven itself can bear witness; you know also the diligence with which I have sought her, and the wish I have felt to have my marriage with her celebrated publicly. But she is not to be found, and my word cannot be considered eternally engaged to a shadow. I am a young man, and am not so blasé as to leave ungathered such pleasures as I find on my path. Before I had ever seen Cornelia I had given my promise to a peasant girl of this village, but whom I was tempted to abandon by the superior charms of Cornelia, giving therein a great proof of my love for the latter, in defiance of the voice of my conscience. Now, therefore, since no one can marry a woman who does not appear, and it is not reasonable that a man should eternally run after a wife who deserts him, lest he should take to his arms one who abhors him, I would have you consider, Signor Lorenzo, whether I can give you any further satisfaction for an affront which was never intended to be one; and further, I would have you give me your permission to accomplish my first promise, and solemnise my marriage with the peasant girl, who is now in this house."

While the duke spoke this, Lorenzo's frequent change of colour, and the difficulty with which he forced himself to retain his seat, gave manifest proof that anger was taking possession of all his senses. The same feelings agitated Don Antonio and Don Juan, who were resolved not to permit the duke to fulfil his intention, even should they be compelled to prevent it by depriving him of life. Alfonso, reading these resolves in their faces, resumed: "Endeavour to calm yourself, Signor Lorenzo; and before you answer me one word, I will have you see the beauty of her whom I desire to take to wife, for it is such that you cannot refuse your consent, and it might suffice, as you will acknowledge, to excuse a graver error than mine."

So saying, the duke rose, and repaired to the apartment where Cornelia was awaiting him in all the splendour of her beauty and rich decorations. No sooner was he gone than Don Juan also rose, and laying both hands on the arms of Lorenzo's chair, he said to him, "By St. James of Galicia, by the true faith of a Christian, and by my honour as a gentleman, Signor Lorenzo, I will as readily allow the duke to fulfil his project as I will become a worshipper of Mahomed. Here, in this spot, he shall yield up his life at my hands, or he shall redeem the promise given to your sister, the lady Cornelia. At the least, he shall give us time to seek her; and until we know to a certainty that she is dead, he shall not marry."

"That is exactly my own view," replied Lorenzo. "And I am sure," rejoined Don Juan, "that it will be the determination of my comrade, Don Antonio, likewise."

While they were thus speaking, Cornelia appeared at the door between the duke and the priest, each of whom led her by one hand. Behind them came Sulpicia, her waiting woman, whom the duke had summoned from Ferrara to attend her lady, with the infant's nurse, and the Spaniards' housekeeper. When Lorenzo saw his sister, and had assured himself it was indeed Cornelia,—for at first the apparently impossible character of the occurrence had forbidden his belief,—he staggered on his feet, and cast himself at those of the duke, who, raising him, placed him in the arms of his delighted sister, whilst Don Juan and Don Antonio hastily applauded the duke for the clever trick he had played upon them all.

Alfonso then took the infant from Sulpicia, and, presenting it to Lorenzo, he said, "Signor and brother, receive your nephew, my son, and see whether it please you to give permission for the public solemnisation of my marriage with this peasant girl—the only one to whom I have ever been betrothed."

To repeat the replies of Lorenzo would be never to make an end, and the rather if to these we added the questions of Don Juan, the remarks of Don Antonio, the expressions of delight uttered by the priest, the rejoicing of Sulpicia, the satisfaction of the housekeeper who had made herself the counsellor of Cornelia, the exclamations of the nurse, and the astonishment of Fabio, with the general happiness of all.

The marriage ceremony was performed by the good priest, and Don Juan de Gamboa gave away the bride; but it was agreed among the parties that this marriage also should be kept secret, until he knew the result of the malady under which the duchess-dowager was labouring; for the present, therefore, it was determined that Cornelia should return to Bologna with her brother. All was done as thus agreed on; and when the duchess-dowager died, Cornelia made her entrance into Ferrara, rejoicing the eyes of all who beheld her: the mourning weeds were exchanged for festive robes, the two housekeepers were enriched, and Sulpicia was married to Fabio. For Don Antonio and Don Juan, they were sufficiently rewarded by the services they had rendered to the duke, who offered them two of his cousins in marriage, with rich dowries. But they replied, that the gentlemen of the Biscayan nation married for the most part in their own country; wherefore, not because they despised so honourable a proffer, which was not possible, but that they might not depart from a custom so laudable, they were compelled to decline that illustrious alliance, and the rather as they were still subject to the will of their parents, who had, most probably, already affianced them.

The duke admitted the validity of their excuses, but, availing himself of occasions warranted by custom and courtesy, he found means to load the two friends with rich gifts, which he sent from time to time to their house in Bologna. Many of these were of such value, that although they might have been refused for fear of seeming to receive a payment, yet the appropriate manner in which they were presented, and the particular periods at which Alfonso took care that they should arrive, caused their acceptance to be easy, not to say inevitable; such, for example, were those despatched by him at the moment of their departure for their own country, and those which he gave them when they came to Ferrara to take their leave of him.

At this period, the Spanish gentlemen found Cornelia the mother of two little girls, and the duke more enamoured of his wife than ever. The duchess gave the diamond cross to Don Juan, and the gold agnus to Don Antonio, both of whom had now no choice but to accept them. They finally arrived without accident in their native Spain, where they married rich, noble, and beautiful ladies; and they never ceased to maintain a friendly correspondence with the duke and duchess of Ferrara, and with Lorenzo Bentivoglio, to the great satisfaction of all parties.

END OF THE LADY CORNELIA.

[2] Cardinal Albornoz founded a college in the university of Bologna, expressly for the Spaniards, his countrymen.

[3] A gesture of contempt or playfulness, as the case may be, and which consists in a certain twist of the fingers and thumb.

[4] The original is benditos, which sometimes means simpleton, but is here equivalent to the Italian beato, and must be rendered as in the text.

[5] Albricias: "Largess!" "Give reward for good tidings."

RINCONETE AND CORTADILLO:

Or, Peter of the Corner and the Little Cutter.

At the Venta or hostelry of the Mulinillo, which is situate on the confines of the renowned plain of Alcudia, and on the road from Castile to Andalusia, two striplings met by chance on one of the hottest days of summer. One of them was about fourteen or fifteen years of age; the other could not have passed his seventeenth year. Both were well formed, and of comely features, but in very ragged and tattered plight. Cloaks they had none; their breeches were of linen, and their stockings were merely those bestowed on them by Nature. It is true they boasted shoes; one of them wore alpargates,[6] or rather dragged them along at his heels; the other had what might as well have been shackles for all the good they did the wearer, being rent in the uppers, and without soles. Their respective head-dresses were a montera[7] and a miserable sombrero, low in the crown and wide in the brim. On his shoulder, and crossing his breast like a scarf, one of them carried a shirt, the colour of chamois leather; the body of this garment was rolled up and thrust into one of its sleeves: the other, though travelling without incumbrance, bore on his chest what seemed a large pack, but which proved, on closer inspection, to be the remains of a starched ruff, now stiffened with grease instead of starch, and so worn and frayed that it looked like a bundle of hemp.

Within this collar, wrapped up and carefully treasured, was a pack of cards, excessively dirty, and reduced to an oval form by repeated paring of their dilapidated corners. The lads were both much burned by the sun, their hands were anything but clean, and their long nails were edged with black; one had a dudgeon-dagger by his side; the other a knife with a yellow handle.

These gentlemen had selected for their siesta the porch or penthouse commonly found before a Venta; and, finding themselves opposite each other, he who appeared to be the elder said to the younger, "Of what country is your worship, noble Sir, and by what road do you propose to travel?" "What is my country, Señor Cavalier," returned the other, "I know not; nor yet which way my road lies."

"Your worship, however, does not appear to have come from heaven," rejoined the elder, "and as this is not a place wherein a man can take up his abode for good, you must, of necessity, be going further." "That is true," replied the younger; "I have, nevertheless, told you only the veritable fact; for as to my country, it is mine no more, since all that belongs to me there is a father who does not consider me his child, and a step-mother who treats me like a son-in-law. With regard to my road, it is that which chance places before me, and it will end wherever I may find some one who will give me the wherewithal to sustain this miserable life of mine."

"Is your worship acquainted with any craft?" inquired the first speaker. "With none," returned the other, "except that I can run like a hare, leap like a goat, and handle a pair of scissors with great dexterity."

"These things are all very good, useful, and profitable," rejoined the elder. "You will readily find the Sacristan of some church who will give your worship the offering-bread of All Saints' Day, for cutting him his paper flowers to decorate the Monument[8] on Holy Thursday."

"But that is not my manner of cutting," replied the younger. "My father, who, by God's mercy, is a tailor and hose maker, taught me to cut out that kind of spatterdashes properly called Polainas, which, as your worship knows, cover the fore part of the leg and come down over the instep. These I can cut out in such style, that I could pass an examination for the rank of master in the craft; but my ill luck keeps my talents in obscurity."

"The common lot, Señor, of able men," replied the first speaker, "for I have always heard that it is the way of the world to let the finest talents go to waste; but your worship is still at an age when this evil fortune may be remedied, and the rather since, if I mistake not, and my eyes do not deceive me, you have other advantageous qualities which it is your pleasure to keep secret." "It is true that I have such," returned the younger gentleman, "but they are not of a character to be publicly proclaimed, as your worship has very judiciously observed."

"But I," rejoined the elder, "may with confidence assure you, that I am one of the most discreet and prudent persons to be found within many a league. In order to induce your worship to open your heart and repose your faith on my honour, I will enlist your sympathies by first laying bare my own bosom; for I imagine that fate has not brought us together without some hidden purpose. Nay, I believe that we are to be true friends from this day to the end of our lives.

"I, then, Señor Hidalgo, am a native of Fuenfrida, a place very well known, indeed renowned for the illustrious travellers who are constantly passing it. My name is Pedro del Rincon,[9] my father is a person of quality, and a Minister of the Holy Crusade, since he holds the important charge of a Bulero or Buldero,[10] as the vulgar call it. I was for some time his assistant in that office, and acquitted myself so well, that in all things concerning the sale of bulls I could hold my own with any man, though he had the right to consider himself the most accomplished in the profession. But one day, having placed my affections on the money produced by the bulls, rather than on the bulls themselves, I took a bag of crowns to my arms, and we two departed together for Madrid.

"In that city, such are the facilities that offer themselves, I soon gutted my bag, and left it with as many wrinkles as a bridegroom's pocket-handkerchief. The person who was charged with the collection of the money, hastened to track my steps; I was taken, and met with but scant indulgence; only, in consideration of my youth, their worships the judges contented themselves with introducing me to the acquaintance of the whipping-post, to have the flies whisked from my shoulders for a certain time, and commanding me to abstain from revisiting the Court and Capital during a period of four years. I took the matter coolly, bent my shoulders to the operation performed at their command, and made so much haste to begin my prescribed term of exile, that I had no time to procure sumpter mules, but contented myself with selecting from my valuables such as seemed most important and useful.

"I did not fail to include this pack of cards among them,"—here the speaker exhibited that oviform specimen already mentioned—"and with these I have gained my bread among the inns and taverns between Madrid and this place, by playing at Vingt-et-un. It is true they are somewhat soiled and worn, as your worship sees; but for him who knows how to handle them, they possess a marvellous virtue, which is, that you never cut them but you find an ace at the bottom; if your worship then is acquainted with the game, you will see what an advantage it is to know for certain that you have an ace to begin with, since you may count it either for one or eleven; and so you may be pretty sure that when the stakes are laid at twenty-one, your money will be much disposed to stay at home.

"In addition to this, I have acquired the knowledge of certain mysteries regarding Lansquenet and Reversis, from the cook of an ambassador who shall be nameless,—insomuch that, even as your worship might pass as master in the cutting of spatterdashes, so could I, too, take my degrees in the art of flat-catching.

"With all these acquirements, I am tolerably sure of not dying from hunger, since, even in the most retired farm-house I come to, there is always some one to be found who will not refuse himself the recreation of a few moments at cards. We have but to make a trial where we are; let us spread the net, and it will go hard with us if some bird out of all the Muleteers standing about do not fall into it. I mean to say, that if we two begin now to play at Vingt-et-un as though we were in earnest, some one will probably desire to make a third, and, in that case, he shall be the man to leave his money behind him."

"With all my heart," replied the younger lad: "and I consider that your excellency has done me a great favour by communicating to me the history of your life. You have thereby made it impossible for me to conceal mine, and I will hasten to relate it as briefly as possible. Here it is, then:—

"I was born at Pedroso, a village situate between Salamanca and Medina del Campo. My father is a tailor, as I have said, and taught me his trade; but from cutting with the scissors I proceeded—my natural abilities coming in aid—to the cutting of purses. The dull, mean life of the village, and the unloving conduct of my mother-in-law, were besides but little to my taste. I quitted my birthplace, therefore, repaired to Toledo to exercise my art, and succeeded in it to admiration; for there is not a reliquary suspended to the dress, not a pocket, however carefully concealed, but my fingers shall probe its contents, or my scissors snip it off, though the owner were guarded by the eyes of Argus.

"During four months I spent in Toledo, I was never trapped between two doors, nor caught in the fact, nor pursued by the runners of justice, nor blown upon by an informer. It is true that, eight days ago, a double spy[11] did set forth my distinguished abilities to the Corregidor, and the latter, taking a fancy to me from his description, desired to make my acquaintance; but I am a modest youth, and do not wish to frequent the society of personages so important. Wherefore I took pains to excuse myself from visiting him, and departed in so much haste, that I, like yourself, had no time to procure sumpter-mules or small change —nay, I could not even find a return-chaise, nor so much as a cart."

"Console yourself for these omissions," replied Pedro del Rincon; "and since we now know each other, let us drop these grand and stately airs, and confess frankly that we have not a blessed farthing between us, nor even shoes to our feet."

"Be it so," returned Diego Cortado, for so the younger boy called himself. "Be it so; and since our friendship, as your worship Señor Rincon is pleased to say, is to last our whole lives, let us begin it with solemn and laudable ceremonies,"—saying which, Diego rose to his feet, and embraced the Señor Rincon, who returned the compliment with equal tenderness and emotion.

They then began to play at Vingt-et-un with the cards above described, which were certainly "free from dust and straw,"[12] as we say, but by no means free from grease and knavery; and after a few deals, Cortado could turn up an ace as well as Rincon his master. When things had attained this point, it chanced that a Muleteer came out at the porch, and, as Rincon had anticipated, he soon proposed to make a third in their game.

To this they willingly agreed, and in less than half an hour they had won from him twelve reals and twenty-two maravedis, which he felt as sorely as twelve stabs with a dagger and twenty-two thousand sorrows. Presuming that the young chaps would not venture to defend themselves, he thought to get back his money by force; but the two friends laying hands promptly, the one on his dudgeon dagger and the other on his yellow handled knife, gave the Muleteer so much to do, that if his companions had not hastened to assist him, he would have come badly out of the quarrel.

At that moment there chanced to pass by a company of travellers on horseback, who were going to make their siesta at the hostelry of the Alcalde, about half a league farther on. Seeing the affray between the Muleteer with two boys, they interposed, and offered to take the latter in their company to Seville, if they were going to that city.

"That is exactly where we desire to go," exclaimed Rincon, "and we will serve your worships in all that it shall please you to command." Whereupon, without more ado, they sprang before the mules, and departed with the travellers, leaving the Muleteer despoiled of his money and furious with rage, while the hostess was in great admiration of the finished education and accomplishments of the two rogues, whose dialogue she had heard from beginning to end, while they were not aware of her presence.

When the hostess told the Muleteer that she had heard the boys say the cards they played with were false, the man tore his beard for rage, and would have followed them to the other Venta, in the hope of recovering his property; for he declared it to be a serious affront, and a matter touching his honour, that two boys should have cheated a grown man like him. But his companions dissuaded him from doing what they declared would be nothing better than publishing his own folly and incapacity; and their arguments, although they did not console the Muleteer, were sufficient to make him remain where he was.

Meanwhile Cortado and Rincon displayed so much zeal and readiness in the service of the travellers, that the latter gave them a lift behind them for the greater part of the way. They might many a time have rifled the portmanteaus of their temporary masters, but did not, lest they should thereby lose the happy opportunity of seeing Seville, in which city they greatly desired to exercise their talents. Nevertheless, as they entered Seville—which they did at the hour of evening prayer, and by the gate of the custom-house, on account of the dues to be paid, and the trunks to be examined—Cortado could not refrain from making an examination, on his own account, of the valise which a Frenchman of the company carried with him on the croup of his mule. With his yellow-handled weapon, therefore, he gave it so deep and broad a wound in the side that its very entrails were exposed to view; and he dexterously drew forth two good shirts, a sun-dial, and a memorandum book, things that did not greatly please him when he had leisure to examine them. Thinking that since the Frenchman carried that valise on his own mule, it must needs contain matters of more importance than those he had captured, Cortado would fain have looked further into it, but he abstained, as it was probable that the deficiency had been already discovered, and the remaining effects secured. Before performing this feat the friends had taken leave of those who had fed them on their journey, and the following day they sold the two shirts in the old clothes' market, which is held at the gate of the Almacen or arsenal, obtaining twenty reals for their booty.

Having despatched this business, they went to see the city, and admired the great magnificence and vast size of its principal church, and the vast concourse of people on the quays, for it happened to be the season for loading the fleet. There were also six galleys on the water, at sight of which the friends could not refrain from sighing, as they thought the day might come when they should be clapped on board one of those vessels for the remainder of their lives. They remarked the large number of basket-boys, porters, &c., who went to and fro about the ships, and inquired of one among them what sort of a trade it was—whether it was very laborious—and what were the gains.

An Asturian, of whom they made the inquiry, gave answer to the effect that the trade was a very pleasant one, since they had no harbour-dues to pay, and often found themselves at the end of the day with six or seven reals in their pocket, with which they might eat, drink, and enjoy themselves like kings. Those of his calling, he said, had no need to seek a master to whom security must be given, and you could dine when and where you please, since, in the city of Seville, there is not an eating-house, however humble, where you will not find all you want at any hour of the day.

The account given by the Asturian was by no means discouraging to the two friends, neither did his calling seem amiss to them; nay, rather, it appeared to be invented for the very purpose of enabling them to exercise their own profession in secresy and safety, on account of the facilities it offered for entering houses. They consequently determined to buy such things as were required for the instant adoption of the new trade, especially as they could enter upon it without undergoing any previous scrutiny.

In reply to their further inquiries, the Asturian told them that it would be sufficient if each had a small porter's bag of linen, either new or second-hand, so it was but clean, with three palm-baskets, two large and one small, wherein to carry the meat, fish, and fruit purchased by their employers, while the bag was to be used for carrying the bread. He took them to where all these things were sold; they supplied themselves out of the plunder of the Frenchman, and in less than two hours they might have been taken for regular graduates in their new profession, so deftly did they manage their baskets, and so jauntily carry their bags. Their instructor furthermore informed them of the different places at which they were to make their appearance daily: in the morning at the shambles, and at the market of St. Salvador; on fast-days at the fish-market; every afternoon on the quay, and on Thursdays at the fair.

All these lessons the two friends carefully stored in their memory, and the following morning both repaired in good time to the market of St. Salvador. Scarcely had they arrived before they were remarked by numbers of young fellows of the trade, who soon perceived, by the shining brightness of their bags and baskets, that they were new beginners. They were assailed with a thousand questions, to all which they replied with great presence of mind and discretion. Presently up came two customers, one of whom had the appearance of a Student, the other was a Soldier; both were attracted by the clean and new appearance of their baskets; and he who seemed to be a student beckoned Cortado, while the soldier engaged Rincon. "In God's name be it!"[13] exclaimed both the novices in a breath—Rincon adding, "It is a good beginning of the trade, master, since it is your worship that is giving me my hansel." "The hansel shall not be a bad one," replied the soldier, "seeing that I have been lucky at cards of late, and am in love. I propose this day to regale the friends of my lady with a feast, and am come to buy the materials." "Load away, then, your worship," replied Rincon, "and lay on me as much as you please, for I feel courage enough to carry off the whole market; nay, if you should desire me to aid in cooking what I carry, it shall be done with all my heart."

The soldier was pleased with the boy's ready good-will, and told him that if he felt disposed to enter his service he would relieve him from the degrading office he then bore; but Rincon declared, that since this was the first day on which he had tried it, he was not willing to abandon the work so soon, or at least until he had seen what profit there was to be made of it; but if it did not suit him, he gave the gentleman his word that he would prefer the service offered him even to that of a Canon.

The soldier laughed, loaded him well, and showed him the house of his lady, bidding him observe it well that he might know it another time, so that he might be able to send him there again without being obliged to accompany him. Rincon promised fidelity and good conduct; the soldier gave him three quartos,[14] and the lad returned like a shot to the market, that he might lose no opportunity by delay. Besides, he had been well advised in respect of diligence by the Asturian, who had likewise told him that when he was employed to carry small fish, such as sprats, sardines, or flounders, he might very well take a few for himself and have the first taste of them, were it only to diminish his expenses of the day, but that he must do this with infinite caution and prudence, lest the confidence of the employers should be disturbed; for to maintain confidence was above all things important in their trade.

But whatever haste Rincon had made to return, he found Cortado at his post before him. The latter instantly inquired how he had got on. Rincon opened his hand and showed the three quartos; when Cortado, thrusting his arm into his bosom, drew forth a little purse which appeared to have once been of amber-coloured silk, and was not badly filled. "It was with this," said he, "that my service to his reverence the Student has been rewarded—with this and two quartos besides. Do you take it, Rincon, for fear of what may follow."

Cortado had scarcely given the purse in secret to his companion, before the Student returned in a great heat, and looking in mortal alarm. He no sooner set eyes on Cortado, than, hastening towards him, he inquired if he had by chance seen a purse with such and such marks and tokens, and which had disappeared, together with fifteen crowns in gold pieces, three double reals, and a certain number of maravedis in quartos and octavos. "Did you take it from me yourself," he added, "while I was buying in the market, with you standing beside me?"

To this Cortado replied with perfect composure, "All I can tell you of your purse is, that it cannot be lost, unless, indeed, your worship has left it in bad hands."

"That is the very thing, sinner that I am," returned the Student. "To a certainty I must have left it in bad hands, since it has been stolen from me." "I say the same," rejoined Cortado, "but there is a remedy for every misfortune excepting death. The best thing your worship can do now is to have patience, for after all it is God who has made us, and after one day there comes another. If one hour gives us wealth, another takes it away; but it may happen that the man who has stolen your purse may in time repent, and may return it to your worship, with all the interest due on the loan."

"The interest I will forgive him," exclaimed the Student; and Cortado resumed:—"There are, besides, those letters of excommunication, the Paulinas;[15] and there is also good diligence in seeking for the thief, which is the mother of success. Of a truth, Sir, I would not willingly be in the place of him who has stolen your purse; for if your worship have received any of the sacred orders, I should feel as if I had been guilty of some great crime—nay of sacrilege—in stealing from your person."

"Most certainly the thief has committed a sacrilege," replied the Student, in pitiable tones; "for although I am not in orders, but am only a Sacristan of certain nuns, yet the money in my purse was the third of the income due from a chapelry, which I had been commissioned to receive by a priest, who is one of my friends, so that the purse does, in fact, contain blessed and sacred money."

"Let him eat his sin with his bread," exclaimed Rincon at that moment; "I should be sorry to become bail for the profit he will obtain from it. There will be a day of judgment at the last, when all things will have to pass, as they say, through the holes of the colander, and it will then be known who was the scoundrel that has had the audacity to plunder and make off with the whole third of the revenue of a chapelry! But tell me, Mr. Sacristan, on your life, what is the amount of the whole yearly income?"

"Income to the devil, and you with it,[16]" replied the Sacristan, with more rage than was becoming; "am I in a humour to talk to you about income? Tell me, brother, if you know anything of the purse; if not, God be with you—I must go and have it cried."

"That does not seem to me so bad a remedy," remarked Cortado; "but I warn your worship not to forget the precise description of the purse, nor the exact sum that it contains; for if you commit the error of a single mite, the money will never be suffered to appear again while the world is a world, and that you may take for a prophecy."

"I am not afraid of committing any mistake in describing the purse," returned the Sacristan, "for I remember it better than I do the ringing of my bells, and I shall not commit the error of an atom." Saying this, he drew a laced handkerchief from his pocket to wipe away the perspiration which rained down his face as from an alembic; but no sooner had Cortado set eyes on the handkerchief, than he marked it for his own.

When the Sacristan had got to a certain distance, therefore, Cortado followed, and having overtaken him as he was mounting the steps of a church, he took him apart, and poured forth so interminable a string of rigmarole, all about the theft of the purse, and the prospect of recovering it, that the poor Sacristan could do nothing but listen with open mouth, unable to make head or tail of what he said, although he made him repeat it two or three times.

Cortado meanwhile continued to look fixedly into the eyes of the Sacristan, whose own were rivetted on the face of the boy, and seemed to hang, as it were, on his words. This gave Cortado an opportunity to finish his job, and having cleverly whipped the handkerchief out of the pocket, he took leave of the Sacristan, appointing to meet him in the evening at the same place, for he suspected that a certain lad of his own height and the same occupation, who was a bit of a thief, had stolen the purse, and he should be able to ascertain the fact in a few days, more or less.

Somewhat consoled by this promise, the Sacristan took his leave of Cortado, who then returned to the place where Rincon had privily witnessed all that had passed. But a little behind him stood another basket-boy, who had also seen the whole transaction; and at the moment when Cortado passed the handkerchief to Rincon, the stranger accosted the pair.

"Tell me, gallant gentlemen," said he, "are you admitted to the Mala Entrada,[17] or not?"

"We do not understand your meaning, noble Sir," replied Rincon.

"How! not entered, brave Murcians?" replied the other.

"We are neither of Murcia[18] nor of Thebes," replied Cortado. "If you have anything else to say to us, speak; if not, go your ways, and God be with you."

"Oh, your worships do not understand, don't you?" said the porter; "but I will soon make you understand, and even sup up my meaning with a silver spoon. I mean to ask you, gentlemen, are your worships thieves? But why put the question, since I see well that you are thieves; and it is rather for you to tell me how it is that you have not presented yourselves at the custom-house of the Señor Monipodio."

"Do they then pay duty on the right of thieving in this country, gallant Sir?" exclaimed Rincon.

"If they do not pay duty, at least they make them register themselves with the Señor Monipodio, who is the father, master, and protector of thieves; and I recommend you to come with me and pay your respects to him forthwith, or, if you refuse to do that, make no attempt to exercise your trade without his mark and pass-word, or it will cost you dearly."

"I thought, for my part," remarked Cortado, "that the profession of thieving was a free one, exempt from all taxes and port dues; or, at least, that if we must pay, it is something to be levied in the lump, for which we give a mortgage upon our shoulders and our necks; but since it is as you say, and every land has its customs, let us pay due respect to this of yours; we are now in the first country of the world, and without doubt the customs of the place must be in the highest degree judicious. Wherefore your worship may be pleased to conduct us to the place where this gentleman of whom you have spoken is to be found. I cannot but suppose, from what you say, that he is much honoured, of great power and influence, of very generous nature, and, above all, highly accomplished in the profession."

"Honoured, generous, and accomplished! do you say?" replied the boy: "aye, that he is; so much so, that during the four years that he has held the seat of our chief and father, only four of us have suffered at Finibusterry;[19] some thirty or so, and not more, have lost leather; and but sixty-two have been lagged."

"Truly, Sir," rejoined Rincon, "all this is Hebrew to us; we know no more about it than we do of flying."

"Let us be jogging, then," replied the new-comer, "and on the way I will explain to you these and other things, which it is requisite you should know as pat as bread to mouth;" and, accordingly, he explained to them a whole vocabulary of that thieves' Latin which they call Germanesco, or Gerigonza, and which their guide used in the course of his lecture,—by no means a short one, for the distance they had to traverse was of considerable length.

On the road, Rincon said to his new acquaintance, "Does your worship happen to be a Thief?"

"Yes," replied the lad, "I have that honour, for the service of God and of all good people; but I cannot boast of being among the most distinguished, since I am as yet but in the year of my novitiate."

"It is news to me," remarked Cortado, "that there are thieves for the service of God and of good people."

"Señor," the other replied, "I don't meddle with theology; but this I know, that every one may serve

25

God in his vocation, the more so as daddy Monipodio keeps such good order in that respect among all his children."

"His must needs be a holy and edifying command," rejoined Rincon, "since it enjoins thieves to serve God."

"It is so holy and edifying," exclaimed the stranger, "that I don't believe a better will ever be known in our trade. His orders are that we give something by way of alms out of all we steal, to buy oil for the lamp of a highly venerated image, well known in this city; and we have really seen great things result from that good work. Not many days ago, one of our cuatreros had to take three ansias for having come the Murcian over a couple of roznos, and although he was but a poor weak fellow, and ill of the fever to boot, he bore them all without singing out, as though they had been mere trifles. This we of the profession attribute to his particular devotion to the Virgin of the Lamp, for he was so weak, that, of his own strength, he could not have endured the first desconcierto of the hangman's wrist. But now, as I guess, you will want to know the meaning of certain words just used; I will take physic before I am sick—that is to say, give you the explanation before you ask for it.

"Be pleased to know then, gentlemen, that a cuatrero is a stealer of cattle, the ansia is the question or torture. Roznos—saving your presence—are asses, and the first desconcierto is the first turn of the cord which is given by the executioner when we are on the rack. But we do more than burn oil to the Virgin. There is not one of us who does not recite his rosary carefully, dividing it into portions for each day of the week. Many will not steal at all on a Friday, and on Saturdays we never speak to any woman who is called Mary."

"All these things fill me with admiration," replied Cortado; "but may I trouble your worship to tell me, have you no other penance than this to perform? Is there no restitution to make?"

"As to restitution," returned the other, "it is a thing not to be mentioned; besides, it would be wholly impossible, on account of the numerous portions into which things stolen have to be divided before each one of the agents and contractors has received the part due to him. When all these have had their share, the original thief would find it difficult to make restitution. Moreover, there is no one to bid us do anything of that kind, seeing that we do not go to confession. And if letters of excommunication are out against us, they rarely come to our knowledge, because we take care not to go into the churches while the priests are reading them, unless, indeed, it be on the days of Jubilee, for then we do go, on account of the vast profits we make from the crowds of people assembled on that occasion."

"And proceeding in this manner," observed Cortado, "your worships think that your lives are good and holy?"

"Certainly! for what is there bad in them?" replied the other lad! "Is it not worse to be a heretic or a renegade? or to kill your father or mother?"

"Without doubt," admitted Cortado; "but now, since our fate has decided that we are to enter this brotherhood, will your worship be pleased to step out a little, for I am dying to behold this Señor Monipodio, of whose virtues you relate such fine things."

"That wish shall soon be gratified," replied the stranger, "nay even from this place we can perceive his house: but your worships must remain at the door until I have gone in to see if he be disengaged, since these are the hours at which he gives audience."

"So be it," replied Rincon; and the thief preceding them for a short distance, they saw him enter a house which, so far from being handsome, had a very mean and wretched appearance. The two friends remained at the door to await their guide, who soon reappeared, and called to them to come in. He then bade them remain for the present in a little paved court, or patio,[20] so clean and carefully rubbed that the red bricks shone as if covered with the finest vermilion. On one side of the court was a three-legged stool, before which stood a large pitcher with the lip broken off, and on the top of the pitcher was placed a small jug equally dilapidated. On the other side lay a rush mat, and in the middle was a fragment of crockery which did service as the recipient of some sweet basil.

The two boys examined these moveables attentively while awaiting the descent of the Señor Monipodio, but finding that he delayed his appearance, Rincon ventured to put his head into one of two small rooms which opened on the court. There he saw two fencing foils, and two bucklers of cork hung upon four nails; there was also a great chest, but without a lid or anything to cover it, with three rush mats extended on the floor. On the wall in face of him was pasted a figure of Our Lady—one of the coarsest of prints—and beneath it was a small basket of straw, with a little vessel of white earthenware sunk into the wall. The basket Rincon took to be a poor box, for receiving alms, and the little basin he supposed to be a receptacle for holy water, as in truth they were.

While the friends thus waited, there came into the court two young men of some twenty years each; they were clothed as students, and were followed soon afterwards by two of the basket boys or porters, and a blind man. Neither spoke a word to the other, but all began to walk up and down in the court. No long time elapsed before there also came in two old men clothed in black serge, and with spectacles on their noses, which gave them an air of much gravity, and made them look highly respectable: each held in his hand a rosary, the beads of which made a ringing sound. Behind these men came an old woman wearing a long and ample gown, who, without uttering a word, proceeded at once to the room wherein was the figure of Our Lady. She then took holy water with the greatest devotion, placed herself on her knees before the Virgin, and after remaining there a considerable time, first kissed the soil thrice, and then rising, lifted her arms and eyes towards heaven, in which attitude she remained a certain time longer. She then dropped her alms into the little wicker case—and that done, she issued forth among the company in the patio.

Finally there were assembled in the court as many as fourteen persons of various costumes and different professions. Among the latest arrivals were two dashing and elegant youths with long moustachios, hats of immense brims, broad collars, stiffly starched, coloured stockings, garters with great bows and fringed ends, swords of a length beyond that permitted by law, and each having a pistol in his belt, with a buckler hanging on his arm. No sooner had these men entered, than they began to look askance at Rincon and Cortado, whom they were evidently surprised to see there, as persons unknown to themselves. At length the new-comers accosted the two friends, asking if they were of the brotherhood. "We are so," replied Rincon, "and the very humble servants of your worships besides."

At this moment the Señor Monipodio honoured the respectable assembly with his welcome presence. He appeared to be about five or six-and-forty years old, tall, and of dark complexion; his eyebrows met on his forehead, his black beard was very thick, and his eyes were deeply sunk in his head. He had come down in his shirt, through the opening of which was seen a hairy bosom, as rough and thick set as a forest of brushwood. Over his shoulders was thrown a serge cloak, reaching nearly to his feet, which were cased in old shoes, cut down to make slippers; his legs were covered with a kind of linen gaiters, wide and ample, which fell low upon his ankles. His hat was that worn by those of the Hampa, bell-formed in the crown, and very wide in the brim.[21] Across his breast was a leather baldric, supporting a broad, short sword of the perrillo fashion.[22] His hands were short and coarse, the fingers thick, and the nails much flattened: his legs were concealed by the gaiters, but his feet were of immoderate size, and the most clumsy form. In short, he was the coarsest and most repulsive barbarian ever beheld. With him came the conductor of the two friends; who, taking Rincon and Cortado each by a hand, presented them to Monipodio, saying, "These are the two good boys of whom I spoke to your worship, Señor Monipodio. May it please your worship to examine them, and you will see how well they are prepared to enter our brotherhood." "That I will do willingly," replied Monipodio.

But I had forgotten to say, that when Monipodio had first appeared, all those who were waiting for him, made a deep and long reverence, the two dashing cavaliers alone excepted, who did but just touch their hats, and then continued their walk up and down the court.

Monipodio also began to pace up and down the patio, and, as he did so, he questioned the new disciples as to their trade, their birthplace, and their parents. To this Rincon replied, "Our trade is sufficiently obvious, since we are here before your worship; as to our country, it does not appear to me essential to the matter in hand that we should declare it, any more than the names of our parents, since we are not now stating our qualifications for admission into some noble order of knighthood."

"What you say, my son, is true, as well as discreet," replied Monipodio; "and it is, without doubt, highly prudent to conceal those circumstances; for if things should turn out badly, there is no need to have placed upon the books of register, and under the sign manual of the justice-clerk, 'So and so, native of such a place, was hanged, or made to dance at the whipping-post, on such a day,' with other announcements of the like kind, which, to say the least of them, do not sound agreeable in respectable ears. Thus, I repeat, that to conceal the name and abode of your parents, and even to change your own proper appellation, are prudent measures. Between ourselves there must, nevertheless, be no concealment: for the present I will ask your names only, but these you must give me."

Rincon then told his name, and so did Cortado: whereupon Monipodio said, "Henceforward I request and desire that you, Rincon, call yourself Rinconete, and you, Cortado, Cortadillo; these being names which accord, as though made in a mould, with your age and circumstances, as well as with our ordinances, which make it needful that we should also know the names of the parents of our comrades, because it is our custom to have a certain number of masses said every year for the souls of our dead, and of the benefactors of our society; and we provide for the payment of the priests who say them, by setting apart a share of our swag for that purpose.

"These masses, thus said and paid for, are of great service to the souls aforesaid. Among our benefactors we count the Alguazil, who gives us warning; the Advocate, who defends us; the Executioner, who takes pity upon us when we have to be whipped, and the man who, when we are running along the street, and the people in full cry after us bawling 'Stop thief,' throws himself between us and our pursuers, and checks the torrent, saying, 'Let the poor wretch alone, his lot is hard enough; let him go, and his crime will be his punishment.' We also count among our benefactors the good wenches who aid us by their labours while we are in prison, or at the galleys; our fathers, and the mothers who brought us into the world; and, finally, we take care to include the Clerk of the Court, for if he befriend us, there is no crime which he will not find means to reduce to a slight fault, and no fault which he does not prevent from being punished. For all these our brotherhood causes the sanctimonies (ceremonies) I have named to be soleciced (solemnised) every year, with all possible grandiloquence."

"Certainly," replied Rinconete (now confirmed in that name), "certainly that is a good work, and entirely worthy of the lofty and profound genius with which we have heard that you, Señor Monipodio, are endowed. Our parents still enjoy life; but should they precede us to the tomb, we will instantly give notice of that circumstance to this happy and highly esteemed fraternity, to the end that you may have 'sanctimonies soleciced' for their souls, as your worship is pleased to say, with the customary 'grandiloquence.'"

"And so shall it be done," returned Monipodio, "if there be but a piece of me left alive to look to it."

He then called their conductor, saying, "Hallo! there, Ganchuelo![23] Is the watch set?" "Yes," replied the boy; "three sentinels are on guard, and there is no fear of a surprise." "Let us return to business, then," said Monipodio. "I would fain know from you, my sons, what you are able to do, that I may assign you an employment in conformity with your inclinations and accomplishments."

"I," replied Rinconete, "know a trick or two to gammon a bumpkin; I am not a bad hand at hiding what a pal has prigged; I have a good eye for a gudgeon; I play well at most games of cards, and have all the best turns of the pasteboard at my finger ends; I have cut my eye teeth, and am about as easy to lay hold of as a hedgehog; I can creep through a cat-hole or down a chimney, as I would enter the door of my father's house; and will muster a million of tricks better than I could marshal a regiment of soldiers; and flabbergast the knowingest cove a deal sooner than pay back a loan of two reals."

"These are certainly the rudiments," admitted Monipodio, "but all such things are no better than old lavender flowers, so completely worn out of all savour that there is not a novice who may not boast of being a master in them. They are good for nothing but to catch simpletons who are stupid enough to run their heads against the church steeple; but time will do much for you, and we must talk further together. On the foundation already laid you shall have half a dozen lessons; and I then trust in God that you will turn out a famous craftsman, and even, mayhap, a master."

"My abilities shall always be at your service, and that of the gentlemen who are our comrades," replied Rinconete; and Monipodio then turned towards Cortadillo

"And you, Cortadillo, what may you be good for?" he inquired; to which Cortadillo replied, "For my part I know the trick called 'put in two, and take out five,' and I can dive to the bottom of a pocket with great precision and dexterity." "Do you know nothing more?" continued Monipodio. "Alas, no, for my sins, that is all I can do," admitted Cortadillo, "Do not afflict yourself, nevertheless," said the master; "you are arrived at a good port, where you will not be drowned, and you enter a school in which you can hardly fail to learn all that is requisite for your future welfare. And now as to courage: how do you feel yourselves provided in that respect, my children?" "How should we be provided," returned Rinconete, "but well and amply? We have courage enough to attempt whatever may be demanded in our art and profession." "But I would have you to possess a share of that sort which would enable you to suffer as well as to dare," replied Monipodio, "which would carry you, if need were, through a good half dozen of ansias without opening your lips, and without once saying 'This mouth is mine.'" "We already know what the ansias are, Señor Monipodio," replied Cortadillo, "and are prepared for all; since we are not so ignorant but that we know very well, that what the tongue says, the throat must pay for; and great is the grace heaven bestows on the bold man (not to give him a different name), in making his life or death depend upon the discretion of his tongue, as though there were more letters in a No than an Aye."

"Halt there, my son; you need say no more," exclaimed Monipodio at this point of the discourse. "The words you have just uttered suffice to convince, oblige, persuade, and constrain me at once to admit you both to full brotherhood, and dispense with your passing through the year of novitiate."

"I also am of that opinion," said one of the gaily-dressed Bravos; and this was the unanimous feeling of the whole assembly. They therefore requested that Monipodio would immediately grant the new brethren the enjoyment of all the immunities of their confraternity, seeing that their good mien and judicious discourse proved them to be entirely deserving of that distinction.

Monipodio replied, that, to satisfy the wishes of all, he at once conferred on those new-comers all the privileges desired, but he exhorted the recipients to remember that they were to hold the favour in high esteem, since it was a very great one: consisting in the exemption from payment of the media anata, or tax levied on the first theft they should commit, and rendering them free of all the inferior occupations of their office for the entire year. They were not obliged, that is to say, to bear messages to a brother of higher grade, whether in prison or at his own residence. They were permitted to drink their wine without water, and to make a feast when and where they pleased, without first demanding permission of their principal. They were, furthermore, to enter at once on a full share of whatever was brought in by the superior brethren, as one of themselves—with many other privileges, which the new comers accepted as most signal favours, and on the possession of which they were felicitated by all present, in the most polite and complimentary terms.

While these pleasing ceremonies were in course of being exchanged, a boy ran in, panting for breath, and cried out, "The Alguazil of the vagabonds is coming direct to the house, but he has none of the Marshalsea men with him."

"Let no one disturb himself," said Monipodio. "This is a friend; never does he come here for our injury. Calm your anxiety, and I will go out to speak with him." At these words all resumed their self-possession, for they had been considerably alarmed; and Monipodio went forth to the door of his house, where he found the Alguazil, with whom he remained some minutes in conversation, and then returned to the company. "Who was on guard to-day," he asked, "in the market of San Salvador?" "I was," replied the conductor of our two friends, the estimable Ganchuelo. "You!" replied Monipodio. "How then does it happen that you have not given notice of an amber-coloured purse which has gone astray there this morning, and has carried with it fifteen crowns in gold, two double reals, and I know not how many quartos?"

"It is true," replied Ganchuelo, "that this purse has disappeared, but it was not I took it, nor can I imagine who has done so." "Let there be no tricks with me," exclaimed Monipodio; "the purse must be found, since the Alguazil demands it, and he is a friend who finds means to do us a thousand services in the course of the year." The youth again swore that he knew nothing about it, while Monipodio's choler began to rise, and in a moment flames seemed to dart from his eyes. "Let none of you dare," he shouted, "to venture on infringing the most important rule of our order, for he who does so shall pay for it with his life. Let the purse be found, and if any one has been concealing it to avoid paying the dues, let him now give it up. I will make good to him all that he would have been entitled to, and out of my own pocket too; for, come what may, the Alguazil must not be suffered to depart without satisfaction." But Ganchuelo could do no more than repeat, with all manner of oaths and imprecations, that he had neither taken the purse, nor ever set eyes on it.

All this did but lay fuel on the flame of Monipodio's anger, and the entire assembly partook of his emotions; the honourable members perceiving that their statutes were violated, and their wise ordinances infringed. Seeing, therefore, that the confusion and alarm had now got to such a height, Rinconete began to think it time to allay it, and to calm the anger of his superior, who was bursting with rage. He took counsel for a moment with Cortadillo, and receiving his assent, drew forth the purse of the Sacristan, saying:—

"Let all questions cease, gentlemen: here is the purse, from which nothing is missing that the Alguazil has described, since my comrade Cortadillo prigged it this very day, with a pocket-handkerchief into the bargain, which he borrowed from the same owner." Thereupon Cortadillo produced the handkerchief before the assembled company.

Seeing this, Monipodio exclaimed "Cortadillo the Good! for by that title and surname shall you henceforward be distinguished. Keep the handkerchief, and I take it upon myself to pay you duly for this service; as to the purse, the Alguazil must carry it away just as it is, for it belongs to a Sacristan who happens to be his relation, and we must make good in his case the proverb, which says, 'To him who gives thee the entire bird, thou canst well afford a drumstick of the same.' This good Alguazil can save us from more mischief in one day than we can do him good in a hundred."

All the brotherhood with one voice approved the spirit and gentlemanly proceeding of the two new comers, as well as the judgment and decision of their superior, who went out to restore the purse to the Alguazil. As to Cortadillo, he was confirmed in his title of the Good, much as if the matter had concerned a Don Alonzo Perez de Guzman, surnamed the Good, who from the walls of Tarifa threw down to his enemy the dagger that was to destroy the life of his only son.[24]

When Monipodio returned to the assembly he was accompanied by two girls, with rouged faces, lips reddened with carmine, and necks plastered with white. They wore short camlet cloaks, and exhibited airs of the utmost freedom and boldness. At the first glance Rinconete and Cortadillo could see what was the profession of these women. They had no sooner entered, than they hurried with open arms, the one to Chiquiznaque, the other to Maniferro; these were the two bravos, one of whom bore the latter name because he had an iron hand, in place of one of his own, which had been cut off by the hand of justice. These two men embraced the girls with great glee, and inquired if they had brought the wherewithal to moisten their throats. "How could we think of neglecting that, old blade!" replied one of the girls, who was called Gananciosa.[25] "Silvatillo, your scout, will be here before long with the clothes-basket, crammed with whatever good luck has sent us."

And true it was; for an instant afterwards, a boy entered with a clothes-basket covered with a sheet.

The whole company renewed their rejoicings on the arrival of Silvatillo, and Monipodio instantly ordered that one of the mats should be brought from the neighbouring chamber, and laid out in the centre of the court. Furthermore he commanded that all the brotherhood should take places around it, in order that while they were taking the wrinkles out of their stomachs, they might talk about business.

To this proposal the old woman, who had been kneeling before the image, replied, "Monipodio, my son, I am not in the humour to keep festival this morning, for during the last two days I have had a giddiness and pain in my head, that go near to make me mad; I must, besides, be at our Lady of the Waters before mid-day strikes, having to accomplish my devotions and offer my candles there, as well as at the crucifix of St. Augustin; for I would not fail to do either, even though it were to snow all day and blow a hurricane. What I came here for is to tell you, that last night the Renegade and Centipede brought to my house a basket somewhat larger than that now before us; it was as full as it could hold of fine linen, and, on my life and soul, it was still wet and covered with soap, just as they had taken it from under the nose of the washerwoman, so that the poor fellows were perspiring and breathless beneath its weight. It would have melted your heart to see them as they came in, with the water streaming from their faces, and they as red as a couple of cherubs. They told me, besides, that they were in pursuit of a cattle-dealer, who had just had some sheep weighed at the slaughter-house, and they were then hastening off to see if they could not contrive to grab a great cat[26] which the dealer carried with him. They could not, therefore, spare time to count the linen, or take it out of the basket but they relied on the rectitude of my conscience; and so may God grant my honest desires, and preserve us all from the power of justice, as these fingers have refrained from touching the basket, which is as full as the day it was born."

"We cannot doubt it, good mother," replied Monipodio. "Let the basket remain where it is; I will come at nightfall to fetch it away, and will then ascertain the quantity and quality of its contents, giving to every one the portion, due to him, faithfully and truly, as it is my habit to do."

"Let it be as you shall command," rejoined the old woman; "and now, as it is getting late, give me something to drink, if you have it there—something that will comfort this miserable stomach, which is almost famishing for want."

"That you shall have, and enough of it, mother," exclaimed Escalanta, the companion of Gananciosa: and, uncovering the basket, she displayed a great leather bottle, containing at least two arrobas[27] of wine, with a cup made of cork, in which you might comfortably carry off an azumbre,[28] or honest half-gallon of the same. This Escalanta now filled, and placed it in the hands of the devout old woman, who took it in both her own, and, having blown away a little froth from the surface, she said,—

"You have poured out a large quantity, Escalanta, my daughter; but God will give me strength." Whereupon, without once taking breath, and at one draught, she poured the whole from the cup down her throat. "It is real Guadalcanal,"[29] said the old woman, when she had taken breath; "and yet it has just a tiny smack of the gypsum. God comfort you, my daughter, as you have comforted me; I am only afraid that the wine may do me some mischief, seeing that I have not yet broken my fast."

"No, mother; it will do nothing of the kind," returned Monipodio, "for it is three years old at the least."

"May the Virgin grant that I find it so," replied the old woman. Then turning to the girls, "See, children," she said "whether you have not a few maravedis to buy the candles for my offerings of devotion. I came away in so much haste, to bring the news of the basket of linen, that I forgot my purse, and left it at home."

"Yes, Dame Pipota,"—such was the name of the old woman,—"I have some," replied Gananciosa; "here are two cuartos for you, and with one of them I beg you to buy a candle for me, which you will offer in my name to the Señor St. Michael, or if you can get two with the money, you may place the other at the altar of the Señor St. Blas, for those two are my patron-saints. I also wish to give one to the Señora Santa Lucia, for whom I have a great devotion, on account of the eyes;[30] but I have no more change to-day, so it must be put off till another time, when I will square accounts with all."

"And you will do well, daughter," replied the old woman. "Don't be niggard, mind. It is a good thing to carry one's own candles before one dies, and not to wait until they are offered by the heirs and executors of our testament."

"You speak excellently, Mother Pipota," said Escalanta; and, putting her hand into her pocket, she drew forth a cuarto, which she gave the old woman, requesting her to buy two candles for her likewise, and offer them to such saints as she considered the most useful and the most likely to be grateful. With this old Pipota departed, saying,

"Enjoy yourselves, my dears, now while you have time, for old age will come and you will then weep for the moments you may have lost in your youth, as I do now. Commend me to God in your prayers, and I will remember you, as well as myself, in mine, that he may keep us all, and preserve us in this dangerous trade of ours from all the terrors of justice." These words concluded, the old woman went her way.

Dame Pipota having disappeared, all seated themselves round the mat, which Gananciosa covered with the sheet in place of a table-cloth. The first thing she drew from the basket was an immense bunch of radishes; this was followed by a couple of dozens or more of oranges and lemons; then came a great earthen pan filled with slices of fried ling, half a Dutch cheese, a bottle of excellent olives, a plate of shrimps, and a large dish of craw-fish, with their appropriate sauce of capers, drowned in pepper-vinegar: three loaves of the whitest bread from Gandul completed the collation. The number of guests at this breakfast was fourteen, and not one of them failed to produce his yellow-handled knife, Rinconete alone excepted, who drew his dudgeon dagger instead. The two old men in serge gowns, and the lad who had been the guide of the two friends, were charged with the office of cupbearers, pouring the wine from the bottle into the cork cup.

But scarcely had the guests taken their places, before they were all startled, and sprang up in haste at the, sound of repeated knocks at the door. Bidding them remain quiet, Monipodio went into one of the lower rooms, unhooked a buckler, took his sword in his hand, and, going to the door, inquired, in a rough and threatening voice, "Who is there?"

"All right Señor! it is I, Tagarote,[31] on sentry this morning," replied a voice from without. "I come to tell you that Juliana de Cariharta[32] is coming, with her hair all about her face, and crying her eyes out, as though some great misfortune had happened to her."

He had scarcely spoken when the girl he had named came sobbing to the door, which Monipodio opened for her, commanding Tagarote to return to his post; and ordering him, moreover, to make less noise and uproar when he should next bring notice of what was going forward,—a command to which the boy promised attention.

Cariharta, a girl of the same class and profession with those already in presence, had meanwhile entered the court, her hair streaming in the wind, her eyes swollen with tears, and her face covered with contusions and bruises. She had no sooner got into the Patio, than she fell to the ground in a fainting fit. Gananciosa and Escalanta[33] sprang to her assistance, unfastened her dress, and found her breast and shoulders blackened and covered with marks of violence. After they had thrown water on her face, she soon came to herself, crying out as she did so, "The justice of God and the king on that shameless thief, that cowardly cut-purse, and dirty scoundrel, whom I have saved from the gibbet more times than he has hairs in his beard. Alas! unhappy creature that I am! see for what I have squandered my youth, and spent the flower of my days! For an unnatural, worthless, and incorrigible villain!"

"Recover yourself, and be calm, Cariharta," said Monipodio; "I am here to render justice to you and to all. Tell me your cause of complaint, and you shall be longer in relating the story than I will be in taking vengeance. Let me know if anything has happened between you and your respeto;[34] and if you desire to be well and duly avenged. You have but to open your mouth."

"Protector!" exclaimed the girl. "What kind of a protector is he? It were better for me to be protected in hell than to remain any longer with that lion among sheep, and sheep among men! Will I ever eat again with him at the same table, or live under the same roof? Rather would I give this flesh of mine, which he has put into the state you shall see, to be devoured alive by raging beasts." So saying, she pulled up her petticoats to her knees, and even a little higher, and showed the wheals with which she was covered. "That's the way," she cried, "that I have been treated by that ungrateful Repolido,[35] who owes more to me than to the mother that bore him.

"And why do you suppose he has done this? Do you think I have given him any cause?—no, truly. His only reason for serving me so was, that being at play and losing his money, he sent Cabrillas, his scout, to me for thirty reals, and I could only send him twenty-four. May the pains and troubles with which I earned them be counted to me by heaven in remission of my sins! But in return for this civility and kindness, fancying that I had kept back part of what he chose to think I had got, the blackguard lured me out to the fields this morning, beyond the king's garden, and there, having stripped me among the olive trees, he took off his belt, not even removing the iron buckle—oh that I may see him clapped in irons and chains!—and with that he gave me such an unmerciful flogging, that he left me for dead; and that's a true story, as the marks you see bear witness."

Here Cariharta once more set up her pipes and craved for justice, which was again promised to her by Monipodio and all the bravos present.

The Gananciosa then tried her hand at consoling the victim; saying to her, among other things—"I would freely give my best gown that my fancy man had done as much by me; for I would have you know, sister Cariharta, if you don't know it yet, that he who loves best thrashes best; and when these scoundrels whack us and kick us, it is then they most devoutly adore us. Tell me now, on our life, after having beaten and abused you, did not Repolido make much of you, and give you more than one caress?"

"More than one!" replied the weeping girl; "he gave me more than a hundred thousand, and would have given a finger off his hand if I would only have gone with him to his posada; nay, I even think that the tears were almost starting from his eyes after he had leathered me."

"Not a doubt of it," replied Gananciosa; "and he would weep now to see the state he has put you into: for men like him have scarcely committed the fault before repentance begins. You will see, sister, if he does not come here to look for you before we leave the place; and see if he does not beg you to forgive what has passed, and behave to you as meek and as humble as a lamb."

"By my faith," observed Monipodio, "the cowardly ruffian shall not enter these doors until he has made full reparation for the offence he has committed. How dare he lay a hand on poor Cariharta, who for cleanliness and industry is a match for Gananciosa herself, and that is saying everything."

"Alas! Señor Monipodio," replied Juliana, "please do not speak too severely of the miserable fellow; for, hard as he is, I cannot but love him as I do the very folds of my heart; and the words spoken in his behalf by my friend Gananciosa have restored the soul to my body. Of a truth, if I consulted only my own wishes, I should go this moment and look for him."

"No, no," replied Gananciosa, "you shall not do so by my counsel; for to do that would make him proud; he would think too much of himself, and would make experiments upon you as on a dead body. Keep quiet, sister, and in a short time you will see him here repentant, as I have said; and if not, we will write verses on him that shall make him roar with rage."

"Let us write by all means," returned Juliana, "for I have a thousand things to say to him."

"And I will be your secretary, if need be," rejoined Monipodio, "for although I am no poet, yet a man has but to tuck up the sleeves of his shirt, set well to work, and he may turn off a couple of thousand verses in the snapping of a pair of scissors. Besides, if the rhymes should not come so readily as one might wish, I have a friend close by, a barber, who is a great poet, and will trim up the ends of the verses at an hour's notice. At present, however, let us go finish our repast; all the rest can be done afterwards."

Juliana was not unwilling to obey her superior, so they all fell to again at the O-be-joyful with so much goodwill that they soon saw the bottom of the basket and the dregs of the great leather bottle. The old ones drank sine fine, the younger men to their hearts' content, and the ladies till they could drink no more. When all was consumed, the two old men begged permission to take their leave, which Monipodio allowed them to do, but charged them to return punctually, for the purpose of reporting all they should see or hear that could be useful to the brotherhood; they assured him they would by no means fail in their duty, and then departed.

After these gentlemen had left the company, Rinconete, who was of a very inquiring disposition, begged leave to ask Monipodio in what way two persons so old, grave, and formal as those he had just seen, could be of service to their community. Monipodio replied, that such were called "Hornets" in their jargon, and that their office was to poke about all parts of the city, spying out such places as might be eligible for attempts to be afterwards made in the night-time. "They watch people who receive money from the bank or treasury," said he, "observe where they go with it, and, if possible, the very place in which it is deposited. When this is done, they make themselves acquainted with the thickness of the walls, marking out the spot where we may most conveniently make our guzpataros, which are the holes whereby we contrive to force an entrance. In a word, these persons are among the most useful of the brotherhood: and they receive a fifth of all that the community obtains by their intervention, as his majesty does, on treasure trove. They are, moreover, men of singular integrity and rectitude. They lead a respectable life, and enjoy a good reputation, fearing God and regarding the voice of their consciences, insomuch that not a day passes over their heads in which they have not heard mass with extraordinary devotion. There are, indeed, some of them so conscientious, that they content themselves with even less than by our rules would be their due. Those just gone are of this number. We have two others, whose trade it is to remove furniture; and as they are daily employed in the conveyance of articles for persons who are changing their abode, they know all the ins and outs of every house in the city, and can tell exactly where we may hope for profit and where not."

"That is all admirable," replied Rinconete, "and greatly do I desire to be of some use to so noble a confraternity."

"Heaven is always ready to favour commendable desires," replied Monipodio.

While the two were thus discoursing, a knock was heard at the door, and Monipodio went to see who might be there. "Open, Sor[36] Monipodio—open," said a voice without; "it is I, Repolido."

Cariharta hearing this voice, began to lift up her own to heaven, and cried out, "Don't open the door, Señor Monipodio; don't let in that Tarpeian mariner—that tiger of Ocaña."[37]

Monipodio opened the door, nevertheless, in despite of her cries; when Cariharta, starting to her feet, hurried away, and hid herself in the room where the bucklers were hung up. There, bolting the door, she bawled from her refuge, "Drive out that black-visaged coward, that murderer of innocents, that white-livered terror of house-lambs, who durst not look a man in the face."

Repolido was meanwhile kept back by Maniferro and Chiquiznaque, as he struggled with all his might to get into the room where Cariharta was hidden. But when he saw that to be impossible, he called to her from without, "Come, come, let us have done with this, my little sulky; by your life, let us have peace, as you would wish to be married." "Married!" retorted the lady, "married to you too! Don't you wish you may get it? See what kind of a string he's playing on now. I would rather be married to a dead notomy." "Oh, bother!" exclaimed Repolido; "let us have done with this, for it is getting late; take care of being too much puffed up at hearing me speak so gently, and seeing me so meek; for, by the light of heaven, if my rage should get steeple-high, the relapse will be worse than the first fit. Come down from your stilts, let us all have done with our tantrums, and not give the devil a dinner."

"I will give him a supper to boot, if he will take you from my sight to some place where I may never set eyes on you more," exclaimed the gentle Juliana from within.

"Haven't I told you once to beware, Madame Hemp-sack? By the powers, I suspect I must serve out something to you by the dozen, though I make no charge for it."

Here Monipodio interposed: "In my presence," he said, "there shall be no violence. Cariharta will come out, not for your threats, but for my sake, and all will go well. Quarrels between people who love each other are but the cause of greater joy and pleasure when peace is once made. Listen to me, Juliana, my daughter; listen to me, my Cariharta. Come out to us, for the love of your friend Monipodio, and I will make Repolido beg your pardon on his knees."

"Ah! if he will do that," exclaimed Escalanta, "we shall then be all on his side, and will entreat Juliana to come out."

"If I am asked to beg pardon in a sense of submission that would dishonour my person," replied Repolido, "an army of lansquenets would not make me consent; but if it be merely in the way of doing pleasure to Cariharta, I do not say merely that I would go on my knees, but I would drive a nail into my forehead to do her service."

At these words Chiquiznaque and Maniferro began to laugh, and Repolido, who thought they were making game of him, cried out in a transport of rage, "Whoever shall laugh or think of laughing at anything whatsoever that may pass between Cariharta and myself, I say that he lies, and that he will have lied every time he shall laugh or think of laughing."

Hearing this, Chiquiznaque and Maniferro looked at each other and scowled so sternly, that Monipodio saw things were likely to come to a crisis unless he prevented it. Throwing himself, therefore, into the midst of the group, he cried out, "No more of this, gentlemen! have done with all big words; grind them up between your teeth; and since those that have been said do not reach to the belt, let no one here apply them to himself."

"We are very sure," replied Chiquiznaque, "that such admonitions neither have been nor will be uttered for our benefit; otherwise, or if it should be imagined that they were addressed to us, the tambourine is in hands that would well know how to beat it."

"We also, Sor Chiquiznaque, have our drum of Biscay," retorted Repolido, "and, in case of need, can make the bells as well as another. I have already said, that whoever jests in our matters is a liar: and whoever thinks otherwise, let him follow me; with a palm's length of my sword I will show him that what is said is said." Having uttered these words, Repolido turned towards the outer door, and proceeded to leave the place.

Cariharta had meanwhile been listening to all this, and when she found that Repolido was departing in anger, she rushed out, screaming, "Hold him, hold him,—don't let him go, or he will be showing us some more of his handiwork; can't you see that he is angry? and he is a Judas Macarelo in the matter of bravery. Come here, Hector of the world and of my eyes!" With these words, Cariharta threw herself upon the retiring bravo, and held him with all her force by his cloak. Monipodio lent her his aid, and between them they contrived to detain him.

Chiquiznaque and Maniferro, undetermined whether to resume the dispute or not, stood waiting apart to see what Repolido would do, and the latter perceiving himself to be in the hands of Monipodio and Cariharta, exclaimed, "Friends should never annoy friends, nor make game of friends, more especially when they see that friends are vexed."

"There is not a friend here," replied Maniferro, "who has any desire to vex a friend; and since we

33

are all friends, let us give each other the hand like friends." "Your worships have all spoken like good friends," added Monipodio, "and as such friends should do; now finish by giving each other your hands like true friends."

All obeyed instantly, whereupon Escalanta, whipping off her cork-soled clog, began to play upon it as if it had been a tambourine. Gananciosa, in her turn, caught up a broom, and, scratching the rushes with her fingers, drew forth a sound which, if not soft or sweet, yet agreed very well with the beating of the slipper. Monipodio then broke a plate, the two fragments of which he rattled together in such fashion as to make a very praiseworthy accompaniment to the slipper and the broom.

Rinconete and Cortadillo stood in much admiration of that new invention of the broom, for up to that time they had seen nothing like it. Maniferro perceived their amazement, and said to them, "The broom awakens your admiration,—and well it may, since a more convenient kind of instrument was never invented in this world, nor one more readily formed, or less costly. Upon my life, I heard a student the other day affirm, that neither the man who fetched his wife out of hell—Negrofeo, Ogrofeo, or what was he called—nor that Marion who got upon a dolphin, and came out of the sea like a man riding on a hired mule—nor even that other great musician who built a city with a hundred gates and as many posterns—never a one of them invented an instrument half so easy of acquirement, so ready to the touch, so pleasing and simple as to its frets, keys, and chords, and so far from troublesome in the tuning and keeping in accord; and by all the saints, they swear that it was invented by a gallant of this very city, a perfect Hector in matters of music."

"I fully believe all you say," replied Rinconete, "but let us listen, for our musicians are about to sing. Gananciosa is blowing her nose, which is a certain sign that she means to sing."

And she was, in fact, preparing to do so. Monipodio had requested her to give the company some of the Seguidillas most in vogue at the moment. But the first to begin was Escalanta, who sang as follows, in a thin squeaking voice:—

"For a boy of Sevilla,
Red as a Dutchman,
All my heart's in flame."

To which Gananciosa replied, taking up the measure as she best might—

"For the little brown lad,
With a good bright eye,
Who would not lose her name?"

Then Monipodio, making great haste to perform a symphony with his pieces of platter, struck in—

"Two lovers dear, fall out and fight,
But soon, to make their peace, take leisure,
And all the greater was the row,
So much the greater is the pleasure."

But Cariharta had no mind to enjoy her recovered happiness in silence and fingering another clog, she also entered the dance, joining her voice to those of her friends, in the following words—

"Pause, angry lad! and do not beat me more,
For 'tis thine own dear flesh that thou dost baste,
If thou but well consider, and—"

"Fair and soft," exclaimed Repolido, at that moment, "give us no old stories, there's no good in that. Let bygones be bygones! Choose another gait, girl; we've had enough of that one."

The canticle, for a moment interrupted by these words, was about to recommence, and would not, apparently, have soon come to an end, had not the performers been disturbed by violent knocks at the door. Monipodio hastened to see who was there, and found one of his sentinels, who informed him that at the end of the street was the alcalde of criminal justice, with the little Piebald and the Kestrel (two catchpolls, who were called neutral, since they did the community of robbers neither good nor harm), marching before him.

The joyous company within heard the report of their scout, and were in a terrible fright. Escalanta and Cariharta put on their clogs in great haste, Gananciosa threw down her broom, and Monipodio his broken plate, every instrument sinking at once into silence. Chiquiznaque lost his joyous grin, and stood dumb as a fish; Repolido trembled with fear, and Maniferro looked pale with anxiety. But these various demonstrations were exhibited only for a moment,—in the next, all that goodly brotherhood had disappeared. Some rushed across a kind of terrace, and gained another court; others clambered over the roof, and so passed into a neighbouring alley. Never did the sound of a fowling piece, or a sudden peal of thunder, more effectually disperse a flock of careless pigeons, than did the news of the alcalde's arrival that select company assembled in the house of the Señor Monipodio. Rinconete and Cortadillo, not knowing whither to flee, stood in their places waiting to see what would be the end of that sudden storm, which finished simply enough by the return of the sentinel, who came to say that the alcalde had passed through the whole length of the street without seeming to have any troublesome suspicions respecting them, or even appearing to think of their house at all.

While Monipodio was in the act of receiving this last report, there came to the door a gentleman in the prime of youth, and dressed in the half-rustic manner suitable to the morning, or to one residing in the country. Monipodio caused this person to enter the house with himself; he then sent to look for Chiquiznaque, Repolido, and Maniferro, with orders that they should come forth from their hiding places, but that such others as might be with them should remain where they were.

Rinconete and Cortadillo having remained in the court, could hear all the conversation which took place between Monipodio and the gentleman who had just arrived, and who began by inquiring how it happened that the job he had ordered had been so badly done. At this point of the colloquy, Chiquiznaque appeared, and Monipodio asked him if he had accomplished the work with which he had been entrusted—namely, the knife-slash of fourteen stitches.[38]

"Which of them was it," inquired Chiquiznaque, "that of the merchant at the Cross-ways?" "Exactly," replied the gentleman. "Then I'll tell you how the matter went," responded the bravo. "Last night, as I watched before the very door of his house, and the man appeared just before to the ringing of the Ave Maria, I got near him, and took the measure of his face with my eyes; but I perceived it was so small that it was impossible, totally impossible, to find room in it for a cut of fourteen stitches. So that, perceiving myself unable to fulfil my destructions"—"Instructions you mean," said the gentleman;— "Well, well, instructions if you will," admitted Chiquiznaque,—"seeing that I could not find room for the number of stitches I had to make, because of the narrowness, I say, and want of space in the visage of the merchant, I gave the cut to a lacquey he had with him, to the end that I might not have my journey for nothing; and certainly his allowance may pass for one of the best quality."

"I would rather you had given the master a cut of seven stitches than the servant one of fourteen," remarked the gentleman. "You have not fulfilled the promise made me, but the thirty ducats which I gave you as earnest money, will be no great loss." This said, he saluted the two ruffians and turned to depart, but Monipodio detained him by the cloak of mixed cloth which he wore on his shoulders, saying: "Be pleased to stop, Señor cavalier, and fulfil your promise, since we have kept our word with strict honour and to great advantage. Twenty ducats are still wanting to our bargain, and your worship shall not go from this place until you have paid them, or left us something of equal value in pledge."

"Do you call this keeping your word," said the gentleman, "making a cut on the servant when you should have made it on the master?"

"How well his worship understands the business," remarked Chiquiznaque. "One can easily see that he does not remember the proverb which says: 'He who loves Beltran, loves his dog likewise.'"

"But what has this proverb to do with the matter?" inquired the gentleman.

"Why, is it not the same thing as to say, 'He who loves Beltran ill, loves his dog ill too?' Now the master is Beltran, whom you love ill, and the servant is his dog; thus in giving the cut to the dog I have given it to Beltran, and our part of the agreement is fulfilled; the work has been properly done, and nothing remains but to pay for it on the spot and without further delay."

"That is just what I am ready to swear to," cried Monipodio; "and you, friend Chiquiznaque, have taken all that you have said from my mouth; wherefore let not your worship, Señor gallant, be making difficulties out of trifles with your friends and servants. Take my advice and pay us what is our due. After that, if your worship would like to have another cut given to the master, of as many stitches as the space can contain, consider that they are already sewing up the wound."

"If it be so," said the gentleman, "I will very willingly pay the whole sum."

"Make no more doubt of it than of my being a good Christian, for Chiquiznaque will set the mark on his face so neatly, that he shall seem to have been born with it."

"On this promise, then, and with this assurance," replied the gentleman, "receive this chain in pledge for the twenty ducats before agreed on, and for forty other ducats which I will give you for the cut that is to come. The chain weighs a thousand reals, and it may chance to remain with you altogether, as I have an idea that I shall want fourteen stitches more before long."

Saying this, he took a chain from his neck, and put it into the hands of Monipodio, who found immediately by the weight and touch that it was not gold made by the chemist, but the true metal. He received it accordingly with great pleasure and much courtesy, for Monipodio was particularly well-bred. The execution of the work to be done for it was committed to Chiquiznaque, who declared that it should be delayed no longer than till the arrival of night. The gentleman then departed, well satisfied with his bargain.

Monipodio now summoned the confraternity from the hiding places into which their terror had driven them. When all had entered, he placed himself in the midst of them, drew forth a memorandum book from the hood of his cloak, and as he himself could not read, he handed it to Rinconete, who opened it, and read as follows:—

"Memoranda of the cuts to be given this week.

"The first is to the merchant at the Cross-ways, and is worth fifty crowns, thirty of which have been received on account. Secutor,[39] Chiquiznaque.

"I believe there are no others, my son," said Monipodio; "go on and look for the place where it is written, 'Memoranda of blows with a cudgel.'" Rinconete turned to that heading, and found under it this entry:—"To the keeper of the pot-house called the Trefoil, twelve blows, to be laid on in the best style, at a crown a-piece, eight of which crowns have been received; time of execution, within six days. Secutor, Maniferro."

"That article may be scratched out of the account," remarked Maniferro, "for to-night I shall give the gentleman his due."

"Is there not another, my son?" asked Monipodio.

"There is," replied Rinconete, and he read as follows:—

"To the hunch-backed Tailor, called by the nick-name Silguero,[40] six blows of the best sort for the lady whom he compelled to leave her necklace in pledge with him. Secutor, the Desmochado." [41]

"I am surprised to find this article still on the account," observed Monipodio, "seeing that two days have elapsed since it ought to have been taken off the book; and yet the secutor has not done his work. Desmochado must be indisposed."

"I met him yesterday," said Maniferro. "He is not ill himself, but the Hunchback has been so, and being confined to the house on that account, the Desmochado has been unable to encounter him."

"I make no doubt of it," rejoined Monipodio, "for I consider the Desmochado to be so good a workman, that but for some such reasonable impediment he would certainly before this have finished a job of much greater importance. Is there any more, my boy?" "No, Señor," replied Rinconete. "Turn over, then, till you find the 'Memorandum of miscellaneous damages.'"

Rinconete found the page inscribed "Memorandum of miscellaneous damages," namely, Radomagos,[42] greasing with oil of juniper, clapping on sanbenitos[43] and horns, false alarms, threatened stabbings, befoolings, calomels,[44] &c. &c.

"What do you find lower down?" inquired Monipodio. "I find, 'Greasing with oil of juniper at the house in—'" "Don't read the place or name of the house," interrupted Monipodio, "tor we know where it is, and I am myself the tuautem and secutor of this trifling matter; four crowns have already been given on account, and the total is eight." "That is exactly what is here written," replied Rinconete. "A little lower down," continued the boy, "I find 'Horns to be attached to the house—'" "Read neither the name nor the place where," interrupted Monipodio. "It is quite enough that we offer this outrage to the people in question; we need not make it public in our community, for that would be an unnecessary load on your consciences. I would rather nail a hundred horns, and as many sanbenitos, on a man's door, provided I were paid for my work, than once tell that I had done so, were it to the mother that bore me." "The executor of this is Nariqueta,"[45] resumed Rinconete. "It is already done and paid for," said Monipodio; "see if there be not something else, for if my memory is not at fault, there ought to be a fright of the value of twenty crowns. One half the money has already been paid, and the work is to be done by the whole community, the time within which it is to come off being all the current month. Nor will we fail in our duty; the commission shall be fulfilled to the very letter without missing a tilde,[46] and it will be one of the finest things that has been executed in this city for many years. Give me the book, boy, I know there is nothing more, and it is certain that business is very slack with us just now; but times will mend, and we shall perhaps have more to do than we want. There is not a leaf on the tree that moves without the will of God, and we cannot force people to avenge themselves, whether they will or not. Besides, many a man has the habit of being brave in his own cause, and does not care to pay for the execution of work which he can do as well with his own hands."

"That is true," said Repolido; "but will your worship, Señor Monipodio, see what you have for us to do, as it is getting late, and the heat is coming on at more than a foot-pace."

"What you have now to do is this," rejoined Monipodio: "Every one is to return to his post of the week, and is not to change it until Sunday. We will then meet here again, and make the distribution of all that shall have come in, without defrauding any one. To Rinconete and Cortadillo I assign for their district, until Sunday, from the Tower of Gold, all without the city, and to the postern of the Alcazar, where they can work with their fine flowers.[47] I have known those who were much less clever than they appear to be, come home daily with more than twenty reals in small money, to say nothing of silver, all made with a single pack, and that four cards short. Ganchuelo will show them the limits of their district, and even though they should extend it as far as to San Sebastian, or Santelmo, there will be no great harm done, although it is perhaps of more equal justice that none should enter on the domain of another."

The two boys kissed his hand in acknowledgment of the favour he was doing them; and promised to perform their parts zealously and faithfully, and with all possible caution and prudence.

Monipodio then drew from the hood of his cloak a folded paper, on which was the list of the brotherhood, desiring Rinconete to inscribe his name thereon, with that of Cortadillo; but as there was no escritoire in the place, he gave them the paper to take with them, bidding them enter the first apothecary's shop they could find, and there write what was needful: "Rinconete, and Cortadillo," namely, "comrades; novitiate; none; Rinconete, a florist; Cortadillo, a bassoon-player."[48] To this was to be added the year, month, and day, but not the parents or birthplace.

At this moment one of the old hornets came in and said, "I come to tell your worships that I have just now met on the steps, Lobillo[49] of Malaga, who tells me that he has made such progress in his art as to be capable of cheating Satan himself out of his money, if he have but clean cards. He is so ragged and out of condition at this moment, that he dares not instantly make his appearance to register himself, and pay his respects as usual, but will be here without fail on Sunday."

"I have always been convinced," said Monipodio, "that Lobillo would some day become supereminent in his art, for he has the best hands for the purpose that have ever been seen; and to be a good workman in his trade, a man should be possessed of good tools, as well as capacity for learning."

"I have also met the Jew," returned the hornet; "he wears the garb of a priest, and is at a tavern in the Street of the Dyers, because he has learned that two Peruleros[50] are now stopping there. He wishes to try if he cannot do business with them, even though it should be but in a trifling way to begin; for from small endeavours often come great achievements. He, too, will be here on Sunday, and will then give an account of himself."

"The Jew is a keen hawk too," observed Monipodio, "but it is long since I have set eyes on him, and he does not do well in staying away, for, by my faith, if he do not mend, I will cut his crown for him. The scoundrel has received orders as much as the Grand Turk, and knows no more Latin than my grandmother. Have you anything further to report?"

The old man replied that he had not. "Very well," said Monipodio; "Take this trifle among you," distributing at the same time some forty reals among those assembled, "and do not fail to be here on Sunday, when there shall be nothing wanting of the booty." All returned him thanks. Repolido and Cariharta embraced each other; so did Maniferro and Escalanta, and Chiquiznaque and Gananciosa; and all agreed that they would meet that same evening, when they left off work at the house of Dame Pipota, whither Monipodio likewise promised to repair, for the examination of the linen announced in the morning, before he went to his job with the juniper oil.

The master finally embraced Rinconete and Cortadillo, giving them his benediction; he then dismissed them, exhorting them to have no fixed dwelling or known habitation, since that was a precaution most important to the safety of all. Ganchuelo accompanied the friends for the purpose of guiding them to their districts, and pointing out the limits thereof. He warned them on no account to miss the assembly on Sunday, when it seemed that Monipodio intended to give them a lecture on matters concerning their profession. That done, the lad went away, leaving the two novices in great astonishment at all they had seen.

Now Rinconete, although very young, had a good understanding, and much intelligence. Having often accompanied his father in the sale of his bulls, he had acquired the knowledge of a more refined language than that they had just been hearing, and laughed with all his heart as he recalled the expressions used by Monipodio, and the other members of the respectable community they had entered. He was especially entertained by the solecising sanctimonies; and by Cariharta calling Repolido a Tarpeian Mariner, and a Tiger of Ocaña. He was also mightily edified by the expectation of Cariharta that the pains she had taken to earn the twenty-four reals would be accepted in heaven as a set-off against her sins, and was amazed to see with what security they all counted on going to heaven by means of the devotions they performed, notwithstanding the many thefts, homicides, and other offences against God and their neighbour which they were daily committing. The boy laughed too with all his heart, as he thought of the good old woman Pipota, who suffered the basket of stolen linen to be concealed in her house, and then went to place her little wax candles before the images of the saints, expecting thereby to enter heaven full dressed in her mantle and clogs.

But he was most surprised at the respect and deference which all these people paid to Monipodio, whom he saw to be nothing better than a coarse and brutal barbarian. He recalled the various entries which he had read in the singular memorandum-book of the burly thief, and thought over all the various occupations in which that goodly company was hourly engaged. Pondering all these things, he could not but marvel at the carelessness with which justice was administered in that renowned city of Seville, since such pernicious hordes and inhuman ruffians were permitted to live there almost openly.

He determined to dissuade his companion from continuing long in such a reprobate course of life. Nevertheless, led away by his extreme youth, and want of experience, he remained with these people for some months, during which there happened to him adventures which would require much writing to detail them; wherefore I propose to remit the description of his life and adventures to some other occasion, when I will also relate those of his master, Monipodio, with other circumstances connected with the members of that infamous academy, which may serve as warnings to those who read them.

END OF PETER OF THE CORNER AND THE LITTLE CUTTER.

[6] The alpargates are a kind of sandal made of cord.

[7] Montera, a low cap, without visor or front to shade the eyes.

[8] The Monument is a sort of temporary theatre, erected in the churches during Passion Week, and on which the passion of the Saviour is represented.

[9] Peter of the Corner; rincon meaning a corner, or obscure nook.

[10] The Spanish authorities, under the pretext of being at perpetual war with Infidels, still cause "Bulls of the Crusade," to the possession of which certain indulgences are attached, to be publicly sold in obscure villages. The product of these sales was originally expended on the wars with the Moors, but from the time when Granada fell into the hands of the Spaniards, it has been divided between the church and state. The bulls are carried about by hawkers, who are called "Buleros."—Viardot.

[11] An alguazil, who, while in the service of justice, is also in that of the thieves. He betrays them, nevertheless, whenever it suits his purpose to do so:

[12] "Clean from dust and straw"—limpios de polvo y paja—is a phrase equivalent to "free of the king's dues."

[13] This is a formula used in Spain by those who do a thing for the first time.—Viardot.

[14] The Quarto contains four Maravedis.

[15] Paulinas are the letters of excommunication despatched by the ecclesiastical courts for the discovery of such things as are supposed to be stolen or maliciously concealed.

[16] (This footnote is missing from the printed edition.)

[17] Mala Entrada, the evil way.

[18] In the slang dialect of Spain, Murcian and Murcia, mean thief, and the land of thieves.

[19] In finibus terræ, that is to say, at the gallows, or garotte, which to the thief is the end of the earth and all things.

[20] The Patio, familiar to all who have visited Seville, as forming the centre of the houses, and which serves in summer as the general sitting-room, so to speak, of the family.

[21] The Braves of the Hampa were a horde of ruffians principally Andalusians; they formed a society ready to commit every species of wrong and violence.

[22] The perrillo, or "little dog," was the mark of Julian del Rey, a noted armourer of Toledo, by birth a Morisco.

[23] Ganchuelo is the diminutive of gancho, a crimp.

[24] Our readers will perceive that this relates to the atrocity committed by the Infant Don Juan of Castille, who, while in revolt against his brother, Sancho IV., appeared before the city of Tarifa with an army, chiefly composed of Mahometans; finding the infant son of the governor, Don Alonzo Perez de Guzman, at nurse in a neighbouring village, he took the child, and bearing him to the foot of the walls, called on Guzman to surrender the place on pain of seeing his infant slaughtered before his eyes in case of refusal. The only reply vouchsafed by Don Alonzo was the horrible one alluded to in the text. He detached his own dagger from its belt, and threw it to Don Juan, when the sanguinary monster, far from respecting the fidelity of his opponent, seized the weapon, and pierced the babe to the heart as he had threatened to do This anecdote is related, with certain variations, in Conde, "La Dominacion de los Arabes en Espana."—See English Translation, vol. iii.

[25] The winner.

[26] A large purse made of cat-skin.

[27] The arroba holds about thirty-two pints.

[28] The azumbre is two quarts.

[29] A favourite wine, grown on the shore of the Manzanares.

[30] The Virgin Martyr, Santa Lucia, had her eyes burnt out of her head, and is regarded, in the Catholic Church, as particularly powerful in the cure of all diseases of the eyes. She is usually represented as bearing her eyes on a salver, which she holds in her hand.

[31] The quill-driver.

[32] Fat-face, puff-cheeks, or any other term describing fulness of face, in the least complimentary manner.

[33] The clamberer.

[34] Protector, or more exactly "bully,"—to defend and uphold in acts of fraud and violence.

[35] Dandy.

[36] Sor the contraction of Señor.

[37] "Ocaña" is a city at no great distance from Madrid; and if the lady has placed her tiger there, instead of in Hyrcania, as she doubtless intended, it is of course because her emotions had troubled her memory. The "Tarpeian mariner" is a fine phrase surely, but its meaning is not very clear.

[38] "At that time," remarks Viardot, "while wounds were still sewed up by the surgeons, the importance or extent of the cut made was estimated by the number of the stitches."

[39] Secutor for executor.

[40] The goldfinch.

[41] The lop-eared, or mutilated; alluding, generally, to losses suffered at the hands of justice.

[42] Radomagos, phials or bottles of ink, vitriol, and other injurious matters, cast on the face, person, or clothes.

[43] Most of our readers will remember that the "sanbenito" is the long coat or robe, painted over with flames, which is worn by heretics whom the Inquisition has condemned and given over to the civil power.

[44] Calomels, for calumnies

[45] The flat-nose.

[46] The tilde is the mark placed over the Spanish letter n, as in Señor.

[47] Tricks of cheatery at cards.

[48] Cutpurse.

[49] The wolf-cub.

[50] For Peruvians, which the American merchants were then called.

THE LICENTIATE VIDRIERA; OR, DOCTOR GLASS-CASE.

Two students were one day passing along the banks of the Tormes, when they found a boy, about eleven years old, dressed as a labourer, and sleeping under a tree. They sent a servant to wake him, and when he had well opened his eyes, they asked him whence he came, and what he was doing, to be lying asleep and defenceless in that lonely place. The boy replied, that he had forgotten the name of his birthplace, but was going to Salamanca, there to seek a master whom he might serve, on condition of being permitted and aided to pursue his studies.

The gentlemen then asked if he could read, and he replied that he could, and write also.

"It is not from want of memory, then, that you have forgotten the name of your country," remarked the students.

"Let the cause be what it may," replied the boy, "neither that nor the name of my parents shall be known to any one until I can do honour to them both."

"But in what manner do you propose to do them honour?" inquired the gentlemen.

"By the results of my studies," said the boy, "and when I have rendered myself famous by the learning I mean to acquire; for I have heard that some men have made themselves bishops by their studies."

This reply moved the two gentlemen to receive the lad into their service, and take him with them to Salamanca, giving him such facilities for studying as it is not unusual for masters to afford in that university to those who serve them.

The youth subsequently informed his masters, that they might call him Thomas Rodaja; whence the students judged him to be the son of some poor labourer. A day or two after their meeting, they caused him to be clothed in a suit of black; and, in the course of a few weeks, he gave proof of extraordinary talent. He was, besides, very grateful, and laboured so earnestly in the service of his masters, that although in fact exceedingly attentive to his studies, it might well have been thought that he did nothing but wait upon those he served.

Now the good service of the valet led the masters to treat him well; Thomas soon became their companion rather than servant, and, during eight years, all of which he passed with them, he acquired for himself so high a reputation in the university, by his great ability and excellent conduct, that he was beloved and esteemed by those of every rank.

The principal object of Rodaja's study was the law, but he was almost equally distinguished in polite learning, and his memory was matter of marvel to all; and the correctness of his views on all subjects was not less remarkable.

The time had now arrived when the studies of his masters were completed, and they returned to their birthplace, which was one of the most important cities of Andalusia. They took Rodaja with them, and he remained in their company for some time; but, assailed by a perpetual longing to return to his studies at Salamanca,—a city that enchains the will of all who have tasted the amenities of life in that fair seat of learning—he entreated permission of his masters to depart for that purpose. With their usual kindness, they accorded him the favour he desired, and took such measures in his behalf that by their bounty he was supplied with a sufficiency to support him in the university for three years.

Rodaja took his leave with manifest proofs of gratitude, and departed from Malaga, for that was the native city of his masters, without further delay. Descending the declivity of the Zambra on the road to Antequera, he chanced to encounter a gentleman on horseback, gaily accoutred in a rich travelling dress, and attended by two servants, also on horseback, whose company he joined; their journey thenceforward lay in the same direction, and the gentleman accepted Thomas as his comrade.[51] They discoursed of various matters, and, in a short time, Rodaja gave such proof of his quality as much delighted his fellow-traveller; while the latter, on his part, soon proved himself to be a kind and courteous man. He told Rodaja that he was a captain of infantry in the service of the king, and that his ensign was then completing their company at Salamanca. He praised the life of a soldier in the highest terms, describing, with much encomium, the many cities and other places visited by those who lead that life. Among other themes of which he spoke were the beauty of Naples, the feasting and pleasures of Palermo, the rich abundance of Milan, and the frequent festivals held in other parts of Lombardy—not omitting the good cheer of the numerous hostelries—in the description of which he broke forth rapturously in the Tuscan language, discoursing of Macarela, Macarroni, and Polastri, with the most cordial goodwill. He expatiated largely on the free enjoyment of life in Italy, and on the pleasures of the soldier's life in general, which he exalted to the skies; but he did not say a word of the chilling night-watch, the perils of the assault, the terrors of battle, the hunger and privation endured in blockades and sieges, or the ruin caused by mines, with other matters of similar kind whereof he might have spoken, but which he passed over in silence—although there are those who would consider such things as having something to do with the life of the soldier, not to call them its principal features. In a word, he said so much on the subject, that the resolution of our Thomas Rodaja began to waver, and his inclination went near to fix itself on that life, which is so near a neighbour to death.

The captain, whose name was Don Diego de Valdivia, charmed, on his part, with the handsome looks, cheerful manners, and admirable abilities of Rodaja, entreated him to accompany the march into Italy, were it only for the purpose of seeing the country. He offered him his table, and even, if he would adopt the military life, he proposed to procure him a pair of colours; nay, he assured him that those of his own regiment would soon be vacant, and should be at his service.

But little persuasion was required to induce Rodaja's acceptance of a part of this offer. Weighing it in his mind, he considered that it would be well to see Italy and Flanders, to say nothing of other countries, since travel contributes to increase knowledge and discretion. He thought, too, that although he should spend three, or even four years in that occupation, yet these, added to the few he then counted, would not make him so old but that he might afterwards return to his studies. These and other considerations had their weight, and the opportunity being so much to his taste, Rodaja finally told the captain that he would go with him into Italy; but it must be on condition of being left at perfect liberty. He would not consent to enlist under his banner, nor to have his name enrolled in the books of the regiment, that he might not be subjected to the restraints of service. The captain represented that his being inscribed on the lists was a matter which involved no duty, and that he would thereby obtain all the appointments, with the regular pay accorded to his rank; while he, Don Diego, would take care that he should have leave of absence whenever he might demand it. Yet Rodaja was not to be moved from his determination. "For this," said he, "would be to act against the dictates of my conscience and of yours, señor captain; I would, besides, much rather go free than be attached to military service in any manner."

"A conscience so scrupulous is more suitable to the cowl of a monk than the helmet of a soldier," said Don Diego, laughing; "but let it be as you will, so we but remain comrades."

The first night of their journey they had passed at Antequera, and making long stages each day, they speedily arrived at the place where the captain was to join his company. All arrangements being completed, the company began its march with four others to Carthagena, quartering at such places as fell in their way.

And now Rodaja could not fail to remark the authority assumed by the commissaries; the intractable character of many among the captains; the rapacity of the quartermasters, and the unreasonable nature of their demands; the fashion in which the paymasters managed their accounts; the complaints of the people; the traffic in and exchange of billets; the insolence of the undisciplined troops; their quarrels with the other guests at the inns; the requisition of more rations and other stores than were rightful or necessary; and, finally, the almost inevitable consequences of all this. Much besides came under his observation, which he could not but see to be in every way wrong and injurious.

For Rodaja himself, he had now abandoned the garb of a student, and dressed himself parrot-fashion (as we say), conforming to such things as the life around him presented. The many books he had possessed were now reduced to the "Orisons of Our Lady," and a "Garcilaso without Comments," which he carried in two of his pockets.

The party with which he travelled arrived at Carthagena much earlier than he desired, for the varied life he led was very pleasant, and each day brought something new and agreeable. At Carthagena the troops embarked in four galleys for Naples; and in his cabin, also, Kodaja made many observations on the strange life passed in those maritime houses, where, for the most part, a man is devoured by vermin and destroyed by rats, vexed by the sailors, robbed by the galley-slaves, and tormented by the swell of the waters. He endured terrible fear from violent storms and tempests, more especially in the Gulf of Lyons, where they had two, by one of which they were cast on the Island of Corsica, while the other drove them back upon Toulon, in France. At last, weary and half-drowned, they reached land in the darkness of the night, and with great difficulty arrived at the most peaceful and beautiful city of Genoa.

Having disembarked, and hastily visited a church to return thanks for their safety, the captain with all his comrades adjourned to a tavern, where they quickly forgot past storms and tempests in present rejoicing and feasting.

Here they learned to appreciate the respective merits of the different wines presented to them by their active and voluble host; the delicacy of Trebbiano, the fine body of Montefiascone, the purity of Asperino, the generous spirit of the wines from Candia and Soma, and the strength of those from the Cincovinas, or Five Vineyards. Neither did they disregard the sweetness and amenity of the Señora Guarnacha, or the rustic bloom of the Centola, not forgetting even in this bright array the humble Romanesco, which likewise came in for its meed of praise.

The host having passed in review all these and other wines, of many various qualities, offered besides to place before his guests, without having any recourse to magic, and not as one marks down places on a map, but in all their vivid reality, Madriga, Coca, Alacjos, and the imperial, rather than royal city—that favourite abode of the god of smiles—Ciudad Real. He furthermore offered Esquibias, Alanis, Cazalla, Guadalcanal, and Membrilla, without forgetting the wines of Ribadavia or of Descargamaria. At a word, the host offered and even gave them more wines than Bacchus himself could have stored in all his cellars.

Nor was the good Thomas unmindful of the admiration due to the radiant locks of the Genoese maidens, renowned for those fair tresses, while he likewise appreciated the obliging and cheerful disposition of the male inhabitants, and was never weary of expatiating on the beauty of the city itself, which, as you look at it from the sea, appears to hold the houses enchased amidst the rocks, as diamonds are set in gold.

The day after their arrival, such of the companies as were destined for Piedmont were disembarked; Rodaja, however, had no wish to proceed thither, but determined to go from Genoa by land to Rome and Naples, and return by the way of Our Lady of Loretto to the great and magnificent Venice, and thence to Milan and Piedmont, where it was agreed that he should rejoin Don Diego, if the latter had not previously been compelled to set off for Flanders, as was expected.

Two days after these arrangements were made, Rodaja took leave of the captain, and in five days from that time he reached Florence, having first seen Lucca, a city which is small but very well built, and one where Spaniards are more kindly received and better treated than in any other part of Italy.

With Florence Rodaja was infinitely delighted, as well for the pleasantness of its position as for its sumptuous buildings, its fine river, agreeable streets, and cleanliness of aspect. He remained there but four days, and then departed for Rome, the queen of cities and mistress of the world, whose temples he visited, whose relics he adored, and whose grandeur he admired: and as from the claws of the lion you may judge of its mass and force, so did Rodaja infer the greatness of Rome from the fragments of her marbles—her statues, broken or entire—her arches, fallen or fractured—her baths, crumbled to ruin—her magnificent porticos and vast amphitheatres—her renowned and holy river, which ever fills the banks with water to the brim, while it blesses them with innumerable remains of the martyrs whose bodies have found a burial beneath its waves. Nor did our traveller fail to estimate the beauty of the bridges, which one might fancy to be admiring each other, or the streets, which, by their very names alone, claim authority and pre-eminence over those of all other cities in the world: the Via Flaminia, for example, the Via Julia, the Appia, and others of the same character.

No less was Rodaja satisfied with the division of those hills which exist within the city itself, the Cælian, the Quirinal, the Vatican, and the other four, whose very names bear evidence to the Roman greatness and majesty. He took careful note, moreover, of that authority which attaches to the College of Cardinals, and of the dignity represented in the person of the Supreme Pontiff; nor did he suffer to pass unnoticed that great concourse and variety of men from all nations ever congregated within the walls of the city.

All these things Rodaja admired, reflected on, and arranged in the order of their importance; and having made the station of the Seven Churches, confessed to a Penitentiary, and kissed the feet of his Holiness, he departed, well loaded with Agnus Deis and legends, determining thence to proceed to Naples.

But the time was one of important changes and much disorder; this rendered the roads dangerous for all desiring to enter or travel out of Rome; and as he had come to the city by land, so he now resolved to depart by sea, wherefore, proceeding to the port of Ostia, he there embarked, and having reached Naples, added to the satisfaction which he had previously felt at seeing Rome, that of finding himself in a city, in his estimation, and in the opinion of all who have seen it, the finest in Europe, or even in the whole world.

From Naples, Rodaja proceeded to Sicily, where he visited Palermo and Messina; the first of these cities he admired for the advantages of its position and its beauty, and the second for the convenience of its port; while to the whole island he could not but offer the tribute of his praise for that abundance which causes it to be justly denominated the granary of all Italy.

Returning from Sicily to Naples and Rome, Rodaja thence proceeded to Our Lady of Loretto, in whose Holy Temple he could see neither walls nor partitions, since every part was covered with crutches, biers, shrouds, chains, padlocks, fetters, and locks of hair; with arms, hands, legs, or busts in wax, to say nothing of pictures and prints, all giving manifest indication of the mercies and favours innumerable which hundreds of men have received in that place from the hand of God, by the intercession of his Divine Mother, whose sacred Image (there preserved) He has been pleased to exalt and sanction by a vast number of miracles, which have been performed in recompense of the devotion of her votaries; for by them it is that the walls of her house have been adorned in the manner described.[52]

Here Rodaja beheld that very chamber of the Virgin, wherein was delivered the most stupendous embassy ever heard or witnessed by all the heavens, all the angels, and all the archangels, or other inhabitants of the everlasting abodes.

From this place our traveller proceeded to Ancona, where he embarked and repaired to Venice, a city which, had Columbus never appeared in the world, would certainly be still supposed to have no equal; but, by the favour of heaven, and thanks to the great Fernando Cortez who conquered Mexico, the magnificent Venice has now found a city that may be compared to herself. The streets of these two renowned capitals, which are almost wholly of water, make them the admiration and terror of all mankind—that of Europe dominating the old world, and that of America the new. For of the former it would appear that her riches are infinite, her position impregnable, her government most wise, the abundance of her products inexhaustible; in a word, she is herself, as a whole, and in all her parts, entirely worthy of that fame for greatness and majesty which has penetrated to all the regions of the world: the justice of the praise bestowed on Venice is, besides, accredited by her renowned arsenal, wherein are constructed her potent galleys, with other vessels of which the number is not to be told.

To our curious traveller the delights and pastimes found in Venice had almost proved fatal as those of Calypso, since they had nearly caused him to forget his first intentions. Yet when he had passed a month in that enchanting place, he found resolution to continue his journey, passing by Ferrara, Parma, and Placentia, to Milan, that workshop of Vulcan—that grudge and despair of France—that superb city of which more wonders are reported than words can tell, her own grandeur being increased by that of her famous Temple, and by the marvellous abundance of all things necessary to human life that are to be found therein.

From Milan, Rodaja journeyed to Asti, where he arrived in very good time, since the regiment of Don Diego was to depart for Flanders on the following day. He was received very kindly by his friend the captain, with whom he passed into Flanders, and arrived at Antwerp, a city no less worthy of admiration than those which he had seen in Italy. He visited Ghent and Brussels likewise, finding the whole country preparing to take arms, and well disposed to enter on the campaign of the following year.

Rodaja having now seen all that he had desired to behold, resolved to return to his native Spain, and to the city of Salamanca, there to complete his studies. He had no sooner determined than he instantly put his purpose into execution, to the great regret of his friend, who, finding him resolved to depart, entreated him at least to write him word of his safe arrival, and likewise of his future success. This Rodaja promised to do, and then returned to Spain through France, but he did not see Paris, which was at that time in arms. At length he arrived at Salamanca, where he was well received by his friends, and with the facilities which they procured him, he continued his studies until he finally attained to the degree of doctor of laws.

Now it chanced that, about this time, there arrived in Salamanca one of those ladies who belong to all the points of the compass; she was besides well furnished with devices of every colour. To the whistle and bird-call of this fowler there instantly came flocking all the birds of the place; nor was there a vade mecum[53] who refrained from paying a visit to that gay decoy. Among the rest our Thomas was informed that the Señora said she had been in Italy and Flanders when he, to ascertain if he were acquainted with the dame, likewise paid her a visit. She, on her part, immediately fell in love with Rodaja, but he rejected her advances, and never approached her house but when led thither by others, and almost by force. Attending much more zealously to his studies than his amusements, he did not in any manner return her affection, even when she had made it known to him by the offer of her hand and all her possessions.

Seeing herself thus scorned, and perceiving that she could not bend the will of Rodaja by ordinary means, the woman determined to seek others, which in her opinion would be more efficacious, and must, as she thought, ensure the desired effect. So, by the advice of a Morisca woman, she took a Toledan quince, and in that fruit she gave him one of those contrivances called charms, thinking that she was thereby forcing him to love her; as if there were, in this world, herbs, enchantments, or words of power, sufficient to enchain the free-will of any creature. These things are called charms, but they are in fact poisons: and those who administer them are actual poisoners, as has been proved by sundry experiences.

In an unhappy moment Rodaja ate the quince, but had scarcely done so when he began to tremble from head to foot as if struck by apoplexy, remaining many hours before he could be brought to himself. At the end of that time he partially recovered, but appeared to have become almost an idiot. He complained, with a stammering tongue and feeble voice, that a quince which he had eaten had poisoned him, and also found means to intimate by whom it had been given, when justice at once began to move in quest of the criminal; but she, perceiving the failure of her attempt, took care to hide herself, and never appeared again.

Six months did Thomas remain confined to his bed; and during that time he not only became reduced to a skeleton, but seemed also to have lost the use of his faculties. Every remedy that could be thought of was tried in his behalf; but although the physicians succeeded in curing the physical malady, they could not remove that of the mind; so that when he was at last pronounced cured, he was still afflicted with the strangest madness that was ever heard of among the many kinds by which humanity has been assailed. The unhappy man imagined that he was entirely made of glass; and, possessed with this idea, when any one approached him he would utter the most terrible outcries, begging and beseeching them not to come near him, or they would assuredly break him to pieces, as he was not like other men but entirely of glass from head to foot.

In the hope of rousing him from this strange hallucination, many persons, without regard to his prayers and cries, threw themselves upon him and embraced him, bidding him observe that he was not broken for all that. But all they gained by this was to see the poor creature sink to the earth, uttering lamentable moans, and instantly fall into a fainting fit, from which he could not be recovered for several hours; nay, when he did recover, it was but to renew his complaints, from which he never desisted but to implore that such a misfortune might not be suffered to happen again.

He exhorted every one to speak to him from a great distance; declaring that on this condition they might ask him what they pleased, and that he could reply with all the more effect, now he was a man of glass and not of flesh and bones, since glass, being a substance of more delicate subtlety, permits the soul to act with more promptitude and efficacy than it can be expected to do in the heavier body formed of mere earth.

Certain persons then desiring to ascertain if what he had said were true, asked him many questions of great difficulty respecting various circumstances; to all these he replied with the utmost acuteness, insomuch that his answers awakened astonishment in the most learned professors of medicine and philosophy whom that university could boast. And well they might be amazed at seeing a man who was subject to so strange an hallucination as that of believing himself to be made of glass, still retain such extraordinary judgment on other points as to be capable of answering difficult questions with the marvellous propriety and truth which distinguished the replies of Rodaja.

The poor man had often entreated that some case might be given to him wherein he might enclose the brittle vase of his body, so that he might not break it in putting on the ordinary clothing. He was consequently furnished with a surplice of ample width, and a cloth wrapper, which he folded around him with much care, confining it to his waist with a girdle of soft cotton, but he would not wear any kind of shoes. The method he adopted to prevent any one from approaching him when they brought him food, was to fix an earthen pot into the cleft of a stick prepared for that purpose, and in this vessel he would receive such fruits as the season presented. He would not eat flesh or fish; nor would he drink anything but the water of the river, which he lapped from his hands.

In passing through the streets, Rodaja was in the habit of walking carefully in the middle of them, lest a tile should fall from the houses upon his head and break it. In the summer he slept in the open air, and in the winter he lodged at one of the inns, where he buried himself in straw to his throat, remarking that this was the most proper and secure bed for men of glass. When it thundered, Rodaja trembled like an aspen leaf, and would rush out into the fields, not returning to the city until the storm had passed.

His friends kept him shut up for some time, but perceiving that his malady increased, they at last complied with his earnest request that they would let him go about freely; and he might be seen walking through the streets of the city, dressed as we have described, to the astonishment and regret of all who knew him.

The boys soon got about him, but he kept them off with his staff, requesting them to speak to him from a distance, lest they should break him, seeing that he, being a man of glass, was exceedingly tender and brittle. But far from listening to his request, the boys, who are the most perverse generation in the world, soon began to throw various missiles and even stones at him, notwithstanding all his prayers and exclamations. They declared that they wished to see if he were in truth of glass, as he affirmed; but the lamentations and outcries of the poor maniac induced the grown persons who were near to reprove and even beat the boys, whom they drove away for the moment, but who did not fail to return at the next opportunity.

One day, that a horde of these tormentors had pursued him with more than their usual pertinacity, and had worn out his patience, he turned to them, saying—"What do you want with me you varlets? more obstinate than flies, more disgusting than Chinches,[54] and bolder than the boldest fleas. Am I, perchance, the Monte Testacio[55] of Rome, that you cast upon me so many potsherds and tiles?" But Rodaja was followed by many who kept about him for the purpose of hearing him reply to the questions asked, or reprove the questioner, as the case might be. And after a time, even the boys found it more amusing to listen to his words than to throw tiles at him; when they gave him, for the most part, somewhat less annoyance.

The maniac Bodaja was one day passing through the Ropery at Salamanca, when a woman who was working there accosted him, and said, "By my soul, Señor Doctor, I am sorry for your misfortune, but what shall I do for you, since, try as I may, I cannot weep?" To which Rodaja, fixedly regarding her, gravely replied, "Filiæ Jerusalem, plorate super vos et super filios vestros." The husband of the ropeworker was standing by, and comprehending the reply, he said to Rodaja, "Brother Glasscase, for so they tell me you are to be called, you have more of the rogue than the fool in you!" "You are not called on to give me an obolus," rejoined Rodaja, "for I have not a grain of the fool about me!" One day that he was passing near a house well known as the resort of thieves and other disorderly persons, he saw several of the inhabitants assembled round the door, and called out, "See, here you have baggage belonging to the army of Satan, and it is lodged in the house of hell accordingly."

A man once asked him what advice he should give to a friend whose wife had left him for another, and who was in great sorrow for her loss. "You shall bid him thank God," replied Rodaja, "for the favour he has obtained, in that his enemy is removed from his house."

"Then you would not have him go seek her?" inquired the other.

"Let him not even think of doing so," returned Rodaja, "for if he find her, what will he have gained but the perpetual evidence of his dishonour?"

"And what shall I do to keep peace with my own wife?" inquired the same person.

"Give her all that she can need or rightfully claim," said the maniac, "and let her be mistress of every person and thing thy house contains, but take care that she be not mistress of thyself."

A boy one day said to him, "Señor Glasscase, I have a mind to run away from my father, and leave my home for ever, because he beats me." "I would have thee beware, boy," replied Rodaja; "the stripes given by a father are no dishonour to the son, and may save him from those of the hangman, which are indeed a disgrace."

Intelligence of his peculiar state, with a description of the replies he gave, and the remarks he uttered, was much spread abroad, more especially among those who had known him in different parts, and great sorrow was expressed for the loss of a man who had given so fair a promise of distinction. A person of high rank then at Court wrote to a friend of his at Salamanca, begging that Rodaja might be sent to him at Valladolid, and charging his friend to make all needful arrangements for that purpose. The gentleman consequently accosted Vidriera the next time he met him, and said, "Señor Glasscase, you are to know that a great noble of the Court is anxious to have you go to Valladolid;" whereupon Rodaja replied, "Your worship will excuse me to that nobleman, and say that I am not fit to dwell at Court, nor in the Palace, because I have some sense of shame left, and do not know how to flatter." He was nevertheless persuaded to go, and the mode in which he travelled was as follows: a large pannier of that kind in which glass is transported was prepared, and in this Rodaja was placed, well defended by straw, which was brought up to his neck, the opposite pannier being carefully balanced by means of stones, among which appeared the necks of bottles, since Rodaja desired it to be understood that he was sent as a vessel of glass. In this fashion he journeyed to Valladolid, which city he entered by night, and was not unpacked until he had first been carefully deposited in the house of the noble who had requested his presence.

By this gentleman he was received with much kindness, and the latter said to him, "You are extremely welcome, Doctor Glasscase; I hope you have had a pleasant journey." Rodaja replied, that no journey could be called a bad one if it took you safe to your end, unless indeed it were that which led to the gallows.

Being one day shown the Falconry, wherein were numerous falcons and other birds of similar kind, he remarked that the sport pursued by means of those birds was entirely suitable to great nobles, since the cost was as two thousand to one of the profit.

When it pleased Rodaja to go forth into the city, the nobleman caused him to be attended by a servant, whose office it was to protect him from intrusion, and see that he was not molested by the boys of the place, by whom he was at once remarked; indeed but few days had elapsed before he became known to the whole city, since he never failed to find a reply for all who questioned or consulted him.

Among those of the former class, there once came a student, who inquired if he were a poet, to which Rodaja replied, that up to the moment they had then arrived at, he had neither been so stupid nor so bold as to become a poet. "I do not understand what you mean by so stupid or so bold, Señor Glasscase," rejoined the student; to which Rodaja made answer, "I am not so stupid as to be a bad poet, nor so bold as to think myself capable of being a good one." The student then inquired in what estimation he held poets, to which he answered that he held the poets themselves in but little esteem; but as to their art, that he esteemed greatly. His hearer inquiring further what he meant by that, Rodaja said that among the innumerable poets, by courtesy so called, the number of good ones was so small as scarcely to count at all, and that as the bad were not true poets, he could not admire them: but that he admired and even reverenced greatly the art of poetry, which does in fact comprise every other in itself, since it avails itself of all things, and purifies and beautifies all things, bringing its own marvellous productions to light for the advantage, the delectation, and the wonder of the world, which it fills with its benefits. He added further, "I know thoroughly to what extent, and for what qualities, we ought to estimate the good poet, since I perfectly well remember those verses of Ovid, wherein he says:—

"'Cura ducum fuerunt olim regumque poetæ,
Præmiaque antiqui magna tulere chori.
Sanctaque majestas, et erat venerabile nomen
Vatibus; et largæ sæpe dabantur opes.'
And still less do I forget the high quality of the poets whom Plato calls the interpreters of the Gods, while Ovid says of them—
"'Est deus in nobis; agitante calescimus illo.'
And again—
"'At sacri vates et divum cura vocamur.'
"These things are said of good poets; but, as respects the bad ones—the gabbling pretenders—what can we say, save only that they are the idiocy and the arrogance of the world.

"Who is there that has not seen one of this sort when he is longing to bring forth some sonnet to the ears of his neighbours? How he goes round and round them with—'Will your worships excuse me if I read you a little sonnet, which I made one night on a certain occasion; for it appears to me, although indeed it be worth nothing, to have yet a certain something—a je ne scai quoi of pretty, and pleasing.' Then shall he twist his lips, and arch his eyebrows, and make a thousand antics, diving into his pockets meanwhile and bringing out half a hundred scraps of paper, greasy and torn, as if he had made a good million of sonnets; he then recites that which he proffered to the company, reading it in a chanting and affected voice.

"If, perchance, those who hear him, whether because of their knowledge or their ignorance, should fail to commend him, he says, 'Either your worships have not listened to the verses, or I have not been able to read them properly, for indeed and in truth they deserve to be heard;' and he begins, as before, to recite his poem, with new gestures and varied pauses.

"Then to hear these poetasters censure and tear one another to pieces! And what shall I say of the thefts committed by these cubs and whelps of modern pretence on the grave and ancient masters of the art, or of their malevolent carpings at those excellent persons of their own day in whom shines the true light of poetry; who, making a solace and recreation of their arduous labours, prove the divinity of their genius and the elevation of their thoughts to the despite and vexation of these ignorant pretenders, who presume to judge that of which they know nothing, and abhor the beauties which they are not able to comprehend? What will you have me esteem in the nullity which seeks to find place for itself under the canopy spread for others—in the ignorance which is ever leaning for support on another man's chair?"

Rodaja was once asked how it happened that poets are always poor; to which he replied, "That if they were poor, it was because they chose to be so, since it was always in their power to be rich if they would only take advantage of the opportunities in their hands. For see how rich are their ladies," he added; "have they not all a very profusion of wealth in their possession? Is not their hair of gold, their brows of burnished silver, their eyes of the most precious jewels, their lips of coral, their throats of ivory and transparent crystal? Are not their tears liquid pearls, and where they plant the soles of their feet do not jasmine and roses spring up at the moment, however rebellious and sterile the earth may previously have been? Then what is their breath but pure amber, musk, and frankincense? Yet to whom do all these things belong, if not to the poets? They are, therefore, manifest signs and proofs of their great riches."

In this manner he always spoke of bad poets; as to the good ones, he was loud in their praise, and exalted them above the horns of the moon.

Being at San Francisco, he one day saw some very indifferent pictures, by an incapable hand; whereupon he remarked that the good painters imitate nature, while the bad ones have the impertinence to daub her face.

Having planted himself one day in front of a bookseller's shop with great care, to avoid being broken, he began to talk to the owner, and said, "This trade would please me greatly, were it not for one fault that it has." The bookseller inquiring what that might be, Rodaja replied, "It is the tricks you play on the writers when you purchase the copyright of a book, and the sport you make of the author if, perchance, he desire to print at his own cost. For what is your method of proceeding? Instead of the one thousand five hundred copies which you agree to print for him, you print three thousand; and when the author supposes that you are selling his books, you are but disposing of your own."

One of those men who carry sedan-chairs, once standing by while Rodaja was enumerating the faults committed by various trades and occupations, remarked to the latter, "Of us, Señor Doctor, you can find nothing amiss to say." "Nothing," replied Rodaja, "except that you are made acquainted with more sins than are known to the confessor; but with this difference, that the confessor learns them to keep all secret, but you to make them the public talk of the taverns."

A muleteer who heard this, for all kinds of people were continually listening to him, said aloud, "There is little or nothing that you can say of us, Señor Phial, for we are people of great worth, and very useful servants to the commonwealth." To which the man of glass replied, "The honour of the master exalts the honour of the servant. You, therefore, who call those who hire your mules your masters, see whom you serve, and what honour you may borrow from them, for your employers are some of the dirtiest rubbish that this earth endures.

"Once, when I was not a man of glass, I was travelling on a mule which I had hired, and I counted in her master one hundred and twenty-one defects, all capital ones, and all enemies to the human kind. All muleteers have a touch of the ruffian, a spice of the thief, and a dash of the mountebank. If their masters, as they call those they take on their mules, be of the butter-mouthed kind, they play more pranks with them than all the rogues of this city could perform in a year. If they be strangers, the muleteers rob them; if students, they malign them; if monks, they blaspheme them; but if soldiers, they tremble before them. These men, with the sailors, the carters, and the arrieros or pack carriers, lead a sort of life which is truly singular, and belongs to themselves alone.

"The carter passes the greater part of his days in a space not more than a yard and a half long, for there cannot be much more between the yoke of his mules and the mouth of his cart. He is singing for one half of his time, and blaspheming the other; and if he have to drag one of his wheels out of a hole in the mire, he is more aided, as it might seem, by two great oaths than by three strong mules.

"The mariners are a pleasant people, but little like those of the towns, and they can speak no other language than that used in ships. When the weather is fine they are very diligent, but very idle, when it is stormy. During the tempest they order much and obey little. Their ship, which is their mess-room, is also their god, and their pastime is the torment endured by sea-sick passengers.

"As to the mule-carriers, they are a race which has taken out a divorce from all sheets, and has married the pack-saddle. So diligent and careful are these excellent men, that to save themselves from losing a day, they will lose their souls. Their music is the tramp of a hoof; their sauce is hunger; their matins are an exchange of abuse and bad words; their mass is—to hear none at all."

While speaking thus, Rodaja stood at an apothecary's door, and turning to the master of the shop, he said, "Your worship's occupation would be a most salutary one if it were not so great an enemy to your lamps."

"Wherein is my trade an enemy to my lamps?" asked the apothecary.

"In this way," replied Rodaja; "whenever other oils fail you, immediately you take that of the lamp, as being the one which most readily comes to hand. But there is, indeed, another fault in your trade, and one that would suffice to ruin the most accredited physician in the world." Being asked what that was, he replied that an apothecary never ventured to confess, or would admit, that any drug was absent from his stock; and so, if he have not the medicine prescribed, he makes use of some other which, in his opinion, has the same virtues and qualities; but as that is very seldom the case, the medicine, being badly compounded, produces an effect contrary to that expected by the physician.

Rodaja was then asked what he though, of the physicians themselves, and he replied as follows: "Honora medicum propter necessitatem, etenim creavit cum altissimus: à Deo enim est omnis medela, et a rege accipiet donationem: disciplina medici exaltavit caput illius, et in conspectu magnatum collaudabitur. Altissimus de terra creavit medicinam, et vir prudens non abhorrebit illam. Thus," he added, "speaketh the Book of Ecclesiasticus, of Medicine, and good Physicians; but of the bad ones we may safely affirm the very contrary, since there are no people more injurious to the commonwealth than they are. The judge may distort or delay the justice which he should render us; the lawyer may support an unjust demand; the merchant may help us to squander our estate, and, in a word, all those with whom we have to deal in common life may do us more or less injury; but to kill us without fear and standing quietly at his ease; unsheathing no other sword than that wrapped in the folds of a recipe, and without being subject to any danger of punishment, that can be done only by the physician; he alone can escape all fear of the discovery of his crimes, because at the moment of committing them he puts them under the earth. When I was a man of flesh, and not of glass, as I now am, I saw many things that might be adduced in support of what I have now said, but the relation of these I refer to some other time."

A certain person asked him what he should do to avoid envying another, and Rodaja bade him go to sleep, for, said he, "While you sleep you will be the equal of him whom you envy."

It happened on a certain occasion that the Criminal Judge passed before the place where Rodaja stood. There was a great crowd of people, and two alguazils attended the magistrate, who was proceeding to his court, when Rodaja inquired his name. Being told, he replied, "Now, I would lay a wager that this judge has vipers in his bosom, pistols in his inkhorn, and flashes of lightning in his hands, to destroy all that shall come within his commission. I once had a friend who inflicted so exorbitant a sentence in respect to a criminal commission which he held, that it exceeded by many carats the amount of guilt incurred by the crime of the delinquents. I inquired of him wherefore he had uttered so cruel a sentence, and committed so manifest an injustice? To which he replied that he intended to grant permission of appeal, and that in this way he left the field open for the Lords of the Council to show their mercy by moderating and reducing that too rigorous punishment to its due proportions. But I told him it would have been still better for him to have given such a sentence as would have rendered their labour unnecessary, by which means he would also have merited and obtained the reputation of being a wise and exact judge."

Among the number of those by whom Rodaja, as I have said, was constantly surrounded, was an acquaintance of his own, who permitted himself to be saluted as the Señor Doctor, although Thomas knew well that he had not taken even the degree of bachelor. To him, therefore, he one day said, "Take care, gossip mine, that you and your title do not meet with the Fathers of the Redemption, for they will certainly take possession of your doctorship as being a creature unrighteously detained captive."

"Let us behave well to each other, Señor Glasscase," said the other, "since you know that I am a man of high and profound learning."

"I know you rather to be a Tantalus in the same," replied Rodaja; "for if learning reach high to you, you are never able to plunge into its depths."

He was one day leaning against the stall of a tailor, who was seated with his hands before him, and to whom he said—

"Without doubt, Señor Maeso,[56] you are in the way to salvation."

"From what symptom do you judge me to be so, Señor Doctor?" inquired the tailor.

"From the fact that, as you have nothing to do, so you have nothing to lie about, and may cease lying, which is a great step."

Of the shoemakers he said, that not one of that trade ever performed his office badly; seeing that if the shoe be too narrow, and pinches the foot, the shoemaker says, "In two hours it will be as wide as an alpargate;" or he declares it right that it should be narrow, since the shoe of a gentleman must needs fit closely; and if it be too wide, he maintains that it still ought to be so, for the ease of the foot, and lest a man should have the gout.

Seeing the waiting-maid of an actress attending her mistress, he said she was much to be pitied who had to serve so many women, to say nothing of the men whom she also had to wait on; and the bystanders requiring to know how the damsel, who had but to serve one, could be said to wait on so many, he replied, "Is she not the waiting-maid of a queen, a nymph, a goddess, a scullery-maid, and a shepherdess? besides that she is also the servant of a page and a lackey? for all these, and many more, are in the person of an actress."

Some one asked Rodaja, who had been the happiest man in the world? To which he answered— "Nemo, seeing that Nemo novit patrem—Nemo sine crimine vivit—Nemo sua sorte contentus—Nemo ascendit in coelum," &c. &c.

Of the fencing masters he said, that they were professors of an art which was never to be known when it was most wanted, since they pretended to reduce to mathematical demonstrations, which are infallible, the angry thoughts and movements of a man's adversaries.

To such men as dyed their beards, Rodaja always exhibited a particular enmity; and one day observing a Portuguese, whose beard he knew to be dyed, in dispute with a Spaniard, to whom he said, "I swear by the beard that I wear on my face," Rodaja called out to him, "Halt there, friend; you should not say that you wear on your face, but that you dye on your face."[57] To another, whose beard had been streaked by an imperfect dye, Doctor Glasscase said, "Your beard is of the true dust-coloured pieball." He related, on another occasion, that a certain damsel, discreetly conforming to the will of her parents, had agreed to marry an old man with a white beard, who, on the evening before his marriage was to take place, thought fit to have his beard dyed, and whereas he had taken it from the sight of his betrothed as white as snow, he presented it at the altar with a colour blacker than that of pitch.

Seeing this, the damsel turned to her parents and requested them to give her the spouse they had promised, saying that she would have him, and no other.

They assured her, that he whom she there saw was the person they had before shewn her, and given her for her spouse: but she refused to believe it, maintaining, that he whom her parents had given her was a grave person, with a white beard: nor was she, by any means, to be persuaded that the dyed man before her was her betrothed, and the marriage was broken off.

Towards Duennas he entertained as great a dislike as towards those who dyed their beards— uttering wonderful things respecting their falsehood and affectation, their tricks and pretences, their simulated scruples and their real wickedness,—reproaching them with their fancied maladies of stomach, and the frequent giddiness with which they were afflicted in the head; nay, even their mode of speaking, was made the subject of his censure; and he declared that there were more turns in their speech than folds in their great togas and wide gowns; finally, he declared them altogether useless, if not much worse.

Being one day much tormented by a hornet which settled on his neck, he nevertheless refused to take it off, lest in seeking to catch the insect he should break himself; but he still complained woefully of the sting. Some one then remarked to him, that it was scarcely to be supposed he would feel it much since his whole person was of glass. But Rodaja replied, that the hornet in question must needs be a slanderer, seeing that slanderers were of a race whose tongues were capable of penetrating bodies of bronze, to say nothing of glass.

A monk, who was enormously fat, one day passed near where Rodaja was sitting, when one who stood by ironically remarked, that the father was so reduced and consumptive, as scarcely to be capable of walking. Offended by this, Rodaja exclaimed, "Let none forget the words of Holy Scripture, 'Nolite tangere Christos meos;' and, becoming still more heated, he bade those around him reflect a little, when they would see, that of the many saints canonised, and placed among the number of the blessed by the Church within a few years in those parts, none had been called the Captain Don Such a one, or the Lawyer Don So and So, or the Count Marquis, or Duke of Such a Place; but all were brother Diego, brother Jacinto, or brother Raimundo: all monks and friars, proceeding, that is to say, from the monastic orders." "These," he added, "are the orange-trees of heaven, whose fruits are placed on the table of God." Of evil-speakers Rodaja said, that they were like the feathers of the eagle which gnaw, wear away, and reduce to nothing, whatever feathers of other birds are mingled with them in beds or cushions, how good soever those feathers may be.

Concerning the keepers of gaming-houses he uttered wonders, and many more than can here be repeated—commending highly the patience of a certain gamester, who would remain all night playing and losing; yea, though of choleric disposition by nature, he would never open his mouth to complain, although he was suffering the martyrdom of Barabbas, provided only his adversary did not cut the cards. At a word, Rodaja uttered so many sage remarks, that, had it not been for the cries he sent forth when any one approached near enough to touch him, for his peculiar dress, slight food, strange manner of eating, and sleeping in the air, or buried in straw, as we have related, no one could have supposed but that he was one of the most acute persons in the world.

He remained more than two years in this condition; but, at the end of that time, a monk of the order of St. Jerome, who had extraordinary powers in the cure of lunacy, nay, who even made deaf and dumb people hear and speak in a certain manner; this monk, I say, undertook the care and cure of Rodaja, being moved thereto by the charity of his disposition. Nor was it long before the lunatic was restored to his original state of judgment and understanding. When the cure was effected, the monk presented his patient with his previous dress of a doctor of laws, exhorting him to return to his earlier mode of life, and assuring him that he might now render himself as remarkable for the force of his intellect, as he had before done for his singular folly.

Thomas returned accordingly to his past pursuits; but, instead of calling himself Rodaja, as before, he assumed the name of Rueda. He had scarcely appeared in the street, before he was recognised by the boys; but seeing him in a dress so different from that he had before worn and been known by, they dared not cry after him or ask him questions, but contented themselves with saying, one to another, "Is not this the madman, Doctor Glasscase? It is certainly he; and though he now looks so discreet, he may be just as mad in this handsome dress as he was in that other. Let us ask him some questions, and get rid of our doubts."

All this was heard by Thomas, who maintained silence, but felt much confused, and hurried along more hastily than he had been wont to do before he regained his senses. The men at length made the same remarks as the boys and before he had arrived at the courts he had a train of more than two hundred persons of all classes following him, being more amply attended than the most popular professor of the university.

Having gained the first court, which is that of the entrance, these people ended by surrounding him completely; when, perceiving that he was so crowded on as no longer to have the power of proceeding, he finally raised his voice, and said—

"Señores, it is true that I am Doctor Glass-case, but not he whom you formerly knew. I am now Doctor Rueda. Misfortunes such as not unfrequently happen in this world, by the permission of heaven, had deprived me of my senses, but the mercy of God has restored them; and by those things which you have heard me say when I was mad, you may judge of what I shall say now that I am become sane. I am a doctor in laws of the university of Salamanca, where I studied in much poverty, but raised myself through all the degrees to that I now hold; but my poverty may serve to assure you that I owe my rank to industry and not to favour. I have come to this great sea of the Court, hoping to swim and get forward and gain the bread of my life; but if you do not leave me I shall be more likely to sink and find my death. For the love of God, I entreat that you follow me no further, since, in doing so, you persecute and injure me. What you formerly enquired of me in the streets, I beg you now to come and ask me at my house, when you shall see that the questions to which I before replied, impromptu, shall be more perfectly answered now that I shall take time to consider."

All listened to him, many left him as he desired, and he returned to his abode with a much smaller train. But it was every day the same: his exhortations availed nothing; and Thomas finally resolved to repair to Flanders, there to support himself by the strength of his arm, since he could no longer profit by that of his intellect.

This resolution he executed accordingly, exclaiming as he departed—"Oh, city and court! you by whom the expectations of the bold pretender are fulfilled, while the hopes of the modest labourer are destroyed; you who abundantly sustain the shameless Buffoon, while the worthy sage is left to die of hunger; I bid you farewell." That said, he proceeded to Flanders, where he finished in arms the life which he might have rendered immortal by letters, and died in the company of his friend the Captain Don Diego, leaving behind him the reputation of a most valiant soldier and upright man.

[51] Don Augustin de Arrieta, a Spanish commentator of our author, informs us that the camarada not only journeyed and lived with his companion of the way, but even slept in the same chamber, and not unfrequently in the same bed.

[52] The ex-votos, or pictures and figures here described, are too familiar to the visitor of Catholic churches to need any explanation.

[53] Student: they are so called from the name given to the portfolio in which they carry their books and papers to the university, and which they always have with them.

[54] The reader will be pleased to guess the name of that insufferable insect which the Spaniards denominate Chinche, and with the English equivalent of which I am unwilling to offend his eyes. Happy, indeed, if he cannot guess; but then he cannot have seen either Seville or Granada, and one might almost encounter an acquaintance with the animal called Chinche rather than renounce them.

[55] Such of our readers as have visited Rome, will remember that enormous mound which is seen rising on the right hand as you leave the city, by the Porta Salaria, and is said to have been formed by the numberless fragments of pottery cast on the spot from time immemorial.

[56] Master.

[57] Here Rodaja spoke mockingly, an impure Portuguese, and not Spanish (olhay, homen, naon,

digais, teno, sino tino). The spirit of the remark (as in some other passages omitted for that reason) consists in a play on words resembling each other in sound, though not in sense, and is necessarily lost in translation.

THE DECEITFUL MARRIAGE

From the Hospital of the Resurrection, which stands just beyond the Puerta del Campo, in Valladolid, there issued one day a soldier, who, by the excessive paleness of his countenance, and the weakness of his limbs, which obliged him to lean upon his sword, showed clearly to all who set eyes on him that, though the weather was not very warm, he must have sweated a good deal in the last few weeks. He had scarcely entered the gate of the city, with tottering steps, when he was accosted by an old friend who had not seen him for the last six months, and who approached the invalid, making signs of the cross as if he had seen a ghost. "What; is all this?" he cried; "do I, indeed, behold the Señor Alferez[58] Campuzano? Is it possible that I really see you in this country? Why, I thought you were in Flanders trailing a pike, instead of hobbling along with your sword for a walking-stick. How pale—how emaciated you look!"

"As to whether I am in this country or elsewhere, Signor Licentiate Peralta, the fact that you now see me is a sufficient answer," replied Campuzano; "as for your other questions, all I can tell you is, that I have just come out of that hospital, where I have been confined for a long time in a dreadful state of health, brought upon me by the conduct of a woman I was indiscreet enough to make my wife."

"You have been married, then?" said Peralta.

"Yes, Señor."

"Married without benefit of clergy, I presume. Marriages of that sort bring their own penance with them."

"Whether it was without benefit of clergy I cannot say," replied the Alferez; "but I can safely aver that it was not without benefit of physic. Such were the torments of body and soul which my marriage brought upon me, that those of the body cost me forty sudations to cure them, and, as for those of the soul, there is no remedy at all that can relieve them. But excuse me, if I cannot hold a long conversation in the street; another day I will, with more convenience, relate to you my adventures, which are the strangest and most singular you ever heard in all the days of your life."

"That will not do," said the licentiate; "I must have you come to my lodgings, and there we will do penance together.[59] You will have an olla, very fit for a sick man; and though it is scantly enough for two, we will make up the deficiency with a pie and a few slices of Rute ham, and, above all, with a hearty welcome, not only now, but whenever you choose to claim it."

Campuzano accepted the polite invitation. They turned into the church of San Lorente and heard mass, and then Peralta took his friend home, treated him as he had promised, repeated his courteous offers, and requested him after dinner to relate his adventures. Campuzano, without more ado, began as follows:—

You remember, Señor Licentiate Peralta, how intimate I was in this city with Captain Pedro de Herrera, who is now in Flanders. "I remember it very well," replied Peralta. Well, one day when we had done dinner in the Posada della Solana, where we lived, there came in two ladies of genteel appearance, with two waiting women: one of the ladies entered into conversation with the Captain, both leaning against a window; the other sat down in a chair beside me, with her veil low down, so that I could not see her face, except so far as the thinness of the texture allowed. I entreated her to do me the favour to unveil, but I could not prevail, which the more inflamed my desire to have sight of her; but what especially increased my curiosity was that, whether on purpose, or by chance, the lady displayed a very white hand, with very handsome rings.

At that time I made a very gallant appearance with that great chain you have seen me wear, my hat with plumes and bands, my flame-coloured military garments, and, in the eyes of my own folly, I seemed so engaging that I imagined all the women must fall in love with me! Well, I implored her to unveil. "Be not importunate," she replied; "I have a house; let a servant follow me; for though I am of more honourable condition than this reply of mine would indicate, yet for the sake of seeing whether your discretion corresponds to your gallant appearance, I will allow you to see me with less reserve." I kissed her hand for the favour she granted me, in return for which I promised mountains of gold. The captain ended his conversation, the ladies went away, and a servant of mine followed them. The captain told me that what the lady had been asking of him was to take some letters to Flanders to another captain, who she said was her cousin, though he knew he was nothing but her gallant.

For my part I was all on fire for the snow-white hands I had seen, and dying for a peep at the face; so I presented myself next day at the door which my servant pointed out to me, and was freely admitted. I found myself in a house very handsomely decorated and furnished, in presence of a lady about thirty years of age, whom I recognised by her hands. Her beauty was not extraordinary, but of a nature well suited to fascinate in conversation; for she talked with a sweetness of tone that won its way through the ears to the soul. I had long tête-à-têtes with her, in which I made love with all my might: I bragged, bounced, swaggered, offered, promised, and made all the demonstrations I thought necessary to work myself into her good graces; but as she was accustomed to such offers and protestations, she listened to them with an attentive, but apparently far from credulous ear. In short, during the four days I continued to visit her, our intercourse amounted only to talking soft nonsense, without my being able to gather the tempting fruit.

In the course of my visits I always found the house free from intruders, and without a vestige of pretended relations or real gallants. She was waited on by a girl in whom there was more of the rogue than the simpleton. At last resolving to push my suit in the style of a soldier, who is about to shift his quarters, I came to the point with my fair one, Doña Estefania de Caycedo (for that is the name of my charmer), and this was the answer she gave me:—"Señor Alferez Campuzano, I should be a simpleton if I sought to pass myself off on you for a saint; I have been a sinner, ay, and am one still, but not in a manner to become a subject of scandal in the neighbourhood or of notoriety in public. I have inherited no fortune either from my parents or any other relation; and yet the furniture of my house is worth a good two thousand five hundred ducats, and would fetch that sum it put up to auction at any moment. With this property I look for a husband to whom I may devote myself in all obedience, and with whom I may lead a better life, whilst I apply myself with incredible solicitude to the task of delighting and serving him; for there is no master cook who can boast of a more refined palate, or can turn out more exquisite ragouts and made-dishes than I can, when I choose to display my housewifery in that way. I can be the major domo in the house, the tidy wench in the kitchen, and the lady in the drawing room: in fact, I know how to command and make myself obeyed. I squander nothing and accumulate a great deal; my coin goes all the further for being spent under my own directions. My household linen, of which I have a large and excellent stock, did not come out of drapers' shops or warehouses; these fingers and those of my maid servants stitched it all, and it would have been woven at home had that been possible. If I give myself these commendations, it is because I cannot incur your censure by uttering what it is absolutely necessary that you should know. In fine, I wish to say that I desire a husband to protect, command, and honour me, and not a gallant to flatter and abuse me: if you like to accept the gift that is offered you, here I am, ready and willing to put myself wholly at your disposal, without going into the public market with my hand, for it amounts to no less to place oneself at the mercy of match-makers' tongues, and no one is so fit to arrange the whole affair as the parties themselves."

My wits were not in my head at that moment, but in my heels. Delighted beyond imagination, and seeing before me such a quantity of property, which I already beheld by anticipation converted into ready money, without making any other reflections than those suggested by the longing that fettered my reason, I told her that I was fortunate and blest above all men since heaven had given me by a sort of miracle such a companion, that I might make her the lady of my affections and my fortune,—a fortune which was not so small, but that with that chain which I wore round my neck, and other jewels which I had at home, and by disposing of some military finery, I could muster more than two thousand ducats, which, with her two thousand five hundred, would be enough for us to retire upon to a village of which I was a native, and where I had relations and some patrimony. Its yearly increase, helped by our money, would enable us to lead a cheerful and unembarrassed life. In fine, our union was at once agreed on; the banns were published on three successive holidays (which happened to fall together), and on the fourth day, the marriage was celebrated in the presence of two friends of mine, and a youth who she said was her cousin, and to whom I introduced myself as a relation with words of great urbanity. Such, indeed, were all those which hitherto I had bestowed on my bride—with how crooked and treacherous an intention I would rather not say; for though I am telling truths, they are not truths under confession which must not be kept back.

My servant removed my trunk from my lodgings to my wife's house. I put by my magnificent chain in my wife's presence; showed her three or four others, not so large, but of better workmanship, with three or four other trinkets of various kinds; laid before her my best dresses and my plumes, and gave her about four hundred reals, which I had, to defray the household expenses. For six days I tasted the bread of wedlock, enjoying myself like a beggarly bridegroom in the house of a rich father-in-law. I trod on rich carpets, lay in holland sheets, had silver candlesticks to light me, breakfasted in bed, rose at eleven o'clock, dined at twelve, and at two took my siesta in the drawing-room. Doña Estefania and the servant girl danced attendance upon me; my servant, whom I had always found lazy, was suddenly become nimble as a deer. If ever Doña Estefania quitted my side, it was to go to the kitchen and devote all her care to preparing fricassees to please my palate and quicken my appetite. My shirts, collars, and handkerchiefs were a very Aranjuez of flowers, so drenched they were with fragrant waters. Those days flew fast, like the years which are under the jurisdiction of time; and seeing myself so regaled and so well treated, I began to change for the better the evil intention with which I had begun this affair.

At the end of them, one morning, whilst I was still in bed with Doña Estefania, there was a loud knocking and calling at the street door. The servant girl put her head out of the window, and immediately popped it in again, saying,—"There she is, sure enough; she is come sooner than she mentioned in her letter the other day, but she is welcome!"

"Who's come, girl?" said I.

"Who?" she replied; "why, my lady Doña Clementa Bueso, and with her señor Don Lope Melendez de Almendarez, with two other servants, and Hortigosa, the dueña she took with her."

"Bless me! Run, wench, and open the door for them," Doña Estefania now exclaimed; "and you, señor, as you love me, don't put yourself out, or reply for me to anything you may hear said against me."

"Why, who is to say anything to offend you, especially when I am by? Tell me, who are these people, whose arrival appears to have upset you?"

"I have no time to answer," said Doña Estefania; "only be assured that whatever takes place here will be all pretended, and bears upon a certain design which you shall know by and by."

Before I could make any reply to this, in walked Doña Clementa Bueso, dressed in lustrous green satin, richly laced with gold, a hat with green, white, and pink feathers, a gold hat-band, and a fine veil covering half her face. With her entered Don Lope Melendez de Almendarez in a travelling suit, no less elegant than rich. The dueña Hortigosa was the first who opened her lips, exclaiming, "Saints and angels, what is this! My lady Doña Clementa's bed occupied, and by a man too! Upon my faith, the señora Doña Estefania has availed herself of my lady's friendliness to some purpose!"

"That she has, Hortigosa," replied Doña Clementa; "but I blame myself for never being on my guard against friends who can only be such when it is for their own advantage."

To all this Doña Estefania replied: "Pray do not be angry, my lady Doña Clementa. I assure you there is a mystery in what you see; and when you are made acquainted with it you will acquit me of all blame."

During this time I had put on my hose and doublet, and Doña Estefania, taking me by the hand, led me into another room. There she told me that this friend of hers wanted to play a trick on that Don Lope who was come with her, and to whom she expected to be married. The trick was to make him believe that the house and everything in it belonged to herself. Once married, it would matter little that the truth was discovered, so confident was the lady in the great love of Don Lope, the property would then be returned; and who could blame her, or any woman, for contriving to get an honourable husband, though it were by a little artifice? I replied that it was a very great stretch of friendship she thought of making, and that she ought to look well to it beforehand, for very probably she might be constrained to have recourse to justice to recover her effects. She gave me, however, so many reasons, and alleged so many obligations by which she was bound to serve Doña Clementa even in matters of more importance, that much against my will, and with sore misgivings, I complied with Doña Estefania's wishes, on the assurance that the affair would not last more than eight days, during which we were to lodge with another friend of hers.

We finished dressing; she went to take her leave of the señora Doña Clementa Bueso and the señor Lope Melendez Almendarez, ordered my servant to follow her with my luggage, and I too followed without taking leave of any one. Doña Estefania stopped at a friend's house, and stayed talking with her a good while, leaving us in the street, till at last a girl came out and told me and my servant to come in. We went up stairs to a small room in which there were two beds so close together that they seemed but one, for the bed-clothes actually touched each other. There we remained six days, during which not an hour passed in which we did not quarrel; for I was always telling her what a stupid thing she had done in giving up her house and goods, though it were to her own mother. One day, when Doña Estefania had gone out, as she said, to see how her business was going on, the woman of the house asked me what was the reason of my wrangling so much with my wife, and what had she done for which I scolded her so much, saying it was an act of egregious folly rather than of perfect friendship. I told her the whole story, how I had married Doña Estefania, the dower she had brought me, and the folly she had committed in leaving her house and goods to Doña Clementa, even though it was for the good purpose of catching such a capital husband as Don Lope. Thereupon the woman began to cross and bless herself at such a rate, and to cry out, "O, Lord! O, the jade!" that she put me into a great state of uneasiness. At last, "Señor Alferez," said she, "I don't know but I am going against my conscience in making known to you what I feel would lie heavy on it if I held my tongue. Here goes, however, in the name of God,—happen what may, the truth for ever, and lies to the devil! The truth is, that Doña Clementa Bueso is the real owner of the house and property which you have had palmed upon you for a dower; the lies are every word that Doña Estefania has told you, for she has neither house nor goods, nor any clothes besides those on her back. What gave her an opportunity for this trick was that Doña Clementa went to visit one of her relations in the city of Plasencia, and there to perform a novenary in the church of our Lady of Guadalupe, meanwhile leaving Doña Estefania to look after her house, for in fact they are great friends. And after all, rightly considered, the poor señora is not to blame, since she has had the wit to get herself such a person as the Señor Alferez for a husband."

Here she came to an end, leaving me almost desperate; and without doubt I should have become wholly so, if my guardian angel had failed in the least to support me, and whisper to my heart that I ought to consider I was a Christian, and that the greatest sin men can be guilty of is despair, since it is the sin of devils. This consideration, or good inspiration, comforted me a little; not so much, however, but that I took my cloak and sword, and went out in search of Doña Estefania, resolved to inflict upon her an exemplary chastisement; but chance ordained, whether for my good or not I cannot tell, that she was not to be found in any of the places where I expected to fall in with her. I went to the church of San Lorente, commended me to our Lady, sat down on a bench, and in my affliction fell into so deep a sleep that I should not have awoke for a long time if others had not roused me. I went with a heavy heart to Doña Clementa's, and found her as much at ease as a lady should be in her own house. Not daring to say a word to her, because Señor Don Lope was present, I returned to my landlady, who told me she had informed Doña Estefania that I was acquainted with her whole roguery; that she had asked how I had seemed to take the news; that she, the landlady, said I had taken it very badly, and had gone out to look for her, apparently with the worst intentions; whereupon Doña Estefania had gone away, taking with her all that was in my trunk, only leaving me one travelling coat. I flew to my trunk, and found it open, like a coffin waiting for a dead body; and well might it have been my own, if sense enough had been left me to comprehend the magnitude of my misfortune.

"Great it was, indeed," observed the licentiate Peralta; "only to think that Doña Estefania carried off your fine chain and hat-band! Well, it is a true saying, 'Misfortunes never come single.'"

I do not so much mind that loss, replied the Alferez, since I may apply to myself the old saw, "My father-in-law thought to cheat me by putting off his squinting daughter upon me; and I myself am blind of an eye."

"I don't know in what respect you can say that?" replied Peralta.

Why, in this respect, that all that lot of chains and gewgaws might be worth some ten or twelve crowns.

"Impossible!" exclaimed the licentiate; "for that which the Señor Alferez wore on his neck must have weighed more than two hundred ducats."

So it would have done, replied the Alferez, if the reality had corresponded with the appearance; but "All is not gold that glitters," and my fine things were only imitations, but so well made that nothing but the touchstone or the fire could have detected that they were not genuine.

"So, then, it seems to have been a drawn game between you and the Señora Doña Estefania," said the licentiate.

So much so that we may shuffle the cards and make a fresh deal. Only the mischief is, Señor Licentiate, that she may get rid of my mock chains, but I cannot get rid of the cheat she put upon me; for, in spite of my teeth, she remains my wife.

"You may thank God, Señor Campuzano," said Peralta, "that your wife has taken to her heels, and that you are not obliged to go in search of her."

Very true; but for all that, even without looking for her, I always find her—in imagination; and wherever I am, my disgrace is always present before me.

"I know not what answer to make you, except to remind you of these two verses of Petrarch:—

"'Che qui prende diletto di far frode,
Non s'ha di lamentar s'altro l'inganna.'

That is to say, whoever makes it his practice and his pleasure to deceive others, has no right to complain when he is himself deceived."

But I don't complain, replied the Alferez; only I pity myself—for the culprit who knows his fault does not the less feel the pain of his punishment. I am well aware that I sought to deceive and that I was deceived, and caught in my own snare; but I cannot command my feelings so much as not to lament over myself. To come, however, to what more concerns my history (for I may give that name to the narrative of my adventures), I learned that Doña Estefania had been taken away by that cousin whom she brought to our wedding, who had been a lover of hers of long standing. I had no mind to go after her and bring back upon myself an evil I was rid of. I changed my lodgings and my skin too within a few days. My eyebrows and eyelashes began to drop; my hair left me by degrees; and I was bald before my time, and stripped of everything; for I had neither a beard to comb nor money to spend. My illness kept pace with my want; and as poverty bears down honour, drives some to the gallows, some to the hospital, and makes others enter their enemies' doors with cringing submissiveness, which is one of the greatest miseries that can befall an unlucky man; that I might not expend upon my cure the clothes that should cover me respectably in health, I entered the Hospital of the Resurrection, where I took forty sudations. They say that I shall get well if I take care of myself. I have my sword; for the rest I trust in God.

The licentiate renewed his friendly offers, much wondering at the things he had heard.

If you are surprised at the little I have told you, Señor Peralta, said the Alferez, what will you say to the other things I have yet to relate, which exceed all imagination, since they pass all natural bounds? I can only tell you that they are such that I think it a full compensation for all my disasters that they were the cause of my entering the hospital, where I saw what I shall now relate to you; and what you can never believe; no; nor anybody else in the world.

All these preambles of the Alferez so excited Peralta's curiosity, that he earnestly desired to hear, in detail, all that remained to be told.

You have no doubt seen, said the Alferez, two dogs going about by night with lanterns along with the Capuchin brethren, to give them light when they are collecting alms.

"I have," replied Peralta.

You have also seen, or heard tell of them, that if alms are thrown from the windows, and happen to fall on the ground, they immediately help with the light and begin to look for what has fallen; that they stop of their own accord before the windows from which they know they are used to receive alms; and that with all their tameness on these occasions, so that they are more like lambs than dogs, they are lions in the hospital, keeping guard with great care and vigilance.

"I have heard that all this is as you say," said Peralta; "but there is nothing in this to move my wonder."

But what I shall now tell you of them, returned the Alferez, is enough to do so; yet, strange as it is, you must bring yourself to believe it. One night, the last but one of my sudation, I heard, and all but saw with my eyes those two dogs, one of which is called Scipio, the other Berganza, stretched on an old mat outside my room. In the middle of the night, lying awake in the dark, thinking of my past adventures and my present sorrows, I heard talking, and set myself to listen attentively, to see if I could make out who were the speakers and what they said. By degrees I did both, and ascertained that the speakers were the dogs Scipio and Berganza.

The words were hardly out of Campuzano's mouth, when the licentiate jumped up and said: "Saving your favour, Señor Campuzano, till this moment I was in much doubt whether or not to believe what you have told me about your marriage; but what you now tell me of your having heard dogs talk, makes me decide upon not believing you at all. For God's sake, Señor Alferez, do not relate such nonsense to any body, unless it be to one who is as much your friend as I am."

Do not suppose I am so ignorant, replied Campuzano, as not to know that brutes cannot talk unless by a miracle. I well know that if starlings, jays, and parrots talk, it is only such words as they have learned by rote, and because they have tongues adapted to pronounce them; but they cannot, for all that, speak and reply with deliberate discourse as those dogs did. Many times, indeed, since I heard them I have been disposed not to believe myself, but to regard as a dream that which, being really awake, with all the five senses which our Lord was pleased to give me, I heard, marked, and finally wrote down without missing a word; whence you may derive proof enough to move and persuade you to believe this verity which I relate. The matters they talked of were various and weighty, such as might rather have been discussed by learned men than by the mouths of dogs; so that, since I could not have invented them out of my own head, I am come, in spite of myself, to believe that I did not dream, and that the dogs did talk.

"Body of me!" exclaimed the licentiate, "are the times of Æsop come back to us, when the cock conversed with the fox, and one beast with another?"

I should be one of them, and the greatest, replied the Alferez, if I believed that time had returned; and so I should be, too, if I did not believe what I have heard and seen, and what I am ready to swear to by any form of oath that can constrain incredulity itself to believe. But, supposing that I have deceived myself, and that this reality was a dream, and that to contend for it is an absurdity, will it not amuse you, Señor Peralta, to see, written in the form of a dialogue, the matters talked of by those dogs, or whoever the speakers may have been?

"Since you no longer insist on having me believe that you heard dogs talk," replied Peralta, "with much pleasure I will hear this colloquy, of which I augur well, since it is reported by a gentlemen of such talents as the Señor Alferez."

Another thing I have to remark, said Campuzano, is, that, as I was very attentive, my apprehension very sensitive, and my memory very retentive (thanks to the many raisins and almonds I had swallowed), I got it all by heart, and wrote it down, word for word, the next day, without attempting to colour or adorn it, or adding or suppressing anything to make it attractive. The conversation took place not on one night only, but on two consecutive nights, though I have not written down more than one dialogue, that which contains the life of Berganza. His comrade Scipio's life, which was the subject of the second night's discourse, I intend to write out, if I find that the first one is believed, or at least not despised. I have thrown the matter into the form of a dialogue to avoid the cumbrous repetition of such phrases as, said Scipio, replied Berganza.

So saying, he took a roll of paper out of his breast pocket, and put it in the hands of the licentiate, who received it with a smile, as if he made very light of all he had heard, and was about to read.

I will recline on this sofa, said the Alferez, whilst you are reading those dreams or ravings, if you will, which have only this to recommend them, that you may lay them down when you grow tired of them.

"Make yourself comfortable," said Peralta; "and I will soon despatch my reading."

The Alferez lay down; the licentiate opened the scroll, and found it headed as follows:—

DIALOGUE BETWEEN SCIPIO AND BERGANZA,

DOGS OF THE HOSPITAL OF THE RESURRECTION IN THE CITY OF VALLADOLID, COMMONLY CALLED THE DOGS OF MAHUDES.

Scip. Berganza, my friend, let us leave our watch over the hospital to-night, and retire to this lonely place and these mats, where, without being noticed, we may enjoy that unexampled favour which heaven has bestowed on us both at the same moment.

Berg. Brother Scipio, I hear you speak, and know that I am speaking to you; yet cannot I believe, so much does it seem to me to pass the bounds of nature.

Scip. That is true, Berganza; and what makes the miracle greater is, that we not only speak but hold intelligent discourse, as though we had souls capable of reason; whereas we are so far from having it, that the difference between brutes and man consists in this, that man is a rational animal and the brute is irrational.

Berg. I hear all you say, Scipio; and that you say it, and that I hear it, causes me fresh admiration and wonder. It is very true that in the course of my life I have many a time heard tell of our great endowments, insomuch that some, it appears, have been disposed to think that we possess a natural instinct, so vivid and acute in many things that it gives signs and tokens little short of demonstrating that we have a certain sort of understanding capable of reason.

Scip. What I have heard highly extolled is our strong memory, our gratitude, and great fidelity; so that it is usual to depict us as symbols of friendship. Thus you will have seen (if it has ever come under your notice) that, on the alabaster tombs, on which are represented the figures of those interred in them, when they are husband and wife, a figure of a dog is placed between the pair at their feet, in token that in life their affection and fidelity to each other was inviolable,

Berg. I know that there have been grateful dogs who have cast themselves into the same grave with the bodies of their deceased masters; others have stood over the graves in which their lords were buried without quitting them or taking food till they died. I know, likewise, that next to the elephant the dog holds the first place in the way of appearing to possess understanding, then the horse, and last the ape.

Scip. True; but you will surely confess that you never saw or heard tell of any elephant, dog, horse, or monkey having talked: hence I infer, that this fact of our coming by the gift of speech so unexpectedly falls within the list of those things which are called portents, the appearance of which indicates, as experience testifies, that some great calamity threatens the nations.

Berg. That being so I can readily enough set down as a portentous token what I heard a student say the other day as I passed through Alcala de Henares.

Scip. What was that?

Berg. That of five thousand students this year attending the university—two thousand are studying medicine.

Scip. And what do you infer from that?

Berg. I infer either that those two thousand doctors will have patients to treat, and that would be a woful thing, or that they must die of hunger.

Scip. Be that as it may, let us talk, portent or no portent; for what heaven has ordained to happen, no human diligence or wit can prevent. Nor is it needful that we should fall to disputing as to the how or the why we talk. Better will it be to make the best of this good clay or good night at home; and since we enjoy it so much on these mats, and know not how long this good fortune of ours may last, let us take advantage of it and talk all night, without suffering sleep to deprive us of a pleasure which I, for my part, have so long desired.

Berg. And I, too; for ever since I had strength enough to gnaw a bone I have longed for the power of speech, that I might utter a multitude of things I had laid up in my memory, and which lay there so long that they were growing musty or almost forgotten. Now, however, that I see myself so unexpectedly enriched with this divine gift of speech, I intend to enjoy it and avail myself of it as much as I can, taking pains to say everything I can recollect, though it be confusedly and helter-skelter, not knowing when this blessing, which I regard as a loan, shall be reclaimed from me.

Scip. Let us proceed in this manner, friend Berganza: to-night you shall relate the history of your life to me, and the perils through which you have passed to the present hour; and to-morrow night, if we still have speech, I will recount mine to you; for it will be better to spend the time in narrating our own lives than in trying to know those of others.

Berg. I have ever looked upon you, Scipio, as a discreet dog and a friend, and now I do so more than ever, since, as a friend, you desire to tell me your adventures and know mine; and, as a discreet dog, you apportion the time in which we may narrate them. But first observe whether any one overhears us.

Scip. No one, I believe; since hereabouts there is a soldier going through a sweating-course; but at this time of night he will be more disposed to sleep than to listen to anything.

Berg. Since then we can speak so securely, hearken; and if I tire you with what I say, either check me or bid me hold my tongue.

Scip. Talk till dawn, or till we are heard, and I will listen to you with very great pleasure, without interrupting you, unless I see it to be necessary.

Berg. It appears to me that the first time I saw the sun was in Seville, in its slaughter-houses, which were outside the Puerta do la Carne; wence I should imagine (were it not for what I shall afterwards tell you) that my progenitors were some of those mastiff's which are bred by those ministers of confusion who are called butchers. The first I knew for a master, was one Nicholas the Pugnosed, a stout, thick-set, passionate fellow, as all butchers are. This Nicholas taught me and other whelps to run at bulls in company with old dogs and catch them by the ears. With great ease I became an eagle among my fellows in this respect.

Scip. I do not wonder, Berganza, that ill-doing is so easily learned, since it comes by a natural obliquity.

Berg. What can I say to you, brother Scipio, of what I saw in those slaughter-houses, and the enormous things that were done in them? In the first place, you must understand that all who work in them, from the lowest to the highest, are people without conscience or humanity, fearing neither the king nor his justice; most of them living in concubinage; carrion birds of prey; maintaining themselves and their doxies by what they steal. On all flesh days, a great number of wenches and young chaps assemble in the slaughtering place before dawn, all of them with bags which come empty and go away full of pieces of meat. Not a beast is killed out of which these people do not take tithes, and that of the choicest and most savoury pickings. The masters trust implicitly in these honest folk, not with the hope that they will not rob them (for that is impossible), but that they may use their knives with some moderation. But what struck me as the worst thing of all, was that these butchers make no more of killing a man than a cow. They will quarrel for straws, and stick a knife into a person's body as readily as they would fell an ox. It is a rare thing for a day to pass without brawls and bloodshed, and even murder. They all pique themselves on being men of mettle, and they observe, too, some punctilios of the bravo; there is not one of them but has his guardian angel in the Plaza de San Francesco, whom he propitiates with sirloins, and beef tongues.

Scip. If you mean to dwell at such length, friend Berganza, on the characteristics and faults of all the masters you have had, we had better pray to heaven to grant us the gift of speech for a year; and even then I fear, at the rate you are going, you will not get through half your story. One thing I beg to remark to you, of which you will see proof when I relate my own adventures; and that is, that some stories are pleasing in themselves, and others from the manner in which they are told; I mean that there are some which give satisfaction, though they are told without preambles and verbal adornments; while others require to be decked in that way and set off by expressive play of features, hands, and voice; whereby, instead of flat and insipid, they become pointed and agreeable. Do not forget this hint, but profit by it in what you are about to say.

Berg. I will do so, if I can, and if I am not hindered by the great temptation I feel to speak; though, indeed, it appears to me that I shall have the greatest difficulty in constraining myself to moderation.

Scip. Be wary with your tongue, for from that member flow the greatest ills of human life.

Berg. Well, then, to go on with my story, my master taught me to carry a basket in my mouth, and to defend it against any one who should attempt to take it from me. He also made me acquainted with the house in which his mistress lived, and thereby spared her servant the trouble of coming to the slaughter-house, for I used to carry to her the pieces of meat he had stolen over night. Once as I was going along on this errand in the gray of the morning, I heard some one calling me by name from a window. Looking up I saw an extremely pretty girl; she came down to the street door, and began to call me again. I went up to her to see what she wanted of me; and what was it but to take away the meat I was carrying in the basket and put an old clog in its place? "Be off with you," she said, when she had done so; "and tell Nicholas the Pugnosed, your master, not to put trust in brutes." I might easily have made her give up what she had taken from me; but I would not put a cruel tooth on those delicate white hands.

Scip. You did quite right; for it is the prerogative of beauty always to be held in respect.

Berg. Well, I went back to my master without the meat and with the old clog. It struck him that I had come back very soon, and seeing the clog, he guessed the trick, snatched up a knife, and flung it at me; and if I had not leaped aside, you would not now be listening to my story. I took to my heels, and was off like a shot behind St. Bernard's, away over the fields, without stopping to think whither my luck would lead me. That night I slept under the open sky, and the following day I chanced to fall in with a flock of sheep. The moment I saw it, I felt that I had found the very thing that suited me, since it appeared to me to be the natural and proper duty of dogs to guard the fold, that being an office which involves the great virtue of protecting and defending the lowly and the weak against the proud and mighty. One of the three shepherds who were with the flock immediately called me to him, and I, who desired nothing better, went up at once to him, lowering my head and wagging my tail. He passed his hand along my back, opened my mouth, examined my fangs, ascertained my age, and told his master that I had all the works and tokens of a dog of good breed. Just then up came the owner of the flock on a gray mare with lance and surge, so that he looked more a coast-guard than a sheep master.

"What dog is that!" said he to the shepherd; "he seems a good one." "You may well say that," replied the man; "for I have examined him closely, and there is not a mark about him but shows that he must be of the right sort. He came here just now; I don't know whose he is, but I know that he does not belong to any of the flocks hereabouts."

"If that be so," said the master, "put on him the collar that belonged to the dog that is dead, and give him the same rations as the rest, treat him kindly that he may take a liking to the fold, and remain with it henceforth." So saying he went away, and the shepherd put on my neck a collar set with steel points, after first giving me a great mess of bread sopped in milk in a trough. At the same time I had a name bestowed on me, which was Barcino. I liked my second master, and my new duty very well; I was careful and diligent in watching the flock, and never quitted it except in the afternoons, when I went to repose under the shade of some tree, or rock, or bank, or by the margin of one of the many streams that watered the country. Nor did I spend those leisure hours idly, but employed them in calling many things to mind, especially the life I had led in the slaughter-house, and also that of my master and all his fellows, who were bound to satisfy the inordinate humours of their mistresses. O how many things I could tell you of that I learned in the school of that she-butcher, my master's lady; but I must pass them over, lest you should think me tedious and censorious.

Scip. I have heard that it was a saying of a great poet among the ancients, that it was a difficult thing to write satires. I consent that you put some point into your remarks, but not to the drawing of blood. You may hit lightly, but not wound or kill; for sarcasm, though it make many laugh, is not good if it mortally wounds one; and if you can please without it, I shall think you more discreet.

Berg. I will take your advice, and I earnestly long for the time when you will relate your own adventures; for seeing how judiciously you correct the faults into which I fall in my narrative, I may well expect that your own will be delivered in a manner equally instructive and delightful. But to take up the broken thread of my story, I say that in those hours of silence and solitude, it occurred to me among other things, that there could be no truth in what I had heard tell of the life of shepherds—of those, at least, about whom my master's lady used to read, when I went to her house, in certain books, all treating of shepherds and shepherdesses; and telling how they passed their whole life in singing and playing on pipes and rebecks, and other old fashioned instruments. I remember her reading how the shepherd of Anfriso sang the praises of the peerless Belisarda, and that there was not a tree on all the mountains of Arcadia on whose trunk he had not sat and sung from the moment Sol quitted the arms of Aurora, till he threw himself into those of Thetis, and that even after black night had spread its murky wings over the face of the earth, he did not cease his melodious complaints. I did not forget the shepherd Elicio, more enamoured than bold, of whom it was said, that without attending to his own loves or his flock, he entered into others' griefs; nor the great shepherd Filida, unique painter of a single portrait, who was more faithful than happy; nor the anguish of Sireno and the remorse of Diana, and how she thanked God and the sage Felicia, who, with her enchanted water, undid that maze of entanglements and difficulties. I bethought me of many other tales of the same sort, but they were not worthy of being remembered.

The habits and occupations of my masters, and the rest of the shepherds in that quarter, were very different from those of the shepherds in the books. If mine sang, it was no tuneful and finely composed strains, but very rude and vulgar songs, to the accompaniment not of pipes and rebecks, but to that of one crook knocked against another, or of bits of tile jingled between the fingers, and sung with voices not melodious and tender, but so coarse and out of tune, that whether singly or in chorus, they seemed to be howling or grunting. They passed the greater part of the day in hunting up their fleas or mending their brogues; and none of them were named Amarillis, Filida, Galatea, or Diana; nor were there any Lisardos, Lausos, Jacintos, or Riselos; but all were Antones, Domingos, Pablos, or Llorentes. This led me to conclude that all those books about pastoral life are only fictions ingeniously written for the amusement of the idle, and that there is not a word of truth in them; for, were it otherwise, there would have remained among my shepherds some trace of that happy life of yore, with its pleasant meads, spacious groves, sacred mountains, handsome gardens, clear streams and crystal fountains, its ardent but no less decorous love-descants, with here the shepherd, there the shepherdess all woe-begone, and the air made vocal everywhere with flutes and pipes and flageolets.

Scip. Enough, Berganza; get back into your road, and trot on.

Berg. I am much obliged to you, friend Scipio; for, but for your hint, I was getting so warm upon the scent, that I should not have stopped till I had given you one whole specimen of those books that had so deceived me. But a time will come when I shall discuss the whole matter more fully and more opportunely than now.

Scip. Look to your feet, and don't run after your tail, that is to say, recollect that you are an animal devoid of reason; or if you seem at present to have a little of it, we are already agreed that this is a supernatural and altogether unparalleled circumstance.

Berg. That would be all very well if I were still in my pristine state of ignorance; but now that I bethink me of what I should have mentioned to you in the beginning of our conversation, I not only cease to wonder that I speak, but I am terrified at the thought of leaving off.

Scip. Can you not tell me that something now that you recollect it?

Berg. It was a certain affair that occurred to me with a sorntess, a disciple of la Camacha de Montilla.

Scip. Let me hear it now, before you proceed with the story of your life.

Berg. No, not till the proper time. Have patience and listen to the recital of my adventures in the order they occurred, for they will afford you more pleasure in that way.

Scip. Very well; tell me what you will and how you will, but be brief.

Berg. I say, then, that I was pleased with my duty as a guardian of the flock, for it seemed to me that in that way I ate the bread of industry, and that sloth, the root and mother of all vices, came not nigh me, for if I rested by day, I never slept at night, the wolves continually assailing us and calling us to arms. The instant the shepherds said to me, "The wolf! the wolf! at him, Barcino," I dashed forward before all the other dogs, in the direction pointed out to me by the shepherds. I scoured the valleys, searched the mountains, beat the thickets, leaped the gullies, crossed the roads, and on the morning returned to the fold without having caught the wolf or seen a glimpse of him, panting, weary, all scratched and torn, and my feet cut with splinters; and I found in the fold either a ewe or a wether slaughtered and half eaten by the wolf. It vexed me desperately to see of what little avail were all my care and diligence. Then the owner of the flock would come; the shepherds would go out to meet him with the skin of the slaughtered animal: the owner would scold the shepherds for their negligence, and order the dogs to be punished for cowardice. Down would come upon us a shower of sticks and revilings; and so, finding myself punished without fault, and that my care, alertness, and courage were of no avail to keep off the wolf, I resolved to change my manner of proceeding, and not to go out to seek him, as I had been used to do, but to remain close to the fold; for since the wolf came to it, that would be the surest place to catch him. Every week we had an alarm; and one dark night I contrived to get a sight of the wolves, from which it was so impossible to guard the fold. I crouched behind a bank; the rest of the dogs ran forward; and from my lurking-place I saw and heard how two shepherds picked out one of the fattest wethers, and slaughtered it in such a manner, that it really appeared next morning as if the executioner had been a wolf. I was horror-struck, when I saw that the shepherds themselves were the wolves, and that the flock was plundered by the very men who had the keeping of it. As usual, they made known to their master the mischief done by the wolf, gave him the skin and part of the carcase, and ate the rest, and that the choicest part, themselves. As usual, they had a scolding, and the dogs a beating. Thus there were no wolves, yet the flock dwindled away, and I was dumb, all which filled me with amazement and anguish. O Lord! said I to myself, who can ever remedy this villany? Who will have the power to make known that the defence is offensive, the sentinels sleep, the trustees rob, and those who guard you kill you?

Scip. You say very true, Berganza; for there is no worse or more subtle thief than the domestic thief; and accordingly there die many more of those who are trustful than of those who are wary. But the misfortune is, that it is impossible for people to get on in the world in any tolerable way without mutual confidence. However, let us drop this subject: there is no need that we should be evermore preaching. Go on.

Berg. I determined then to quit that service, though it seemed so good a one, and to choose another, in which well-doing, if not rewarded, was at least not punished. I went back to Seville, and entered the service of a very rich merchant.

Scip. How did you set about getting yourself a master? As things are now-a-days, an honest man has great difficulty in finding an employer. Very different are the lords of the earth from the Lord of Heaven; the former, before they will accept a servant, first scrutinise his birth and parentage, examine into his qualifications, and even require to know what clothes he has got; but for entering the service of God, the poorest is the richest, the humblest is the best born; and whoso is but disposed to serve him in purity of heart is at once entered in his book of wages, and has such assigned to him as his utmost desire can hardly compass, so ample are they.

Berg. All this is preaching, Scipio.

Scip. Well, it strikes me that it is. So go on.

Berg. With respect to your question, how I set about getting a master: you are aware that humility is the base and foundation of all virtues, and that without it there are none. It smooths inconveniences, overcomes difficulties, and is a means which always conducts us to glorious ends; it makes friends of enemies, tempers the wrath of the choleric, and abates the arrogance of the proud: it is the mother of modesty, and sister of temperance. I availed myself of this virtue whenever I wanted to get a place in any house, after having first considered and carefully ascertained that it was one which could maintain a great dog. I then placed myself near the door; and whenever any one entered whom I guessed to be a stranger, I barked at him; and when the master entered, I went up to him with my head down, my tail wagging, and licked his shoes. If they drove me out with sticks, I took it patiently, and turned with the same gentleness to fawn in the same way on the person who beat me. The rest let me alone, seeing my perseverance and my generous behaviour; and after one or two turns of this kind, I got a footing in the house. I was a good servant: they took a liking to me immediately; and I was never turned out, but dismissed myself, or, to speak more properly, I ran away; and sometimes I met with such a master, that but for the persecution of fortune I should have remained with him to this day.

Scip. It was just in the same way that I got into the houses of the masters I served. It seems that we read men's thoughts.

Berg. I will tell you now what happened to me after I left the fold in the power of those reprobates. I returned, as I have said, to Seville, the asylum of the poor and refuge for the destitute, which embraces in its greatness not only the rude but the mighty and nourishing. I planted myself at the door of a large house belonging to a merchant, exerted myself as usual, and after a few trials gained admission. They kept me tied up behind the door by day, and let me loose at night. I did my duty with great care and diligence, barked at strangers, and growled at those who were not well known. I did not sleep at night, but visited the yards, and walked about the terraces, acting as general guard over our own house and those of the neighbours; and my master was so pleased with my good service, that he gave orders I should be well treated, and have a ration of bread, with the bones from his table, and the kitchen scraps. For this I showed my gratitude by no end of leaps when I saw my master, especially when he came home after being abroad; and such were my demonstrations of joy that my master ordered me to be untied, and left loose day and night. As soon as I was set free, I ran to him, and gambolled all round him, without venturing to lay my paws on him; for I bethought me of that ass in Æsop's Fables, who was ass enough to think of fondling his master in the same manner as his favourite lap-dog, and was well basted for his pains. I understood that fable to signify, that what is graceful and comely in some is not so in others. Let the ribald flout and jeer, the mountebank tumble,—let the common fellow, who has made it his business, imitate the song of birds and the gestures of animals, but not the man of quality, who can deserve no credit or renown from any skill in these things.

Scip. Enough said, Berganza; I understand you; go on.

Berg. Would that others for whom I say this understood me as well! For there is something or other in my nature which makes me feel greatly shocked when I see a cavalier make a buffoon of himself, and taking pride in being able to play at thimblerig, and in dancing the chacona to perfection, I know a cavalier who boasted, that he had, at the request of a sacristan, cut out thirty-two paper ornaments, to stick upon the black cloth over a monument; and he was so proud of his performance that he took his friends to see it, as though he were showing them pennons and trophies taken from the enemy, and hung over the tombs of his forefathers. Well, this merchant I have been telling you of had two sons, one aged twelve, the other about fourteen, who were studying the humanities in the classes of the Company of Jesus. They went in pomp to the college, accompanied by their tutor, and by pages to carry their books, and what they called their Vademecum. To see them go with such parade, on horseback in fine weather, and in a carriage when it rained, made me wonder at the plain manner in which their father went abroad upon his business, attended by no other servant than a negro, and sometimes mounted upon a sorry mule.

Scip. You must know, Berganza, that it is a customary thing with the merchants of Seville, and of other cities also, to display their wealth and importance, not in their own persons, but in those of their sons: for merchants are greater in their shadows than in themselves; and as they rarely attend to anything else than their bargains, they spend little on themselves; but as ambition and wealth burn to display themselves, they show their own in the persons of their sons, maintaining them as sumptuously as if they were sons of princes. Sometimes too they purchase titles for them, and set upon their breasts the mark that so much distinguishes men of rank from the commonalty.

Berg. It is ambition, but a generous ambition that seeks to improve one's condition without prejudice to others.

Scip. Seldom or never can ambition consist with abstinence from injury to others.

Berg. Have we not said that we are not to speak evil of any one?

Scip. Ay, but I don't speak evil of any one.

Berg. You now convince me of the truth of what I have often heard say, that a person of a malicious tongue will utter enough to blast ten families, and calumniate twenty good men; and if he is taken to task for it, he will reply that he said nothing; or, if he did, he meant nothing by it, and would not have said it if he had thought any one would take it amiss. In truth, Scipio, one had need of much wisdom and wariness to be able to entertain a conversation for two hours, without approaching the confines of evil speaking. In my own case, for instance, brute as I am, I see that with every fourth phrase I utter, words full of malice and detraction come to my tongue like flies to wine. I therefore say again that doing and speaking evil are things we inherit from our first parents, and suck in with our mother's milk. This is manifest in the fact, that hardly is a boy out of swaddling clothes before he lifts his hand to take vengeance upon those by whom he thinks himself offended; and the first words he articulates are to call his nurse or his mother a jade.

Scip. That is true. I confess my error, and beg you will forgive it, as I have forgiven you so many. Let us pitch ill-nature into the sea—as the boys say—and henceforth backbite no more. Go on with your story. You were talking of the grand style in which the sons of your master the merchant went to the college of the Company of Jesus.

Berg. I will go on then; and though I hold it a sufficient thing to abstain from ill-natured remarks, yet I propose to use a remedy, which I am told was employed by a great swearer, who repenting of his bad habit, made it a practice to pinch his arm, or kiss the ground as penance, whenever an oath escaped him; but he continued to swear for all that. In like manner, whenever I act contrary to the precept you have given me against evil speaking, and contrary to my own intention to abstain from that practice, I will bite the tip of my tongue, so that the smart may remind me of my fault, and hinder me from relapsing into it.

Scip. If that is the remedy you mean to use, I expect that you will have to bite your tongue so often, that there will be none of it left, and it will be put beyond the possibility of offending.

Berg. At least I will do my best; may heaven make up my deficiencies. Well, to resume: one day my master's sons left a note-book in the court-yard where I was; and as I had been taught to fetch and carry, I took it up, and went after them, resolved to put it into their own hands. It turned out exactly as I desired; for my masters seeing me coming with the note-book in my mouth, which I held cleverly by its string, sent a page to take it from me; but I would not let him, nor quitted it till I entered the hall with it, at which all the students fell a laughing. Going up to the elder of my masters, I put it into his hands, with all the obsequiousness I could, and went and seated myself on my haunches at the door of the hall, with my eyes fixed on the master who was lecturing in the chair. There is some strange charm in virtue; for though I know little or nothing about it, I at once took delight in seeing the loving care and industry with which the reverend fathers taught those youths, shaping their tender minds aright, and guiding them in the path of virtue, which they demonstrated to them along with letters. I observed how they reproved them with suavity, chastised them with mercy, animated them with examples, incited them with rewards, and indulged them with prudence; and how they set before them the loathsomeness of vice and the beauty of virtue, so that abhorring the one and loving the other, they might achieve the end for which they were created.

Scip. You say very well, Berganza; for I have heard tell of this holy fraternity, that for worldly wisdom there are none equal to them; and that as guides and leaders on the road to heaven, few come up to them. They are mirrors of integrity, catholic doctrine, rare wisdom, and profound humility, the base on which is erected the whole edifice of beatitude.

Berg. That is every word true. But to return to my story: my masters were so pleased with my carrying them the note-book, that they would have me do so every day; and thus I enjoyed the life of a king, or even better, having nothing to do but to play with the students, with whom I grew so tame, that they would put their hands in my mouth, and the smallest of them would ride on my back. They would fling their hats or caps for me to fetch, and I would put them into their hands with marks of great delight. They used to give me as much to eat as they could; and they were fond of seeing, when they gave me nuts or almonds, how I cracked them like a monkey, let fall the shells, and ate the kernels. One student, to make proof of my ability, brought me a great quantity of salad in a basket, and I ate it like a human being. It was the winter season, when manchets and mantequillas abound in Seville; and I was so well supplied with them, that many an Antonio was pawned or sold that I might breakfast. In short, I spent a student's life, without hunger or itch, and that is saying everything for it; for if hunger and itch were not identified with the student's life, there would be none more agreeable in the world; since virtue and pleasure go hand in hand through it, and it is passed in learning and taking diversion. This happy life ended too soon for me. It appeared to the professors that the students spent the half-hour between the classes not in studying their lessons, but in playing with me; and therefore they ordered my masters not to bring me any more to the college. I was left at home accordingly, at my old post behind the door; and notwithstanding the order graciously given by the head of the family, that I should be at liberty day and night, I was again confined to a small mat, with a chain round my neck. Ah, friend Scipio, did you but know how sore a thing it is to pass from a state of happiness to one of wretchedness! When sorrows and distresses flood the whole course of life, either they soon end in death, or their continuance begets a habit of endurance, which generally alleviates their greatest rigour; but when one passes suddenly and unexpectedly from a miserable and calamitous lot to one of prosperity and enjoyment, and soon after relapses into his former state of woe and suffering: this is such a poignant affliction, that if it does not extinguish life, it is only to make it a prolonged torment. Well, I returned to my ordinary rations, and to the bones which were flung to me by a negress belonging to the house; but even these were partly filched from me by two cats, who very nimbly snapped up whatever fell beyond the range of my chain. Brother Scipio, as you hope that heaven will prosper all your desires, do suffer me to philosophise a little at present; for unless I utter the reflections which have now occurred to my mind, I feel that my story will not be complete or duly edifying.

Scip. Beware, Berganza, that this inclination to philosophise is not a temptation of the fiend; for slander has no better cloak to conceal its malice than the pretence that all it utters are maxims of philosophers, that evil speaking is moral reproval, and the exposure of the faults of others is nothing but honest zeal. There is no sarcastic person whose life, if you scrutinise it closely, will not be found full of vices and improprieties. And now, after this warning, philosophise as much as you have a mind.

Berg. You may be quite at your ease on that score, Scipio. What I have to remark is, that as I was the whole day at leisure—and leisure is the mother of reflection—I conned over several of those Latin phrases I had heard when I was with my masters at college, and wherewith it seemed to me that I had somewhat improved my mind; and I determined to make use of them as occasion should arise, as if I knew how to talk, but in a different manner from that practised by some ignorant persons, who interlard their conversation with Latin apophthegms, giving those who do not understand them to believe that they are great Latinists, whereas they can hardly decline a noun or conjugate a verb.

Scip. That is not so bad as what is done by some who really understand Latin; some of whom are so absurd, that in talking with a shoemaker or a tailor, they pour out Latin like water.

Berg. On the whole we may conclude, that he who talks Latin before persons who do not understand it, and he who talks it, being himself ignorant of it, are both equally to blame.

Scip. Another thing you may remark, which is that some persons who know Latin are not the less asses for all that.

Berg. No doubt of it; and the reason is clear; for when in the time of the Romans everybody spoke Latin as his mother tongue, that did not hinder some among them from being boobies.

Scip. But to know when to keep silence in the mother tongue, and speak in Latin, is a thing that needs discretion, brother Berganza.

Berg. True; for a foolish word may be spoken in Latin as well as in the vulgar tongue; and I have seen silly literati, tedious pedants, and babblers in the vernacular, who were enough to plague one to death with their scraps of Latin.

Scip. No more of this: proceed to your philosophical remarks.

Berg. They are already delivered.

Scip. How so?

Berg. In those remarks on Latin and the vulgar tongue, which I began and you finished.

Scip. Do you call railing philosophising? Sanctify the unhallowed plague of evil speaking, Berganza, and give it any name you please, it will, nevertheless entail upon us the name of cynics, which means dogs of ill tongue. In God's name, hold your peace, and go on with your story.

Berg. How can I go on with my story, if I hold my peace?

Scip. I mean go on with it in one piece, and don't hang on so many tails to it as to make it look like a polypus.

Berg. Speak correctly, Scipio: one does not say the tails but the arms of a polypus. But to my story: my evil fortune, not content with having torn me from my studies, and from the calm and joyous life I led amid them; not content with having fastened me up behind a door, and transferred me from the liberality of the students to the stinginess of the negress, resolved to rob me of the little ease and comfort I still enjoyed. Look ye, Scipio, you may set it down with me for a certain fact, that ill luck will hunt out and find the unlucky one, though he hides in the uttermost parts of the earth. I have reason to say this; for the negress was in love with a negro, also belonging to the house, who slept in the porch between the street-door and the inner one behind which I was fastened, and they could only meet at night, to which end they had stolen the keys or got false ones. Every night the negress came down stairs, and stopping my mouth with a piece of meat or cheese, opened the door for the negro. For some days, the woman's bribes kept my conscience asleep; for but for them, I began to fear that my ribs would come together, and that I should be changed from a mastiff to a greyhound. But my better nature coming at last to my aid, I bethought me of what was due to my master, whose bread I ate; and that I ought to act as becomes not only honest dogs, but all who have masters to serve.

Scip. There now, Berganza, you have spoken what I call true philosophy; but go on. Do not make too long a yarn—not to say tail of your history.

Berg. But, first of all, pray tell me if you know what is the meaning of the word philosophy? For though I use it, I do not know what the thing really is, only I guess that it is something good.

Scip. I will tell you briefly. The word is compounded of two Greek words, philo, love, and sophia, wisdom; so that it means love of wisdom, and philosopher a lover of wisdom.

Berg. What a deal you know, Scipio. Who the deuce taught you Greek words?

Scip. Truly you are a simpleton, Berganza, to make so much of a matter that is known to every schoolboy; indeed, there are many persons who pretend to know Greek, though they are ignorant of it, just as is the case with Latin.

Berg. I believe it, Scipio; and I would have such persons put under a press, as the Portuguese do with the negroes of Guinea, and have all the juice of their knowledge well squeezed out of them, so that they might no more cheat the world with their scraps of broken Greek and Latin.

Scip. Now indeed, Berganza, you may bite your tongue, and I may do the same; for we do nothing but rail in every word.

Berg. Ay, but I am not bound to do as I have heard that one Charondas, a Tytian, did, who published a law that no one should enter the national assembly in arms, on pain of death. Forgetting this, he one day entered the assembly girt with a sword; the fact was pointed out to him, and, on the instant, he drew his sword, plunged it into his body, and thus he was the first who made the law, broke it, and suffered its penalty. But I made no law; all I did was to promise that I would bite my tongue, if I chanced to utter an acrimonious word; but things are not so strictly managed in these times as in those of the ancients. To-day a law is made, and to-morrow it is broken, and perhaps it is fit it should be so. To-day a man promises to abandon his fault, and to-morrow he falls into a greater. It is one thing to extol discipline, and another to inflict it on one's self; and indeed there is a wide difference between saying and doing. The devil may bite himself, not I; nor have I a mind to perform heroic acts of self-denial here on this mat, where there are no witnesses to commend my honourable determination.

Scip. In that case, Berganza, were you a man you would be a hypocrite, and all your acts would be fictitious and false, though covered with the cloak of virtue, and done only that men might praise you, like the acts of all hypocrites.

Berg. I don't know what I should do if I were a man; but what I do know is that at present I shall not bite my tongue, having so many things yet to tell, and not knowing how or when I shall be able to finish them; but rather fearing that when the sun rises we shall be left groping without the power of speech.

Scip. Heaven forbid it! Go on with your story, and do not run off the road into needless digressions; in that way only you will come soon to the end of it, however long it may be.

Berg. I say, then, that having seen the thievery, impudence, and shameful conduct of the negroes, I determined, like a good servant, to put an end to their doings, if possible, and I succeeded completely in my purpose. The negress, as I have told you, used to come to amuse herself with the negro, making sure of my silence on account of the pieces of meat, bread, or cheese she threw me. Gifts have much power, Scipio.

Scip. Much. Don't digress: go on.

Berg. I remember, when I was a student, to have heard from the master a Latin phrase or adage, as they call it, which ran thus: habet bovem in lingua.

Scip. O confound your Latin! Have you so soon forgotten what we have said of those who mix up that language with ordinary conversation?

Berg. But this bit of Latin comes in here quite pat; for you must know that the Athenians had among their coin one which was stamped with the figure of an ox; and whenever a judge failed to do justice in consequence of having been corrupted, they used to say, "He has the ox on his tongue."

Scip. I do not see the application.

Berg. Is it not very manifest, since I was rendered mute many times by the negress's gifts, and was careful not to bark when she came down to meet her amorous negro? Wherefore I repeat, that great is the power of gifts.

Scip. I have already admitted it; and were it not to avoid too long a digression, I could adduce many instances in point; but I will speak of these another time, if heaven grants me an opportunity of narrating my life to you.

Berg. God grant it! meanwhile I continue. At last my natural integrity prevailed over the negress's bribes; and one very dark night, when she came down as usual, I seized her without barking, in order not to alarm the household; and in a trice I tore her shift all to pieces, and bit a piece out of her thigh. This little joke confined her for eight days to her bed, for which she accounted to her masters by some pretended illness or other. When she was recovered, she came down another night: I attacked her again; and without biting, scratched her all over as if I had been carding wool. Our battles were always noiseless, and the negress always had the worst of them; but she had her revenge. She stinted my rations and my bones, and those of my own body began to show themselves through my skin. But though she cut short my victuals, that did not hinder me from barking; so to make an end of me altogether, she threw me a sponge fried in grease. I perceived the snare, and knew that what she offered me was worse than poison, for it would swell up in the stomach, and never leave it with life. Judging then that it was impossible for me to guard against the insidious attacks of such a base enemy, I resolved to get out of her sight, and put some space between her and me. One day, I found myself at liberty, and without bidding adieu to any of the family, I went into the street; and before I had gone a hundred paces, I fell in with the alguazil I mentioned in the beginning of my story, as being a great friend of my first master Nicholas the butcher. He instantly knew me, and called me by my name. I knew him too, and went up to him with my usual ceremonies and caresses. He took hold of me by the neck, and said to his men, "This is a famous watch-dog, formerly belonging to a friend of mine: let us bring him home." The men said, if I was a watch-dog, I should be of great use to them all, and they wanted to lay hold on me to lead me along; but the alguazil said, it was not necessary, for I knew him, and would follow him. I forgot to tell you, that the spiked collar I wore when I ran away from the flock was stolen from me at an inn by a gipsy, and I went without one in Seville; but my new master put on me a collar all studded with brass. Only consider, Scipio, this change in my fortunes, Yesterday I was a student, and to-day I found myself a bailiff.

Scip. So wags the world, and you need not exaggerate the vicissitudes of fortune, as if there were any difference between the service of a butcher and that of a bailiff. I have no patience when I hear some persons rail at fortune, whose highest hopes never aspired beyond the life of a stable-boy. How they curse their ill-luck, and all to make the hearers believe that they have known better days, and have fallen from some high estate.

Berg. Just so. Now you must know that this alguazil was on intimate terms with an attorney; and the two were connected with a pair of wenches not a bit better than they ought to be, but quite the reverse. They were rather good looking, but full of meretricious arts and impudence. These two served their male associates as baits to fish with. Their dress and deportment was such that you might recognise them for what they were at the distance of a musket shot; they frequented the houses of entertainment for strangers, and the period of the fairs in Cadiz and Seville was their harvest time, for there was not a Breton with whom they did not grapple. Whenever a bumpkin fell into their snares they apprised the alguazil and the attorney to what inn they were going, and the latter then seized the party as lewd persons, but never took them to prison, for the strangers always paid money to get out of the scrape.

One day it happened that Colendres—this was the name of the alguazil's mistress—picked up a Breton, and made an appointment with him for the night, whereof she informed her friend; and they were hardly undressed before the alguazil, the attorney, two bailiffs, and myself entered the room. The amorous pair were sorely disconcerted, and the alguazil, inveighing against the enormity of their conduct, ordered them to dress with all speed, and go with him to prison. The Breton was dismayed, the attorney interceded from motives of compassion, and prevailed on the alguazil to commute the penalty for only a hundred reals. The Breton called for a pair of leather breeches he had laid on a chair at the end of the room, and in which there was money to pay his ransom, but the breeches were not to be seen. The fact was, that when I entered the room, my nostrils were saluted by a delightful odour of ham. I followed the scent, and found a great piece of ham in one of the pockets of the breeches, which I carried off into the street, in order to enjoy the contents without molestation. Having done so, I returned to the house, where I found the Breton vociferating in his barbarous jargon, and calling for his breeches, in one of the pockets of which he said he had fifty gold crowns. The attorney suspected that either Colendres or the bailiffs had stolen the money; the alguazil was of the same opinion, took them aside, and questioned them. None of them knew anything, and they all swore at each other like troopers. Seeing the hubbub, I went back to the street where I had left the breeches, having no use for the money in them; but I could not find them, for some one passing by had no doubt picked them up.

The alguazil, in despair at finding that the Breton had no money to bribe with, thought to indemnify himself by extorting something from the mistress of the house. He called for her, and in she came half dressed, and when she saw and heard the Breton bawling for his money, Colindres crying in her shift, the alguazil storming, the attorney in a passion, and the bailiffs ransacking the room, she was in no very good humour. The alguazil ordered her to put on her clothes and be off with him to prison, for allowing men and women to meet for bad purposes in her house. Then indeed the row grew more furious than ever. "Señor Alguazil and Señor Attorney," said the hostess, "none of your tricks upon me, for I know a thing or two, I tell you. Give me none of your blustering, but shut your mouth, and go your ways in God's name, otherwise by my faith I'll pitch the house out of the windows, and blow upon you all; for I am well acquainted with the Señora Colendres, and I know moreover that for many months past she has been kept by the Señor Alguazil; so don't provoke me to let out any more, but give this gentleman back his money, and let us all part good friends, for I am a respectable woman, and I have a husband with his patent of nobility with its leaden seals all hanging to it, God be thanked! and I carry on this business with the greatest propriety. I have the table of charges hung up where everybody may see it, so don't meddle with me, or by the Lord I'll soon settle your business. It is no affair of mine if women come in with my lodgers; they have the keys of their rooms, and I am not a lynx to see through seven walls."

My masters were astounded at the harangue of the landlady, and at finding how well acquainted she was with the story of their lives; but seeing there was nobody else from whom they could squeeze money, they still pretended that they meant to drag her to prison. She appealed to heaven against the unreasonableness and injustice of their behaving in that manner when her husband was absent, and he too a man of such quality. The Breton bellowed for his fifty crowns; the bailiffs persisted in declaring that they had never set eyes on the breeches, God forbid! The attorney privately urged the alguazil to search Colindres' clothes, for he suspected she must have possessed herself of the fifty crowns, since it was her custom to grope in the pockets of those who took up with her company. Colindres declared that the Breton was drunk, and that it was all a lie about his money. All in short was confusion, oaths, and bawling, and there would have been no end to the uproar if the lieutenant corregidor had not just then entered the room, having heard the noise as he was going his rounds. He asked what it was all about, and the landlady replied with great copiousness of detail. She told him who was the damsel Colindres (who by this time had got her clothes on), made known the connection between her and the alguazil, and exposed her plundering tricks; protested her own innocence, and that it was never with her consent that a woman of bad repute had entered her house; cried herself up for a saint, and her husband for a pattern of excellence; and called out to a servant wench to run and fetch her husband's patent of nobility out of the chest, that she might show it to the Señor Lieutenant. He would then be able to judge whether the wife of so respectable a man was capable of anything but what was quite correct. If she did keep a lodging-house, it was because she could not help it. God knows if she would not rather have some comfortable independence to live upon at her ease. The lieutenant, tired of her volubility and her bouncing about the patent of gentility, said to her, "Sister hostess, I am willing to believe that your husband is a gentleman, but then you must allow he is only a gentleman innkeeper." The landlady replied with great dignity, "And where is the family in the world, however good its blood may be, but you may pick some holes in its coat?" "Well, all I have to say, sister, is, that you must put on your clothes, and come away to prison." This brought her down from her high flights at once; she tore her hair, cried, screamed, and prayed, but all in vain; the inexorable lieutenant carried the whole party off to prison, that is to say, the Breton, Colindres, and the landlady. I learned afterwards that the Breton lost his fifty crowns, and was condemned besides to pay costs; the landlady had to pay as much more. Colindres was let off scot free, and the very day she was liberated she picked up a sailor, out of whom she made good her disappointment in the affair of the Breton. Thus you see, Scipio, what serious troubles arose from my gluttony.

Scip. Say rather from the rascality of your master.

Berg. Nay but listen, for worse remains to be told, since I am loth to speak ill of alguazil and attorneys.

Scip. Ay, but speaking ill of one is not speaking ill of all. There is many and many an attorney who is honest and upright. They do not all take fees from both parties in a suit; nor extort more than their right; nor go prying about into other people's business in order to entangle them in the webs of the law; nor league with the justice to fleece one side and skin the other. It is not every alguazil that is in collusion with thieves and vagabonds, or keeps a decoy-duck in the shape of a mistress, as your master did. Very many of them are gentlemen in feeling and conduct; neither arrogant nor insolent, nor rogues and knaves, like those who go about inns, measuring the length of strangers' swords, and ruining their owners if they find them a hair's breadth longer than the law allows.[60]

Berg. My master hawked at higher game. He set himself up for a man of valour, piqued himself on making famous captures, and sustained his reputation for courage without risk to his person, but at the cost of his purse. One day at the Puerta de Xeres he fell in, single-handed, with six famous bravoes, whilst I could not render him any assistance, having a muzzle on my mouth, which he made me wear by day and took off at night. I was amazed at his intrepidity and headlong valour. He dashed in and out between the six swords of the ruffians, and made as light of them as if they were so many osier wands. It was wonderful to behold the agility with which he assaulted, his thrusts and parries, and with what judgment and quickness of eye he prevented his enemies from attacking him from behind. In short, in my opinion and that of all the spectators of the fight, he was a very Rhodomont, having fought his men all the way from the Puerta de Xeres to the statues of the college of Maese Rodrigo, a good hundred paces and more. Having put them to flight, he returned to collect the trophies of the battle, consisting of three sheaths, and these he carried to the corregidor, who was then, if I mistake not, the licentiate Sarmiento de Valladares, renowned for the destruction of the Sauceda.[61] As my master walked through the streets, people pointed to him and said, "There goes the valiant man who ventured, singly, to encounter the flower of the bravoes of Andalusia."

He spent the remainder of the day in walking about the city, to let himself be seen, and at night we went to the suburb of Triana, to a street near the powder-mill, where my master, looking about to see if any one observed him, entered a house, myself following him, and in the court-yard we found the six rogues he had fought with, untrussed, and without cloaks or swords. One fellow, who appeared to be the landlord, had a big jar of wine in one hand and a great tavern goblet in the other, and, filling a sparkling bumper, he drank to all the company. No sooner had they set eyes on my master than they all ran to him with open arms. They all drank his health, and he returned the compliment in every instance, and would have done it in as many more had there been occasion—so affable he was and so averse to disoblige any one for trifles. Were I to recount all that took place there—the supper that was served up, the fights and the robberies they related, the ladies of their acquaintance whom they praised or disparaged, the encomiums they bestowed on each other, the absent bravoes whom they named, the clever tricks they played, jumping up from supper to exhibit their sleight of hand, the picked words they used, and, finally, the figure of the host, whom all respected as their lord and father,—were I to attempt this, I should entangle myself in a maze, from which I could never extricate myself. I ascertained that the master of the house, whose name was Monipodio, was a regular fence, and that my master's battle of the morning had been preconcerted between him and his opponents, with all its circumstances, including the dropping of the sword-sheaths, which my master now delivered, in lieu of his share of the reckoning. The entertainment was continued almost till breakfast time; and, by way of a final treat, they gave my master information of a foreign bravo, an out-and-outer, just arrived in the city. In all probability he was an abler blade than themselves, and they denounced him from envy. My master captured him the next night as he lay in bed; but had he been up and armed, there was that in his face and figure which told me that he would not have allowed himself to be taken so quietly. This capture, coming close upon the heels of the pretended fight, enhanced the fame of my poltroon of a master, who had no more courage than a hare, but sustained his valorous reputation by treating and feasting; so that all the gains of his office, both fair and foul, were frittered away upon his false renown.

I am afraid I weary you, Scipio, but have patience and listen to another affair that befel him, which I will tell you without a tittle more or less than the truth. Two thieves stole a fine horse in Antequera, brought him to Seville, and in order to sell him without risk, adopted what struck me as being a very ingenious stratagem. They put up at two different inns, and one of them entered a plaint in the courts of law, to the effect that Pedro de Losada owed him four hundred reals, money lent, as appeared by a note of hand, signed by the said Pedro, which he produced in evidence. The lieutenant corregidor directed that Losada should be called upon to state whether or not he acknowledged the note as his own, and if he did, that he should be compelled to pay the amount by seizure of his goods, or go to prison. My master and his friend the attorney were employed in this business. One of the thieves took them to the lodgings of the other, who at once acknowledged his note of hand, admitted the debt, and offered his horse in satisfaction of the amount. My master was greatly taken with the animal, and resolved to have it if it should be sold. The time prescribed by the law being expired, the horse was put up for sale; my master employed a friend to bid for it, and it was knocked down to him for five hundred reals, though well worth twelve or thirteen hundred. Thus one thief obtained payment of the debt which was not due to him, the other a quittance of which he had no need, and my master became possessed of the horse, which was as fatal to him as the famous Sejanus[62] was to his owners.

The thieves decamped at once; and two days afterwards my master, after having repaired the horse's trappings, appeared on his back in the Plaza de San Francisco, as proud and conceited as a bumpkin in his holiday clothes. Everybody complimented him on his bargain, declaring the horse was worth a hundred and fifty ducats as surely as an egg was worth a maravedi. But whilst he was caracolling and curvetting, and showing off his own person and his horse's paces, two men of good figure and very well dressed entered the square, one of whom cried out, "Why, bless my soul! that is my horse Ironfoot, that was stolen from me a few days ago in Antequera." Four servants, who accompanied him, said the same thing. My master was greatly chopfallen; the gentleman appealed to justice, produced his proofs, and they were so satisfactory that sentence was given in his favour, and my master was dispossessed of the horse. The imposture was exposed; and it came out how, through the hands of justice itself, the thieves had sold what they had stolen; and almost everybody rejoiced that my master's covetousness had made him burn his fingers.

His disasters did not end there. That night the lieutenant going his rounds, was informed that there were robbers abroad as far as San Julian's wards. Passing a cross-road he saw a man running away, and taking me by the collar, "At him, good dog!" he said, "At him, boy!" Disgusted as I was with my master's villanies, and eager to obey the lieutenant's orders, I made no hesitation to seize my own master and pull him down to the ground, where I would have torn him to pieces if the thief-takers had not with great difficulty separated us. They wanted to punish me, and even to beat me to death with sticks; and they would have done so if the lieutenant had not bade them let me alone, for I had only done what he ordered me. The warning was not lost upon me, so without taking my leave of anybody, I leaped through an opening in the wall, and before daybreak I was in Mayrena, a place about four leagues from Seville.

There by good luck I fell in with a party of soldiers, who, as I heard, were going to embark at Cartagena. Among them were four of my late master's ruffian friends; one of them was the drummer, who had been a catchpole and a great buffoon, as drummers frequently are. They all knew me and spoke to me, asking after my master as if I could reply; but the one who showed the greatest liking for me was the drummer, and so I determined to attach myself to him, if he would let me, and to accompany the expedition whether they were bound for Italy or Flanders. For in spite of the proverb, a blockhead at home is a blockhead all the world over, you must agree with me that travelling and sojourning among various people makes men wise.

Scip. That is so true that I remember to have heard from a master of mine, a very clever man, that the famous Greek, Ulysses, was renowned as wise solely because he had travelled and seen many men and nations. I therefore applaud your determination to go with the soldiers, wherever they might take you.

Berg. To help him in the display of his jugglery, the drummer began to teach me to dance to the sound of the drum, and to play other monkey tricks such as no other dog than myself could ever have acquired. The detachment marched by very short stages; we had no commissary to control us; the captain was a mere lad, but a perfect gentleman, and a great christian; the ensign had but just left the page's hall at the court; the serjeant was a knowing blade, and a great conductor of companies from the place where they were raised to the port of embarkation. The detachment was full of ruffians whose insolent behaviour, in the places through which we passed, redounded in curses directed to a quarter where they were not deserved. It is the misfortune of the good prince to be blamed by some of his subjects, for faults committed by others of them, which he could not remedy if he would, for the circumstances attendant on war are for the most part inevitably harsh, oppressive, and untoward.

In the course of a fortnight, what with my own cleverness, and the diligence of him I had chosen for my patron, I learned to jump for the king of France, and not to jump for the good-for-nothing landlady; he taught me to curvet like a Neapolitan courser, to move in a ring like a mill horse, and other things which might have made one suspect that they were performed by a demon in the shape of a dog. The drummer gave me the name of the wise dog, and no sooner were we arrived at a halting place, than he went about, beating his drum, and giving notice to all who desired to behold the marvellous graces and performances of the wise dog, that they were to be seen at such a house, for four or eight maravedis a head, according to the greater or less wealth of the place. After these encomiums everybody ran to see me, and no one went away without wonder and delight. My master exulted in the gains I brought him, which enabled him to maintain six of his comrades like princes. The envy and covetousness of the rogues was excited, and they were always watching for an opportunity to steal me, for any way of making money by sport has great charms for many. This is why there are so many puppet showmen in Spain, so many who go about with peep shows, so many others who hawk pens and ballads, though their stock, if they sold it all, would not be enough to keep them for a day; and yet they are to be found in taverns and drinking-shops all the year round, whence I infer that the cost of their guzzling is defrayed by other means than the profits of their business. They are all good-for-nothing vagabonds, bread weevils and winesponges.

Scip. No more of that, Berganza; let us not go over the same ground again. Continue your story, for the night is waning, and I should not like, when the sun rises, that we should be left in the shades of silence.

Berg. Keep it and listen. As it is an easy thing to extend and improve our inventions, my master, seeing how well I imitated a Neapolitan courser, made me housings of gilt leather, and a little saddle, which he fitted on my back; he put on it a little figure of a man, with lance in hand, and taught me to run straight at a ring fixed between two stakes. As soon as I was perfect in that performance, my master announced that on that day the wise dog would run at the ring, and exhibit other new and incomparable feats, which, indeed, I drew from my own invention, not to give my master the lie. We next marched to Montilla, a town belonging to the famous and great christian, Marquis of Priego, head of the house of Aguilar and Montilla. My master was quartered, at his own request, in a hospital; he made his usual proclamation, and as my great fame had already reached the town, the court-yard was filled with spectators in less than an hour. My master rejoiced to see such a plenteous harvest, and resolved to show himself that day a first-rate conjuror. The entertainment began with my leaping through a hoop. He had a willow switch in his hand, and when he lowered it, that was a signal for me to leap; and when he kept it raised, I was not to budge.

On that day (for ever memorable in my life) he began by saying, "Come, my friend, jump for that juvenile old gentleman, you know, who blacks his beard; or, if you won't, jump for the pomp and grandeur of Donna Pimpinela de Plafagonia, who was the fellow servant of the Galician kitchen wench at Valdeastillas. Don't you like that, my boy? Then jump for the bachelor Pasillas, who signs himself licentiate without having any degree. How lazy you are! Why don't you jump? Oh! I understand! I am up to your roguery! Jump, then, for the wine of Esquivias, a match for that of Ciudad Real, St. Martin, and Rivadavia." He lowered the switch, and I jumped in accordance with the signal. Then, addressing the audience, "Do not imagine, worshipful senate," he said, "that it is any laughing matter what this dog knows. I have taught him four-and-twenty performances, the least of which is worth going thirty leagues to see. He can dance the zaraband and the chacona better than their inventor; he tosses off a pint of wine without spilling a drop; he intones a sol, fa, mi, re, as well as any sacristan. All these things, and many others which remain to be told, your worships shall witness during the time the company remains here. At present, our wise one will give another jump, and then we will enter upon the main business."

Having inflamed the curiosity of the audience, or senate, as he called them, with this harangue, he turned to me and said, "Come now, my lad, and go through all your jumps with your usual grace and agility; but this time it shall be for the sake of the famous witch who is said to belong to this place." The words were hardly out of his mouth, when the matron of the hospital, an old woman, who seemed upwards of seventy, screamed out, "Rogue, charlatan, swindler, there is no witch here. If you mean Camacha, she has paid the penalty of her sin, and is where God only knows; if you mean me, you juggling cheat, I am no witch, and never was one in my life; and if I ever was reputed to be a witch, I may thank false witnesses, and the injustice of the law, and a presumptuous and ignorant judge. All the world knows the life of penance I lead, not for any acts of witchcraft, which I have never done, but for other great sins which I have committed as a poor sinner. So get out of the hospital, you rascally sheep-skin thumper, or by all the saints I'll make you glad to quit it at a run." And with that she began to screech at such a rate, and pour such a furious torrent of abuse upon my master, that he was utterly confounded. In fine, she would not allow the entertainment to proceed on any account. My master did not care much about the row, as he had his money in his pocket, and he announced that he would give the performance next day in another hospital. The people went away cursing the old woman, and calling her a witch, and a bearded hag into the bargain. We remained for all that in the hospital that night, and the old woman meeting me alone in the yard, said, "Is that you, Montiel, my son? Is that you?" I looked up as she spoke, and gazed steadily at her, seeing which, she came to me with tears in her eyes, threw her arms round my neck, and would have kissed my mouth if I had allowed her; but I was disgusted, and would not endure it.

Scip. You were quite right, for it is no treat, but quite the reverse, to kiss or be kissed by an old woman.

Berg. What I am now going to relate I should have told you at the beginning of my story, as it would have served to diminish the surprise we felt at finding ourselves endowed with speech. Said the old woman to me, "Follow me, Montiel, my son, that you may know my room; and be sure you come to me to-night, that we may be alone together, for I have many things to tell you of great importance for you to know." I drooped my head in token of obedience, which confirmed her in her belief that I was the dog Montiel whom she had been long looking for, as she afterwards told me. I remained bewildered with surprise, longing for the night to see what might be the meaning of this mystery or prodigy, and as I had heard her called a witch, I expected wonderful things from the interview. At last the time came, and I entered the room, which was small, and low, and dimly lighted by an earthenware lamp. The old woman trimmed it, sat down on a chest, drew me to her, and without speaking a word, fell to embracing me, and I to taking care that she did not kiss me.

"I did always hope in heaven," the old woman began, "that I should see my son before my eyes were closed in the last sleep; and now that I have seen you, let death come when it will, and release me from this life of sorrow. You must know, my son, that there lived in this city the most famous witch in the world, called Camacha de Montilla. She was so perfect in her art, that the Erichtheas, Circes, and Medeas, of whom old histories, I am told, are full, were not to be compared to her. She congealed the clouds when she pleased, and covered the face of the sun with them; and when the whim seized her, she made the murkiest sky clear up at once. She fetched men in an instant from remote lands; admirably relieved the distresses of damsels who had forgot themselves for a moment; enabled widows to console themselves without loss of reputation; unmarried wives, and married those she pleased. She had roses in her garden in December, and gathered wheat in January. To make watercresses grow in a handbasin was a trifle to her, or to show any persons whom you wanted to see, either dead or alive, in a looking-glass, or on the nail of a newborn infant. It was reported that she turned men into brutes, and that she made an ass of a sacristan, and used him really and truly in that form for six years. I never could make out how this was done; for as for what is related of those ancient sorceresses, that they turned men into beasts, the learned are of opinion that this means only that by their great beauty and their fascinations, they so captivated men and subjected them to their humours, as to make them seem unreasoning animals. But in you, my son, I have a living instance to the contrary, for I know that you are a rational being, and I see you in the form of a dog; unless indeed this is done through that art which they call Tropelia, which makes people mistake appearances and take one thing for another.

"Be this as it may, what mortifies me is that neither your mother nor myself, who were disciples of the great Camacha, ever came to know as much as she did, and that not for want of capacity, but through her inordinate selfishness, which could never endure that we should learn the higher mysteries of her art, and be as wise as herself. Your mother, my son, was called Montiela, and next to Camacha, she was the most famous of witches. My name is Cañizares; and, if not equal in proficiency to either of these two, at least I do not yield to them in good will to the art. It is true that in boldness of spirit, in the intrepidity with which she entered a circle, and remained enclosed in it with a legion of fiends, your mother was in no wise inferior to Camacha herself; while, for my part, I was always somewhat timid, and contented myself with conjuring half a legion; but though I say it that should not, in the matter of compounding witches' ointment, I would not turn my back upon either of them, no, nor upon any living who follow our rules. But you must know, my son, ever since I have felt how fast my life is hastening away upon the light wings of time, I have sought to withdraw from all the wickedness of witchcraft in which I was plunged for many years, and I have only amused myself with white magic, a practice so engaging that it is most difficult to forego it. Your mother acted in the same manner; she abandoned many evil practices, and performed many righteous works; but she would not relinquish white magic to the hour of her death. She had no malady, but died by the sorrow brought upon her by her mistress, Camacha, who hated her because she saw that in a short time Montiela would know as much as herself, unless indeed she had some other cause of jealousy not known to me.

"Your mother was pregnant, and her time being come, Camacha was her midwife. She received in her hands what your mother brought forth, and showed her that she had borne two puppy dogs. 'This is a bad business,' said Camacha; 'there is some knavery here. But, sister Montiela, I am your friend, and I will conceal this unfortunate birth; so have patience and get well, and be assured that your misfortune shall remain an inviolable secret.' I was present at this extraordinary occurrence, and was not less astounded than your mother. Camacha went away taking the whelps with her, and I remained to comfort the lying-in woman, who could not bring herself to believe what had happened. At last Camacha's end drew near, and when she felt herself at the point of death, she sent for her and told her how she had turned her sons into dogs on account of a certain grudge she bore her, but that she need not distress herself, for they would return to their natural forms when it was least expected; but this would not happen 'until they shall see the exalted quickly brought low, and the lowly exalted by an arm that is mighty to do it.'

"Your mother wrote down this prophecy, and deeply engraved it in her memory, and so did I, that I might impart it to one of you if ever the opportunity should present itself. And in hopes to recognise you, I have made it a practice to call every dog of your colour by your mother's name, to see if any of them would answer to one so unlike those usually given to dogs; and, this evening, when I saw you do so many things, and they called you the wise dog, and also when you looked up at me upon my calling to you in the yard, I believed that you were really the son of Montiela. It is with extreme pleasure I acquaint you with the history of your birth, and the manner in which you are to recover your original form. I wish it was as easy as it was for the golden ass of Apuleius, who had only to eat a rose for his restoration; but yours depends upon the actions of others, and not upon your own efforts. What you have to do meanwhile, my son, is to commend yourself heartily to God, and hope for the speedy and prosperous fulfilment of the prophecy; for since it was pronounced by Camacha it will be accomplished without any doubt, and you and your brother, if he is alive, will see yourselves as you would wish to be. All that grieves me is that I am so near my end, that I can have no hope of witnessing the joyful event.

"I have often longed to ask my goat how matters would turn out with you at last; but I had not the courage to do so, for he never gives a straightforward answer, but as crooked and perplexing as possible. That is always the way with our lord and master; there is no use in asking him anything, for with one truth he mingles a thousand lies, and from what I have noted of his replies it appears that he knows nothing for certain of the future, but only by way of conjecture. At the same time he so be-fools us that, in spite of a thousand treacherous tricks he plays us, we cannot shake off his influence. We go to see him a long way from here in a great field, where we meet a multitude of warlocks and witches, and are feasted without measure, and other things take place which, indeed and in truth, I cannot bring myself to mention, nor will I offend your chaste ears by repeating things so filthy and abominable. Many are of opinion that we frequent these assemblies only in imagination, wherein the demon presents to us the images of all those things which we afterwards relate as having occurred to us in reality; others, on the contrary, believe that we actually go to them in body and soul; and for my part I believe that both opinions are true, since we know not when we go in the one manner or in the other; for all that happens to us in imagination does so with such intensity, that it is impossible to distinguish between it and reality. Their worships the inquisitors have had sundry opportunities of investigating this matter, in the cases of some of us whom they have had under their hands, and I believe that they have ascertained the truth of what I state.

"I should like, my son, to shake off this sin, and I have exerted myself to that end. I have got myself appointed matron to this hospital; I tend the poor, and some die who afford me a livelihood either by what they leave me, or by what I find among their rags, through the great care I always take to examine them well. I say but few prayers, and only in public, but grumble a good deal in secret. It is better for me to be a hypocrite than an open sinner; for my present good works efface from the memory of those who know me the bad ones of my past life. After all, pretended sanctity injures no one but the person who practises it. Look you, Montiel, my son, my advice to you is this: be good all you can; but if you must be wicked, contrive all you can not to appear so. I am a witch, I do not deny it, and your mother was one likewise; but the appearances we put on were always enough to maintain our credit in the eyes of the whole world. Three days before she died, we were both present at a grand sabbath of witches in a valley of the Pyrenees; and yet when she died it was with such calmness and serenity, that were it not for some grimaces she made a quarter of an hour before she gave up the ghost, you would have thought she lay upon a bed of flowers. But her two children lay heavy at her heart, and even to her last gasp she never would forgive Camacha, such a resolute spirit she had. I closed her eyes and followed her to the grave, and there took my last look at her; though, indeed, I have not lost the hope of seeing her again before I die, for they say that several persons have met her going about the churchyards and the cross-roads in various forms, and who knows but I may fall in with her some time or other, and be able to ask her whether I can do anything for the relief of her conscience?"

Every word that the old hag uttered in praise of her she called my mother went like a knife to my heart; I longed to fall upon her and tear her to pieces, and only refrained from unwillingness that death should find her in such a wicked state. Finally she told me that she intended to anoint herself that night and go to one of their customary assemblies, and inquire of her master as to what was yet to befal me. I should have liked to ask her what were the ointments she made use of; and it seemed as though she read my thoughts, for she replied to my question as though it had been uttered.

"This ointment," she said, "is composed of the juices of exceedingly cold herbs, and not, as the vulgar assert, of the blood of children whom we strangle. And here you may be inclined to ask what pleasure or profit can it be to the devil to make us murder little innocents, since he knows that being baptised they go as sinless creatures to heaven, and every Christian soul that escapes him is to him a source of poignant anguish. I know not what answer to give to this except by quoting the old saying, that some people would give both their eyes to make their enemy lose one. He may do it for sake of the grief beyond imagination which the parents suffer from the murder of their children; but what is still more important to him is to accustom us to the repeated commission of such a cruel and perverse sin. And all this God allows by reason of our sinfulness; for without his permission, as I know by experience, the devil has not the power to hurt a pismire; and so true is this, that one day when I requested him to destroy a vineyard belonging to an enemy of mine, he told me that he could not hurt a leaf of it, for God would not allow him. Hence you may understand when you come to be a man, that all the casual evils that befal men, kingdoms, and cities, and peoples, sudden deaths, shipwrecks, devastations, and all sorts of losses and disasters, come from the hand of the Almighty, and by his sovereign permission; and the evils which fall under the denomination of crime, are caused by ourselves. God is without sin, whence it follows that we ourselves are the authors of sin, forming it in thought, word, and deed; God permitting all this by reason of our sinfulness, as I have already said.

"Possibly you will ask, my son, if so be you understand me, who made me a theologian? And mayhap you will say to yourself, Confound the old hag! why does not she leave off being a witch since she knows so much? Why does not she turn to God, since she knows that he is readier to forgive sin than to permit it? To this I reply, as though you had put the question to me, that the habit of sinning becomes a second nature, and that of being a witch transforms itself into flesh and blood; and amidst all its ardour, which is great, it brings with it a chilling influence which so overcomes the soul as to freeze and benumb its faith, whence follows a forgetfulness of itself, and it remembers neither the terrors with which God threatens it, nor the glories with which he allures it. In fact, as sin is fleshly and sensual, it must exhaust and stupefy all the feelings, and render the soul incapable of rising to embrace any good thought, or to clasp the hand which God in his mercy continually holds out to it. I have one of those souls I have described; I see it clearly; but the empire of the senses enchains my will, and I have ever been and ever shall be bad.

"But let us quit this subject, and go back to that of our unguents. They are of so cold a nature that they take away all our senses when we anoint ourselves with them, we remain stretched on the ground, and then they say we experience all those things in imagination which we suppose to occur to us in reality. Sometimes after we have anointed and changed ourselves into fowls, foals, or deer, we go to the place where our master awaits us. There we recover our own forms and enjoy pleasures which I will not describe, for they are such as the memory is ashamed to recal, and the tongue refuses to relate. The short and the long of it is, I am a witch, and cover my many delinquencies with the cloak of hypocrisy. It is true that if some esteem and honour me as a good woman, there are many who bawl in my ear the name imprinted upon your mother and me by order of an ill-tempered judge, who committed his wrath to the hands of the hangman; and the latter, not being bribed, used his plenary power upon our shoulders. But that is past and gone; and all things pass, memories wear out, lives do not renew themselves, tongues grow tired, and new events make their predecessors forgotten. I am matron of a hospital; my behaviour is plausible in appearance; my unguents procure me some pleasant moments, and I am not so old but that I may live another year, my age being seventy-five. I cannot fast on account of my years, nor pray on account of the swimming in my head, nor go on pilgrimages for the weakness of my legs, nor give alms because I am poor, nor think rightly because I am given to back-biting, and to be able to backbite one must first think evil. I know for all that that God is good and merciful, and that he knows what is in store for me, and that is enough; so let us drop this conversation which really makes me melancholy. Come, my son, and see me anoint myself; for there is a cure for every sorrow; and though the pleasures which the devil affords us are illusive and fictitious, yet they appear to us to be pleasures; and sensual delight is much greater in imagination than in actual fruition, though it is otherwise with true joys."

After this long harangue she got up, and taking the lamp went into another and smaller room. I followed her, filled with a thousand conflicting thoughts, and amazed at what I had heard and what I expected to see. Cañizares hung the lamp against the wall, hastily stripped herself to her shift, took a jug from a corner, put her hand into it, and, muttering between her teeth, anointed herself from her feet to the crown of her head. Before she had finished she said to me, that whether her body remained senseless in that room, or whether it quitted it, I was not to be frightened, nor fail to wait there till morning, when she would bring me word of what was to befal me until I should be a man. I signified my assent by drooping my head; and she finished her unction, and stretched herself on the floor like a corpse. I put my mouth to hers, and perceived that she did not breathe at all. One thing I must own to

70

you, friend Scipio, that I was terribly frightened at seeing myself shut up in that narrow room with that figure before me, which I will describe to you as well as I can.

She was more than six feet high, a mere skeleton covered with a black wrinkled skin. Her dugs were like two dried and puckered ox-bladders; her lips were blackened; her long teeth locked together; her nose was hooked; her eyes starting from her head; her hair hung in elf-locks on her hollow wrinkled cheeks;—in short, she was all over diabolically hideous. I remained gazing on her for a while, and felt myself overcome with horror as I contemplated the hideous spectacle of her body, and the worse occupation of her soul. I wanted to bite her to see if she would come to herself, but I could not find a spot on her whole body that did not fill me with disgust. Nevertheless, I seized her by one heel, and dragged her to the yard, without her ever giving any sign of feeling. There seeing myself at large with the sky above me, my fear left me, or at least abated, so much as to give me courage to await the result of that wicked woman's expedition, and the news she was to bring me. Meanwhile, I asked myself, how comes this old woman to be at once so knowing and so wicked? How is it that she can so well distinguish between casual and culpable evils? How is it that she understands and speaks so much about God, and acts so much from the prompting of the devil? How is it that she sins so much from choice, not having the excuse of ignorance?

In these reflections I passed the night. The day dawned and found us both in the court, she lying still insensible, and I on my haunches beside her, attentively watching her hideous countenance. The people of the hospital came out, and seeing this spectacle, some of them exclaimed, "The pious Cañizares is dead! See how emaciated she is with fasting and penance." Others felt her pulse, and finding that she was not dead, concluded that she was in a trance of holy ecstasy; whilst others said, "This old hag is unquestionably a witch, and is no doubt anointed, for saints are never seen in such an indecent condition when they are lost in religious ecstasy; and among us who know her, she has hitherto had the reputation of a witch rather than a saint." Some curious inquirers went so far as to stick pins in her flesh up to the head, yet without ever awaking her. It was not till seven o'clock that she came to herself; and then finding how she was stuck over with pins, bitten in the heels, and her back flayed by being dragged from her room, and seeing so many eyes intently fixed upon her, she rightly concluded that I had been the cause of her exposure. "What, you thankless, ignorant, malicious villain," she cried, "is this my reward for the acts I did for your mother and those I intended to do for you?" Finding myself in peril of my life under the talons of that ferocious harpy, I shook her off, and seizing her by her wrinkled flank, I worried and dragged her all about the yard, whilst she shrieked for help from the fangs of that evil spirit. At these words, most present believed that I must be one of those fiends who are continually at enmity with good Christians. Some were for sprinkling me with holy water, some were for pulling me off the old woman, but durst not; others bawled out words to exorcise me. The witch howled, I tightened my grip with my teeth, the confusion increased, and my master was in despair, hearing it said that I was a fiend. A few who knew nothing of exorcisms caught up three or four sticks and began to baste me. Not liking the joke, I let go the old woman; in three bounds I was in the street, and in a few more I was outside the town, pursued by a host of boys, shouting, "Out of the way! the wise dog is gone mad." Others said "he is not mad, but he is the devil in the form of a dog." The people of the place were confirmed in their belief that I was a devil by the tricks they had seen me perform, by the words spoken by the old woman when she woke out of her infernal trance, and by the extraordinary speed with which I shot away from them, so that I seemed to vanish from before them like a being of the other world. In six hours I cleared twelve leagues; and arrived at a camp of gipsies in a field near Granada. There I rested awhile, for some of the gipsies who recognised me as the wise dog, received me with great delight, and hid me in a cave, that I might not be found if any one came in search of me; their intention being, as I afterwards learned, to make money by me as my master the drummer had done. I remained twenty days among them, during which I observed their habits and ways of life; and these are so remarkable that I must give you an account of them.

Scip. Before you go any further, Berganza, we had better consider what the witch said to you, and see if there can possibly be a grain of truth in the great lie to which you give credit. Now, what an enormous absurdity it would be to believe that Camacha could change human beings into brutes, or that the sacristan served her for years under the form of an ass. All these things, and the like, are cheats, lies, or illusions of the devil; and if it now seems to ourselves that we have some understanding and reason— since we speak, though we are really dogs or bear that form—we have already said that this is a portentous and unparalleled case; and though it is palpably before us, yet we must suspend our belief until the event determines what it should be. Shall I make this more plain to you? Consider upon what frivolous things Camacha declared our restoration to depend, and that what seems a prophecy to you is nothing but a fable, or one of those old woman's tales, such as the headless horse, and the wand of virtues, which are told by the fireside in the long winter nights; for were it anything else it would already have been accomplished, unless, indeed, it is to be taken in what I have heard called an allegorical sense: that is to say, a sense which is not the same as that which the letter imports, but which, though differing from it, yet resembles it. Now for your prophecy:—"They are to recover their true forms when they shall see the exalted quickly brought low, and the lowly exalted by a hand that is mighty to do it." If we take this in the sense I have mentioned, it seems to me to mean that we shall recover our forms when we shall see those who yesterday were at the top of fortune's wheel, to-day cast down in the mire, and held of little account by those who most esteemed them; so, likewise, when we shall see others who, but two hours ago, seemed sent into the world only to figure as units in the sum of its population, and now are lifted up to the very summit of prosperity. Now, if our return, as you say, is to human form, were to depend on this, why we have already seen it, and we see it every hour. I infer, then, that Camacha's words are to be taken, not in an allegorical, but in a literal, sense; but this will help us out no better, since we have many times seen what they say, and we are still dogs, as you see. And so Camacha was a cheat, Cañizares an artful hag, and Montiela a fool and a rogue—be it said without offence, if by chance she was the mother of us both, or yours, for I won't have her for mine. Furthermore, I say that the true meaning is a game of nine-pins, in which those that stand up are quickly knocked down, and the fallen are set up again, and that by a hand that is able to do it. Now think whether or not in the course of our lives we have ever seen a game of nine-pins, or having seen it, have therefore been changed into men.

Berg. I quite agree with you Scipio, and have a higher opinion of your judgment than ever. From all you have said, I am come to think and believe that all that has happened to us hitherto, and that is now happening, is a dream; but let us not therefore fail to enjoy this blessing of speech, and the great excellence of holding human discourse all the time we may; and so let it not weary you to hear me relate what befel me with the gipsies who hid me in the cave.

Scip. With great pleasure. I will listen to you, that you in your turn may listen to me, when I relate, if heaven pleases, the events of my life.

Berg. My occupation among the gipsies was to contemplate their numberless tricks and frauds, and the thefts they all commit from the time they are out of leading-strings and can walk alone. You know what a multitude there is of them dispersed all over Spain. They all know each other, keep up a constant intelligence among themselves, and reciprocally pass off and carry away the articles they have purloined. They render less obedience to their king than to one of their own people whom they style count, and who bears the surname of Maldonado, as do all his descendants. This is not because they come of that noble line, but because a page belonging to a cavalier of that name fell in love with a beautiful gipsy, who would not yield to his wishes unless he became a gipsy and made her his wife. The page did so, and was so much liked by the other gipsies, that they chose him for their lord, yielded him obedience, and in token of vassalage rendered to him a portion of everything they stole, whatever it might be.

To give a colour to their idleness the gipsies employ themselves in working in iron, and you may always see them hawking pincers, tongs, hammers, fire-shovels, and so forth, the sale of which facilitates their thefts. The women are all midwives, and in this they have the advantage over others, for they bring forth without cost or attendants. They wash their new-born infants in cold water, and accustom them from birth to death to endure every inclemency of weather. Hence they are all strong, robust, nimble leapers, runners, and dancers. They always marry among themselves, in order that their bad practices may not come to be known, except by their own people. The women are well behaved to their husbands, and few of them intrigue except with persons of their own race. When they seek for alms, it is rather by tricks and juggling than by appeals to charity; and as no one puts faith in them, they keep none, but own themselves downright vagabonds; nor do I remember to have ever seen a gipsy-woman taking the sacrament, though I have often been in the churches. The only thoughts of their minds are how to cheat and steal. They are fond of talking about their thefts and how they effected them. A gipsy, for instance, related one day in my presence how he had swindled a countryman as you shall hear:

The gipsy had an ass with a docked tail, and he fitted a false tail to the stump so well that it seemed quite natural. Then he took the ass to market and sold it to a countryman for ten ducats. Having pocketed the money, he told the countryman that if he wanted another ass, own brother to the one he had bought, and every bit as good, he might have it a bargain. The countryman told him to go and fetch it, and meanwhile he would drive that one home. Away went the purchaser; the gipsy followed him, and some how or other, it was not long before he had stolen the ass, from which he immediately whipped off the false tail, leaving only a bare stump. He then changed the halter and saddle, and had the audacity to go and offer the animal for sale to the countryman, before the latter had discovered his loss. The bargain was soon made; the purchaser went into his house to fetch the money to pay for the second ass, and there he discovered the loss of the first. Stupid as he was, he suspected that the gipsy had stolen the animal, and he refused to pay him. The gipsy brought forward as witness the man who had received the alcabala[63] on the first transaction, and who swore that he had sold the countryman an ass with a very

72

bushy tail, quite different from the second one; and an alguazil, who was present, took the gipsy's part so strongly that the countryman was forced to pay for the ass twice over. Many other stories they told, all about stealing beasts of burden, in which art they are consummate masters. In short, they are a thoroughly bad race, and though many able magistrates have taken them in hand, they have always remained incorrigible.

After I had remained with them twenty days, they set out for Murcia, taking me with them. We passed through Granada, where the company was quartered to which my master the drummer belonged. As the gipsies were aware of this, they shut me up in the place where they were lodged. I overheard them talking about their journey, and thinking that no good would come of it, I contrived to give them the slip, quitted Granada, and entered the garden of a Morisco,[64] who gladly received me. I was quite willing to remain with him and watch his garden,—a much less fatiguing business in my opinion than guarding a flock of sheep; and as there was no need to discuss the question of wages, the Morisco soon had a servant and I a master. I remained with him more than a month, not that the life I led with him was much to my liking, but because it gave me opportunities of observing that of my master, which was like that of all the other Moriscoes in Spain. O what curious things I could tell you, friend Scipio, about that half Paynim rabble, if I were not afraid that I should not get to the end of my story in a fortnight! Nay, if I were to go into particulars, two months would not be enough. Some few specimens, however, you shall hear.

Hardly will you find among the whole race one man who is a sincere believer in the holy law of Christianity. Their only thought is how to scrape up money and keep it; and to this end they toil incessantly and spend nothing. The moment a real falls into their clutches, they condemn it to perpetual imprisonment; so that by dint of perpetually accumulating and never spending, they have got the greater part of the money of Spain into their hands. They are the grubs, the magpies, the weasels of the nation. Consider how numerous they are, and that every day they add much or little to their hoards, and that as they increase in number so the amount of their hoarded wealth must increase without end. None of them of either sex make monastic vows, but all marry and multiply, for thrifty living is a great promoter of fecundity. They are not wasted by war or excessive toil; they plunder us in a quiet way, and enrich themselves with the fruits of our patrimonies which they sell back to us. They have no servants, for they all wait upon themselves. They are at no expense for the education of their sons, for all their lore is but how to rob us. From the twelve sons of Jacob, who entered Egypt, as I have heard, there had sprung, when Moses freed them from captivity, six hundred thousand fighting men, besides women and children. From this we may infer how much the Moriscoes have multiplied, and how incomparably greater must be their numbers.

Scip. Means have been sought for remedying the mischiefs you have mentioned and hinted at; and, indeed, I am sure that those which you have passed over in silence, are even more serious than those which you have touched upon. But our commonwealth has most wise and zealous champions, who, considering that Spain produces and retains in her bosom such vipers as the Moriscoes, will, with God's help, provide a sure and prompt remedy for so great an evil. Go on.

Berg. My master being a stingy hunks, like all his caste, I lived like himself chiefly on maize bread and buckwheat porridge; but this penury helped me to gain paradise, in the strange manner you shall hear. Every morning, by daybreak, a young man used to seat himself at the foot of one of the many pomegranate trees. He had the look of a student, being dressed in a rusty suit of threadbare baize, and was occupied in writing in a note book, slapping his forehead from time to time, biting his nails, and gazing up at the sky. Sometimes he was so immersed in reverie, that he neither moved hand nor foot, nor even winked his eyes. One day I drew near him unperceived, and heard him muttering between his teeth. At last, after a long silence, he cried out aloud, "Glorious! The very best verse I ever composed in my life!" and down went something in his note book. From all this, it was plain that the luckless wight was a poet. I approached him with my ordinary courtesies, and when I had convinced him of my gentleness, he let me lie down at his feet, and resumed the course of his thoughts, scratching his head, falling into ecstacies, and then writing as before.

Meanwhile there came into the garden another young man, handsome and well dressed, with papers in his hand, at which he glanced from time to time. The new comer walked up to the pomegranate tree, and said to the poet, "Have you finished the first act?"

"I have just this moment finished it in the happiest manner possible," was the reply.

"How is that?"

"I will tell you! His Holiness the Pope comes forth in his pontificals, with twelve cardinals in purple canonicals—for the action of my comedy is supposed to take place at the season of mutatio caparum, when their eminences are not dressed in scarlet but in purple—therefore propriety absolutely requires that my cardinals should wear purple. This is a capital point, and one on which your common run of writers would be sure to blunder; but as for me I could not go wrong, for I have read the whole Roman ceremonial through, merely that I might be exact as to these dresses."

"But where do you suppose," said the other, "that our manager is to find purple robes for twelve cardinals?"

"If a single one is wanting," cried the poet, "I would as soon think of flying, as of letting my comedy be represented without it. Zounds! is the public to lose that magnificent spectacle! Just imagine the splendid effect on the stage of a supreme Pontiff and twelve grave cardinals, with all the other dignitaries, who will of course accompany them! By heavens, it will be one of the grandest things ever seen on the stage, not excepting even the nosegay of Duraja!"

I now perceived that one of these young men was a poet, and the other a comedian. The latter advised the former that he should cut out a few of his cardinals, if he did not want to make it impossible for the manager to produce the piece. The poet would not listen to this, but said they might be thankful that he had not brought in the whole conclave, to be present at the memorable event which he proposed to immortalise in his brilliant comedy. The player laughed, left him to his occupation, and returned to his own, which was studying a part in a new play. The poet, after having committed to writing some verses of his magnificent comedy, slowly and gravely drew from his pocket some morsels of bread, and about twenty raisins, or perhaps not so many, for there were some crumbs of bread among them, which increased their apparent number. He blew the crumbs from the raisins, and ate them one by one, stalks and all, for I did not see him throw anything away, adding to them the pieces of bread, which had got such a colour from the lining of his pocket, that they looked mouldy, and were so hard that he could not get them down, though he chewed them over and over again. This was lucky for me, for he threw them to me, saying, "Catch, dog, and much good may it do you." Look, said I to myself, what nectar and ambrosia this poet gives me; for that is the food on which they say these sons of Apollo are nourished. In short, great for the most part is the penury of poets; but greater was my need, since it obliged me to eat what he left.

As long as he was busy with the composition of his comedy he did not fail to visit the garden, nor did I want crusts, for he shared them with me very liberally; and then we went to the well, where we satisfied our thirst like monarchs, I lapping, and he drinking out of a pitcher. But at last the poet came no more, and my hunger became so intolerable, that I resolved to quit the Morisco and seek my fortune in the city. As I entered it, I saw my poet coming out of the famous monastery of San Geronimo. He came to me with open arms, and I was no less delighted to see him. He immediately began to empty his pockets of pieces of bread, softer than those he used to, carry to the garden, and to put them between my teeth without passing them through his own. From the softness of the bits of bread, and my having seen my poet come out of the monastery, I surmised that his muse, like that of many of his brethren, was a bashful beggar. He walked into the city, and I followed him, intending to take him for my master if he would let me, thinking that the crumbs from his table might serve to support me, since there is no better or ampler purse than charity, whose liberal hands are never poor.

After some time, we arrived at the house of a theatrical manager, called Angulo the Bad, to distinguish him from another Angulo, not a manager but a player, one of the best ever seen. The whole company was assembled to hear my master's comedy read; but before the first act was half finished, all had vanished, one by one, except the manager and myself, who formed the whole audience. The comedy was such that to me, who am but an ass in such matters, it seemed as though Satan himself had composed it for the utter ruin and perdition of the poet; and I actually shivered with vexation to see the solitude in which his audience had left him. I wonder did his prophetic soul presage to him the disgrace impending over him; for all the players—and there were more than twelve of them—came back, laid hold on the poet, without saying a word, and, had it not been for the authoritative interference of the manager, they would have tossed him in a blanket. I was confounded by this sad turn of affairs, the manager was incensed, the players very merry; and the poor forlorn poet, with great patience, but a somewhat wry face, took the comedy, thrust it into his bosom, muttering, "It is not right to cast pearls before swine," and sadly quitted the place without another word. I was so mortified and ashamed that I could not follow him, and the manager caressed me so much that I was obliged to remain; and within a month I became an excellent performer in interludes and pantomimes. Interludes, you know, usually end with a cudgelling bout, but in my master's theatre they ended with setting me at the characters of the piece, whom I worried and tumbled one over the other, to the huge delight of the ignorant spectators, and my master's great gain.

Oh, Scipio! what things I could tell you that I saw among these players, and two other companies to which I belonged; but I must leave them for another day, for it would be impossible to compress them within moderate limits. All you have heard is nothing to what I could relate to you about these people and their ways, their work and their idleness, their ignorance and their cleverness, and other matters without end, which might serve to disenchant many who idolise these fictitious divinities.

Scip. I see clearly, Berganza, that the field is large; but leave it now, and go on.

Berg. I arrived with a company of players in this city of Valladolid, where they gave me a wound in an interlude that was near being the death of me. I could not revenge myself then, because I was muzzled, and I had no mind to do so afterwards in cold blood; for deliberate vengeance argues a cruel and malicious disposition. I grew weary of this employment, not because it was laborious, but because I saw in it many things which called for amendment and castigation; and, as it was not in my power to remedy them, I resolved to see them no more, but to take refuge in an abode of holiness, as those do who forsake their vices when they can no longer practise them; but better late than never. Well, then, seeing you one night carrying the lantern with that good Christian Mahudes, I noticed how contented you were, how righteous and holy was your occupation. Filled with honest emulation, I longed to follow your steps; and, with that laudable intention, I placed myself before Mahudes, who immediately elected me your companion, and brought me to this hospital. What has occurred to me since I have been here would take some time to relate. I will just mention a conversation I heard between four invalids, who lay in four beds next each other. It will not take long to tell, and it fits in here quite pat.

Scip. Very well; but be quick, for, to the best of my belief, it cannot be far from daylight.

Berg. The four beds were at the end of the infirmary, and in them lay an alchemist, a poet, a mathematician, and one of those persons who are called projectors.

Scip. I recollect these good people well.

Berg. One afternoon, last summer, the windows being closed, I lay panting under one of their beds, when the poet began piteously to bewail his ill fortune. The mathematician asked him what he complained of.

"Have I not good cause for complaint?" he replied. "I have strictly observed the rule laid down by Horace in his Art of Poetry, not to bring to light any work until ten years after it has been composed. Now, I have a work on which I was engaged for twenty years, and which has lain by me for twelve. The subject is sublime, the invention perfectly novel, the episodes singularly happy, the versification noble, and the arrangement admirable, for the beginning is in perfect correspondence with the middle and the end. Altogether it is a lofty, sonorous, heroic poem, delectable and full of matter; and yet I cannot find a prince to whom I may dedicate it—a prince, I say, who is intelligent, liberal, and magnanimous. Wretched and depraved age this of ours!"

"What is the subject of the work?" inquired the alchemist.

"It treats," said the poet, "of that part of the history of king Arthur of England which archbishop Turpin left unwritten, together with the history of the quest of the Sangreal, the whole in heroic measure,—part rhymes, part blank-verse; and in dactyles moreover, that is to say, in dactylic noun substantives, without any admission of verbs."

"For my part, I am not much of a judge in matters of poetry," returned the alchemist, "and therefore I cannot precisely estimate the misfortune you complain of; but in any case it cannot equal my own in wanting means, or a prince to back me and supply me with the requisites, for prosecuting the science of alchemy; but for which want alone I should now be rolling in gold, and richer than ever was Midas, Crassus, or Croesus."

"Have you ever succeeded, Señor Alchemist," said the mathematician, "in extracting gold from the other metals?"

"I have not yet extracted it," the alchemist replied, "but I know for certain that the thing is to be done, and that in less than two months more I could complete the discovery of the philosopher's stone, by means of which gold can be made even out of pebbles."

"Your worships," rejoined the mathematician, "have both of you made a great deal of your misfortunes; but after all, one of you has a book to dedicate, and the other is on the point of discovering the philosopher's stone, by means of which he will be as rich as all those who have followed that course. But what will you say of my misfortune, which is great beyond compare? For two and twenty years I have been in pursuit of the fixed point; here I miss it, there I get sight of it again, and just when it seems that I am down upon it so that it can by no means escape me, I find myself on a sudden so far away from it that I am utterly amazed. It is just the same with the quadrature of the circle. I have been within such a hair's breadth of it, that I cannot conceive how it is that I have not got it in my pocket. Thus I suffer a torment like that of Tantalus, who starves with fruits all round him, and burns with thirst with water at his lip. At one moment I seem to grasp the truth, at another it is far away from me; and, like another Sisyphus, I begin again to climb the hill which I have just rolled down, along with all the mass of my labours."

The projector, who had hitherto kept silence, now struck in. "Here we are," he said, "four complainants, brought together by poverty under the roof of this hospital. To the devil with such callings and employments, as give neither pleasure nor bread to those who exercise them! I, gentlemen, am a projector, and have at various times offered sundry valuable projects to his majesty, all to his advantage, and without prejudice to the realm; and I have now a memorial in which I supplicate his majesty to appoint a person to whom I may communicate a new project of mine, which will be the means of entirely liquidating all his debts. But from the fate which all my other memorials have had, I foresee that this one also will be thrown into the dust-hole. Lest, however, your worships should think me crack-brained, I will explain my project to you, though this be in some degree a publication of my secret.

"I propose that all his majesty's vassals, from the age of fourteen to sixty, be bound once a month, on a certain appointed day, to fast on bread and water; and that the whole expenditure, which would otherwise be made on that day for food, including fruit, meat, fish, wine, eggs, and vegetables, be turned into money, and the amount paid to his majesty, without defrauding him of a doit, as each shall declare on oath. By this means, in the course of twenty years the king will be freed from all debts and incumbrances. The calculation is easily made. There are in Spain more than three millions of persons of the specified age, exclusive of invalids, old, and young, and there is not one of these but spends at least a real and a half daily; however, I am willing to put it at a real only, and less it cannot be, even were they to eat nothing but leeks. Now does it not strike your worships that it would be no bad thing to realise every month three millions of reals, all net and clear as if they were winnowed and sifted? The plan, moreover, instead of a loss to his majesty's subjects, would be a real advantage to them; for by means of their fasts they would make themselves acceptable to God and would serve their king, and some of them even might find it beneficial to their health. The project is in every way admirable, as you must confess; the money too might be collected by parishes, without the cost of tax gatherers and receivers, those plagues and bloodsuckers of the realm."

The others all laughed at the projector's scheme, and even he himself joined in the laugh at last. For my part I found much matter for reflection in the strange conversation I had heard, and in the fact that people such as these usually end their days in a hospital.

Scip. That is true, Berganza. Have you anything more to say?

Berg. Two things more and then I shall have done, for I think day is beginning to dawn. One day I accompanied Mahudes to ask for alms in the house of the corregidor of this city, who is a great cavalier and a very great Christian. We found him alone, and I thought fit to take advantage of that opportunity to give him certain counsels which I had gathered from the lips of an old invalid in this hospital, who was discussing the means of saving from perdition those vagabond girls who take to a life of vice to avoid labour, an intolerable evil demanding an immediate and effectual remedy. Wishing to impart what I had heard to the corregidor, I lifted up my voice, thinking to speak, but instead of articulate speech I barked so loudly that the corregidor called out in a passion to his servants to drive me out of the room with sticks; whereupon one of them caught up a copper syphon, which was the nearest thing at hand, and thrashed me with it so, that I feel it in my ribs to this hour.

Scip. And do you complain of that, Berganza?

Berg. Nay; have I not reason to complain, since I feel the pain even now; and since it appears to me that my good intentions merited no such chastisement?

Scip. Look you, Berganza, no one should interfere where he is not wanted, nor take upon himself a business that in no wise is his concern. Besides, you ought to know, that the advice of the poor, however good it may be, is never taken; nor should the lowly presume to offer advice to the great, who fancy they know everything. Wisdom in a poor man lies under a cloud, and cannot be seen; or if by chance it shines through it, people mistake it for folly, and treat it with contempt.

Berg. You are right, Scipio; and having had the lesson well beaten into me, I will henceforth act accordingly. That same night I entered the house of a lady of quality, who had in her arms a little lap-dog, so very diminutive that she could have hid it in her bosom. The instant it saw me, it flew at me out of its mistress's arms, barking with all its might, and even went so far as to bite my leg. I looked at it with disgust, and said to myself, "If I met you in the street, paltry little animal, either I would take no notice of you at all, or I would make mince meat of you." The little wretch was an example of the common rule—that mean-souled persons when they are in favour are always insolent, and ready to offend those who are much better than themselves, though inferior to them in fortune.

Scip. We have many instances of this in worthless fellows, who are insolent enough under cover of their masters' protection; but if death or any other chance brings down the tree against which they leaned, their true value becomes apparent, since they have no other merit than that borrowed from their patrons; whilst virtue and good sense are always the same, whether clothed or naked, alone or accompanied. But let us break off now; for the light beaming in through those chinks shows that the dawn is far advanced.

Berg. Be it so; and I trust in heaven that to-night we shall find ourselves in a condition to renew our conversation.

The licentiate finished the reading of this dialogue, and the Alferez his nap, both at the same time. "Although this colloquy is manifestly fictitious," said the licentiate, "it is, in my opinion, so well composed, that the Señor Alferez may well proceed with the second part."

"Since you give me such encouragement, I will do so," replied the alferez, "without further discussing the question with you, whether the dogs spoke or not."

"There is no need that we should go over that ground again," said the licentiate. "I admire the art and the invention you have displayed in the dialogue, and that is enough. Let us go to the Espolon,[65] and recreate our bodily eyes, as we have gratified those of our minds."

"With all my heart," said the alferez, and away they went.

[58] Alferez, Ensign.

[59] A common form of invitation, meaning we will partake of a poor repast.

[60] When Cervantes wrote this, a decree had recently been issued limiting the length of the sword.

[61] An old promenade of the city.

[62] The successive owners of this animal were Seius, Dollabella, Cassius, and Anthony. The first of them was executed, the rest committed suicide.

[63] A tax on sales and transfers.

[64] A Christian of Moorish descent.

[65] A promenade on the banks of the Arlozoro at Valladolid.

THE LITTLE GIPSY GIRL.

It would almost seem that the Gitanos and Gitanas, or male and female gipsies, had been sent into the world for the sole purpose of thieving. Born of parents who are thieves, reared among thieves, and educated as thieves, they finally go forth perfected in their vocation, accomplished at all points, and ready for every species of roguery. In them the love of thieving, and the ability to exercise it, are qualities inseparable from their existence, and never lost until the hour of their death.

Now it chanced that an old woman of this race, one who had merited retirement on full pay as a veteran in the ranks of Cacus, brought up a girl whom she called Preciosa, and declared to be her granddaughter. To this child she imparted all her own acquirements, all the various tricks of her art. Little Preciosa became the most admired dancer in all the tribes of Gipsydom; she was the most beautiful and discreet of all their maidens; nay she shone conspicuous not only among the gipsies, but even as compared with the most lovely and accomplished damsels whose praises were at that time sounded forth by the voice of fame. Neither sun, nor wind, nor all those vicissitudes of weather, to which the gipsies are more constantly exposed than any other people, could impair the bloom of her complexion or embrown her hands; and what is more remarkable, the rude manner in which she was reared only served to reveal that she must have sprung from something better than the Gitano stock; for she was extremely pleasing and courteous in conversation, and lively though she was, yet in no wise did she display the least unseemly levity; on the contrary, amidst all her sprightliness, there was at the same time so much genuine decorum in her manner, that in the presence of Preciosa no gitana, old or young, ever dared to sing lascivious songs, or utter unbecoming words.

The grandmother fully perceived what a treasure she had in her grandchild; and the old eagle determined to set her young eaglet flying, having been careful to teach her how to live by her talons. Preciosa was rich in hymns, ballads, seguidillas, sarabands, and other ditties, especially romances, which she sang with peculiar grace; for the cunning grandmother knew by experience that such accomplishments, added to the youth and beauty of her granddaughter, were the best means of increasing her capital, and therefore she failed not to promote their cultivation in every way she could. Nor was the aid of poets wanting; for some there are who do not disdain to write for the gipsies, as there are those who invent miracles for the pretended blind, and go snacks with them in what they gain from charitable believers.

During her childhood, Preciosa lived in different parts of Castile; but in her sixteenth year her grandmother brought her to Madrid, to the usual camping-ground of the gipsies, in the fields of Santa Barbara. Madrid seemed to her the most likely place to find customers; for there everything is bought and sold. Preciosa made her first appearance in the capital on the festival of Santa Anna, the patroness of the city, when she took part in a dance performed by eight gitanas, with one gitano, an excellent dancer, to lead them. The others were all very well, but such was the elegance of Preciosa, that she fascinated the eyes of all the spectators. Amidst the sound of the tambourine and castanets, in the heat of the dance, a murmur of admiration arose for the beauty and grace of Preciosa; but when they heard her sing—for the dance was accompanied with song—the fame of the gitana reached its highest point;

and by common consent the jewel offered as the prize of the best dancer in that festival was adjudged to her. After the usual dance in the church of Santa Maria, before the image of the glorious Santa Anna, Preciosa caught up a tambourine, well furnished with bells, and having cleared a wide circle around her with pirouettes of exceeding lightness, she sang a hymn to the patroness of the day. It was the admiration of all who heard her. Some said, "God bless the girl!" Others, "'Tis a pity that this maiden is a gitana: truly she deserves to be the daughter of some great lord!" Others more coarsely observed, "Let the wench grow up, and she will show you pretty tricks; she is closing the meshes of a very nice net to fish for hearts." Another more good-natured but ill-bred and stupid, seeing her foot so lightly, "Keep it up! keep it up! Courage, darling! Grind the dust to atoms!" "Never fear," she answered, without losing a step; "I'll grind it to atoms."

At the vespers and feast of Santa Anna Preciosa was somewhat fatigued; but so celebrated had she become for beauty, wit, and discretion, as well as for her dancing, that nothing else was talked of throughout the capital. A fortnight afterwards, she returned to Madrid, with three other girls, provided with their tambourines and a new dance, besides a new stock of romances and songs, but all of a moral character; for Preciosa would never permit those in her company to sing immodest songs, nor would she ever sing them herself. The old gitana came with her, for she now watched her as closely as Argus, and never left her side, lest some one should carry her off. She called her granddaughter, and the girl believed herself to be her grandchild.

The young gitanas began their dance in the shade, in the Calle de Toledo, and were soon encircled by a crowd of spectators. Whilst they danced, the old woman gathered money among the bystanders, and they showered it down like stones on the highway; for beauty has such power that it can awaken slumbering charity. The dance over, Preciosa said, "If you will give me four quartos, I will sing by myself a beautiful romance about the churching of our lady the Queen Doña Margarita. It is a famous composition, by a poet of renown, one who may be called a captain in the battalion of poets." No sooner had she said this, than almost every one in the ring cried out, "Sing it, Preciosa; here are my four quartos;" and so many quartos were thrown down for her, that the old gitana had not hands enough to pick them up. When the gathering was ended, Preciosa resumed her tambourine, and sang the promised romance, which was loudly encored, the whole audience crying out with one voice, "Sing again, Preciosa, sing again, and dance for us, girl, thou shalt not want quartos, whilst thou hast the ground beneath thy feet."

Whilst more than two hundred persons were thus looking on at the dance, and listening to the singing of the gitana, one of the lieutenants of the city passed by; and seeing so many people together, he asked what was the occasion of the crowd. Being told that the handsome gitana was singing there, the lieutenant, who was not without curiosity, drew near also to listen, but in consideration of his dignity, he did not wait for the end of the romance. The gitanilla, however, pleased him so much, that he sent his page to tell the old crone to come to his house that evening with her troop, as he wished his wife Doña Clara to hear them. The page delivered the message, and the old gitana promised to attend.

After the performance was ended, and the performers were going elsewhere, a very well-dressed page came up to Preciosa, and giving her a folded paper, said, "Pretty Preciosa, will you sing this romance? It is a very good one, and I will give you others from time to time, by which you will acquire the fame of having the best romances in the world."

"I will learn this one with much willingness," replied Preciosa; "and be sure, señor, you bring me the others you speak of, but on condition that there is nothing improper in them. If you wish to be paid for them, we will agree for them by the dozen; but do not expect to be paid in advance; that will be impossible. When a dozen have been sung, the money for a dozen shall be forthcoming."

"If the Señora Preciosa only pays me for the paper," said the page, "I shall be content. Moreover, any romance which does not turn out so well shall not be counted."

"I will retain the right of choice," said Preciosa; and then she continued her way with her companions up the street, when some gentlemen called and beckoned to them from a latticed window. Preciosa went up and looked through the window, which was near the ground, into a cheerful, well-furnished apartment, in which several cavaliers were walking about, and others playing at various games. "Will you give me a share of your winnings, señors?" said Preciosa, in the lisping accent of the gipsies, which she spoke not by nature but from choice. At the sight of Preciosa, and at the sound of her voice, the players quitted the tables, the rest left off lounging, and all thronged to the window, for her fame had already reached them. "Come in! Let the little gipsies come in," said the cavaliers, gaily; "we will certainly give them a share of our winnings."

"But you might make it cost us dear, señors," said Preciosa.

"No, on the honour of gentlemen," said one, "you may come in, niña, in full security that no one will touch the sole of your shoe. I swear this to you by the order I wear on my breast;" and as he spoke he laid his hand on the cross of the order of Calatrava which he wore.

"If you like to go in, Preciosa," said one of the gitanillas who were with her, "do so by all means; but I do not choose to go where there are so many men."

"Look you, Christina," answered Preciosa, "what you have to beware of is one man alone; where there are so many there is nothing to fear. Of one thing you may be sure, Christina; the woman who is resolved to be upright may be so amongst an army of soldiers. It is well, indeed, to avoid occasions of temptation, but it is not in crowded rooms like this that danger lurks."

"Well then, let us go in, Preciosa," said her companion, "you know more than a witch."

The old gipsy also encouraged them to go in, and that decided the question. As soon as they had entered the room, the cavalier of the order, seeing the paper which Preciosa carried, stretched out his hand to take it. "Do not take it from me," she said: "It is a romance but just given to me, and which I have not yet had time to read."

"And do you know how to read, my girl?" said one of the cavaliers.

"Ay, and to write too," said the old woman. "I have brought up my grandchild as if she was a lawyer's daughter."

The cavalier opened the paper, and finding a gold crown inclosed in it, said, "Truly, Preciosa, the contents of this letter are worth the postage. Here is a crown inclosed in the romance."

"The poet has treated me like a beggar," said Preciosa; "but it is certainly a greater marvel for one of his trade to give a crown than for one of mine to receive it. If his romances come to me with this addition, he may transscribe the whole Romancero General and send me every piece in it one by one. I will weigh their merit; and if I find there is good matter in them, I will not reject them. Read the paper aloud, señor, that we may see if the poet is as wise as he is liberal." The cavalier accordingly read as follows:—

Sweet gipsy girl, whom envy's self
Must own of all fair maids the fairest,
Ah! well befits thy stony heart
The name thou, Preciosa,[66] bearest.
If as in beauty, so in pride
And cruelty thou grow to sight,
Woe worth the land, woe worth the age
Which brought thy fatal charms to light.
A basilisk in thee we see,
Which fascinates our gaze and kills.
No empire mild is thine, but one
That tyrannises o'er our wills.
How grew such charms 'mid gipsy tribes,
From roughest blasts without a shield?
How such a perfect chrysolite
Could humble Manzanares yield?
River, for this thou shalt be famed,
Like Tagus with its golden show,
And more for Preciosa prized
Than Ganges with its lavish flow.
In telling fortunes who can say
What dupes to ruin thou beguilest?
Good luck thou speak'st with smiling lips.
But luckless they on whom thou smilest!
Tis said they're witches every one,
The women of the gipsy race;
And all men may too plainly see
That thou hast witchcraft in thy face.
A thousand different modes are thine
To turn the brain; for rest or move,
Speak, sing, be mute, approach, retire,
Thou kindlest still the fire of love.
The freest hearts bend to thy sway,
And lose the pride of liberty;
Bear witness mine, thy captive thrall,
Which would not, if it could, be free.

These lines, thou precious gem of love,
Whose praise all power of verse transcend,
He who for thee will live or die,
Thy poor and humble lover sends.

"The poem ends with 'poor' in the last line," said Preciosa; "and that is a bad sign. Lovers should never begin by saying that they are poor, for poverty, it strikes me, is a great enemy to love."

"Who teaches you these things, girl?" said one of the cavaliers.

"Who should teach me?" she replied. "Have I not a soul in my body? Am I not fifteen years of age? I am neither lame, nor halt, nor maimed in my understanding. The wit of a gipsy girl steers by a different compass from that which guides other people. They are always forward for their years. There is no such thing as a stupid gitano, or a silly gitana. Since it is only by being sharp and ready that they can earn a livelihood, they polish their wits at every step, and by no means let the moss grow under their feet. You see these girls, my companions, who are so silent. You may think they are simpletons, but put your fingers in their mouths to see if they have cut their wise teeth; and then you shall see what you shall see. There is not a gipsy girl of twelve who does not know as much as one of another race at five-and-twenty, for they have the devil and much practice for instructors, so that they learn in one hour what would otherwise take them a year."

The company were much amused by the gitana's chat, and all gave her money. The old woman sacked thirty reals, and went off with her flock as merry as a cricket to the house of the señor lieutenant, after promising that she would return with them another day to please such liberal gentlemen. Doña Clara, the lieutenant's lady, had been apprised of the intended visit of the gipsies, and she and her doncellas and dueñas, as well as those of another señora, her neighbour, were expecting them as eagerly as one looks for a shower in May. They had come to see Preciosa. She entered with her companions, shining among them like a torch among lesser lights, and all the ladies pressed towards her. Some kissed her, some gazed at her; others blessed her sweet face, others her graceful carriage. "This, indeed, is what you may call golden hair," cried Doña Clara; "these are truly emerald eyes."[67] The señora, her neighbour, examined the gitanilla piecemeal. She made a pepetoria[68] of all her joints and members, and coming at last to a dimple in her chin, she said, "Oh, what a dimple! it is a pit into which all eyes that behold it must fall." Thereupon an esquire in attendance on Doña Clara, an elderly gentleman with a long beard, exclaimed, "Call you this a dimple, señora? I know little of dimples then if this be one. It is no dimple, but a grave of living desires. I vow to God the gitanilla is such a dainty creature, she could not be better if she was made of silver or sugar paste. Do you know how to tell fortunes, niña?"

"That I do, and in three or four different manners," replied Preciosa.

"You can do that too?" exclaimed Doña Clara. "By the life of my lord the lieutenant, you must tell me mine, niña of gold, niña of silver, niña of pearls, niña of carbuncles, niña of heaven, and more than that cannot be said."

"Give the niña the palm of your hand, señora, and something to cross it with," said the old gipsy; "and you will see what things she will tell you, for she knows more than a doctor of medicine."

The señora Tenienta[69] put her hand in her pocket, but found it empty; she asked for the loan of a quarto from her maids, but none of them had one, neither had the señora her neighbour. Preciosa seeing this, said, "For the matter of crosses all are good, but those made with silver or gold are best. As for making the sign of the cross with copper money, that, ladies, you must know lessens the luck, at least it does mine. I always like to begin by crossing the palm with a good gold crown, or a piece of eight, or at least a quarto, for, I am like the sacristans who rejoice when there is a good collection."

"How witty you are," said the lady visitor; then turning to the squire, "Do you happen to have a quarto about you, Señor Contreras? if you have, give it me, and when my husband the doctor comes you shall have it again."

"I have one," replied Contreras, "but it is pledged for two-and-twenty maravedis for my supper; give me so much and I will fly to fetch it."

"We have not a quarto amongst us all," said Doña Clara, "and you ask for two-and-twenty maravedis? Go your ways, Contreras, for a tiresome blockhead, as you always were."

One of the damsels present, seeing the penury of the house, said to Preciosa, "Niña, will it be of any use to make the cross with a silver thimble?"

"Certainly," said Preciosa; "the best crosses in the world are made with silver thimbles, provided there are plenty of them."

"I have one," said the doncella; "if that is enough, here it is, on condition that my fortune be told too."

"So many fortunes to be told for a thimble!" exclaimed the old gipsy. "Make haste, granddaughter, for it will soon be night." Preciosa took the thimble, and began her sooth saying.

Pretty lady, pretty lady,
With a hand as silver fair,
How thy husband dearly loves thee
'Tis superfluous to declare.
Thou'rt a dove, all milk of kindness;
Yet at times too thou canst be
Wrathful as a tiger, or a
Lioness of Barbary.
Thou canst show thy teeth when jealous;
Truly the lieutenant's sly;
Loves with furtive sports to vary
Magisterial gravity.
What a pity! One worth having
Woo'd thee when a maiden fair.
Plague upon all interlopers!
You'd have made a charming pair.
Sooth, I do not like to say it,
Yet it may as well be said;
Thou wilt be a buxom widow;
Twice again shalt thou be wed.
Do not weep, my sweet senora;
We gitanas, you must know,
Speak not always true as gospel
Weep not then sweet lady so.
If the thought is too distressing,
Losing such a tender mate,
Thou hast but to die before him,
To escape a widow's fate.
Wealth abundant thou'lt inherit,
And that quickly, never fear:
Thou shalt have a son, a canon,
—Of what church does not appear;
Not Toledo; no, that can't be;
And a daughter—let me see—
Ay, she'll rise to be an abbess;
—That is, if a nun she be.
If thy husband do not drop off
From this moment in weeks four,
Burgos him, or Salamanca,
Shall behold corregidor.
Meanwhile keep thyself from tripping:
Where thou walkest, many a snare
For the feet of pretty ladies
Naughty gallants lay: beware!
Other things still more surprising
Shall on Friday next be told,
Things to startle and delight thee,
When I've crossed thy palm with gold.

Preciosa having finished this oracular descant for the lady of the house, the rest of the company were all eager to have their fortunes told likewise, but she put them off till the next Friday, when they promised to have silver coin ready for crossing their palms. The señor lieutenant now came in, and heard a glowing account of the charms and accomplishments of the leading gitana. Having made her and her companions dance a little, he emphatically confirmed the encomiums bestowed on Preciosa; and putting his hand in his pocket he groped and rummaged about in it for a while, but at last drew his hand out empty, saying, "Upon my life I have not a doit. Give Preciosa a real, Doña Clara; I will give it you by and by."

"That is all very well, señor," the lady replied; "but where is the real to come from? Amongst us all we could not find a quarto to cross our hands with."

"Well, give her some trinket or another, that Preciosa may come another day to see us, when we will treat her better."

"No," said Doña Clara, "I will give her nothing to-day, and I shall be sure she will come again."

"On the contrary," said Preciosa, "if you give me nothing. I will never come here any more. Sell justice, señor lieutenant, sell justice, and then you will have money. Do not introduce new customs, but do as other magistrates do, or you will die of hunger. Look you, señor, I have heard say that money enough may be made of one's office to pay any mulets that may be incurred,[70] and to help one to other appointments."

"So say and do those who have no conscience," said the lieutenant; "but the judge who does his duty will have no mulet to pay; and to have well discharged his office, will be his best help to obtain another."

"Your worship speaks like a very saint," replied Preciosa; "proceed thus, and we shall snip pieces off your old coats for relics."

"You know a great deal, Preciosa," said the lieutenant; "say no more, and I will contrive that their majesties shall see you, for you are fit to be shown to a king."

"They will want me for a court fool," said the gitanilla, "and as I never shall learn the trade, your pains will be all for nothing. If they wanted me for my cleverness, they might have me; but in some palaces fools thrive better than the wise. I am content to be a gitana, and poor, and let Heaven dispose of me as it pleases."

"Come along, niña," said the old gipsy; "say no more, you have said a great deal already, and know more than I ever taught you. Don't put too fine a point to your wit for fear it should get blunted; speak of things suitable to your years; and don't set yourself on the high ropes, lest you should chance to have a fall."

"The deuce is in these gitanas," said the delighted lieutenant, as they were taking their leave. The doncella of the thimble stopped them for a moment, saying to Preciosa, "Tell me my fortune, or give me back my thimble, for I have not another to work with."

"Señora doncella," replied Preciosa, "count upon your fortune as if it were already told, and provide yourself with another; or else sew no more gussets until I come again on Friday, when I will tell you more fortunes and adventures than you could read in any book of knight errantry."

The gipsies went away, and falling in with numerous workwomen returning from Madrid to their villages as usual at the Ave Maria, they joined company with them, as they always did for the greater security; for the old gipsy lived in perpetual terror lest some one should run away with her granddaughter.

One morning after this as they were returning to Madrid to levy black mail along with other gitanas, in a little valley about five hundred yards from the city, they met a handsome young gentleman richly dressed; his sword and dagger were a blazo of gold; his hat was looped with a jewelled band, and was adorned with plumes of various colours. The gitanas stopped on seeing him, and set themselves to observe his movements at their leisure, wondering much that so fine a cavalier should be alone and on foot in such a place at that early hour. He came up to them, and addressing the eldest gitana, said, "On your life, friend, I entreat you do me the favour to let me say two words in private to you and Preciosa. It shall be for your good."

"With all my heart," said the old woman, "so you do not take us much out of our way, or delay us long;" and calling Preciosa, they withdrew to some twenty paces distance, where they stopped, and the young gentleman thus addressed them: "I am so subdued by the wit and beauty of Preciosa, that after having in vain endeavoured to overcome my admiration, I have at last found the effort impossible. I, señoras (for I shall always give you that title if heaven favours my pretensions), am a knight, as this dress may show you;" and opening his cloak he displayed the insignia of one of the highest orders in Spain; "I am the son of——" (here he mentioned a personage whose name we suppress for obvious reasons), "and am still under tutelage and command. I am an only son, and expect to inherit a considerable estate. My father is here in the capital, looking for a certain post which by all accounts he is on the point of obtaining. Being then of the rank and condition which I have declared to you, I should yet wish to be a great lord for the sake of Preciosa, that I might raise her up to my own level, and make her my equal and my lady. I do not seek to deceive; the love I bear her is too deep for any kind of deception; I only desire to serve her in whatever way shall be most agreeable to her; her will is mine; for her my heart is wax to be moulded as she pleases but enduring as marble to retain whatever impression she shall make upon it. If you believe me I shall fear no discouragement from any other quarter, but if you doubt me, I shall despond. My name is——; my father's I have already given you; he lives in such a house in such a street and you may inquire about him and me of the neighbours, and of others also; for our name and quality are not so obscure but that you may hear of us about the court, and every, where in the capital. I have here a hundred crowns in gold to present to you, as earnest of what I mean to give you hereafter; for a man will be no niggard of his wealth who has given away his very soul."

Whilst the cavalier was speaking, Preciosa watched him attentively, and doubtless she saw nothing to dislike either in his language or his person. Turning to the old woman, she said, "Pardon me, grandmother, if I take the liberty of answering this enamoured señor myself."

"Make whatever answer you please, granddaughter," said the old woman, "for I know you have sense enough for anything." So Preciosa began.

"Señor cavalier," she said, "though I am but a poor gitana and humbly born, yet I have a certain fantastic little spirit within me, which moves me to great things. Promises do not tempt me, nor presents sap my resolution, nor obsequiousness allure, nor amorous wiles ensnare me; and although by my grandmother's reckoning I shall be but fifteen next Michaelmas, I am already old in thought, and have more understanding than my years would seem to promise. This may, perhaps, be more from nature than from experience; but be that as it may, I know that the passion of love is an impetuous impulse, which violently distorts the current of the will, makes it dash furiously against all impediments, and recklessly pursue the desired object. But not unfrequently when the lover believes himself on the point of gaining the heaven of his wishes, he falls into the hell of disappointment. Or say that the object is obtained, the lover soon becomes wearied of his so much desired treasure, and opening the eyes of his understanding he finds that what before was so devoutly adored is now become abhorrent to him. The fear of such a result inspires me with so great a distrust, that I put no faith in words, and doubt many deeds. One sole jewel I have, which I prize more than life, and that is my virgin purity, which I will not sell for promises or gifts, for sold it would be in that case, and if it could be bought, small indeed would be its value. Nor is it to be filched from me by wiles or artifices; rather will I carry it with me to my grave, and perhaps to heaven, than expose it to danger by listening to specious tales and chimeras. It is a flower which nothing should be allowed to sully, even in imagination if it be possible. Nip the rose from the spray, and how soon it fades! One touches it, another smells it, a third plucks its leaves, and at last the flower perishes in vulgar hands. If you are come then, señor, for this booty, you shall never bear it away except bound in the ties of wedlock. If you desire to be my spouse, I will be yours; but first there are many conditions to be fulfilled, and many points to be ascertained.

"In the first place I must know if you are the person you declare yourself to be. Next, should I find this to be true, you must straightway quit your father's mansion, and exchange it for our tents, where, assuming the garb of a gipsy, you must pass two years in our schools, during which I shall be able to satisfy myself as to your disposition, and you will become acquainted with mine. At the end of that period, if you are pleased with me and I with you, I will give myself up to you as your wife; but till then I will be your sister and your humble servant, and nothing more. Consider, señor, that during the time of this novitiate you may recover your sight, which now seems lost, or at least disordered, and that you may then see fit to shun what now you pursue with so much ardour. You will then be glad to regain your lost liberty, and having done so, you may by sincere repentance obtain pardon of your family for your faults. If on these conditions you are willing to enlist in our ranks, the matter rests in your own hands; but if you fail in any one of them, you shall not touch a finger of mine."

The youth was astounded at Preciosa's decision, and remained as if spell-bound, with his eyes bent on the ground, apparently considering what answer he should return. Seeing this, Preciosa said to him, "This is not a matter of such light moment that it can or ought to be resolved on the spot. Return, señor, to the city, consider maturely what is best for you to do; and you may speak with me in this same place any week-day you please, as we are on our way to or from Madrid."

"When Heaven disposed me to love you, Preciosa," replied the cavalier, "I determined to do for you whatever it might be your will to require of me, though it never entered my thoughts that you would make such a demand as you have now done; but since it is your pleasure that I should comply with it, count me henceforth as a gipsy, and put me to all the trials you desire, you will always find me the same towards you as I now profess myself. Fix the time when you will have me change my garb. I will leave my family under pretext of going to Flanders, and will bring with me money for my support for some time. In about eight days I shall be able to arrange for my departure, and I will contrive some means to get rid of my attendants, so as to be free to accomplish my purpose. What I would beg of you (if I might make bold to ask any favour) is that, except to-day for the purpose of inquiring about me and my family, you go no more to Madrid, for I would not that any of the numerous occasions that present themselves there, should deprive me of the good fortune I prize so dearly."

"Not so, señor gallant," said Preciosa: "wherever I go I must be free and unfettered; my liberty must not be restrained or encumbered by jealousy. Be assured, however, that I will not use it to such excess, but that any one may see from a mile off that my honesty is equal to my freedom. The first charge, therefore, I have to impose upon you is, that you put implicit confidence in me; for lovers who begin by being jealous, are either silly or deficient in confidence."

"You must have Satan himself within you, little one," said the old gipsy; "why you talk like a bachelor of Salamanca. You know all about love and jealousy and confidence. How is this? You make me look like a fool, and I stand listening to you as to a person possessed, who talks Latin without knowing it."

"Hold your peace, grandmother," replied Preciosa; "and know that all the things you have heard me say are mere trifles to the many greater truths that remain in my breast."

All that Preciosa said, and the sound sense she displayed, added fuel to the flame that burned in the breast of the enamoured cavalier. Finally, it was arranged that they should meet in the same place on that day sennight, when he would report how matters stood with him, and they would have had time to inquire into the truth of what he had told them. The young gentleman then took out a brocaded purse in which he said there were a hundred gold crowns, and gave it to the old woman; but Preciosa would by no means consent that she should take them.

"Hold your tongue, niña," said her grandmother; "the best proof this señor has given of his submission, is in thus having yielded up his arms to us in token of surrender. To give, upon whatever occasion it may be, is always the sign of a generous heart. Moreover, I do not choose that the gitanas should lose, through my fault, the reputation they have had for long ages of being greedy of lucre. Would you have me lose a hundred crowns, Preciosa? A hundred crowns in gold that one may stitch up in the hem of a petticoat not worth two reals, and keep them there as one holds a rent-charge on the pastures of Estramadura! Suppose that any of our children, grandchildren, or relations should fall by any mischance into the hands of justice, is there any eloquence so sure to touch the ears of the judge as the music of these crowns when they fall into his purse? Three times, for three different offences, I have seen myself all but mounted on the ass to be whipped; but once I got myself off by means of a silver mug, another time by a pearl necklace, and the third time with the help of forty pieces of eight, which I exchanged for quartos, throwing twenty reals into the bargain. Look you, niña, ours is a very perilous occupation, full of risks and accidents; and there is no defence that affords us more ready shelter and succour than the invincible arms of the great Philip: nothing beats the plus ultra.[71] For the two faces of a doubloon, a smile comes over the grim visage of the procurator and of all the other ministers of mischief, who are downright harpies to us poor gitanas, and have more mercy for highway robbers than for our poor hides. Let us be ever so ragged and wretched in appearance, they will not believe that we are poor, but say that we are like the doublets of the gavachos of Belmont, ragged and greasy and full of doubloons."

"Say no more, for heaven's sake, grandmother," said Preciosa; "do not string together so many arguments for keeping the money, but keep it, and much good may it do you. I wish to God you would bury it in a grave out of which it may never return to the light, and that there may never be any need of it. We must, however, give some of it to these companions of ours, who must be tired of waiting so long for us."

"They shall see one coin out of this purse as soon as they will see the Grand Turk," the old woman replied. "The good señor will try if he has any silver coin or a few coppers remaining, to divide amongst them, for they will be content with a little."

"Yes, I have," he said, and he took from his pocket three pieces of eight which he divided among the gitanas, with which they were more delighted than the manager of a theatre when he is placarded as victor in a contest with a rival. Finally it was settled that the party should meet there again in a week, as before mentioned, and that the young man's gipsy name should be Andrew Caballero, for that was a surname not unknown among the gipsies. Andrew (as we shall henceforth call him) could not find courage to embrace Preciosa, but darting his very soul into her with a glance, he went away without it, so to speak, and returned to Madrid. The gipsies followed soon after; and Preciosa, who already felt a certain interest in the handsome and amiable Andrew, was anxious to learn if he was really what he said.

They had not gone far before they met the page of the verses and the gold crown. "Welcome, Preciosa," he said, coming up to her. "Have you read the lines I gave you the other day?"

"Before I answer you a word," said she, "you must, by all you love best, tell me one thing truly."

"Upon that adjuration," he replied, "I could not refuse an answer to any question, though it should cost me my head."

"Well, then, what I want to know is this: are you, perchance, a poet?"

"If I were one, it would certainly be perchance," said the page; "but you must know, Preciosa, that the name of poet is one which very few deserve. Thus I am not a poet, but only a lover of poetry; yet for my own use I do not borrow of others. The verses I gave you were mine, as are these also which I give you now; but I am not a poet for all that—God forbid."

"Is it such a bad thing to be a poet?" Preciosa asked.

"It is not a bad thing," he answered; "but to be a poet and nothing else I do not hold to be very good. We should use poetry like a rich jewel, the owner of which does not wear it every day, or show it to all people, but displays it only at suitable times. Poetry is a beautiful maiden, chaste, honest, discreet, reserved, and never overstepping the limits of perfect refinement. She is fond of solitude; she finds pleasure and recreation among fountains, meadows, trees, and flowers; and she delights and instructs all who are conversant with her."

"I have heard for all that," said Preciosa, "that she is exceedingly poor; something of a beggar in short."

"It is rather the reverse," said the page, "for there is no poet who is not rich, since they all live content with their condition; and that is a piece of philosophy which few understand. But what has moved you, Preciosa, to make this inquiry?"

"I was moved to it, because, as I believe all poets, or most of them, to be poor, that crown which you gave me wrapped up with the verses caused me some surprise; but now that I know that you are not a poet, but only a lover of poetry, it may be that you are rich, though I doubt it, for your propensity is likely to make you run through all you have got. It is a well-known saying, that no poet can either keep or make a fortune."

"But the saying is not applicable to me," said the page. "I make verses, and I am neither rich nor poor; and without feeling it or making a talk about it, as the Genoese do of their invitations, I can afford to give a crown, or even two, to whom I like. Take then, precious pearl, this second paper, and this second crown enclosed in it, without troubling yourself with the question whether I am a poet or not. I only beg you to think and believe that he who gives you this would fain have the wealth of Midas to bestow upon you."

Preciosa took the paper, and feeling a crown within it, she said, "This paper bids fair to live long, for it has two souls within it, that of the crown and that of the verses, which, of course, are full of souls and hearts as usual. But please to understand, Señor Page, that I do not want so many souls; and that unless you take back one of them, I will not receive the other on any account. I like you as a poet and not as a giver of gifts; and thus we may be the longer friends, for your stock of crowns may run out sooner than your verses."

"Well," said the page, "since you will have it that I am poor, do not reject the soul I present to you in this paper, and give me back the crown, which, since it has been touched by your hand, shall remain with me as a hallowed relic as long as I live."

Preciosa gave him the crown, and kept the paper, but would not read it in the street. The page went away exulting in the belief that Preciosa's heart was touched, since she had treated him with such affability.

It being now her object to find the house of Andrew's father, she went straight to the street, which she well knew, without stopping anywhere to dance. About half way down it, she saw the gilded iron balcony which Andrew had mentioned to her, and in it a gentleman of about fifty years of age, of noble presence, with a red cross on his breast. This gentleman seeing the gitanilla, called out, "Come up here, niñas, and we will give you something." These words brought three other gentlemen to the balcony, among whom was the enamoured Andrew. The instant he cast his eyes on Preciosa he changed colour, and well nigh swooned, such was the effect her sudden appearance had upon him. The girls went up stairs, whilst the old woman remained below to pump the servants with respect to Andrew. As they entered the room, the elder gentleman was saying to the others, "This is no doubt the handsome gitanilla who is so much talked of in Madrid."

"It is," said Andrew; "and she is unquestionably the most beautiful creature that ever was seen."

"So they say," said Preciosa, who had overheard these remarks as she came in; "but indeed they must be half out in the reckoning. I believe I am pretty well, but as handsome as they say—not a bit of it!"

"By the life of Don Juanico, my son," said the elder gentleman, "you are far more so, fair gitana."

"And who is Don Juanico, your son?" said Preciosa.

"That gallant by your side," said the cavalier.

"Truly, I thought your worship had sworn by some bantling of two years old," said Preciosa. "What a pretty little pet of a Don Juanico![72] Why he is old enough to be married; and by certain lines on his forehead, I foresee that married he will be before three years are out, and much to his liking too, if in the meantime he be neither lost nor changed."

"Ay, ay," said one of the company; "the gitanilla can tell the meaning of a wrinkle."

During this time, the three gipsy girls, who accompanied Preciosa, had got their heads together and were whispering each other. "Girls," said Christina, "that is the gentleman that gave us the three pieces of eight this morning."

"Sure enough," said they; "but don't let us say a word about it unless he mentions it. How do we know but he may wish to keep it secret?"

Whilst the three were thus conferring together, Preciosa replied to the last remark about wrinkles. "What I see with my eyes, I divine with my fingers. Of the Señor Don Juanico, I know without lines that he is somewhat amorous, impetuous, and hasty; and a great promiser of things that seem impossible. God grant he be not a deceiver, which would be worse than all. He is now about to make a long journey; but the bay horse thinks one thing, and the man that saddles him thinks another thing. Man proposes and God disposes. Perhaps he may think he is bound for Oñez, and will find himself on the way to Gaviboa."

"In truth, gitana," said Don Juan, "you have guessed right respecting me in several points. I certainly intend, with God's will, to set out for Flanders in four or five days, though you forebode that I shall have to turn out of my road; yet I hope no obstacle will occur to frustrate my purpose."

"Say no more, señorito," the gipsy replied; "but commend yourself to God, and all will be well. Be assured I know nothing at all of what I have been saying. It is no wonder if I sometimes hit the mark, since I talk so much and always at random. I wish I could speak to such good purpose as to persuade you not to leave home, but remain quietly with your parents to comfort their old age; for I am no friend to these Flanders expeditions, especially for a youth of your tender years. Wait till you are grown a little more and better able to bear the toils of war; and the rather as you have war enough at home, considering all the amorous conflicts that are raging in your bosom. Gently, gently with you, madcap! Look what you are doing before you marry; and now give us a little dole for God's sake and for the name you bear; for truly I believe you are well born, and if along with this you are loyal and true, then I will sing jubilee for having hit the mark in all I have said to you."

"I told you before, niña," said Don Juan, otherwise Andrew Caballero, "that you were right on every point except as to the fear you entertain that I am not quite a man of my word. In that respect you are certainly mistaken. The word that I pledge in the field I fulfil in the town, or wherever I may be, without waiting to be asked; for no man can esteem himself a gentleman, who yields in the least to the vice of falsehood. My father will give you alms for God's sake and for mine; for in truth I gave all I had this morning to some ladies, of whom I would not venture to assert that they are as obliging as they are beautiful, one of them especially."

Hearing this, Christina said to her companions, "May I be hanged, girls, if he is not talking of the three pieces of eight he gave us this morning."

"No, that can't be," one of them observed; "for he said they were ladies, and we are none; and being so true-spoken as he says he is, he would not lie in this matter."

"Oh, but," said Christina, "that is not a lie of any moment that is told without injury to anybody, but for the advantage and credit of him who tells it. Be that as it may, I see he neither gives us anything, nor asks us to dance."

The old gipsy now came into the room and said, "Make haste, granddaughter; for it is late, and there is much to be done, and more to be said."

"What is it, grandmother?" said Preciosa, "A boy or a girl?"

"A boy, and a very fine one. Come along, Preciosa, and you shall hear marvels."

"God grant the mother does not die of her after pains," said the granddaughter.

"We will take all possible care of her. She has had a very good time, and the child is a perfect beauty."

"Has any lady been confined?" said Andrew's father.

"Yes, señor," replied the old Gitana: "but it is such a secret, that no one knows of it except Preciosa, myself, and one other person. So we cannot mention the lady's name."

"Well, we don't want to know it," said one of the gentlemen present; "but God help the lady who trusts her secret to your tongues, and her honour to your aid."

"We are not all bad," replied Preciosa; "perhaps there may be one among us who piques herself on being as trusty and as true as the noblest man in this room. Let us begone, grandmother; for here we are held in little esteem, though in truth we are neither thieves nor beggars."

"Do not be angry, Preciosa," said Andrew's father. "Of you at least I imagine no one can presume anything ill, for your good looks are warrant for your good conduct. Do me the favour to dance a little with your companions. I have here a doubloon for you with two faces, and neither of them as good as your own, though they are the faces of two kings."

The moment the old woman heard this she cried, "Come along, girls: tuck up your skirts, and oblige these gentlemen." Preciosa took the tambourine, and they all danced with so much grace and freedom, that the eyes of all the spectators were riveted upon their steps, especially those of Andrew, who gazed upon Preciosa as if his whole soul was centred in her; but an untoward accident turned his delight into anguish. In the exertion of the dance, Preciosa let fall the paper given her by the page. It was immediately picked up by the gentleman who had no good opinion of the gipsies. He opened it, and said, "What have we here? A madrigal? Good! Break off the dance, and listen to it; for, as far as I can judge from the beginning, it is really not bad." Preciosa was annoyed at this, as she did not know the contents of the paper; and she begged the gentleman not to read it, but give it back to her. All her entreaties, however, only made Andrew more eager to hear the lines, and his friend read them out as follows:—

Who hath Preciosa seen
Dancing like the Fairy Queen?
Ripplets on a sunlit river
Like her small feet glance and quiver.
When she strikes the timbrel featly,
When she warbles, oh how sweetly!
Pearls from her white hands she showers,
From her rosy lips drop flowers.
Not a ringlet of her hair
But doth thousand souls ensnare.
Not a glance of her bright eyes
But seems shot from Love's own skies.
He in obeisance to this sovereign maid,
His bow and quiver at her feet hath laid.

"Por dios!" exclaimed the reader, "he is a dainty poet who wrote this."

"He is not a poet, señor," said Preciosa, "but a page, and a very gallant and worthy man."

"Mind what you say, Preciosa," returned the other; "for the praises you bestow on the page are so many lance-thrusts through Andrew's heart. Look at him as he sits aghast, thrown back on his chair, with a cold perspiration breaking through all his pores. Do not imagine, maiden, that he loves you so lightly but that the least slight from you distracts him. Go to him, for God's sake, and whisper a few words in his ear, that may go straight to his heart, and recall him to himself. Go on receiving such madrigals as this every day, and just see what will come of it."

It was just as he had said. Andrew had been racked by a thousand jealousies on hearing the verses; and was so overcome that his father observed it, and cried out, "What ails you, Don Juan? You are turned quite pale, and look as if you were going to faint."

"Wait a moment," said Preciosa, "let me whisper certain words in his ear, and you will see that he will not faint." Then bending over him she said, almost without moving her lips, "A pretty sort of gitano you will make! Why, Andrew, how will you be able to bear the torture with gauze,[73] when you are overcome by a bit of paper?" Then making half-a-dozen signs of the cross over his heart, she left him, after which Andrew breathed a little, and told his friends that Preciosa's words had done him good.

Finally, the two-faced doubloon was given to Preciosa, who told her companions that she would change it, and share the amount honourably with them. Andrew's father intreated her to leave him in writing the words she had spoken to his son, as he wished by all means to know them. She said she would repeat them with great pleasure; and that though they might appear to be mere child's play, they were of sovereign virtue to preserve from the heartache and dizziness of the head. The words were these:—

Silly pate, silly pate,
Why run on at this rate?
No tripping, or slipping, or sliding!
Have trusty assurance,
And patient endurance
And ever be frank and confiding.
To ugly suspicion
Refuse all admission,
Nor let it your better sense twist over.
All this if you do
You'll not rue,
For excellent things will ensue,
With the good help of God and St. Christopher.

"Only say these words," she continued, "over any person who has a swimming in the head, making at the same time six signs of the cross over his heart, and he will soon be as sound as an apple."

When the old woman heard the charm, she was amazed at the clever trick played by her granddaughter; and Andrew was still more so when he found that the whole was an invention of her quick wit. Preciosa left the madrigal in the hands of the gentleman, not liking to ask for it, lest she should again distress Andrew; for she knew, without any one teaching her, what it was to make a lover feel the pangs of jealousy. Before she took her leave, she said to Don Juan, "Every day of the week, señor, is lucky for beginning a journey: not one of them is black. Hasten your departure, therefore, as much as you can; for there lies before you a free life of ample range and great enjoyment, if you choose to accommodate yourself to it."

"It strikes me that a soldier's life is not so free as you say," replied Andrew, "but one of submission rather than liberty. However, I will see what I can do."

"You will see more than you think for," said Preciosa; "and may God have you in his keeping, and lead you to happiness, as your goodly presence deserves."

These farewell words filled Andrew with delight; the gitanas went away no less gratified, and shared the doubloon between them, the old woman as usual taking a part and a half, both by reason of her seniority, as because she was the compass by which they steered their course on the wide sea of their dances, pleasantry, and tricks.

At last the appointed day of meeting came, and Andrew arrived in the morning at the old trysting place, mounted on a hired mule, and without any attendant. He found Preciosa and her grandmother waiting for him, and was cordially welcomed by them. He begged they would take him at once to the rancho,[74] before it was broad day, that he might not be recognised should he be sought for. The two gitanas, who had taken the precaution to come alone, immediately wheeled round, and soon arrived with him at their huts. Andrew entered one of them, which was the largest in the rancho, where he was forthwith assisted by ten or twelve gitanos, all handsome strapping young fellows, whom the old woman had previously informed respecting the new comrade who was about to join them. She had not thought it necessary, to enjoin them to secrecy; for, as we have already said, they habitually observed it with unexampled sagacity and strictness. Their eyes were at once on the mule, and said one of them, "We can sell this on Thursday in Toledo."

"By no means," said Andrew; "for there is not a hired mule in Madrid, or any other town, but is known to all the muleteers that tramp the roads of Spain."

"Por dios, señor Andrew," said one of the gang, "if there were more signs and tokens upon the mule than are to precede the day of judgment, we will transform it in such a manner that it could not be known by the mother that bore it, or the master that owned it."

"That maybe," said Andrew; "but for this time you must do as I recommend. This mule must be killed, and buried where its bones shall never be seen."

"Put the innocent creature to death!" cried another gipsy. "What a sin! Don't say the word, good Andrew; only do one thing. Examine the beast well, till you have got all its marks well by heart; then let me take it away, and if in two hours from this time you are able to know, it again, let me be basted like a runaway negro."

"I must insist upon the mule's being put to death," said Andrew, "though I were ever so sure of its transformation. I am in fear of being discovered unless it is put under ground. If you object for sake of the profit to be made by selling it, I am not come so destitute to this fraternity but that I can pay my footing with more than the price of four mules."

"Well, since the Señor Andrew Caballero will have it so," said the other gitano, "let the sinless creature die, though God knows how much it goes against me, both because of its youth, for it has not yet lost mark of mouth, a rare thing among hired mules, and because it must be a good goer, for it has neither scars on its flank nor marks of the spur."

The slaughter of the mule was postponed till night, and the rest of the day was spent in the ceremonies of Andrew's initiation. They cleared out one of the best huts in the encampment, dressed it with boughs and rushes, and seating Andrew in it on the stump of a cork tree, they put a hammer and tongs in his hands, and made him cut two capers to the sound of two guitars. They then bared one of his arms, tied round it a new silk ribbon through which they passed a short stick, and gave it two turns gently, after the manner of the garotte with which criminals are strangled. Preciosa was present at all this, as were many other gitanas, old and young, some of whom gazed at Andrew with admiration, others with love, and such was his good humour, that even the gitanos took most kindly to him.

These ceremonies being ended, an old gipsy took Preciosa by the hand, and setting her opposite Andrew, spoke thus: "This girl, who is the flower and cream of all beauty among the gitanas of Spain, we give to you either for your wife or your mistress, for in that respect you may do whatever shall be most to your liking, since our free and easy life is not subject to squeamish scruples or to much ceremony. Look at her well, and see if she suits you, or if there is anything in her you dislike; if there is, choose from among the maidens here present the one you like best, and we will give her to you. But bear in mind that once your choice is made, you must not quit it for another, nor make or meddle either with the married women or the maids. We are strict observers of the law of good fellowship; none among us covets the good that belongs to another. We live free and secure from the bitter plague of jealousy; and though incest is frequent amongst us there is no adultery. If a wife or a mistress is unfaithful, we do not go ask the courts of justice to punish; but we ourselves are the judges and executioners of our wives and mistresses, and make no more ado about killing and burying them in the mountains and desert places than if they were vermin. There are no relations to avenge them, no parents to call us to account for their deaths. By reason of this fear and dread, our women learn to live chaste; and we, as I have said, feel no uneasiness about their virtue.

"We have few things which are not common to us all, except wives and mistresses, each of whom we require to be his alone to whom fortune has allotted her. Among us divorce takes place, because of old age as well as by death. Any man may if he likes leave a woman who is too old for him, and choose one more suitable to his years. By means of these and other laws and statutes we contrive to lead a merry life. We are lords of the plains, the corn fields, the woods, mountains, springs, and rivers. The mountains yield us wood for nothing, the orchards fruit, the vineyards grapes, the gardens vegetables, the fountains water, the rivers fish, the parks feathered game; the rocks yield us shade, the glades and valleys fresh air, and the caves shelter. For us the inclemencies of the weather are zephyrs, the snow refreshment, the rain baths, the thunder music, and the lightning torches. For us the hard ground is a bed of down; the tanned skin of our bodies is an impenetrable harness to defend us; our nimble limbs submit to no obstacle from iron bars, or trenches, or walls; our courage is not to be twisted out of us by cords, or choked by gauze,[75] or quelled by the rack.

"Between yes and no we make no difference when it suits our convenience to confound them; we always pride ourselves more on being martyrs than confessors. For us the beasts of burden are reared in the fields, and pockets are filled in the cities. No eagle or other bird of prey pounces more swiftly on its quarry than we upon opportunities that offer us booty. And finally, we possess many qualities which promise us a happy end; for we sing in prison, are silent on the rack, work by day, and by night we thieve, or rather we take means to teach all men that they should exempt themselves from the trouble of seeing where they put their property. We are not distressed by the fear of losing our honour, or kept awake by ambition to increase it. We attach ourselves to no parties; we do not rise by day-light to attend levees and present memorials, or to swell the trains of magnates, or to solicit favours. Our gilded roofs and sumptuous palaces are these portable huts; our Flemish pictures and landscapes are those which nature presents to our eyes at every step in the rugged cliffs and snowy peaks, the spreading meads and leafy groves. We are rustic astronomers, for as we sleep almost always under the open sky, we can tell every hour by day or night. We see how Aurora extinguishes and sweeps away the stars from heaven, and how she comes forth with her companion the dawn, enlivening the air, refreshing the water, and moistening the earth; and after her appears the sun gilding the heights, as the poet sings, and making the mountains smile. We are not afraid of being left chilly by his absence, when his rays fall aslant upon us, or of being roasted when they blaze down upon us perpendicularly. We turn the same countenance to sun and frost, to dearth and plenty. In conclusion, we are people who live by our industry and our wits, without troubling ourselves with the old adage, 'The church, the sea, or the king's household.' We have all we want, for we are content with what we have.

"All these things have I told you, generous youth, that you may not be ignorant of the life to which you are come, and the manners and customs you will have to profess, which I have here sketched for you in the rough. Many other particulars, no less worthy of consideration, you will discover for yourself in process of time."

Here the eloquent old gitano closed his discourse, and the novice replied, that he congratulated himself much on having been made acquainted with such laudable statutes; that he desired to make profession of an order so based on reason and politic principles; that his only regret was that he had not sooner come to the knowledge of so pleasant a life; and that from that moment he renounced his knighthood, and the vain glory of his illustrious lineage, and placed them beneath the yoke, or beneath the laws under which they lived, forasmuch as they so magnificently recompensed the desire he had to serve them, in bestowing upon him the divine Preciosa, for whom he would surrender many crowns and wide empires, or desire them only for her sake.

Preciosa spoke next: "Whereas these señores, our lawgivers," she said, "have determined, according to their laws that I should be yours, and as such have given me up to you, I have decreed, in accordance with the law of my own will, which is the strongest of all, that I will not be so except upon the conditions heretofore concerted between us two. You must live two years in our company before you enjoy mine, so that you may neither repent through fickleness, nor I be deceived through precipitation. Conditions supersede laws; those which I have prescribed you know; if you choose to keep them, I may be yours, and you mine; if not, the mule is not dead, your clothes are whole, and not a doit of your money is spent. Your absence from home has not yet extended to the length of a day; what remains you may employ in considering what best suits you. These señores may give up my body to you, but not my soul, which is free, was born free, and shall remain free. If you remain, I shall esteem you much; if you depart, I shall do so no less; for I hold that amorous impulses run with a loose rein, until they are brought to a halt by reason or disenchantment. I would not have you be towards me like the sportsman, who when he has bagged a hare thinks no more of it, but runs after another. The eyes are sometimes deceived; at first sight tinsel looks like gold; but they soon recognise the difference between the genuine and the false metal. This beauty of mine, which you say I possess, and which you exalt above the sun, and declare more precious than gold, how do I know but that at a nearer view it will appear to you a shadow, and when tested will seem but base metal? I give you two years to weigh and ponder well what will be right to choose or reject. Before you buy a jewel, which you can only get rid of by death, you ought to take much time to examine it, and ascertain its faults or its merits. I do not assent to the barbarous licence which these kinsmen of mine have assumed, to forsake their wives or chastise them when the humour takes them; and as I do not intend to do anything which calls for punishment, I will not take for my mate one who will abandon me at his own caprice."

"You are right, Preciosa," said Andrew; "and so if you would have me quiet your fears and abate your doubts, by swearing not to depart a jot from the conditions you prescribe, choose what form of oath I shall take, or what other assurance I shall give you, and I will do exactly as you desire."

"The oaths and promises which the captive makes to obtain his liberty are seldom fulfilled when he is free," returned Preciosa; "and it is just the same, I fancy, with the lover, who to obtain his desire will promise the wings of Mercury, and the thunderbolts of Jove; and indeed a certain poet promised myself no less, and swore it by the Stygian lake. I want no oaths or promises, Señor Andrew, but to leave everything to the result of this novitiate. It will be my business to take care of myself, if at any time you should think of offending me."

"Be it so," said Andrew. "One request I have to make of these señores and comrades mine, and that is that they will not force me to steal anything for a month or so; for it strikes me that it will take a great many lessons to make me a thief."

"Never fear, my son," said the old gipsy; "for we will instruct you in such a manner that you will turn out an eagle in our craft; and when you have learned it, you will like it so much, that you will be ready to eat your hand, it will so itch after it. Yes, it is fine fun to go out empty-handed in the morning, and to return loaded at night to the rancho."

"I have seen some return with a whipping," said Andrew.

"One cannot catch trouts dry shod," the old man replied: "all things in this life have their perils: the acts of the thief are liable to the galleys, whipping, and the scragging-post; but it is not because one ship encounters a storm, or springs a leak, that others should cease to sail the seas. It would be a fine thing if there were to be no soldiers, because war consumes men and horses. Besides, a whipping by the hand of justice is for us a badge of honour, which becomes us better worn on the shoulders than on the breast. The main point is to avoid having to dance upon nothing in our young days and for our first offences; but as for having our shoulders dusted, or thrashing the water in a galley, we don't mind that a nutshell. For the present, Andrew, my son, keep snug in the nest under the shelter of our wings; in due time, we will take you out to fly, and that where you will not return without a prey; and the short and the long of it is, that by and by you will lick your fingers after every theft."

"Meanwhile," said Andrew, "as a compensation for what I might bring in by thieving during the vacation allowed me, I will divide two hundred gold crowns among all the members of the rancho."

The words were no sooner out of his mouth, than several gitanos caught him up in their arms, hoisted him upon their shoulders, and bore him along, shouting, "Long life to the great Andrew, and long life to Preciosa his beloved!" The gitanas did the same with Preciosa, not without exciting the envy of Christina, and the other gitanillas present; for envy dwells alike in the tents of barbarians, the huts of shepherds, and the palaces of princes; and to see another thrive who seems no better than oneself is a great weariness to the spirit.

This done, they ate a hearty dinner, made an equitable division of the gift money, repeated their praises of Andrew, and exalted Preciosa's beauty to the skies. When night fell, they broke the mule's neck, and buried it, so as to relieve Andrew of all fear of its leading to his discovery; they likewise buried with it the trappings, saddle, bridle, girths and all, after the manner of the Indians, whose chief ornaments are laid in the grave with them.

Andrew was in no small astonishment at all he had seen and heard, and resolved to pursue his enterprise without meddling at all with the customs of his new companions, so far as that might be possible. Especially he hoped to exempt himself, at the cost of his purse, from participating with them in any acts of injustice. On the following day, Andrew requested the gipsies to break up the camp, and remove to a distance from Madrid; for he feared that he should be recognised if he remained there. They told him they had already made up their minds to go to the mountains of Toledo, and thence to scour all the surrounding country, and lay it under contribution. Accordingly they struck their tents, and departed, offering Andrew an ass to ride; but he chose rather to travel on foot, and serve as attendant to Preciosa, who rode triumphantly another ass, rejoicing in her gallant esquire; whilst he was equally delighted at finding himself close to her whom he had made the mistress of his freedom.

O potent force of him who is called the sweet god of bitterness—a title given him by our idleness and weakness—how effectually dost thou enslave us! Here was Andrew, a knight, a youth of excellent parts, brought up at court, and maintained in affluence by his noble parents; and yet since yesterday such a change has been wrought in him that he has deceived his servants and friends; disappointed the hopes of his parents; abandoned the road to Flanders, where he was to have exercised his valour and increased the honours of his line; and he has prostrated himself at the feet of a girl, made himself the lackey of one who, though exquisitely beautiful, is after all a gitana! Wondrous prerogative of beauty, which brings down the strongest will to its feet, in spite of all its resistance!

In four days' march, the gipsies arrived at a pleasant village, within two leagues of the great Toledo, where they pitched their camp, having first given some articles of silver to the alcalde of the district, as a pledge that they would steal nothing within all his bounds, nor do any other damage that might give cause of complaint against them. This done, all the old gitanas, some young ones, and the men, spread themselves all over the country, to the distance of four or five leagues from the encampment. Andrew went with them to take his first lesson in thievery; but though they gave him many in that expedition, he did not profit by any of them. On the contrary, as was natural in a man of gentle blood, every theft committed by his masters wrung his very soul, and sometimes he paid for them out of his own pocket, being moved by the tears of the poor people who had been despoiled. The gipsies were in despair at this behavior: it was in contravention, they said, of their statutes and ordinances, which prohibited the admission of compassion into their hearts; because if they had any they must cease to be thieves,—a thing which was not to be thought of on any account. Seeing this, Andrew said he would go thieving by himself; for he was nimble enough to run from danger, and did not lack courage to encounter it; so that the prize or the penalty of his thieving would be exclusively his own.

The gipsies tried to dissuade him from this good purpose, telling him that occasions might occur in which he would have need of companions, as well to attack as to defend; and that one person alone could not make any great booty. But in spite of all they could say, Andrew was determined to be a solitary robber; intending to separate from the gang, and purchase for money something which he might say he had stolen, and thus burden his conscience as little as possible. Proceeding in this way, in less than a month, he brought more gain to the gang than four of the most accomplished thieves in it. Preciosa rejoiced not a little to see her tender lover become such a smart and handy thief; but for all that she was sorely afraid of some mischance, and would not have seen him in the hands of justice for all the treasures of Venice; such was the good feeling towards him which she could not help entertaining, in return for his many good offices and presents. After remaining about a month in the Toledan district, where they reaped a good harvest, the gipsies entered the wealthy region of Estramadura.

Meanwhile Andrew frequently held honourable and loving converse with Preciosa, who was gradually becoming enamoured of his good qualities; while, in like manner, his love for her went on increasing, if that were possible: such were the virtues, the good sense and beauty of his Preciosa. Whenever the gipsies engaged in athletic games, he carried off the prize for running and leaping: he played admirably at skittles and at ball, and pitched the bar with singular strength and dexterity. In a short while, his fame spread through all Estramadura, and there was no part of it where they did not speak of the smart young gitano Andrew, and his graces and accomplishments. As his fame extended, so did that of Preciosa's beauty; and there was no town, village, or hamlet, to which they were not invited, to enliven their patron saints' days, or other festivities. The tribe consequently became rich, prosperous, and contented, and the lovers were happy in the mere sight of each other.

It happened one night, when the camp was pitched among some evergreen oaks, a little off the highway, they heard their dogs barking about the middle watch, with unusual vehemence. Andrew and some others got up to see what was the matter, and found a man dressed in white battling with them, whilst one of them held him by the leg. "What the devil brought you here, man," said one of the gipsies, after they had released him, "at such an hour, away from the high road? Did you come to thieve? If so, you have come to the right door?"

"I do not come to thieve; and I don't know whether or not I am off the road, though I see well enough that I am gone astray," said the wounded man. "But tell me, señores, is there any venta or place of entertainment where I can get a night's lodging, and dress the wounds which these dogs have given me?"

"There is no venta or public place to which we can take you," replied Andrew; "but as for a night's lodging, and dressing your wounds, that you can have at our ranchos. Come along with us; for though we are gipsies, we are not devoid of humanity."

"God reward you!" said the man: "take me whither you please, for my leg pains me greatly." Andrew lifted him up, and carried him along with the help of some of the other compassionate gipsies; for even among the fiends there are some worse than others, and among many bad men you may find one good.

It was a clear moonlight night, so that they could see that the person they carried was a youth of handsome face and figure. He was dressed all in white linen, with a sort of frock of the same material belted round his waist. They arrived at Andrew's hut or shed, quickly kindled a fire, and fetched Preciosa's grandmother to attend to the young man's hurts. She took some of the dogs' hairs, fried them in oil, and after washing with wine the two bites she found on the patient's left leg, she put the hairs and the oil upon them, and over this dressing a little chewed green rosemary. She then bound the leg up carefully with clean bandages, made the sign of the cross over it, and said, "Now go to sleep, friend and with the help of God your hurts will not signify."

Whilst they were attending to the wounded man, Preciosa stood by, eyeing him with great curiosity, whilst he did the same by her, insomuch that Andrew took notice of the eagerness with which he gazed; but he attributed this to the extraordinary beauty of Preciosa, which naturally attracted all eyes. Finally, having done all that was needful for the youth, they left him alone on a bed of dry hay, not caring to question him then as to his road, or any other matter.

As soon as all the others were gone, Preciosa called Andrew aside, and said to him, "Do you remember, Andrew, a paper I let fall in your house, when I was dancing with my companions, and which caused you, I think, some uneasiness?"

"I remember it well," said Andrew; "it was a madrigal in your praise, and no bad one either."

"Well, you must know, Andrew, that the person who wrote those verses is no other than the wounded youth we have left in the hut. I cannot be mistaken, for he spoke to me two or three times in Madrid, and gave me too a very good romance. He was then dressed, I think, as a page,—not an ordinary one, but like a favourite of some prince. I assure you, Andrew, he is a youth of excellent understanding, and remarkably well behaved; and I cannot imagine what can have brought him hither, and in such a garb."

"What should you imagine, Preciosa, but that the same power which has made me a gitano, has made him put on the dress of a miller, and come in search of you? Ah, Preciosa! Preciosa! how plain it begins to be that you pride yourself on having more than one adorer. If this be so, finish me first, and then kill off this other, but do not sacrifice both at the same time to your perfidy."

"God's mercy, Andrew, how thin-skinned you are! On how fine a thread you make your hopes and my reputation hang, since you let the cruel sword of jealousy so easily pierce your soul. Tell me, Andrew, if there were any artifice or deceit in this case, could I not have held my tongue about this youth, and concealed all knowledge of him? Am I such a fool that I cannot help telling you what should make you doubt my integrity and good behaviour? Hold your tongue, Andrew, in God's name, and try to-morrow to extract from this cause of your alarm whither he is bound, and why he is come hither. It may be that you are mistaken in your suspicion, though I am not mistaken in what I told you of the stranger. And now for your greater satisfaction—since it is come to that pass with me that I seek to satisfy you— whatever be the reason of this youth's coming, send him away at once. All our people obey you, and none of them will care to receive him into their huts against your wish. But if this fails, I give you my word not to quit mine, or let myself be seen by him, or by anybody else from whom you would have me concealed. Look you, Andrew, I am not vexed at seeing you jealous, but it would vex me much to see you indiscreet."

"Unless you see me mad, Preciosa," said Andrew, "any other demonstration would be far short of showing you what desperate havoc jealousy can make of a man's feelings. However, I will do as you bid me, and find out what this señor page-poet wants, whither he is going, and whom he is in search of. It may be, that unawares he may let me get hold of some end of thread which shall lead to the discovery of the whole snare which I fear he is come to set for me."

"Jealousy, I imagine," said Preciosa, "never leaves the understanding clear to apprehend things as they really are. Jealousy always looks through magnifying glasses, which make mountains of molehills, and realities of mere suspicions. On your life, Andrew, and on mine, I charge you to proceed in this matter, and all that touches our concerns, with prudence and discretion; and if you do, I know that you will have to concede the palm to me, as honest, upright, and true to the very utmost."

With these words she quitted Andrew, leaving him impatient for daylight, that he might receive the confession of the wounded man, and distracted in mind by a thousand various surmises. He could not believe but that this page had come thither attracted by Preciosa's beauty; for the thief believes that all men are such as himself. On the other hand, the pledge voluntarily made to him by Preciosa appeared so highly satisfactory, that he ought to set his mind quite at ease, and commit all his happiness implicitly to the keeping of her good faith. At last day appeared: he visited the wounded man; and after inquiring how he was, and did his bites pain him, he asked what was his name, whither he was going, and how it was he travelled so late and so far off the road. The youth replied that he was better, and felt no pain so that he was able to resume his journey. His name was Alonzo Hurtado; he was going to our Lady of the Peña de Francia, on a certain business; he travelled by night for the greater speed; and having missed his way, he had come upon the encampment, and been worried by the dogs that guarded it. Andrew did not by any means consider this a straightforward statement: his suspicions returned to plague him; and, said he, "Brother, if I were a judge, and you had been brought before me upon any charge which would render necessary such questions as those I have put to you, the reply you have given would oblige me to apply the thumb-screw. It is nothing to me who you are, what is your name, or whither you are going: I only warn you, that if it suits your convenience to lie on this journey, you should lie with more appearance of truth. You say you are going to La Peña de Francia, and you leave it on the right hand more than thirty leagues behind this place. You travel by night for sake of speed, and you quit the high road, and strike into thickets and woods where there is scarcely a footpath. Get up, friend, learn to lie better, and go your ways, in God's name. But in return for this good advice I give you, will you not tell me one truth? I know you will, you are such a bad hand at lying. Tell me, are you not one I have often seen in the capital, something between a page and a gentleman? One who has the reputation of being a great poet, and who wrote a romance and a sonnet upon a gitanilla who some time ago went about Madrid, and was celebrated for her surpassing beauty? Tell me, and I promise you, on the honour of a gentleman gipsy, to keep secret whatever you may wish to be so kept. Mind you, no denial that you are the person I say will go down with me; for the face I see before me is unquestionably the same I saw in Madrid. The fame of your talents made me often stop to gaze at you as a distinguished man, and therefore your features are so strongly impressed on my memory, though your dress is very different from that in which I formerly saw you. Don't be alarmed, cheer up, and don't suppose you have fallen in with a tribe of robbers, but with an asylum, where you may be guarded and defended from all the world. A thought strikes me; and if it be as I conjecture, you have been lucky in meeting me above all men. What I conjecture is, that being in love with Preciosa—that beautiful young gipsy, to whom you addressed the verses—you have come in search of her; for which I don't think a bit the worse of you, but quite the reverse: for gipsy though I am, experience has shown me how far the potent force of love reaches, and the transformations it makes those undergo whom it brings beneath its sway and jurisdiction. If this be so, as I verily believe it is, the fair gitanilla is here."

"Yes, she is here; I saw her last night," said the stranger. This was like a death-blow to Andrew; for it seemed at once to confirm all his suspicions.

"I saw her last night," the young man repeated; "but I did not venture to tell her who I was, for it did not suit my purpose."

"So, then," said Andrew, "you are indeed the poet of whom I spoke."

"I am: I neither can nor will deny it. Possibly it may be that where I thought myself lost I have come right to port, if, as you say, there is fidelity in the forests, and hospitality in the mountains."

"That there is, beyond doubt," said Andrew; "and among us gipsies the strictest secrecy in the world. On that assurance, señor, you may unburden your breast to me: you will find in mine no duplicity whatever. The gitanilla is my relation, and entirely under my control. If you desire her for a wife, myself and all other relations will be quite willing; and if for a mistress, we will not make any squeamish objections, provided you have money, for covetousness never departs from our ranchos."

"I have money," the youth replied; "in the bands of this frock, which I wear girt round my body, there are four hundred gold crowns."

This was another mortal blow for Andrew, who assumed that the stranger could carry so large a sum about him for no other purpose than to purchase possession of the beloved object. With a faltering tongue he replied, "That is a good lump of money; you have only to discover yourself, and go to work: the girl is no fool, and will see what a good thing it will be for her to be yours."

"O friend," exclaimed the youth, "I would have you know that the power which has made me change my garb is not that of love, as you say, nor any longing for Preciosa; for Madrid has beauties who know how to steal hearts and subdue souls as well as the handsomest gitanas, and better; though I confess that the beauty of your kinswoman surpasses any I have ever seen. The cause of my being in this dress, on foot, and bitten by dogs, is not love but my ill luck."

Upon this explanation, Andrew's downcast spirit began to rise again; for it was plain that the wind was in quite a different quarter from what he had supposed. Eager to escape from this confusion, he renewed his assurances of secrecy, and the stranger proceeded thus:—

"I was in Madrid, in the house of a nobleman, whom I served not as a master but as a relation. He had an only son and heir, who treated me with great familiarity and friendship, both on account of our relationship, and because we were both of the same age and disposition. This young gentleman fell in love with a young lady of rank, whom he would most gladly have made his wife, had it not been for his dutiful submission to the will of his parents, who desired him to marry into a higher family. Nevertheless, he continued furtively to pay court to the lady of his choice, carefully concealing his proceedings from all eyes but mine. One night, which ill luck must have especially selected for the adventure I am about to relate to you, as we were passing by the lady's house, we saw ranged against it two men of good figure apparently. My kinsman wished to reconnoitre them, but no sooner had he made a step towards them than their swords were out, their bucklers ready, and they made at us, whilst we did the same on our side, and engaged them with equal arms. The fight did not last long, neither did the lives of our two opponents; for two thrusts, urged home by my kinsman's jealousy and my zeal in his defence, laid them both low—an extraordinary occurrence, and such as is rarely witnessed. Thus involuntarily victorious, we returned home, and taking all the money we could, set off secretly to the church of San Geronimo, waiting to see what would happen when the event was discovered next day, and what might be the conjectures as to the persons of the homicides.

"We learned that no trace of our presence on the scene had been discovered, and the prudent monks advised us to return home, so as not by our absence to arouse any suspicion against us. We had already resolved to follow their advice, when we were informed that the alcaldes of the court had arrested the young lady and her parents; and that among their domestics, whom they examined, one person, the young lady's attendant, had stated that my kinsman visited her mistress by night and by day. Upon this evidence they had sent in search of us; and the officers not finding us, but many indications of our flight, it became a confirmed opinion throughout the whole city, that we were the very men who had slain the two cavaliers, for such they were, and of very good quality. Finally, by the advice of the count, my relation, and of the monks, after remaining hid a fortnight in the monastery, my comrade departed in company with a monk, himself disguised as one, and took the road to Aragon, intending to pass over to Italy, and thence to Flanders, until he should see what might be the upshot of the matter. For my part, thinking it well to divide our fortunes, I set out on foot, in a different direction, and in the habit of a lay brother, along with a monk, who quitted me at Talavera. From that city I travelled alone, and missed my way, till last night I reached this wood, when I met with the mishap you know. If I asked for La Peña de Francia, it was only by way of making some answer to the questions put to me; for I know that it lies beyond Salamanca."

"True," observed Andrew, "you left it on your right, about twenty leagues from this. So you see what a straight road you were taking, if you were going thither."

"The road I did intend to take was that to Seville; for there I should find a Genoese gentleman, a great friend of the count my relation, who is in the habit of exporting large quantities of silver ingots to Genoa; and my design is, that he should send me with his carriers, as one of themselves, by which means I may safely reach Carthagena, and thence pass over to Italy; for two galleys are expected shortly to ship some silver. This is my story, good friend: was I not right in saying it is the result of pure ill luck, rather than disappointed love? Now if these señores gitanos will take me in their company to Seville, supposing they are bound thither, I will pay them handsomely; for I believe that I should travel more safely with them, and have some respite from the fear that haunts me."

"Yes, they will take you," said Andrew; "or if you cannot go with our band—for as yet I know not that we are for Andalusia—you can go with another which we shall fall in with in a couple of days; and if you give them some of the money you have about you, they will be able and willing to help you out of still worse difficulties." He then left the young man, and reported to the other gipsies what the stranger desired, and the offer he had made of good payment for their services.

They were all for having their guest remain in the camp; but Preciosa was against it; and her grandmother said, that she could not go to Seville or its neighbourhood, on account of a hoax she had once played off upon a capmaker named Truxillo, well known in Seville. She had persuaded him to put himself up to his neck in a butt of water, stark naked, with a crown of cypress on his head, there to remain till midnight, when he was to step out, and look for a great treasure, which she had made him believe was concealed in a certain part of his house. When the good cap-maker heard matins ring, he made such haste to get out of the butt, lest he should lose his chance, that it fell with him, bruising his flesh, and deluging the floor with water, in which he fell to swimming with might and main, roaring out that he was drowning. His wife and his neighbours ran to him with lights, and found him striking out lustily with his legs and arms. "Help! help!" he cried; "I am suffocating;" and he really was not far from it, such was the effect of his excessive fright. They seized and rescued him from his deadly peril. When he had recovered a little, he told them the trick the gipsy woman had played him; and yet for all that, he dug a hole, more than a fathom deep, in the place pointed out to him, in spite of all his neighbours could say; and had he not been forcibly prevented by one of them, when he was beginning to undermine the foundations of the house, he would have brought the whole of it down about his ears. The story spread all over the city; so that the little boys in the streets used to point their fingers at him, and shout in his ears the story of the gipsy's trick, and his own credulity. Such was the tale told by the old gitana, in explanation of her unwillingness to go to Seville.

The gipsies, knowing from Andrew that the youth had a sum of money about him, readily assented to his accompanying them, and promised to guard and conceal him as long as he pleased. They determined to make a bend to the left, and enter La Mancha and the kingdom of Murcia. The youth thanked them cordially, and gave them on the spot a hundred gold crowns to divide amongst them, whereupon they became as pliant as washed leather. Preciosa, however, was not pleased with the continuance among them of Don Sancho, for that was the youth's name, but the gipsies changed it to Clement. Andrew too was rather annoyed at this arrangement; for it seemed to him that Clement had given up his original intention upon very slight grounds; but the latter, as if he read his thoughts, told him that he was glad to go to Murcia, because it was near Carthagena, whence, if galleys arrived there, as he expected, he could easily pass over to Italy. Finally, in order to have him more under his own eye, to watch his acts, and scrutinise his thoughts, Andrew desired to have Clement for his own comrade, and the latter accepted this friendly offer as a signal favour. They were always together, both spent largely, their crowns came down like rain; they ran, leaped, danced, and pitched the bar better than any of their companions, and were more than commonly liked by the women of the tribe, and held in the highest respect by the men.

Leaving Estramadura they entered La Mancha, and gradually traversed the kingdom of Murcia. In all the villages and towns they passed through, they had matches at ball-playing, fencing, running, leaping, and pitching the bar; and in all these trials of strength, skill, and agility Andrew and Clement were victorious, as Andrew alone had been before. During the whole journey, which occupied six weeks, Clement neither found nor sought an opportunity to speak alone with Preciosa, until one day when she and Andrew were conversing together, they called him to them, and Preciosa said, "The first time you came to our camp I recognised you, Clement, and remembered the verses you gave me in Madrid; but I would not say a word, not knowing with what intention you had come among us. When I became acquainted with your misfortune, it grieved me to the soul, though at the same time it was a relief to me; for I had been much disturbed, thinking that as there was a Don Juan in the world who had become a gipsy, a Don Sancho might undergo transformation in like manner. I speak this to you, because Andrew tells me he has made known to you who he is, and with what intention he turned gipsy." (And so it was, for Andrew had acquainted Clement with his whole story, that he might be able to converse with him on the subject nearest to his thoughts.) "Do not think that my knowing you was of little advantage to you, since for my sake, and in consequence of what I said of you, our people the more readily admitted you amongst them, where I trust in God you may find things turn out according to your best wishes. You will repay me, I hope, for this good will on my part, by not making Andrew ashamed of having set his mind so low, or representing to him how ill he does in persevering in his present way of life; for though I imagine that his will is enthralled to mine, still it would grieve me to see him show signs, however slight, of repenting what he has done."

"Do not suppose, peerless Preciosa," replied Clement, "that Don Juan acted lightly in revealing himself to me. I found him out beforehand: his eyes first disclosed to me the nature of his feelings; I first told him who I was, and detected that enthralment of his will which you speak of; and he, reposing a just confidence in me, made his secret mine. He can witness whether I applauded his determination and his choice; for I am not so dull of understanding, Preciosa, as not to know how omnipotent is beauty; and yours, which surpasses all bounds of loveliness, is a sufficient excuse for all errors, if error that can be called for which there is so irresistible a cause. I am grateful to you, señora, for what you have said in my favour; and I hope to repay you by hearty good wishes that you may find a happy issue out of your perplexities, and that you may enjoy the love of your Andrew, and Andrew that of his Preciosa, with the consent of his parents; so that from so beautiful a couple there may come into the world the finest progeny which nature can form in her happiest mood. This is what I shall always desire, Preciosa; and this is what I shall always say to your Andrew, and not anything which could tend to turn him from his well-placed affections."

With such emotion did Clement utter these words, that Andrew was in doubt whether they were spoken in courtesy only, or from love; for the infernal plague of jealousy is so susceptible that it will take offence at the motes in the sunbeams; and the lover finds matter for self-torment in everything that concerns the beloved object. Nevertheless, he did not give way to confirmed jealousy; for he relied more on the good faith of his Preciosa than on his own fortune, which, in common with all lovers, he regarded as luckless, so long as he had not obtained the object of his desires. In fine, Andrew and Clement continued to be comrades and friends, their mutual good understanding being secured by Clement's upright intentions, and by the modesty and prudence of Preciosa, who never gave Andrew an excuse for jealousy. Clement was somewhat of a poet, Andrew played the guitar a little, and both were fond of music. One night, when the camp was pitched in a valley four leagues from Murcia, Andrew seated himself at the foot of a cork-tree, and Clement near him under an evergreen oak. Each of them had a guitar; and invited by the stillness of the night, they sang alternately, Andrew beginning the descant, and Clement responding.

ANDREW.
Ten thousand golden lamps are lit on high,
Making this chilly night
Rival the noon-day's light;
Look, Clement, on yon star-bespangled sky,
And in that image see,
If so divine thy fancy be,
That lovely radiant face,
Where centres all of beauty and of grace.
CLEMENT
Where centres all of beauty and of grace,
And where in concord sweet
Goodness and beauty meet,
And purity hath fixed its dwelling-place.
Creature so heavenly fair,
May any mortal genius dare,
Or less than tongue divine,
To praise in lofty, rare, and sounding line?
ANDREW
To praise in lofty, rare, and sounding line
Thy name, gitana bright!
Earth's wonder and delight,
Worthy above the empyrean vault to shine;
Fain would I snatch from Fame
The trump and voice, whose loud acclaim
Should startle every ear,
And lift Preciosa's name to the eighth sphere.
CLEMENT
To lift Preciosa's fame to the eighth sphere
Were meet and fit, that so
The heavens new joy might know
Through all their shining courts that name to hear,
Which on this earth doth sound
Like music spreading gladness round,
Breathing with charm intense
Peace to the soul and rapture to the sense.

It seemed as though the freeman and the captive were in no haste to bring their tuneful contest to conclusion, had not the voice of Preciosa, who had overheard them, sounded from behind in response to theirs. They stopped instantly, and remained listening to her in breathless attention. Whether her words were delivered impromptu, or had been composed some time before, I know not; however that may be, she sang the following lines with infinite grace, as though they were made for the occasion.

While in this amorous emprise
An equal conflict I maintain,
'Tis higher glory to remain
Pure maid, than boast the brightest eyes.
The humblest plant on which we tread,
If sound and straight it grows apace,
By aid of nature or of grace

May rear aloft towards heaven its head.
In this my lowly poor estate,
By maiden honour dignified,
No good wish rests unsatisfied;
Their wealth I envy not the great.
I find not any grief or pain
In lack of love or of esteem;
For I myself can shape, I deem,
My fortunes happy in the main.
Let me but do what in me lies
The path of rectitude to tread;
And then be welcomed on this head
Whatever fate may please the skies.
I fain would know if beauty hath
Such high prerogative, to raise
My mind above the common ways,
And set me on a loftier path.
If equal in their souls they be,
The humblest hind on earth may vie
In honest worth and virtue high
With one of loftiest degree.
What inwardly I feel of mine
Doth raise me all that's base above;
For majesty, be sure, and love
Do not on common soil recline.

Preciosa having ended her song, Andrew and Clement rose to meet her. An animated conversation ensued between the three; and Preciosa displayed so much intelligence, modesty, and acuteness, as fully excused, in Clement's opinion, the extraordinary determination of Andrew, which he had before attributed more to his youth than his judgment. The next morning the camp was broken up, and they proceeded to a place in the jurisdiction of Murcia, three leagues from the city, where a mischance befel Andrew, which went near to cost him his life.

After they had given security in that place, according to custom, by the deposit of some silver vessels and ornaments, Preciosa and her grandmother, Christina and two other gitanillas, Clement, and Andrew, took up their quarters in an inn, kept by a rich widow, who had a daughter aged about seventeen or eighteen, rather more forward than handsome. Her name was Juana Carducha. This girl having seen the gipsies dance, the devil possessed her to fall in love with Andrew to that degree that she proposed to tell him of it, and take him for a husband, if he would have her, in spite of all her relations. Watching for an opportunity to speak to him, she found it in a cattle-yard, which Andrew had entered in search of two young asses, when she said to him, hurriedly, "Andrew" (she already knew his name), "I am single and wealthy. My mother has no other child: this inn is her own; and besides it she has large vineyards, and several other houses. You have taken my fancy; and if you will have me for a wife, only say the word. Answer me quickly, and if you are a man of sense, only wait, and you shall see what a life we shall lead."

Astonished as he was at Carducha's boldness, Andrew nevertheless answered her with the promptitude she desired, "Señora doncella, I am under promise to marry, and we gitanos intermarry only with gitanas. Many thanks for the favour you would confer on me, of which I am not worthy."

Carducha was within two inches of dropping dead at this unwelcome reply, to which she would have rejoined, but that she saw some of the gitanos come into the yard. She rushed from the spot, athirst for vengeance. Andrew, like a wise man, determined to get out of her way, for he read in her eyes that she would willingly give herself to him with matrimonial bonds, and he had no wish to find himself engaged foot to foot and alone in such an encounter; accordingly, he requested his comrades to quit the place that night. Complying with his wishes as they always did, they set to work at once, took up their securities again that evening, and decamped. Carducha, seeing that Andrew was going away and half her soul with him, and that she should not have time to obtain the fulfilment of her desires, resolved to make him stop by force, since he would not do so of good will. With all the cunning and secrecy suggested to her by her wicked intentions, she put among Andrew's baggage, which she knew to be his, a valuable coral necklace, two silver medals, and other trinkets belonging to her family. No sooner had the gipsies left the inn than she made a great outcry, declaring that the gipsies had robbed her, till she brought about her the officers of justice and all the people of the place. The gipsies halted, and all swore that they had no stolen property with them, offering at the same time to let all their baggage be searched. This made the old gipsy woman very uneasy, lest the proposed scrutiny should lead to the discovery of Preciosa's trinkets and Andrew's clothes, which she preserved with great care. But the good wench Carducha quickly put an end to her fears on that head, for before they had turned over two packages, she said to the men, "Ask which of these bundles belongs to that gipsy who is such a great dancer. I saw him enter my room twice, and probably he is the thief."

Andrew knew it was himself she meant, and answered with a laugh, "Señora doncella, this is my bundle, and that is my ass. If you find in or upon either of them what you miss, I will pay you the value sevenfold, beside submitting to the punishment which the law awards for theft."

The officers of justice immediately unloaded the ass, and in the turn of a hand discovered the stolen property, whereat Andrew was so shocked and confounded that he stood like a stone statue. "I was not out in my suspicions," said Carducha; "see with what a good looking face the rogue covers his villany." The alcalde, who was present, began to abuse Andrew and the rest of the gipsies, calling them common thieves and highwaymen. Andrew said not a word, but stood pondering in the utmost perplexity, for he had no surmise of Carducha's treachery. At last, an insolent soldier, nephew to the alcalde, stepped up to him, saying "Look at the dirty gipsy thief! I will lay a wager he will give himself airs as if he were an honest man, and deny the robbery, though the goods have been found in his hands. Good luck to whoever sends the whole pack of you to the galleys. A fitter place it will be for this scoundrel, where he may serve his Majesty, instead of going about dancing from place to place, and thieving from venta to mountain. On the faith of a soldier, I have a mind to lay him at my feet with a blow."

So saying, without more ado he raised his hand, and gave Andrew such a buffet as roused him from his stupor, and made him recollect that he was not Andrew Caballero but Don Juan and a gentleman; therefore, flinging himself upon the soldier with sudden fury, he snatched his sword from its sheath, buried it in his body, and laid him dead at his feet. The people shouted and yelled; the dead man's uncle, the alcalde, was frantic with rage; Preciosa fainted, and Andrew, regardless of his own defence, thought only of succouring her. As ill luck would have it, Clement was not on the spot, having gone forward with some baggage, and Andrew was set upon, by so many, that they overpowered him, and loaded him with heavy chains. The alcalde would gladly have hanged him on the spot, but was obliged to send him to Murcia, as he belonged to the jurisdiction of that city. It was not, however, till the next day that he was removed thither, and meanwhile he was loaded with abuse and maltreatment by the alcalde and all the people of the place. The alcalde, moreover, arrested all the rest of the gipsies he could lay hands on, but most of them had made their escape, among others Clement, who was afraid of being seized and discovered. On the following morning the alcalde, with his officers and a great many other armed men, entered Murcia with a caravan of gipsy captives, among whom were Preciosa and poor Andrew, who was chained on the back of a mule, and was handcuffed and had a fork fixed under his chin. All Murcia flocked to see the prisoners, for the news of the soldier's death had been received there; but so great was Preciosa's beauty that no one looked upon her that day without blessing her. The news of her loveliness reached the corregidor's lady, who being curious to see her, prevailed on her husband to give orders that she should not enter the prison to which all the rest of the gipsies were committed. Andrew was thrust into a dark narrow dungeon, where, deprived of the light of the sun and of that which Preciosa's presence diffused, he felt as though he should leave it only for his grave. Preciosa and her grand-mother were taken to the corregidor's lady, who at once exclaiming, "Well might they praise her beauty," embraced her tenderly, and never was tired of looking at her. She asked the old woman what was the girl's age. "Fifteen, within a month or two, more or less," was the reply. "That would be the age of my poor Constantia," observed the lady. "Ah, amigas! how the sight of this young girl has brought my bereavement back afresh to my mind."

Upon this, Preciosa took hold of the corregidora's bands, kissed them repeatedly, bathed them with tears, and said, "Señora mia, the gitano who is in custody is not in fault, for he had provocation. They called him a thief, and he is none; they gave him a blow on the face, though his is such a face that you can read in it the goodness of his soul. I entreat you, señora, to see that justice is done him, and that the señor corregidor is not too hasty in executing upon him the penalty of the law. If my beauty has given you any pleasure, preserve it for me by preserving the life of the prisoner, for with it mine ends too. He is to be my husband, but just and proper impediments have hitherto prevented our union. If money would avail to obtain his pardon, all the goods of our tribe should be sold by auction, and we would give even more than was asked of us. My lady, if you know what love is, and have felt and still feel it for your dear husband, have pity on me who love mine tenderly and honestly."

All the while Preciosa was thus speaking she kept fast hold of the corregidora's hands, and kept her tearful eyes fixed on her face, whilst the lady gazed on her with no less wistfulness, and wept as she did. Just then the corregidor entered, and seeing his wife and Preciosa thus mingling their tears, he was surprised as much by the scene as by the gitanilla's beauty. On his asking the cause of her affliction, Preciosa let go the lady's hands, and threw herself at the corregidor's feet, crying, "Mercy, mercy, señor! If my husband dies, I die too. He is not guilty; if he is, let me bear the punishment; or if that cannot be, at least let the trial be delayed until means be sought which may save him; for as he did not sin through malice, it may be that heaven in its grace will send him safety." The corregidor was still more surprised to hear such language from the gitanilla's lips, and but that he would not betray signs of weakness, he could have wept with her.

While all this was passing, the old gitana was busily turning over a great many things in her mind, and after all this cogitation, she said, "Wait a little, your honour, and I will turn these lamentations into joy, though it should cost me my life;" and she stepped briskly out of the room. Until she returned, Preciosa never desisted from her tears and entreaties that they would entertain the cause of her betrothed, being inwardly resolved that she would send to his father that he might come and interfere in his behalf.

The old gipsy woman returned with a little box under her arm, and requested that the corregidor and his lady would retire with her into another room, for she had important things to communicate to them in secret. The corregidor imagined she meant to give him information respecting some thefts committed by the gipsies, in order to bespeak his favour for the prisoner, and he instantly withdrew with her and his lady to his closet, where the gipsy, throwing herself on her knees before them both, began thus:

"If the good news I have to give to your honours be not worth forgiveness for a great crime I have committed, I am here to receive the punishment I deserve. But before I make my confession, I beg your honours will tell me if you know these trinkets;" and she put the box which contained those belonging to Preciosa into the corregidor's hands. He opened it, and saw those childish gewgaws, but had no idea what they could mean. The corregidora looked at them, too, with as little consciousness as her husband, and merely observed that they were the ornaments of some little child. "That is true," replied the gipsy, "and to what child they belonged is written in this folded paper." The corregidor hastily opened the paper, and read as follows:—

"The child's name was Doña Constanza de Acevedo y de Menesis; her mother's, Doña Guiomar de Menesis; and her father's, D. Fernando de Acevedo, knight of the order of Calatrava. She disappeared on the day of the Lord's Ascension, at eight in the morning, in the year one thousand five hundred and ninety-five. The child had upon her the trinkets which are contained in this box."

Instantly, on hearing the contents of the paper, the corregidora recognised the trinkets, put them to her lips, kissed them again and again, and swooned away; and the corregidor was too much occupied in assisting her to ask the gitana for his daughter. "Good woman, angel rather than gitana," cried the lady when she came to herself, "where is the owner of these baubles?"

"Where, señora?" was the reply. "She is in your own house. That young gipsy who drew tears from your eyes is their owner, and is indubitably your own daughter, whom I stole from your house in Madrid on the day and hour named in this paper."

On hearing this, the agitated lady threw off her clogs, and rushed with open arms into the sala, where she found Preciosa surrounded by her doncellas and servants, and still weeping and wailing. Without a word she caught her hurriedly in her arms, and examined if she had under her left breast a mark in the shape of a little white mole with which she was born, and she found it there enlarged by time. Then, with the same haste, she took off the girl's shoe, uncovered a snowy foot, smooth as polished marble, and found what she sought; for the two smaller toes of the right foot were joined together by a thin membrane, which the tender parents could not bring themselves to let the surgeon cut when she was an infant. The mole on the bosom, the foot, the trinkets, the day assigned for the kidnapping, the confession of the gitana, and the joy and emotion which her parents felt when they first beheld her, confirmed with the voice of truth in the corregidora's soul that Preciosa was her own daughter: clasping her therefore in her arms, she returned with her to the room where she had left the corregidor and the old gipsy. Preciosa was bewildered, not knowing why she had made all those investigations, and was still more surprised when the lady raised her in her arms, and gave her not one kiss, but a hundred.

Doña Guiomar at last appeared with her precious burthen in her husband's presence, and transferring the maiden from her own arms to his, "Receive, Señor, your daughter Constanza," she said; "for your daughter she is without any doubt, since I have seen the marks on the foot and the bosom; and stronger even than these proofs is the voice of my own heart ever since I set eyes on her."

"I doubt it not," replied the corregidor, folding Preciosa in his arms, "for the same sensations have passed through my heart as through yours; and how could so many strange particulars combine together unless it were by a miracle?"

The people of the house were now lost in wonder, going about and asking each other, "What is all this?" but erring widely in their conjectures; for who would have imagined that the gitanilla was the daughter of their lord? The corregidor told his wife and daughter and the old gipsy that he desired the matter should be kept secret until he should himself think fit to divulge it. As for the old gipsy, he assured her that he forgave the injury she had done him in stealing his treasure, since she had more than made atonement by restoring it. The only thing that grieved him was that, knowing Preciosa's quality, she should have betrothed her to a gipsy, and worse than that, to a thief and murderer. "Alas, señor mio," said Preciosa, "he is neither a gipsy nor a thief, although he has killed a man, but then it was one who had wounded his honour, and he could not do less than show who he was, and kill him."

"What! he is not a gipsy, my child?" said Doña Guiomar.

"Certainly not," said the old gitana; and she related the story of Andrew Caballero, that he was the son of Don Francisco de Cárcamo, knight of Santiago; that his name was Don Juan de Cárcamo, of the same order; and that she had kept his clothes after he had changed them for those of a gipsy. She likewise stated the agreement which Preciosa and Don Juan had made not to marry until after two years of mutual trial; and she put in their true light the honourable conduct of both, and the suitable condition of Don Juan.

The parents were as much surprised at this as at the recovery of their daughter. The corregidor sent the gitana for Don Juan's clothes, and she came back with them accompanied by a gipsy who carried them. Previously to her return, Preciosa's parents put a thousand questions to her, and she replied with so much discretion and grace, that even though they had not recognised her for their child, they must have loved her. To their inquiry whether she had any affection for Don Juan, she replied, not more than that to which she was bound in gratitude towards one who had humbled himself to become a gipsy for her sake; but even this should not extend farther than her parents desired. "Say no more, daughter Preciosa," said her father; "(for I wish you to retain this name of Preciosa in memory of your loss and your recovery); as your father, I take it upon myself to establish you in a position not derogatory to your birth."

Preciosa sighed, and her mother shrewdly suspecting that the sigh was prompted by love for Don Juan, said to the corregidor, "Since Don Juan is a person of such rank, and is so much attached to our daughter, I think, señor, it would not be amiss to bestow her upon him."

"Hardly have we found her to-day," he replied, "and already would you have us lose her? Let us enjoy her company for a while at least, for when she marries she will be ours no longer but her husband's."

"You are right, señor," said the lady. "but give orders to bring out Don Juan, for he is probably lying in some filthy dungeon."

"No doubt he is," said Preciosa, "for as a thief and homicide, and above all as a gipsy, they will have given him no better lodging."

"I will go see him," said the corregidor, "as if for the purpose of taking his confession. Meanwhile, señora, I again charge you not to let any one know this history until I choose to divulge it, for so it behoves my office." Then embracing Preciosa he went to the prison where Don Juan was confined, and entered his cell, not allowing any one to accompany him.

He found the prisoner with both legs in fetters, handcuffed, and with the iron fork not yet removed from beneath his chin. The cell was dark, only a scanty gleam of light passing into it from a loop-hole near the top of the wall. "How goes it, sorry knave?" said the corregidor, as he entered. "I would I had all the gipsies in Spain leashed here together to finish them all at once, as Nero would have beheaded all Rome at a single blow. Know, thou thief, who art so sensitive on the point of honour, that I am the corregidor of this city, and come to know from thee if thy betrothed is a gitanilla who is here with the rest of you?"

Hearing this Andrew imagined that the corregidor had surely fallen in love with Preciosa; for jealousy is a subtle thing, and enters other bodies without breaking or dividing them. He replied, however, "If she has said that I am her betrothed, it is very true; and, if she has said I am not her betrothed, she has also spoken the truth; for it is not possible that Preciosa should utter a falsehood."

"Is she so truthful then?" said the corregidor. "It is no slight thing to be so and be a gitana. Well, my lad, she has said that she is your betrothed, but that she has not yet given you her hand; she knows that you must die for your crime, and she has entreated me to marry her to you before you die, that she may have the honour of being the widow of so great a thief as yourself."

"Then, let your worship do as she has requested," said Andrew; "for so I be married to her, I will go content to the other world, leaving this one with the name of being hers."

"You must love her very much?"

"So much," replied the prisoner, "that whatever I could say of it would be nothing to the truth. In a word, señor corregidor, let my business be despatched. I killed the man who insulted me; I adore this young gitana; I shall die content if I die in her grace, and God's I know will not be wanting to us, for we have both observed honourably and strictly the promise we made each other."

"This night then I will send for you," said the corregidor, "and you shall marry Preciosa in my house, and to-morrow morning you shall be on the gallows. In this way I shall have complied with the demands of justice and with the desire of you both." Andrew thanked him; the corregidor returned home, and told his wife what had passed between them.

During his absence Preciosa had related to her mother the whole course of her life; and how she had always believed she was a gipsy and the old woman's grand-daughter; but that at the same time she had always esteemed herself much more than might have been expected of a gitana. Her mother bade her say truly, was she very fond of Don Juan? With great bashfulness and with downcast eyes she replied that, having considered herself a gipsy, and that she should better her condition by marrying a knight of Santiago, and one of such station as Don Juan de Cárcamo, and having, moreover, learned by experience his good disposition and honourable conduct, she had sometimes looked upon him with the eyes of affection; but that as she had said once for all, she had no other will than that which her parents might approve.

Night arrived; and about ten they took Andrew out of prison without handcuffs and fetters, but not without a great chain with which his body was bound from head to foot. In this way he arrived, unseen by any but those who had charge of him, in the corregidor's house, was silently and cautiously admitted into a room, and there left alone. A confessor presently entered and bade him confess, as he was to die next day. "With great pleasure I will confess," replied Andrew; "but why do they not marry me first? And if I am to be married, truly it is a sad bridal chamber that awaits me."

Doña Guiomar, who heard all this, told her husband that the terrors he was inflicting on Don Juan were excessive, and begged he would moderate them, lest they should cost him his life. The corregidor assented, and called out to the confessor that he should first marry the gipsy to Preciosa, after which the prisoner would confess, and commend himself with all his heart to God, who often rains down his mercies at the moment when hope is most parched and withering. Andrew was then removed to a room where there was no one but Doña Guiomar, the corregidor, Preciosa, and two servants of the family. But when Preciosa saw Don Juan in chains, his face all bloodless, and his eyes dimmed with recent weeping, her heart sank within her, and she clutched her mother's arm for support. "Cheer up, my child," said the corregidora, kissing her, "for all you now see will turn to your pleasure and advantage." Knowing nothing of what was intended, Preciosa could not console herself; the old gipsy was sorely disturbed, and the bystanders awaited the issue in anxious suspense.

"Señor Vicar," said the corregidor, "this gitano and gitana are the persons whom your reverence is to marry."

"That I cannot do," replied the priest, "unless the ceremony be preceded by the formalities required in such cases. Where have the banns been published? Where is the license of my superior, authorising the espousals?"

"The inadvertance has been mine," said the corregidor; "but I will undertake to get the license from the bishop's deputy."

"Until it comes then, your worships will excuse me," said the priest, and without another word, to avoid scandal, he quitted the house, leaving them all in confusion.

"The padre has done quite right," said the corregidor, "and it may be that it was by heaven's providence, to the end that Andrew's execution might be postponed; for married to Preciosa he shall assuredly be, but first the banns must be published, and thus time will be gained, and time often works a happy issue out of the worst difficulties. Now I want to know from Andrew, should matters take such a turn, that without any more of those shocks and perturbations, he should become the husband of Preciosa, would he consider himself a happy man, whether as Andrew Caballero, or as Don Juan de Cárcamo?"

As soon as Don Juan heard himself called by his true name, he said, "Since Preciosa has not chosen to confine herself to silence, and has discovered to you who I am, I say to you, that though my good fortune should make me monarch of the world, she would still be the sole object of my desires; nor would I aspire to have any blessing besides, save that of heaven."

"Now for this good spirit you have shown, Señor Don Juan de Cárcamo, I will in fitting time make Preciosa your lawful wife, and at present I bestow her upon you in that expectation, as the richest jewel of my house, my life, and my soul; for in her I bestow upon you Doña Constanza de Acevedo Menesis, my only daughter, who, if she equals you in love, is nowise inferior to you in birth."

Andrew was speechless with astonishment, while in a few words Doña Guiomar related the loss of her daughter, her recovery, and the indisputable proofs which the old gipsy woman had given of the kidnapping. More amazed than ever, but filled with immeasurable joy, Don Juan embraced his father and mother-in-law, called them his parents and señores, and kissed Preciosa's hands, whose tears called forth his own. The secret was no longer kept; the news was spread abroad by the servants who had been present, and reached the ears of the alcalde, the dead man's uncle, who saw himself debarred of all hope of vengeance, since the rigour of justice could not be inflicted on the corregidor's son-in-law. Don Juan put on the travelling dress which the old woman had preserved; his prison and his iron chain were exchanged for liberty and chains of gold; and the sadness of the incarcerated gipsies was turned into joy, for they were all bailed out on the following day. The uncle of the dead man received a promise of two thousand ducats on condition of his abandoning the suit and forgiving Don Juan. The latter, not forgetting his comrade Clement, sent at once in quest of him, but he was not to be found, nor could anything be learned of him until four days after, when authentic intelligence was obtained that he had embarked in one of two Genoese galleys that lay in the port of Cartagena, and had already sailed. The corregidor informed Don Juan, that he had ascertained that his father, Don Francisco de Cárcanio, had been appointed corregidor of that city, and that it would be well to wait until the nuptials could be celebrated with his consent and approbation. Don Juan was desirous to conform to the corregidor's wishes, but said that before all things he must be made one with Preciosa. The archbishop granted his license, requiring that the banns should be published only once.

The city made a festival on the wedding-day, the corregidor being much liked, and there were illuminations, bullfights, and tournaments. The old woman remained in the house of her pretended grandchild, not choosing to part from Preciosa. The news reached Madrid, and Don Francisco de Cárcamo learned that the gipsy bridegroom was his son, and that Preciosa was the gitanilla he had seen in his house. Her beauty was an excuse in his eyes for the levity of his son, whom he had supposed to be lost, having ascertained that he had not gone to Flanders. Besides, he was the more reconciled when he found what a good match Don Juan had made with the daughter of so great and wealthy a cavalier as was Don Fernando de Acevedo. He hastened his departure in order to see his children, and within twenty days he was in Murcia. His arrival renewed the general joy; the lives of the pair were related, and the poets of that city, which numbers some very good ones, took it upon them to celebrate the extraordinary event along with the incomparable beauty of the gitanilla; and the licentiate Pozo wrote in such wise, that Preciosa's fame will endure in his verses whilst the world lasts. I forgot to mention that the enamoured damsel of the inn owned that the charge of theft she had preferred against Andrew was not true, and confessed her love and her crime, for which she was not visited with any punishment, because the joyous occasion extinguished revenge and resuscitated clemency.

[66] Piedra preciosa, precious stone.

[67] It is hard to say what "exquisite reason" Cervantes can have had for likening a girl's eyes to emeralds above all other gems. He uses the phrase elsewhere, apparently without any ironical meaning.

[68] A dish, in which a fowl is served up disjointed.

[69] The wife of the teniente, or lieutenant.

[70] It was formerly the custom in Spain that a civil officer on giving up his post, should remain for a certain time in the place where he had served, to answer any charges of maladministration that might be brought against him.

[71] After the discovery of America the Spanish dollar was marked with the pillars of Hercules and the legend "PLUS ULTRA."

[72] Juanico, diminutive of Juan; Johnny.

[73] One of the ways in which the torture was formerly administered in Spain, was by making the patient swallow pieces of gauze in water.

[74] Gipsy encampment.

[75] See note, p. 200.

THE GENEROUS LOVER.

"O lamentable ruins of the ill-fated Nicosia,[76] still moist with the blood of your valorous and unfortunate defenders! Were you capable of feeling, we might jointly bewail our disasters in this solitude, and perhaps find some relief for our sorrows in mutually declaring them. A hope may remain that your dismantled towers may rise again, though not for so just a defence as that in which they fell; but I, unfortunate! what good can I hope for in my wretched distress, even should I return to my former state? Such is my hard fate, that in freedom I was without happiness, and in captivity I have no hope of it."

These words were uttered by a captive Christian as he gazed from an eminence on the ruined walls of Nicosia; and thus he talked with them, comparing his miseries with theirs, as if they could understand him,—a common habit with the afflicted, who, carried away by their imaginations, say and do things inconsistent with all sense and reason. Meanwhile there issued from a pavilion or tent, of which there were four pitched in the plain, a young Turk, of good-humoured and graceful appearance, who approached the Christian, saying, "I will lay a wager, friend Ricardo, that the gloomy thoughts you are continually ruminating have led you to this place."

"It is true," replied Ricardo, for that was the captive's name; "but what avails it, since, go where I will, I find no relief from them; on the contrary, the sight of yonder ruins have given them increased force."

"You mean the ruins of Nicosia?"

"Of course I do, since there are no others visible here."

"Such a sight as that might well move you to tears," said the Turk; "for any one who saw this famous and plenteous isle of Cyprus about two years ago, when its inhabitants enjoyed all the felicity that is granted to mortals, and who now sees them exiled from it, or captive and wretched, how would it be possible not to mourn over its calamity? But let us talk no more of these thing's, for which there is no remedy, and speak of your own, for which I would fain find one. Now I entreat you, by what you owe me for the good-will I have shown you, and for the fact that we are of the same country, and were brought up together in boyhood, that you tell me what is the cause of your inordinate sadness. For even, admitting that captivity alone is enough to sadden the most cheerful heart in the world, yet I imagine that your sorrows have a deeper source; for generous spirits like yours do not yield to ordinary misfortunes so much as to betray extraordinary grief on account of them. Besides, I know that you are not so poor as to be unable to pay the sum demanded for your ransom; nor are you shut up in the castles of the Black Sea as a captive of consideration, who late or never obtains the liberty he sighs for. Since, then, you are not deprived of the hope of freedom, and yet manifest such deep despondency, I cannot help thinking that it proceeds from some other cause than the loss of your liberty. I entreat you to tell me what is that cause, and I offer you my help to the utmost of my means and power. Who knows but that it was in order that I might serve you that fortune induced me to wear this dress which I abhor.

"You know, Ricardo, that my master is the cadi (which is the same thing as the bishop) of this city. You know, too, how great is his power, and my influence with him. Moreover, you are not ignorant of the ardent desire I feel not to die in this creed, which I nominally profess; but if it can be done in no other way, I propose to confess and publicly cry aloud my faith in Jesus Christ, from which I lapsed by reason of my youth and want of understanding. Such a confession I know will cost me my life, which I will give freely, that I may not lose my soul. From all this I would have you infer, and be assured, that my friendship may be of some use to you. But that I may know what remedies or palliations your case may admit of, it is necessary that you explain it to me, as the sick man does to the doctor, taking my word for it, that I will maintain the strictest secrecy concerning it."

Ricardo, who had listened in silence all this while, finding himself at last obliged to reply, did so as follows: "If, as you have guessed rightly, respecting my misfortune, friend Mahmoud," (that was the Turk's name,) "so also you could hit upon the remedy for it, I should think my liberty well lost, and would not exchange my mischance for the greatest imaginable good fortune. But I know that it is such, that though all the world should know the cause whence it proceeds, no one ever would make bold to find for it a remedy, or even an alleviation. That you may be satisfied of this truth, I will relate my story to you, as briefly as I can; but before I enter upon the confused labyrinth of my woes, tell me what is the reason why my master, Hassan Pasha, has caused these pavilions to be pitched here in the plain, before he enters Nicosia, to which he has been appointed pasha, as the Turks call their viceroys."

"I will satisfy you briefly," replied Mahmoud. "You must know, then, that it is the custom among the Turks, for those who are sent as viceroys of any province, not to enter the city in which their predecessor dwells until he quits it, and leaves the new comer to take up his residence freely; and when the new pasha has done so, the old one remains encamped beyond the walls, waiting the result of the inquiry into his administration, which is made without his being able to interfere, and avail himself of bribery or affection, unless he has done so beforehand. The result of the inquiry, enrolled on a sealed parchment, is then given to the departing pasha, and this he must present to the Sublime Porte, that is to say, the court in front of the grand council of the Turk. It is then read by the vizier pasha and the four lesser pashas, (or, as we should say, by the president and members of the royal council,) who punish or reward the bearer according to its contents; though, if these are not favourable, he buys off his punishment with money. If there is no accusation against him, and he is not rewarded, as commonly happens, he obtains by means of presents the post he most desires; for, at that court, offices are not bestowed by merit, but for money; everything is bought and sold. The bestowers of office fleece the receivers; but he who purchases a post, makes enough by it to purchase another which promises more profit.

"Everything proceeds as I tell you; in this empire all is violence: a fact which betokens that it will not be durable; but, as I full surely believe, it is our sins that uphold it, the sins, I mean, of those who imprudently and forwardly offend God, as I am doing: may he forgive me in his mercy!

"It is, then, for the reason I have stated that your master, Hassan Pasha, has been encamped here four days, and if the Pasha of Nicosia has not come out as he should have done, it is because he has been very ill. But he is now better, and he will come out to-day or to-morrow without fail, and lodge in some tents behind this hill, which you have not seen, after which your master will immediately enter the city. And now I have replied to the question you put to me."

"Listen, then, to my story," said Ricardo, "but I know not if I shall be able to fulfil my promise to be brief, since my misfortune is so vast that it cannot be comprised within any reasonable compass of words. However, I will do what I may and as time allows. Let me ask you, in the first place, if you knew in our town of Trapani, a young lady whom fame pronounced to be the most beautiful woman in Sicily? A young lady, I say, of whom the most ingenious tongues, and the choicest wits declared that her beauty was the most perfect ever known in past ages or the present, or that may be looked for in the future. One, of whom the poets sang that she had hair of gold, that her eyes were two shining suns, her cheeks roses, her teeth pearls, her lips rubies, her neck alabaster; and that every part of her made with the whole, and the whole with every part, a marvellous harmony and consonance, nature diffusing all over her such an exquisite sweetness of tone and colour, that envy itself could not find a fault in her. How is it possible, Mahmoud, that you have not already named her? Surely you have either not listened to me, or when you were in Trapani you wanted common sensibility."

"In truth, Ricardo," replied Mahmoud, "if she whom you have depicted in such glowing colours is not Leonisa, the daughter of Rodolfo Florencio, I know not who she is, for that lady alone was famed as you have described."

"Leonisa it is, Mahmoud," exclaimed Ricardo; "Leonisa is the sole cause of all my bliss and all my sorrow; it is for her, and not for the loss of liberty, that my eyes pour forth incessant tears, my sighs kindle the air, and my wailings weary heaven and the ears of men. It is she who makes me appear in your eyes a madman, or at least a being devoid of energy and spirit. This Leonisa, so cruel to me, was not so to another, and this is the cause of my present miserable plight. For you must know that, from my childhood, or at least from the time I was capable of understanding, I not only loved, but adored and worshipped her, as though I knew no other deity on earth. Her parents and relations were aware of my affection for her, and never showed signs of disapproving it, for they knew that my designs were honourable and virtuous; and I know that they often said as much to Leonisa, in order to dispose her to receive me as her betrothed; but she had set her heart on Cornelio, the son of Ascanio Rotulo, whom you well know—a spruce young gallant, point de vice in his attire, with white hands, curly locks, mellifluous voice, amorous discourse—made up, in short, of amber and sugar-paste, garnished with plumes and brocade. She never cared to bestow a look on my less dainty face, nor to be touched in the least by my assiduous courtship; but repaid all my affection with disdain and abhorrence; whilst my love for her grew to such an extreme, that I should have deemed my fate most blest if she had killed me by her scorn, provided she did not bestow open, though maidenly, favours on Cornelio. Imagine the anguish of my soul, thus lacerated by her disdain, and tortured by the most cruel jealousy. Leonisa's father and mother winked at her preference for Cornelio, believing, as they well might, that the youth, fascinated by her incomparable beauty, would chose her for his wife, and thus they should have a wealthier son-in-law than myself. That he might have been; but they would not have had one (without arrogance, be it said) of better birth than myself, or of nobler sentiments or more approved worth.

"Well, in the course of my wooing, I learned one day last May, that is to say, about a year ago, that Leonisa and her parents, and Cornelio and his, accompanied by all their relations and servants had gone to enjoy themselves in Ascanio's garden, close to the sea shore on the road to the Saltpits.

"I know the place well," interrupted Mahmoud, "and passed many a merry day there in better times. Go on, Ricardo."

"The moment I received information of this party, such an infernal fury of jealousy possessed my soul that I was utterly distraught, as you will see, by what I straightway did; and that was to go to the garden, where I found the whole party taking their pleasure, and Cornelio and Leonisa seated together under a nopal-tree, a little apart from the rest.

"What were their sensations on seeing me I know not, all I know is that my own were such that a cloud came over my sight, and I was like a statue without power of speech or motion. But this torpor soon gave way to choler, which roused my heart's blood, and unlocked my hands and my tongue. My hands indeed were for a while restrained by respect for that divine face before me; but my tongue at least broke silence.

"'Now hast thou thy heart's content,' I cried, 'O mortal enemy of my repose, thine eyes resting with so much composure on the object that makes mine a perpetual fountain of tears! Closer to him! Closer to him, cruel girl! Cling like ivy round that worthless trunk. Comb and part the locks of that new Ganymede, thy lukewarm admirer. Give thyself up wholly to the capricious boy on whom thy gaze is fixed, so that losing all hope of winning thee I may lose too the life I abhor. Dost thou imagine, proud, thoughtless girl, that the laws and usages which are acknowledged in such cases by all mankind, are to give way for thee alone? Dost thou imagine that this boy, puffed up with his wealth, vain of his looks, presuming upon his birth, inexperienced from his youth, can preserve constancy in love, or be capable of estimating the inestimable, or know what riper years and experience know? Do not think it. One thing alone is good in this world, to act always consistently, so that no one be deceived unless it be by his own ignorance. In extreme youth there is much inconstancy; in the rich there is pride; in the arrogant, vanity; in men who value themselves on their beauty, there is disdain; and in one who unites all these in himself, there is a fatuity which is the mother of all mischief.

"'As for thee, boy, who thinkest to carry off so safely a prize more due to my earnest love than to thy idle philandering, why dost thou not rise from that flowery bank, and tear from my bosom the life which so abhors thine? And that not for the insult thou puttest upon myself, but because thou knowest not how to prize the blessing which fortune bestows upon thee. 'Tis plain, indeed, how little thou esteemest it, since thou wilt not budge to defend it for fear of ruffling the finical arrangement of thy pretty attire. Had Achilles been of as placid temper as thou art, Ulysses would certainly have failed in his attempt, for all his show of glittering arms and burnished helmets. Go, play among thy mother's maids; they will help thee to dress thy locks and take care of those dainty hands that are fitter to wind silk than to handle a sword.'

"In spite of all these taunts Cornelio never stirred from his seat, but remained perfectly still, staring at me as if he was bewitched. The loud tones in which I spoke had brought round us all the people who were walking in the garden, and they arrived in time to hear me assail Cornelio with many other opprobrious terms. Plucking up heart, at last, from the presence of numbers, most of whom were his relations, servants, or friends, he made a show as if he would rise; but before he was on his feet my sword was out, and I attacked not him only but all who were before me. The moment Leonisa saw the gleam of my sword she swooned away, which only exasperated my frantic rage. I know not whether it was that those whom I assailed contented themselves with acting on the defensive as against a raving madman, or that it was my own good luck and adroitness, or Heaven's design to reserve me for greater ills, but the fact was that I wounded seven or eight of those who came under my hand. As for Cornelio, he made such good use of his heels that he escaped me.

"In this imminent danger, surrounded by enemies who were now incensed to vengeance, I was saved by an extraordinary chance; but better would it have been to have lost my life on the spot than to be saved in order to suffer hourly death. On a sudden the garden was invaded by a great number of Turkish corsairs, who had landed in the neighbourhood without being perceived by the sentinels in the castles on the coast, or by our cruisers. As soon as my antagonists descried them they left me, and escaped with all speed. Of all the persons in the garden the Turks captured only three, besides Leonisa, who was still in her swoon. As for me, I fell into their hands after receiving four ugly wounds, which, however, I had revenged by laying four Turks dead upon the ground.

"The Turks having effected this onslaught with their usual expedition, returned to their galleys, ill-satisfied with a success which had cost them so dear. Having set sail they quickly arrived at Fabiana, where mustering their hands to see who was missing, they found that they had lost four Levantine soldiers whom they esteemed their best men. They resolved to revenge the loss on me, and the commander of the galley immediately ordered the yard-arm to be lowered in order to hang me. Leonisa was present at all this. She had come to her senses, and seeing herself in the power of the corsairs, she stood weeping and wringing her delicate hands, without saying a word, but listening if she could understand what was said by the Turks. One of the Christian slaves at the oar told her in Italian that the captain had ordered that Christian to be hanged, pointing to me, because he had killed in his own defence four of the best soldiers belonging to the galley. On hearing this, Leonisa (it was the first time she showed any pity for me) bade the captive tell the Turks not to hang me, for they would lose a large ransom, but return at once, to Trapani, where it would be paid them. This, I say, was the first, as it will also be the last mark of compassion bestowed on me by Leonisa, and all for my greater woe.

"The Turks believed what the captive told them: interest got the better of their resentment, and they returned next morning with a flag of peace. I passed a night of the greatest anguish, not so much from the pain of my wounds, as from thinking of the danger in which my fair and cruel enemy was placed among those barbarians. When we arrived at the town one galley entered the port, the other remained in the offing. The Christian inhabitants lined the whole shore, and the effeminate Cornelio stood watching from a distance what was going on in the galley. My steward immediately came to treat for my ransom, and I told him on no account to bargain for it but for that of Leonisa, for which he should offer all I was worth. I furthermore ordered him to return to shore, and toll Leonisa's parents that they might leave it to him to treat for their daughter's liberation, and give themselves no trouble about the matter.

"The chief captain, who was a Greek renegade named Yusuf, demanded six thousand crowns for Leonisa and four thousand for me, adding that he would not give up the one without the other. He asked this large sum, as I afterwards ascertained, because he was in love with Leonisa, and did not wish to ransom her, but to give me and a thousand crowns to boot to the other captain, with whom he was bound to share equally whatever prizes they made, and to keep Leonisa for himself as valued at five thousand crowns. It was for this reason that he appraised us both at ten thousand.

"Leonisa's parents made no offer at all, relying on my promise, nor did Cornelio so much as open his lips on the matter. After much bargaining my steward agreed to pay five thousand crowns for Leonisa and three for me, and Yusuf accepted this offer at the persuasion of the other captain and of all his men. But as my agent had not so large an amount in ready money, he asked for three days to get it in, being resolved to expend all I possessed rather than fail to rescue us. Yusuf was glad of this, thinking that something might possibly occur in the interval to prevent the completion of the bargain, and he departed for the isle of Fabiana, saying that in three days he would return for the money. But fortune, never weary of persecuting me, ordained that a Turkish sentinel descried from the highest point of the island, far out at sea, six vessels which appeared to be either the Maltese squadron or one belonging to Sicily. He ran down to give warning, and as quick as thought the Turks who were on shore, some cooking their dinners, some washing their linen, embarked again, heaved anchor, got out their oars, hoisted sail, and heading in the direction of Barbary, in less than two hours lost sight of the galleys. I leave you to conjecture, friend Mahmoud, what I suffered in that voyage, so contrary to my expectation, and more when we arrived the following day at the south-west of the isle of Pantanalea. There the Turks landed, and the two captains began to divide all the prizes they had made. All this was for me a lingering death.

"When Leonisa's turn and mine came, Yusuf gave Fatallah (the other captain) myself and six other Christians, four of them fit for the oar, and two very handsome Corsican boys, as an equivalent for Leonisa, whom he himself retained; Fatallah being content with that arrangement. I was present at all this, but knew not what they said, though I saw what they did, nor should I have then understood the nature of the partition, had not Fatallah come up to me and said in Italian, 'Christian, you now belong to me; you have cost me two thousand crowns; if you desire your liberty you must pay me four thousand, or else die here.' I asked him if the Christian maiden was his also. He said she was not, but that Yusuf had kept her with the intention to make her a Moor and marry her; and this was true, for I was told the same thing by one of the Christian rowers, who understood Turkish very well, and had overheard the conversation that had passed between Yusuf and Fatallah. I told my master to take measures for possessing himself of the maiden, and that I would give him for her ransom alone ten thousand gold crowns. He replied that it was impossible, but he would let Yusuf know the large sum I had offered for the Christian girl, and perhaps he would be tempted to change his intention and ransom her. He did so, and ordered all his crew to go on board again immediately, for he intended to sail to Tripoli, to which city he belonged. Yusuf also determined to make for Biserta, and they all embarked with as much speed as they use when they discover galleys to give them chase or merchant craft to plunder. They had reason for this haste, for the weather seemed to be changing, and to threaten a storm.

"Leonisa was ashore, but not where I could see her, until just as we were embarking we met at the water side. Her new master and newer lover led her by the hand, and as she set foot on the ladder that reached from the shore to the galley, she turned her eyes upon me. Mine were fixed on her, and such a pang of mingled tenderness and grief came over me that a mist overspread my eyes, and I fell senseless on the ground. I was told afterwards that Leonisa was affected in the same way, for she fell off the ladder into the sea, into which Yusuf plunged after her and brought her out in his arms. This was told me in my master's galley into which I had been carried insensible. When I came to my senses, and found myself there, and saw the other galley steering a different course and carrying off the half of my soul or rather the whole of it, my heart sank within me again; again I cursed my unhappy fate, and clamorously invoked death, till my master, annoyed by my loud lamentations, threatened me with a great stick if I did not hold my tongue. I restrained my tears and groans, believing that the force with which I compressed them would make them burst a passage for my soul, which so longed to quit this miserable body. But my misfortune did not end here. The storm which had been foreseen suddenly burst upon us. The wind veered round to the south and blew in our teeth with such violence that we were forced to quit our course and run before it.

"It was the captain's intention to make for the island and take shelter under its northern shore, but in this he was disappointed; for such was the fury of the storm that although before it we had been making way continually for two days and nights, yet in little more than fourteen hours we saw ourselves again within six or seven miles of the island, and driving helplessly against it, not where the shore was low, but just where the rocks were highest and threatened us with inevitable death. We saw near us the other galley, on board of which was Leonisa, and all its Turk and captive rowers straining every nerve to keep themselves off the rocks. Ours did the same, but with more success than the crew of our consort, who, spent with toil, and vanquished in the desperate struggle with the elements, let fall their oars, and suffered themselves to drift ashore, where the galley struck with such violence that it was dashed to pieces before our eyes.

"Night began to close in, and such were the shrieks of those who were drowning, and the alarm of those on board our galley, that none of our captain's orders were heard or executed. All the crew did, was to keep fast hold of their oars, turn the vessel's head to the wind, and let go two anchors, in hopes to delay for a little while the death that seemed certain. Whilst all were in dread of dying, with me it was quite the reverse; for in the fallacious hope of seeing in the other world her who had so lately departed from this, every instant the galley delayed to founder or drive ashore was to me an age of agony. I watched every billow that dashed by us and over us, to see if they bore the body of the unfortunate Leonisa. I will not detain you, Mahmoud, with a recital of the tortures that distracted my soul in that long and bitter night; it is enough to say that they were such that had death come, it would have had little to do in bereaving me of life.

"Day broke with every appearance of worse weather than ever, and we found that our vessel had shifted its course considerably, having drifted away from the rocks and approached a point of the island. Setting all of us to work, both Turks and Christians, with renewed hope and strength, in six hours we doubled the point, and found ourselves in calmer water, so that we could better use our oars; and the Turks saw a prospect of going on shore to see if there were any remains of the galley that had been wrecked the night before. But Heaven denied me the consolation I hoped for in seeing in my arms the body of Leonisa. I asked a renegade, who was about to land, to look for it and see if it had been cast on the strand. But, as I have said, Heaven denied me this consolation, for at that moment the wind rose with such fresh fury that the shelter of the island was no longer of any avail to us.

"Seeing this, Fatallah would no longer strive against the fortune that so persecuted him. He ordered some sail to be spread, turned the prow to the sea and the poop to the wind, and himself taking the helm, let the vessel run over the wide sea, secure of not being crossed in his way by any impediment. The oars were all placed in their regular positions, the whole crew was seated on the benches, and no one else was seen on foot in the whole galley but the boatswain, who had lashed himself strongly amidship for his greater security. The vessel flew so swiftly that in three days and nights, passing in sight of Trapani, Melazo, and Palermo, she entered the straits of Messina, to the dismay of all on board, and of the spectators on shore. Not to be as long-winded as the storm that buffeted us, I will only say that wearied, famishing, and exhausted by such a long run, almost all round the island of Sicily, we arrived at Tripoli, where my master, before he had divided the booty with his partners, and accounted to the king for one-fifth part, according to custom, was seized with such a pleurisy that in three days it carried him off to hell.

"The king of Tripoli, and the alcayde of the Grand Turk, who, as you know, is heir to all those who die without natural heirs, immediately took possession of all Fatallah's effects. I became the property of the then viceroy of Tripoli, who a fortnight afterwards received the patent appointing him viceroy of Cyprus, and hither I am come with him without any intention of redeeming myself. He has often told me to do so, since I am a man of station, as Fatallah's soldiers informed him; I have never complied, but have declared that he was deceived by those who had exaggerated my means. If you would have me tell you my whole purpose, Mahmoud, you must know that I desire not to turn in any direction in which I may find any sort of consolation, but that the sad thoughts and memories which have never left me since the death of Leonisa may become so identified with my captive life that it may never afford me the least pleasure. And if it is true that continual sorrow must at last wear out itself, or him who suffers it, mine cannot fail to wear me out, for I am resolved to give it such free scope that in a few days it shall put an end to the wretched life I endure so unwillingly.

"This is, brother Mahmoud, my sad story; this is the cause of my sighs and tears; judge now if it is enough to draw them forth from my inmost vitals, and to engender them in the desolation of my afflicted heart, Leonisa is dead, and with her all my hope; and though whilst she lived it hung by the merest thread, yet, yet—"

Here the speaker's voice faltered, so that he could not utter another word, or restrain the tears which coursed each other down his cheeks so fast that they bedewed the ground. Mahmoud mingled his own with them; and when the paroxysm had somewhat abated, he tried to console Ricardo with the best suggestions he could offer; but the mourner cut them short, saying, "What you have to do, friend, is to advise me how I shall contrive to fall into disgrace with my master, and with all those I have to do with, so that, being abhorred by him and by them, I may be so maltreated and persecuted that I may find the death I so much long for."

"I have now," said Mahmoud, "experienced the truth of the common saying, that what is deeply felt is well expressed, though it is true that sometimes excess of feeling paralyses the tongue. Be that as it may, friend Ricardo,—whether your woes inspire your language, or your language exalts your woes,—you shall always find in me a true friend, to aid or to counsel, though my youth, and the folly I committed in assuming this garb, cry aloud that I am little to be relied on in this capacity. I will try, however, to prove that such a conclusion is unfounded; and though you do not desire either counsel or help, I will not the more desist from doing what your case requires, just as people give a sick man not what he asks for, but what is good for him. There is no one who has more power and influence in this city than my master, the Cadi; not even your own master, who comes to it as viceroy, will have so much. This being the case, I may say that I am the most powerful person here, since I can do what I please with my master. I mention this because it may be that I shall so contrive with him that you shall become his property, and being constantly with me, time will tell us what we had best do, both for your consolation, if you will or can be consoled, and to enable me to exchange the life I lead here for a better one."

"I thank you, Mahmoud, for the friendship you offer me," replied Ricardo, "though I well know that, do what you may, it will avail nothing. But let us quit this subject, and go to the tents, for, as I perceive, great numbers of people are coming forth from the city; no doubt it is the old viceroy who is quitting it to give place to my master."

"It is so," said Mahmoud. "Come then, Ricardo, and you will see the ceremony of the reception."

"Come on," said Ricardo; "perhaps I shall have need of you, if the superintendent of my master's slaves have missed me, for he is a Corsican renegade of no very tender heart."

Here the conversation ended, and the two friends reached the tents, just as the new pasha was coming out to receive his predecessor, Ali Pasha. The latter came attended by all the janissaries who have formed the garrison of Nicosia ever since the Turks have had possession of it, in number about five hundred. They marched in two divisions, the one armed with guns, the other with drawn scimetars. Arrived at the tent of Hassan, the new Pasha, they all surrounded it. Ali made a low obeisance to Hassan, who returned the salutation, but did not bow so low. Ali then entered Hassan's tent, and the Turks placed the new Pasha on a powerful steed, richly caparisoned, and led him round the tents, and up and down the plain; vociferating in their own language, "Long live Sultan Soliman, and Hassan Pasha, his representative!" which cry they frequently repeated, and each time louder and louder. This part of the ceremony being ended, they brought Hassan back to Ali's tent, where the two pashas and the cadi remained alone together for an hour to consult, as Mahmoud informed Ricardo, as to what was to be done upon some works which Ali had begun. Afterwards the cadi appeared at the door of the tent, and proclaimed in Turkish, Arabic, and Greek, that all who desired to crave justice or make any other appeal against Ali Pasha, might now enter freely, for there was Hassan Pasha, sent by the Grand Signor to be viceroy of Cyprus, who would accord them all reason and justice.

In conformity with this permission the janissaries opened a passage to the door of the tent, and every one entered who pleased. Mahmoud made Ricardo go in along with him, for being Hassan's slave his entrance was not opposed. Several Greek Christians and some Turks appeared as appellants, but all upon such trifling matters, that the cadi despatched most of them without the formality of written declarations, rejoinders, and replications. It is, in fact, the custom of the Turks that all causes, except those which relate to marriage, shall be immediately and summarily decided, rather by the rules of common sense than of legal precedent; and among these barbarians (if such they are in this respect) the cadi is the sole judge in all cases, cuts short the pleadings, gives sentence in a breath, and there is no appeal from his decision. Presently a khawass (that is to say, a Turkish alguazil) entered and said that a Jew stood without, at the door of the tent, with a most beautiful Christian maiden for sale. The cadi gave orders to admit him. The khawass withdrew and immediately returned, accompanied by a Jew of venerable appearance, who led by the hand a young woman clothed in the Moorish dress, which became her so well that the most richly arrayed women of Fez or Morocco could not be compared with her, though in the art of adorning themselves they surpass all the other women of Africa, not excepting even those of Algiers, with all their profusion of pearls.

The face of the female slave was covered with a mask of crimson taffety. On her naked ankles she wore two rings, apparently of pure gold; and two others, set with large pearls, on her arms, which shone through the sleeves of a transparent camisole. Her whole dress was rich, gay, and graceful. Struck by her appearance, the first thing the cadi and the pashas did, was to bid the Jew make the Christian uncover her face. She did so, and disclosed a countenance which, like the sun bursting through thick clouds which have long obscured it, dazzled the eyes and gladdened the hearts of the beholders. But on none did that marvellous light produce such an effect as on the woe-worn Ricardo, for he saw before him no other than his cruel and beloved Leonisa, whom he had so often and with such bitter tears bewailed as dead.

At the unexpected sight of such unparalleled loveliness, Ali felt his heart transfixed; Hassan's was pierced with as deep a wound; nor did the cadi's escape scatheless, but, even more deeply smitten than the two pashas, he could not take his eyes off the Christian's face. All three were seized at the same moment with an absolute determination to possess her; and without stopping to inquire how, or where, or when, she had come into the hands of the Jew, they bade him name her price. Four thousand doblas, he replied. The words were no sooner out of the Jew's mouth than Ali Pasha said he would give the price, and that the Jew had only to go to his tent to fetch the money. Hassan Pasha, however, who looked as if he had no mind to lose her, though she were to cost him his life, interposed and said, "I myself will give the four thousand doblas demanded by the Jew, though I would not interfere with Ali's bargain or oppose his wishes, were I not compelled by motives the imperious force and obligation of which he will himself acknowledge. This exquisitely beautiful slave is not for us, but for the Grand Signor alone, and therefore I say that I purchase her in his name. Let us see now who will be so bold as to dispute the purchase with me."

"That will I," replied Ali, "for it is for that very purpose I buy her of the Jew; and it suits me the better to make the present to his Highness, as I have the opportunity of taking her to Constantinople in a few days, and thus winning the favour of the Sultan; for being, as you see, Hassan, a man without employment, I must seek means for obtaining one; whereas, you are secure in that respect for three years, since to-day you enter upon the government of this rich realm of Cyprus. On these grounds, and as I was the first to offer the price demanded for the slave, it stands to reason, Hassan, that you should yield her to me."

"The satisfaction I shall feel in purchasing and sending her to the Sultan," said Hassan, "is so much the greater, as I shall do it without being prompted by any motives of interest whatever. And as for a convenient means of sending her to Constantinople, she shall go thither in a galley manned only by my own slaves."

Ali now started up in wrath, and, clutching his scimetar, cried out, "Since we both intend the same thing, Hassan, namely, to present this Christian to the Grand Signor, and since I was the first purchaser, reason and justice require that you should leave her to me; if you will not, this blade in my hand shall defend my right, and punish your audacity."

The cadi, who had been closely watching this contest, and who was himself no less inflamed with desire than either of the pashas, bethought him how he might remain possessor of the prize, without giving any cause to suspect his insidious designs. Rising therefore to his feet, he stepped between the two angry pashas. "Be quiet, Hassan," he said; "calm yourself, Ali; here am I who can and will arrange your differences in such wise that you shall both have your intentions fulfilled, the Sultan shall be gratified as you desire, and shall be under obligations to you both alike for your loyal and acceptable homage."

The two pashas submitted at once to the cadi, as they would have done even had the terms he imposed appeared harder to them, such is the respect which is paid to their elders by those of that accursed sect. The cadi then continued his address to them. "Ali," said he, "you say that you want this Christian to present her to the Grand Signor; and Hassan says the same. You allege that, having been the first to offer the price required, she ought to be yours; but Hassan denies this; and though he does not know how to assign valid grounds for his claim, yet I find that he has the same as yourself, namely, the intention, which doubtless must have arisen within him at the same time as within yourself, to purchase the slave for the self-same purpose; only you had the advantage of him in being the first to declare yourself. This, however, is no reason why he should be out and out defrauded of the benefit of his good-will, and therefore I am of opinion that it will be well to arrange matters between you in this wise: let the slave be bought by you both; and since she is to belong to the Grand Signor, for whom you buy her, it will be for him to dispose of her. Meanwhile, you Hassan shall pay two thousand doblas, and you Ali another two thousand, and the slave shall remain in my custody, so that I may send her in the name of you both to Constantinople, and thus I too shall not be without some reward for my presence and aid on this occasion. Accordingly, I undertake to send her at my own cost in a style worthy of the great sovereign to whom she is to be presented; and I will write to the Grand Signor a true account of all that has occurred here, and of the good-will you have shown in his service."

The two enamoured pashas could find no pretext for gainsaying this decision; and though it thwarted their desires, they were constrained to submit, each of them comforting himself with the hope, however doubtful, that he would succeed at last. Hassan, who was to remain viceroy of Cyprus, resolved to make such presents to the cadi as would induce him to give up the slave. Ali formed other plans, and as he flattered himself that he should carry them into successful operation, they both professed themselves satisfied, and paid the Jew two thousand doblas each on the spot. The Jew then said that he had sold the slave, but not the clothes she wore, which were worth another two thousand doblas; and this indeed was true, for her hair which she wore partly loose on her shoulders, and partly braided on her forehead, was most gracefully interwoven with strings of pearls; her bracelets and anklets too were set with very large pearls, and her green satin robe was heavily flounced and embroidered with gold. In short, all agreed that the Jew had set a low price on the dress, and the cadi, to show himself no less liberal than the two pashas, said that he would pay for it, that the slave might appear before the Grand Signor as she then stood. The two competitors agreed in approving of this, each of them believing that slave, dress, and all would soon be his own.

It is impossible to describe Ricardo's feelings, when he saw the treasure of his soul thus put up for sale, and found that he had regained it only to lose it more cruelly. He knew not whether he was asleep or awake, and could not believe his own eyes; for it seemed incredible that they should have so unexpectedly before them her whom he had supposed to have disappeared for ever. "Do you know her?" he whispered in Mahmoud's ear.

"No! I do not," was the reply.

"Then I must tell you that it is Leonisa."

"What do you say, Ricardo?" exclaimed Mahmoud.

"I say it is Leonisa."

"Say no more; fortune is proving your friend, and all is turning out for the best, for she is to remain in my master's custody."

"What think you? Shall I place myself where I may be seen by her?"

"By no means, lest you give her a sudden shock; nor must you let it be known that you have seen her, for that might disconcert the plan I have in view."

"I will do as you advise," said Ricardo, turning away his eyes, and carefully avoiding those of Leonisa, which were meanwhile bent upon the ground. Presently the cadi went up to her, and taking her by the hand, delivered her to Mahmoud, ordering him to take her into the city and give her up to his lady, Halema, with directions to keep her as a slave of the Grand Signor, Mahmoud obeyed and left Ricardo alone, following with his eyes the star of his soul, until it disappeared behind the walls of Nicosia. He then went up to the Jew, and asked him where he had bought that Christian slave, or how he had become possessed of her. The Jew replied that he had bought her in the island of Pantanalea, of some Turks who had been shipwrecked there. Ricardo would have pursued his inquiries, but the Jew was called away to give the pashas the very same information which Ricardo so much longed to obtain.

During the long walk from the tents to the city Mahmoud conversed with Leonisa in Italian, and asked her whence she came. She replied that she belonged to the illustrious city of Trapani, and that her parents were noble and wealthy, though as for herself she was utterly unfortunate. Mahmoud then asked her if she knew a gentleman of birth and fortune in that city, named Ricardo. On hearing that name a sigh escaped her that seemed to come from the bottom of her heart. "I know him," she replied, "to my sorrow."

"Why to your sorrow?"

"Because it was to his sorrow that he knew me, and for my misfortune."

"Perhaps," said Mahmoud, "you may also know in the same city another gentleman of very amiable disposition, the son of very wealthy parents, and himself a person of great spirit, liberality, and discretion. His name is Cornelio."

"Him too I know, and of him still more than Ricardo I may say that I know him to my sorrow. But who are you, sir, who know these gentlemen and inquire of me respecting them? Doubtless, Heaven, in compassion for the trouble and mischances I have undergone, has sent me to a place where, if they do not cease, at least I may find a person to console me for them."

"I am a native of Palermo," said Mahmoud, "brought by various chances to wear this garb, and to be in appearance so different from what I am in my secret soul. I know the gentlemen in question, because not many days ago they were with me. Cornelio was captured by some Moors of Tripoli, and sold by them to a Turk who brought him to this island, whither he came to trade, for he is a merchant of Rhodes, and so highly satisfied was he with Cornelio, and such was the confidence he reposed in his truth and integrity, that he entrusted him with his whole property."

"He will be sure to take care of it," said Leonisa, "for he takes very good care of his own. But tell me, señor, how or with whom did Ricardo come to this island?"

"He came," said Mahmoud, "with a corsair who had captured him in a garden on the coast near

Trapani, and along with him a damsel, whose name I never thought of asking, though the corsair often spoke to me in praise of her beauty. Ricardo remained here some days with his master until the latter went to visit the tomb of Mahomet, which is in the city of Almedina,[77] and then Ricardo fell into such a sickness that his master left him with me, as being my countryman, that I might take care of him until the return of the pilgrim to Cyprus, should that happen; or else I was to send Ricardo to Constantinople, when his master should advise me of his arrival there. But heaven ordered it otherwise; for the unfortunate Ricardo died in a few days, always invoking to the last the name of one Leonisa, whom he had told me he loved more than his life and soul. She had been drowned, he said, in the wreck of a galley on the coast of the island of Pantanalea; and he never ceased to deplore her death till his grief destroyed him, for that in fact was the only malady I discovered in him."

"Tell me, señor," said Leonisa, "in the conversations you had with the other young man, did he sometimes name this Leonisa? Did he relate the manner in which he and she and Ricardo were captured?"

"He did name her," replied Mahmoud, "and asked me if there had been brought to this island a Christian of that name, of such and such appearance; for if so he should like to ransom her, provided her owner had been undeceived as to his notion that she was richer than she really was, or should it chance that having enjoyed her, he held her in less esteem. If her price did not exceed three or four hundred crowns, he would pay it gladly, because he had once had some regard for her."

"It must have been very little," said Leonisa, "since it was worth no more than four hundred crowns. Ricardo was more generous. Heaven forgive her who was the cause of his death, and that was myself; for I am the unhappy maiden whom he wept as dead, and God knows how I should rejoice were he alive, that I might repay him by letting him see how I felt for his misfortunes. Yes, señor, I am the little loved of Cornello, the truly wept of Ricardo, whom various chances have brought to the miserable state in which I now am; but through all my perils, by the favour of Heaven, I have preserved my honour unsullied, and that consoles me in my misery. I know not at this moment where I am, nor who is my master, nor what my adverse fates have determined is to become of me. I entreat you, therefore, señor, by the Christian blood that flows in your veins, that you will advise me in my difficulties; for though they have already taught me something by experience, yet they are so great and never-ending, that I know not what to do."

Mahmoud assured her he would do what he could to help her to the best of his understanding and his power. He acquainted her with the nature of the dispute there had been between the pashas concerning her, and how she was now in the keeping of his master the cadi, who was to send her to Constantinople to the Grand Turk Selim; but that he trusted that the true God, in whom he, though a bad Christian, believed, would dispose of her otherwise. He advised her to conciliate Halima, the wife of his master the cadi, with whom she was to remain until she was sent to Constantinople, and of whose character he gave her some details. Having given her this and other useful counsel, he arrived at the cadi's house, and delivered her over to Halima along with his master's message.

The Moorish woman received her well, seeing her so beautiful and so handsomely dressed, and Mahmoud returned to the tents, where he recounted to Ricardo, point by point, all that had passed between himself and Leonisa; and the tears came into his eyes when he spoke of the feeling displayed by Leonisa, when he told her that Ricardo was dead. He stated how he had invented the story of Cornelio's captivity, in order to see what impression it made on her; and in what disparaging terms she had spoken of him. All this was balm to Ricardo's afflicted heart.

"I remember, friend Mahmoud," he said, "an anecdote related to me by my father; you know how ingenious he was, and you have heard how highly he was honoured by the emperor, Charles V., whom he always served in honourable posts in peace and war. He told me that when the emperor was besieging Tunis, a Moorish woman was brought to him one day in his tent, as a marvel of beauty, and that some rays of the sun, entering the tent, fell upon her hair, which vied with them in its golden lustre; a rare thing among the Moorish women, whose hair is almost universally black. Among many other Spanish gentlemen present on that occasion, there were two of distinguished talent as poets, the one an Andalusian, the other a Catalan. Struck with admiration at the sight before him, the Andalusian began to extemporise some verses, but stopped short in the middle of the last line, unable to finish them for want of a rhyme; whereupon the Catalan, who saw his embarrassment, caught the line as it were out of his mouth, finished it, continued the thought, and completed the poem. This incident came into my mind when I saw the exquisitely beautiful Leonisa enter the pasha's tent obscuring not only the rays of the sun, but the whole firmament with all its stars."

"Gently, gently, friend Ricardo," said Mahmoud; "I am afraid if you praise your mistress at that rate you will seem to be a heathen rather than a Christian."

"Well, tell me then," said Ricardo, "what you think of doing in our business. Whilst you were conducting Leonisa to Halima, a Venetian renegade who was in the pasha's tent, and who understands Turkish very well, explained to me all that had passed between them. Above all things, then, we must try to find some means of preventing Leonisa's being sent to the Grand Signor."

"The first thing to be done is to have you transferred to my master," said Mahmoud, "and then we will consider what next."

The keeper of Hassan's Christian slaves now came up and took Ricardo away with him. The cadi returned to the city with Hassan, who in a few days made out the report on Ali's administration, and gave it to him under seal that he might depart to Constantinople. Ali went away at once, laying strict injunctions on the cadi to send the captive without delay to the sultan, along with such a letter as would be serviceable to himself. The cadi promised all this with a treacherous heart, for it was inflamed for the fair Christian. Ali went away full of false hopes, leaving Hassan equally deluded by them. Mahmoud contrived that Ricardo should pass into the possession of his master; but day after day stole on, and Ricardo was so racked with longing to see Leonisa, that he could have no rest. He changed his name to Mario, that his own might not reach her ears before he saw her, which, indeed, was a very difficult thing, because the Moors are exceedingly jealous, and conceal the faces of their women from the eyes of all men; it is true they are not so scrupulous with regard to Christian slaves, perhaps, because being slaves they do not regard them as men.

Now it chanced that one day the lady Halima saw her slave Mario, and gazed so much upon him that his image regained printed on her heart. Not very well satisfied with the languid embraces of her old husband, she readily gave admission to a reprehensible desire, and as readily communicated it to Leonisa, whom she liked much for her agreeable temper, and treated with great respect as a slave of the Grand Signor. She told her how the cadi had brought home a Christian captive of such graceful manners and appearance, that she had never set eyes on a more engaging man in all her life; she understood that he was a chilidi (that is, a gentleman) of the same country as her renegade Mahmoud, and she knew not how to make known to him her inclination, so that the Christian might not despise her for her voluntary declaration. Leonisa asked what was the captive's name, and being told that it was Mario, she replied, "If he was a gentleman, and of the place they say, I should know him; but there is no one of that name in Trapani. But let me see him, and speak with him, lady, and I will tell you who he is, and what may be expected of him."

"It shall be so," said Halima. "On Friday, when the cadi is at prayers in the mosque, I will make Mario come in here where you may speak to him alone, and if you can give him a hint of my desires you will do so in the best way you can."

Not two hours after this conversation the cadi sent for Mahmoud and Mario, and with no less earnestness than Halima had unbosomed herself to Leonisa, the amorous graybeard opened his own to his two slaves, asking their advice as to what he should do to enjoy the Christian and cheat the Grand Signor, to whom she belonged, for he would sooner die a thousand deaths, than give her up to him. So earnestly did the reverend Turk declare his passion that he inspired his two slaves with no less earnestness, though their purposes were quite the reverse of his. It was settled between them that Mario, as a countryman of the fair Christian's, should take it in hand to solicit her on the cadi's part; and that if that failed, the latter should use force, since she was in his power, and afterwards account for not sending her to Constantinople by pretending that she was dead. The cadi was highly delighted with the advice of his two slaves, and with all imaginable alacrity he gave Mahmoud his freedom on the spot, and promised to bequeath him half his property when he died. To Mario likewise he promised, in case of success his liberty and money enough to enable him to return home a wealthy man.

If he was liberal in promises, his slaves were prodigal; they would bring down the moon to him from Heaven, much more Leonisa, if only he gave them an opportunity of speaking with her. "Mario shall have one whenever he pleases," said the cadi, "for I will make Halima go for some days to the house of her parents, who are Greek Christians, and when she is away I will order the porter to admit Mario into the house as often as he pleases, and I will tell Leonisa that she may converse with her countryman whenever she has a mind." Thus did the wind begin to shift in Ricardo's favour, his master and mistress working for him without knowing it; and the first who began was Halima, as was to be expected of her, for it is the nature of women ever to be prompt and bold where their pleasures are concerned.

That same day the cadi told Halima that she might pay a visit to her parents, and stay with them some time if she liked; but elated as she was with the false hopes given her by Leonisa, she was so far from wishing to visit her parents, that she would not have cared to go to the imaginary paradise of Mahomet. She replied then that she had no such wish at that moment; when she had she would mention it, and then she would take the Christian maiden with her. "That you must not," replied the cadi, "for it is not right that the Grand Signor's slave should be seen by any one, much less should she converse with

Christians; for you know that when she comes into the Sultan's possession she will be shut up in the seraglio, and must become a Turk whether she will or not."

"As she will be in my company," said Halima, "there will be no harm in her being in the house of my parents, or conversing with them. I do so myself, and I am not less a good Turk for all that. Besides, I do not intend to remain with them more than four or five days at most, for my love for you will not allow me to be so long without seeing you." Here the conversation dropped, the cadi not venturing to make any further objection, for fear of rousing her suspicions.

Friday being come, he went to the mosque, from which he was sure not to return for about four hours. He was no sooner gone than Halima sent for Mario; but a Corsican slave who acted as porter, would not have admitted him into the court-yard if Halima had not called out to let him pass, whereupon he came in confused and trembling as if he were going to encounter a host of enemies. Leonisa was seated at the foot of a great marble staircase, in the dress in which she had appeared before the pashas. Her right arm resting on her knee supported her head, and her back was towards the door by which Mario entered, so that though he advanced to where she sat, she did not see him.

Ricardo cast his eyes all round the place when he entered; all was silence and solitude till he turned his gaze to where Leonisa sat. Instantly he was seized with a thousand conflicting emotions. He was within twenty paces of the object of his soul's desire; but he was a captive, and the glory of his life was in the power of another. Thus agitated with fear and exultation, joy and sadness, he advanced towards her slowly, until Leonisa suddenly turned round and her eyes met his earnest gaze. He stopped, unable to move another step. Leonisa, who believed him to be dead, was struck with awe and consternation at seeing him so unexpectedly before her. With her eyes still fixed upon him and without turning her back, she retreated up four or five stairs, took a little cross from her breast, kissed it again and again, and crossed herself repeatedly, as though a being from the other world stood before her. Ricardo presently recovered himself, and perceiving from Leonisa's gestures what was the cause of her terror, he said, "It grieves me, beautiful Leonisa, that the news which Mahmoud gave you of my death was not true, so that I might be free from the fear I now feel lest the rigour you have also shown towards me still subsists entire. Set your mind at ease, lady, and come down; and if you will do what you have never yet done— approach me—you will see that I am not a phantom. I am Ricardo, Leonisa,—Ricardo the happy, if you will bid him be so."

Here Leonisa put her finger to her lips, giving Ricardo to understand that he should be silent or speak more low. Gathering a little courage, he drew near enough to hear her whisper thus: "Speak softly, Mario (for so I hear you are now called): talk of nothing but what I talk of, and bear in mind that if we are overheard it will be the cause of our never meeting again. I believe that Halima, our mistress, is listening to us: she has told me that she adores you, and has sent me here as her intercessor. If you will respond to her desires, you will consult the interest of your body more than of your soul; and if you will not, you must feign to do so, were it only because I request it, and for sake of what is due to the declared desires of a woman."

"Never did I think, never could I imagine, beauteous Leonisa," replied Ricardo, "that you could ever ask anything of me with which I should find it impossible to comply; but this present request of yours has undeceived me. Is the inclination so slight a thing that it can be moved this way or that at pleasure? Or would it become a man of truth and honour to feign in matters of such weight? If you think that such things can or ought to be done, be it as you will, since it is for you to command and for me to obey; and that it may not be said I failed to do so with regard to the first order you laid upon me, I will impose silence on the voice of my honour, and will pretend to return Halima's passion, as you desire, if I may thereby secure the blessing of seeing you; and you have only to signify as much to her in such terms as you shall think proper. In return for this sacrifice, to me the greatest possible, I entreat you to tell me briefly how you escaped from the hands of the corsairs, and fell into those of the Jew who sold you."

"The recital of my misfortunes," Leonisa answered, "demands more time than we have now at our disposal; nevertheless, I will tell you some particulars. The day after we parted company, Yusuf's galley was driven back by a contrary wind to the island of Pantanalea, where we also saw your galley, but ours, in spite of all efforts, was driven upon the rocks. My master, seeing death so near, quickly emptied two water-casks, closed them tightly, lashed them together with ropes, and placed me between them. Then stripping off his clothes he took another cask in his arms, and passing round his body a rope attached to the casks on which I was placed, he boldly plunged into the sea. I had not the courage to follow his example, but another Turk pushed me in. I fell senseless into the water, and did not recover until I found myself on land, in the arms of two Turks, who held me with my mouth downwards, discharging a great quantity of water which I had swallowed. I opened my eyes, and looking wildly round me, the first thing I saw was Yusuf lying beside me with his skull shattered, having, as I afterwards learned, been dashed head foremost against the rocks.

"The Turks told me that they had hawled me ashore by the rope, more dead than alive. Only eight persons escaped out of the unfortunate galley. We remained eight days on the island, during which the Turks treated me with as much respect as if I were their sister. We lay hid in a cave, the Turks being afraid of being captured by some of the Christian garrison of a fort in the island, and we supported ourselves with biscuits from the foundered galley which the waves cast ashore, and which the men collected by night. It happened for my misfortune that the commandant of the fort had died a few days before, and that there were in it only twenty soldiers; this fact we learned from a boy whom the Turks captured as he was amusing himself gathering shells on the shore. At the end of eight days a Moorish vessel, of the kind which the Turks call caramuzal, hove in sight; the Turks quitted their hiding-place, and made signals which were recognised by the crew of the caramuzal. They landed, and hearing from their countrymen an account of their disasters, they took us all on board, where there was a very rich Jew, to whom the whole cargo, or the greater part of it, belonged, consisting of carpets, stuffs, and other wares, which are commonly exported by the Jews from Barbary to the Levant. The vessel carried us to Tripoli, and during the voyage I was sold to the Jew, who gave two thousand doubloons, an excessive price; but the Jew was made liberal by the love he conceived for me.

"After leaving the Turks in Tripoli, the vessel continued its voyage, and the Jew began to importune me with his solicitations, which I treated with the scorn they deserved. Despairing, therefore, of success, he resolved to get rid of me upon the first opportunity; and knowing that the two pashas, Ali and Hassan, were in this island, where he could sell his goods as well as in Scio, whither he had been bound, he landed here in hopes of disposing of me to one of the two pashas, with which view he had me dressed as you now see me. I find that I have been purchased by the cadi, for the purpose of being presented to the Grand Turk, which causes me no little dread. Here I heard of your pretended death, which, if you will believe me, grieved me to the soul; yet I envied rather than pitied you, not from ill will towards you, for, if insensible to love, I am yet neither unfeeling nor ungrateful, but because I believed that your sorrows were all at an end."

"You would be right, lady," said Ricardo, "were it not that death would have robbed me of the bliss of seeing you again. The felicity of this moment is more to me than any blessing that life or death could bring me, that of eternity alone excepted. My master, the cadi, into whose hands I have fallen by as strange a series of adventures as your own, is just in the same disposition towards you as Halima is towards me, and has deputed me to be the interpreter of his feelings. I accepted the office, not with the intention of serving his wishes, but my own in obtaining opportunities to speak with you. Only see, Leonisa, to what a pass our misfortunes have brought us; you to ask from me what you know to be impossible; and me to propose to you what I would give my life not to obtain, dear as that life is to me now, since I have the happiness to behold you."

"I know not what to say to you, Ricardo," replied Leonisa, "nor what issue we can find from the labyrinth in which we are involved. I can only say that we must practise, what would not be expected from us, dissimulation and deceit. I will repeat to Halima some phrases on your part which will rather encourage than make her despair; and you may tell the cadi whatever you think may serve, with safety to my honour, to keep him in his delusion. And since I place my honour in your hands, you may be assured that I have preserved it intact, in spite of all the perils and trials I have undergone. Opportunity to converse together will be easily afforded us, and to me this will be most pleasing, provided you never address me on the subject of your suit; from the moment you do so, I shall cease to see you; for I would not have you suppose that my spirit is so weak as to be swayed by captivity. With the favour of heaven, I hope to prove like gold which becomes the purer the more it is passed through the furnace. Be content with the assurance I have given you, that I shall no longer look upon you with repugnance, as I used to do; for I must tell you, Ricardo, that I always found you somewhat more arrogant and presumptuous than became you. I confess, also, that I was deceived, and that my eyes being now opened, if the experiment were to be made over again, perhaps I should be more humane to you, within the bounds of honour. Go now, and God be with you; for I am afraid lest Halima may have been listening to us, and she understands something of our language."

"I fully acknowledge the propriety of all you have said, lady," replied Ricardo. "I am infinitely obliged for the explanation you have given me, and perhaps time will show you how profoundly respectful is the adoration I profess for you. Rely upon me that I will deal in the best manner with the cadi, and do you do the same with Halima. Believe me, lady, since I have seen you, there has sprung up in my heart an assured hope that we shall soon achieve our freedom; and so I commend you to God's keeping, deferring to another time to tell you the events by which fortune brought me to this place, after we were parted."

They now separated, Leonisa well pleased with Ricardo's modest behaviour, and he overjoyed at having heard from her lips words unmixed with harshness. Halima, meanwhile, had shut herself up in her room, and was praying to Mahomet for Leonisa's success in the commission she had given her. The cadi was in the mosque, burning, like his wife, with desire, and anxiously awaiting the answer to be brought him by the slave he had sent to speak to Leonisa, and whom Mahmoud was to admit to her presence for that purpose, even though Halima was at home. Leonisa inflamed Halima's impure desires, giving her very good hopes that Mario would do all she wished, but telling her that two months must elapse before he could consent to what he longed for even more than herself; and that he asked that delay that he might complete a course of devotion for the recovery of his freedom. Halima was satisfied with this excuse, but begged Leonisa to tell her dear Mario to spare himself the trouble and her the delay he proposed, for she would give him, at once, whatever the cadi required for his ransom.

Before Ricardo went with his answer to his master, he consulted Mahmoud as to what it should be. They agreed between them that it should be as discouraging as possible, and that he should advise the cadi to take the girl as soon as possible to Constantinople, and accomplish his wishes on the way by fair means or by force. Moreover, that in order to prevent the unpleasant consequences that might ensue from supplanting the sultan, it would be well to purchase another slave, then pretend, or contrive on the voyage, that Leonisa should fall sick, and throw the newly-purchased Christian woman into the sea by night, with all possible secrecy, giving out that the person who had died was Leonisa, the sultan's slave. All this might be done in such a manner that the truth should never be known, and the cadi would remain blameless in the sultan's eyes, and have the full enjoyment of his desires. The wretched old cadi, who was so blinded by his passion that he would have listened to any absurdity they proposed, eagerly fell in with this scheme as one full of promise; and so indeed it was, but not as he imagined; for the intention of his two advisers was to make off with the boat, and pitch the old fool into the sea.

But a difficulty occurred to the cadi, one of the greatest in his eyes that could possibly be. It occurred to him that his wife would not let him go to Constantinople without her; but presently he got over this obstacle by saying, that instead of buying a Christian woman to put to death in Leonisa's name, he would make Halima serve his turn, for he longed with all his heart to be rid of her. Mahmoud and Ricardo agreed to this expedient as readily as he proposed it, and this being finally settled, the cadi that same day imparted to his wife his design of setting out at once for Constantinople, to present the Christian captive to the Sultan, who, he expected would, in his munificence, make him grand cadi of Cairo or Constantinople. Halima, with great alacrity, expressed her approval of his intention, believing that Mario would be left at home; but when the cadi told her that he would take both him and Mahmoud along with him, she changed her mind, and began to dissuade him from what she had before advised; and finally, she told him that unless she went with him she would not allow him to go at all. The cadi had great satisfaction in complying with her desire, for he thought he would soon get rid of a burden that hung like a millstone round his neck.

All this while Hassan Pasha was indefatigable in pressing the cadi to give up the slave girl to him, in return for which he offered him mountains of gold, and had already made him a present of Ricardo, whose ransom he valued at two thousand crowns. Moreover, to facilitate the transfer, he suggested to the cadi the same expedient which the latter had himself devised, namely, that when the Grand Turk sent for Leonisa he should pretend she was dead. But all the pasha's gifts, promises, and entreaties, had no other effect on the cadi than to increase his eagerness to hasten his departure. Tormented therefore by his own desires, by Hassan's importunities, and by those of Halima (for she, too, was amusing herself with vain hopes) he made such despatch that in twenty days he had equipped a brigantine of fifteen benches, which he manned with able Turkish mariners and some Greek Christians. He put all his wealth on board it; Halima, too, left nothing of value behind her, and asked her husband to let her take her parents with her that they might see Constantinople. Halima entertained the same designs as Mahmoud and Ricardo; she intended, with their help, to seize the brigantine, but would not make this known to them until she found herself actually embarked. Afterwards she proposed to land among Christians, return to her old creed, and marry Ricardo; for she had reason to suppose that bringing so much wealth with her, he would not fail to take her to wife on her again becoming a Christian.

Ricardo had another interview with Leonisa, and made known to her the whole scheme they had projected; and she in return apprised him of the designs of Halima, who kept no secret from Leonisa. After mutual injunctions of secrecy, they bade each other adieu until the day of embarkation. When it arrived, Hassan escorted the party to the shore with all his soldiers, and did not leave them until they had set sail. Even then he never took his eyes off the brigantine until it was out of sight. It almost seemed as if the sighs heaved by the enamoured mussulman swelled the gale, and impelled with more force the sails that were wafting away his soul. But as love had allowed him no rest, but plenty of time to consider what he should do to escape being killed by the vehemence of his unsatisfied desire, he immediately put in operation a plan he had long matured. He put fifty soldiers, all trusty men, bound to him by many favours received and expected, on board a vessel of seventeen benches, which he had secretly fitted out in another port; and he ordered them to pursue and capture the brigantine with all its wealth, and put every soul on board to the sword, with the exception of Leonisa, whom he desired to have as his own sole share of the immense booty. He also ordered them to sink the brigantine, so that no trace of her fate might remain.

Animated with the hope of plunder the soldiers proceeded with the utmost alacrity to execute the pasha's orders, which seemed the more easy as the crew of the brigantine were unarmed, not anticipating any such encounter. It had been now two days under sail, which seemed two centuries to the cadi, who would fain, on the very first of them, have carried his design into effect. But his two slaves represented to him the absolute necessity that Leonisa should first fall sick in order to give colour to the report of her death, and that the feigned malady ought to last some days. The cadi was much more disposed to say that she died suddenly, finish the whole job at once, despatch his wife, and allay the raging fire that was consuming his vitals; but he was obliged to submit to the advice of his two counsellors.

Meanwhile, Halima had declared her design to Mahmoud and Ricardo, who had signified their readiness to accomplish it when passing the Crosses of Alexandria, or entering the castles of Anatolia; but so intolerably did the cadi importune them, that they made up their minds to do so upon the first opportunity that offered. After they had been six days at sea the cadi thought that Leonisa's feigned malady had lasted quite long enough, and was very urgent with them that they should finish with Halima on the following day, and to quiet him they promised that they would do so. But when that day came, which, as they expected, was to witness the accomplishment of their own secret plans, or to be the last of their lives, they suddenly discovered a vessel giving chase to them, with all speed of sails and oars. They were afraid it was a Christian corsair, from which neither party had any good to expect; for if it were one, the mussulmans would be made captive, and the Christians, though left at liberty, would be plundered of everything. Mahmoud and Ricardo, however, took comfort in the prospect of freedom for Leonisa and themselves; nevertheless, they were not without fear of the insolence of the corsairs, for people who abandon themselves to such practices, whatever be their religion or law, are invariably cruel and brutal. The cadi's crew made preparation to defend themselves; but without quitting their oars, and still doing all in their power to escape; but the vessel in chase gained upon them so fast that in less than two hours it was within cannon-shot. Seeing her so close, they lowered their sails, stood to their arms, and awaited the assault, though the cadi told them they had nothing to fear, for the stranger was under Turkish colours and would do them no harm. He then gave orders to hoist the white flag of peace.

Just then Mahmoud chanced to turn his head, and espied another galley of some twenty benches apparently, bearing down upon them from the west. He told the cadi, and some Christians at the oar said that this was a vessel of their own people. The confusion and alarm was now doubled, and all awaited the issue in anxious suspense, not knowing whether to hope or fear it. I fancy the cadi, just then, would have gladly foregone all his amorous hopes to be safe again in Nicosia, so great was his perplexity. It did not last long however; for the first galley, without paying the least regard to the flag of peace, or to what was due to a community in religion, bore down upon his brigantine with such fury as nearly to send it to the bottom. The cadi then perceived that the assailants were soldiers of Nicosia, and guessing what was the real state of the case, he gave himself up for lost; and had it not been for the greed of the soldiers, who fell to plundering in the first instance, not a soul would have been left alive. Suddenly, however, while they were busy with all their might in pillaging, a voice cried out in Turkish, "To arms! to arms! Here's a Christian galley bearing down upon us!" And this indeed was true, for the galley which Mahmoud had descried to the westward was bearing furiously down upon Hassan's under Christian colours; but before it came to close quarters it hailed the latter.

"What galley is that?"

"Hassan Pasha's, viceroy of Cyprus."

"How comes it, then, that you, being mussulmans are plundering this brigantine, on board of which, as we know, is the cadi of Nicosia?"

The reply to this was that they only knew that the pasha had ordered them to take it, and that they, as his soldiers, had done his bidding. The commander of the galley under Christian colours having now ascertained what he wanted to know, desisted from attacking Hassan's and fell upon the cadi's brigantine, killed ten of its Turkish crew at the first volley, and immediately boarded it with great impetuosity. Then the cadi discovered that his assailant was no Christian, but Ali Pasha, Leonisa's lover, who had been laying wait to carry her off, and had disguised himself and his soldiers as Christians, the better to conceal his purpose.

The cadi, finding himself thus assailed on all sides, began loudly to exert his lungs. "What means this, Ali Pasha, thou traitor?" he cried. "How comes it that, being a mussulman, thou attackest me in the garb of a Christian? And you, perfidious soldiers of Hassan, what demon has moved you to commit so great an outrage? How dare you, to please the lascivious appetite of him who sent you, set yourselves against your sovereign?" At these words, the soldiers on both sides lowered their arms, looked upon and recognised each other, for they had all served under one captain and one flag. Confounded by the cadi's words, and by their conscious criminality, they sheathed their blades, and seemed quite discomfited. Ali alone shut his eyes and his ears to everything, and rushing upon the cadi, dealt him such a stroke on the head with his scimetar, that, but for the hundred ells of stuff that formed his turban, he would certainly have cleft it in two. As it was, he knocked the cadi down among the rower's benches, where he lay, exclaiming amid his groans, "O cruel renegade! Enemy of the Prophet! Can it be that there is no true mussulman left to avenge me? Accursed one! to lay violent hands on thy cadi, on a minister of Mahomet!"

The cadi's denunciations made a strong impression on the minds of Hassan's soldiers, who, fearing besides that Ali's men would despoil them of the booty they already looked upon as their own, determined to put all to the hazard of battle. Suddenly they fell upon Ali's men with such vehemence that, although the latter were the stronger party, they soon thinned the number's considerably; the survivors, however, quickly rallied, and so well avenged their slaughtered comrades, that barely four of Hassan's men remained alive, and those too badly wounded. Ricardo and Mahmoud, who had been watching the fight, putting their heads out every now and then at the cabin hatchway, seeing now that most of the Turks were dead, and the survivors all wounded, and that they might very easily be mastered, called upon Halima's father and two of his nephews to aid them in seizing the vessel. Then arming themselves with the dead men's scimetars, they rushed amidships, shouting "Liberty! Liberty!" and with the help of the stout Christian rowers, they soon despatched all the Turks. Then they boarded Ali Pasha's galley. He had been one of the first slain in the last conflict, a Turk having cut him down in revenge for the cadi, and the galley being defenceless, they took possession of it with all its stores.

By Ricardo's advice, all the valuables on board the brigantine and Hassan's galley were transhipped to Ali's, that being the largest of the three vessels, with plenty of stowage room, and a good sailer. The rowers, too, were Christians, and being highly delighted with the acquisition of their freedom, and with the gifts which Ricardo liberally divided amongst them, they offered to carry him to Trapani, or to the end of the world, if he desired it. After this, Mahmoud and Ricardo, exulting in their success, went to Halima, and told her that if she desired to return to Cyprus they would give her her own brigantine, with its full complement of men, and half the wealth she had put on board it; but as her affection for Ricardo was unabated, she replied that she would rather go with them to Christian lands, whereat her parents were exceedingly rejoiced.

The cadi having by this time got upon his legs again, he, too, had his choice given him either to go into Christendom or return to Nicosia in his own vessel. He replied that, "as fortune had reduced him to his present situation, he thanked them for the boon of his liberty; and that he desired to go to Constantinople to complain to the Grand Signor of the outrage he had received at the hands of Ali and Hassan." But when he heard that Halima was leaving him, and intended to go back to Christianity, he was almost beside himself. Finally, they put him on board his own vessel, supplying him abundantly with all accessories for his voyage, and even giving him back some of his own sequins; and he took leave of them all with the intention of returning to Nicosia; but first he entreated that Leonisa would embrace him, declaring that if she would graciously grant him that favour, it would wipe out the recollection of all his misfortunes. All joined in entreating Leonisa to grant him what he so earnestly desired, since she might do so without prejudice to her honour. She complied, and the cadi besought her to lay her hands on his head, that he might have hopes of his wound being healed.

These adieux concluded, and having scuttled Hassan's galley, they sailed away with a favouring breeze and soon lost sight of the brigantine, on the deck of which stood the unlucky cadi, watching with swimming eyes how the wind was wafting away his property, his delight, his wife, and his whole soul. With very different feelings did Ricardo and Mahmoud pursue their way. They passed in sight of Alexandria, and without shortening sail, or needing to have recourse to their oars, they touched at Corfu, where they took in water; and then without more delay they left behind them the ill-famed Acroceraunian rocks, and descried afar off Paquino, a promontory of the most fertile Trinacria, at sight of which, and of the illustrious island of Malta, their prosperous barque seemed to fly across the waters. In fine, fetching a compass round the island, in four days afterwards they made Lampadosa, and then the island where Leonisa had been shipwrecked, at sight of which she almost swooned.

On the following day the beloved native land they so longed for gladdened their eyes and their hearts. Their spirits rose tumultuously with this new joy, one of the greatest that can be known in this life, to return safe and sound to one's country after long captivity; and one which may compare with it is that of victory achieved over its enemies. There was in the galley a chest full of flags and streamers of various colours, with which Ricardo had the rigging adorned. Soon after daybreak they were within less than a league of the city, when taking to their oars, and uttering every now and then joyous cries, they advanced to the harbour, the shore of which was immediately lined by a great concourse of people; for the gaily adorned galley had been so long in sight, that the whole town had come down to observe it more closely.

Meanwhile, Ricardo had entreated Leonisa to dress herself just as she had appeared in the tent before the two pashas, for he wished to play off a pleasant trick upon his relations. She did so, adding jewels to jewels, pearls to pearls, and beauty to beauty (for it increases with the satisfaction of the heart), to the renewed admiration and astonishment of all. Ricardo and Mahmoud also dressed themselves in the Turkish costume, and made the crew put on the garments of the dead Turks. It was about eight o'clock when they entered the harbour, and the morning was so calm and clear that it seemed as though it were intent on beholding this joyful arrival.

Before coming into port, Ricardo fired a salute with the three pieces belonging to the galley, which were one gun amidships, and two falconets; the town returned the salute with an equal number. The whole shore was in lively commotion, watching the approach of the gaily decked galley; but when they had a nearer view of it, and saw by the white turbans of the pretended mussulmans that it was a Turkish craft, there was a general alarm. Suspecting some stratagem, the people flew to arms, all the soldiers in the town were marched down to the port, and the cavalry scoured the coast. Highly amused at all this, the navigators held on their course, entered the port, and anchored close to the shore. Then running out a plank they all stepped ashore one after the other as if in procession, and falling on their knees kissed the ground with tears of joy—a clear proof to all who witnessed their proceedings that they were no Turks. When all the crew were out of the vessel, Halima with her father and mother, and her two nephews, followed next, all dressed as Turks; and the beautiful Leonisa, her face covered with a crimson veil, and escorted on either side by Mahmoud and Ricardo, closed the procession, while the eyes of the whole multitude were fixed upon her. They too did as the others had done, and knelt and kissed the ground.

Presently the captain and governor of the city advanced towards them, perceiving that they were the principal persons belonging to the vessel. The moment he set eyes on Ricardo he recognised him, ran to him with open arms, and embraced him with the liveliest demonstrations of joy. With the governor came Cornelio and his father, Leonisa's parents and relations, and those of Ricardo, all of whom were among the principal persons in the city. Ricardo returned the governor's embrace and his cordial greeting; held out his hand to Cornelio (who had changed colour at sight of him, and almost quaked for fear), and, holding Leonisa also by the hand, thus addressed the bystanders: "Under your favour, gentlemen, I beg that, before we enter the city and the temple to return the thanks so justly due to our Lord for the great mercies vouchsafed to us in our distresses, that you will listen to a few words I have to say to you." The governor bade him say on, for all present would listen to him with pleasure and in silence. All the principal people then formed a circle round him, and he addressed them as follows:—

"You must well remember, gentlemen, the misfortune which befel me some months ago in the garden of the Salt Pits, and the loss of Leonisa: nor can you have forgotten the exertions I made to procure her liberation, since, regardless of my own, I offered all I was worth for her ransom. But this seeming generosity is not to be imputed to me as a merit, since I did but offer my fortune for the ransom of my soul. What has since happened to us both requires more time to relate, a more convenient season, and a speaker less agitated than myself. For the present, let it suffice to tell you that after various extraordinary adventures, and after a thousand disappointments of our hopes of relief, merciful Heaven has, without any merit of ours, restored us to our beloved country, with hearts full of joy and with abundance of wealth. It is not from this, nor from the recovery of my freedom, that springs the incomparable pleasure I now experience, but from that which I imagine this sweet enemy of mine in peace and in war enjoys on seeing herself restored to freedom and to her birth-place. Yet, I rejoice in the general joy of those who have been my companions in misery; and though grievous disasters are apt to alter the disposition and debase worthy minds, it has not been so with the fair destroyer of my hopes, for with more fortitude and invincibility than can well be told, she has passed through the wrecking sea of her disasters and the encounters of my ardent though honourable importunities.

"But to return to the point from which I set out: I offered my fortune for her ransom, and with it the surrender of my soul's desires; I strove for her liberation, and ventured more for her than for my own life. All these things might seem to be obligations of some moment, but I will not have them regarded in that light; what I would have so considered, is that which I now do;" and so saying, he raised his hand and respectfully withdrew the veil from Leonisa's face—it was like removing a cloud from before the sun—and then he continued: "See, Cornelio; here I present to you the prize which you should value above all precious things on earth; and here, beauteous Leonisa, I present to you him

118

whom you have always borne in memory. This is what I would have you all esteem as generosity, in comparison with which to give fortune, life, and honour, is nothing.

"Take her, O fortunate youth, take her; and if your understanding can reach the height of comprehending the greatness of her worth, esteem yourself the most fortunate of mankind. With her I will also give you my whole share of what Heaven has bestowed on us all; it will exceed, as I fully believe, thirty thousand crowns. You may enjoy it all freely and at your ease, and Heaven grant you to do so for many happy years. For my hapless self, since I am left without Leonisa, it is my pleasure to be poor. To want Leonisa, is to find life superfluous."

Here he ceased speaking, as if his tongue clove to the roof of his mouth, but soon afterwards, before any one else had spoken, he exclaimed, "Good heavens! how toil and trouble confuse the understanding! In the eagerness of my desire to do right, I have spoken inconsiderately, for no one can be generous in disposing of what is not his own. What authority have I over Leonisa to give her to another? Or how can I bestow what is so far from being mine? Leonisa is her own mistress, and so much so, that failing her parents (long and happily may they live), her wishes could have no opposition to encounter. Should they meet an imaginary obstacle in the obligations which she, in her good feeling, may think she is under to me, from this moment I cancel them, and declare them null and void. I unsay, then, what I have said, and I give Cornelio nothing, for I cannot; only I confirm the transfer of my property made to Leonisa, without desiring any other recompense than that she will believe in the sincerity of my honourable sentiments towards her, and be assured that they never had an aim unbecoming her incomparable virtue, her worth, and her infinite beauty."

Ricardo closed his speech with these words, and Leonisa thus replied, "If you imagine, Ricardo, that I bestowed any favour on Cornelio during the time when you were enamoured of me and jealous, think that it was in all honour, as being done by the express desire of my parents, who wished to have him for their son-in-law. If you are satisfied with this explanation, I am sure you are no less so with what you have yourself experienced as to my virtue and modesty. I say this, Ricardo, that you may know that I have always been mistress of myself, and subject to no one else except my parents, whom I now entreat humbly, as is meet, to grant me leave and license to dispose of what your magnanimous generosity has given me."

Her parents said she might do so, for they relied on her great discretion that she would make such use of it as would always redound to her honour and advantage. "With that permission, then," said Leonisa, "I beg it may not be taken amiss if I choose rather to seem overbold than ungrateful; and so, worthy Ricardo, my inclination, hitherto coy, perplexed, and dubious, declares in your favour, that the world may know that women are not all ungrateful. I am yours, Ricardo, and yours I will be till death, unless better knowledge move you to refuse me your hand."

Ricardo was almost beside himself to hear her speak thus, and could make no other reply than by falling on his knees before her, grasping her hands, and kissing them a thousand times, with delicious tears. Cornelio wept with vexation, Leonisa's parents for joy, and all the bystanders for admiration and sympathy.

The bishop, who was present, led them with his blessing to the church, and dispensing with the usual forms, married them at once. The whole city overflowed with gladness, which it testified that night by a splendid illumination, and for many days following in jousts and rejoicings given by the relations of Ricardo and Leonisa. Halima, who had lost all hope of having Ricardo for her husband, was content to become the wife of Mahmoud, having returned with him to the bosom of the church. Her parents and her two nephews were, by Ricardo's bounty, presented with so much out of his share of the spoil as sufficed to maintain them for the rest of their lives. In a word, all were happy to their heart's content; and the fame of Ricardo, spreading beyond the limits of Sicily, extended throughout all Italy and beyond it. He was universally known as the Generous Lover, and his renown is still prolonged in the persons of the many sons borne to him by Leonisa, who was a rare example of discretion, virtue, modesty, and beauty.

[76] A city of Cyprus, taken from the Venetians by the Turks in 1570.
[77] A mistake. The prophet's tomb is in Mecca. Medina was his birthplace.
THE SPANISH-ENGLISH LADY.

Among the spoils which the English carried off from the city of Cadiz,[78] was a little girl of about seven years old. An English gentleman, named Clotald, commander of a squadron of vessels, took her to London without the knowledge of the Earl of Essex, and in defiance of his general orders. The parents complained to the earl of the loss of their child, and implored him, since he had declared that property alone should be seized, and the persons of the inhabitants should be left free, they should not, besides being reduced to poverty, suffer the additional misery of being deprived of their daughter, who was the very light of their eyes. The earl caused it to be proclaimed throughout his whole army, that whoever had possession of the child, should restore her on pain of death; but no threatened penalties could constrain Clotald to obey; in spite of them, he kept the child concealed in his ship, being fascinated, though in a Christian manner, with the incomparable beauty of Isabella, as she was called. In fine, her inconsolable parents were left to mourn her loss, and Clotald, rejoicing beyond measure, returned to London, and presented the pretty child to his wife, as the richest prize he had brought home from the war.

It happened fortunately that all the members of Clotald's household were catholics in secret, though in public they affected to follow the religion of the state. Clotald had a son about twelve years old, named Richard, who was brought up by his parents to love and fear God, and to be very stedfast in the truths of the catholic faith. Catherine, the wife of Clotald, a noble, Christian, and prudent lady, conceived such an affection for Isabella, that she reared her as if she was her own daughter; and the child was so well endowed by nature, that she readily learned all they taught her. Time and the kind treatment she received, gradually wore out from her recollection that which her parents had bestowed upon her; not so much so, however, but that she often thought of them with a sigh. Though she learned English, she did not forget her native tongue, for Clotald took care to bring Spaniards secretly to his house to converse with her, and thus it was, that without ceasing to speak Spanish, she became as proficient in English as if she had been born in London.

After having learned all kinds of work becoming a young lady of good birth, she was taught to read and write more than passably well; but what she excelled in above all, was in playing all sorts of instruments suitable to her sex, with extraordinary perfection of musical taste and skill, and with the accompaniment of a voice which Heaven had endowed with such melody that when she chanted she enchanted. All these graces, natural and acquired, gradually inflamed the heart of Richard, whom she loved and respected as the son of her lord. At first his affection for her was like that of a brother for a sister, but when she reached her twelfth year, this feeling had changed into a most ardent desire to possess her, but only in the honourable way of becoming her lawful spouse; for Isabella's incomparable virtue made it hopeless to obtain her in any other way, nor would he have done so even, if he could, for his own noble disposition, and the high estimation in which he held her, forbade any bad thought to take root in his soul.

A thousand times he determined to make known his passion to his father and mother, and as often broke his resolution, knowing that they had destined him to be the husband of a young Scotch lady of great wealth and good family, who, like themselves, secretly professed the catholic faith; and it seemed clear to him, that after having betrothed him to a lady of rank, they would not think of bestowing him on a slave, if that name could be applied to Isabella. Agitated by these distressing reflections, not knowing what course to pursue or whom to consult, he fell into a melancholy that nearly cost him his life. But thinking it was a very cowardly thing to let himself die without making any kind of effort for his own relief, he strove to gather up courage enough to declare his feelings to Isabella.

Everybody in the house was grieved for Richard's illness for he was beloved by them all, and by his parents to the utmost degree, both because he was their only child, and because his virtues, his worth, and good sense deserved all their affection. The physicians could not make out the nature of his complaint, nor could he himself venture to declare it. At last, one day when Isabella entered his room alone, to attend upon him, he said to her, with a faltering voice and stammering tongue, "Lovely Isabella, your worth, your great virtue, and exceeding beauty, have brought me to the state you see; if you would not have me perish in the worst agonies that can be imagined, say that you return the love I feel for you, and consent to my fondest desire, which is to make you secretly my wife; for I fear that my parents, not knowing your merits as I do, would refuse me a blessing to me so indispensable. If you will give me your word to be mine, I here pledge you my own, as a true catholic Christian, to be yours; and though our union be deferred, as deferred it shall be until it can take place with the church's sanction and that of my parents, yet the thought that you will surely be mine, will be enough to restore me to health, and to keep my spirits buoyant until the happy day arrives."

Whilst Richard was speaking, Isabella stood with downcast eyes, and when he had ceased, she replied with equal modesty and good sense, "Ever since Heaven, in its anger or its mercy (I know not which), withdrew me from my parents, Señor Richard, and gave me to yours, I have resolved, in gratitude for the infinite kindness they have bestowed upon me, never to act in opposition to their wishes; and without their consent, I should regard the inestimable boon you desire to confer upon me, not as a good but as an evil fortune. Should it ever be my happy destiny to be acknowledged by them as worthy of you, be assured that my heart shall be yours; but till that time comes, or should it never come, let it console you to know that the dearest wish of my soul will ever be that you may know every blessing which Heaven can bestow upon you." She said no more, but from that moment began the

120

convalescence of Richard, and the revival of his parents' drooping hopes.

The youthful pair took courteous leave of each other, he with tears in his eyes, and she wondering in her soul to see that of Richard captive to her love. As for him, having been raised from his sick bed by a miracle, as it seemed to his parents, he would no longer conceal from them the state of his feelings, but disclosed it one day to his mother, and ended a long conversation by declaring that they might as well put him to death as refuse him Isabella, for it amounted to the same thing. He extolled the virtues of Isabella in such terms, that he almost brought his mother to think that in becoming her son's wife she would have the worst of the bargain. Accordingly she gave Richard good hopes that she would prevail on his father to assent to his wishes, as she herself did; in this she succeeded, for by repeating to her husband all Richard's arguments, she easily induced him to approve of the young man's design, and to find excuses for breaking off the match with the Scotch lady.

At this time Isabella was fourteen and Richard twenty; but even in that early spring time of their youth, they were old in sense and judgment. It wanted but four days of the time appointed by Richard's parents when he should bend his neck to the holy yoke of matrimony; and wise and fortunate did they deem themselves in choosing their prisoner to be their daughter, esteeming her virtues to be a better dower than the great wealth of the Scotch lady. The preparations for the wedding were all made, the relations and friends of the family were invited, and nothing remained but to make known the intended match to the Queen, no marriage between persons of noble blood being lawful without her knowledge and consent; but making no doubt of obtaining the royal licence, they put off applying for it to the last. Things being in this state, their joy was disturbed one evening by the appearance of one of the Queen's servants with an order to Clotald from her Majesty, requiring his appearance before her next morning with his Spanish prisoner. He replied that he would cheerfully obey her Majesty's command. The messenger retired, and left the family in great perturbation; "Alas," said dame Catherine, "what if the Queen knows that I have brought up this girl as a Catholic, and thence infers that we are all of us Christians in this house! For, if her Majesty asks her what she has learned during the eight years she has been with us, what answer can she give with all her discretion, poor timid girl, that will not condemn us?"

"Be under no fear on that account, dear lady," said Isabella; "for I trust in the divine goodness and mercy of Heaven, that it will put such words into my mouth as will not only not condemn you, but redound to your advantage."

Richard trembled as if he foreboded some calamity. Clotald cast about for some encouragement to allay his grievous fears, and found none but in his great trust in God and in the prudence of Isabella, whom he earnestly entreated to try in every possible way to avoid convicting them of being Catholics; for, though their spirits were willing to encounter martyrdom, yet their flesh was weak and recoiled from the bitter trial. Isabella assured them over and over again that they might set their minds at rest; what they apprehended should not befal them through her instrumentality; for though she knew not then what answer she should make to the questions that should be put to her on the morrow, she had a lively and confident hope that she would reply in such a manner as would be for their good.

Many were the comments and surmises they made that night on this unwelcome incident, and especially it occurred to them that, if the Queen knew they were Catholics, she would not have sent them so mild a message; it seemed reasonable to infer from it, that she only desired to see Isabella, the fame of whose incomparable beauty and accomplishments, known to every one in the capital, must have reached her Majesty's ears. Clotald and his wife confessed to themselves, however, that they had done wrong in not presenting her at court, and they thought the best excuse they could make for this, was to say that ever since she had come into their hands, they had destined her to be the wife of their son. But even this would be acknowledging themselves culpable, since it would appear that they arranged the marriage without the Queen's leave; but such an offence would probably not incur any severe punishment. In this way, they comforted themselves, and they resolved that Isabella should not be dressed humbly like a prisoner, but in rich bridal attire, such as became the betrothed of a gentleman of importance Ike their son. Next day accordingly they dressed Isabella in the Spanish style, in a robe of green satin with a long train, and slashes lined with cloth of gold and looped with the pearls, the whole being adorned with precious stones; a diamond necklace and girdle, with a fan such as is carried by Spanish ladies; and for head dress her own luxuriant golden hair entwined with diamonds and pearls.

In that sumptuous attire, with her sprightly air and marvellous beauty, she made her appearance in London in a handsome coach, fascinating the eyes and souls of all who beheld her. Clotald, his wife, and Richard rode with her in the coach, and many noble relations of the family escorted her on horseback, Clotald desiring that all these honours should be paid to his prisoner, in order that the queen might treat her as his son's betrothed. When they arrived at the palace, and entered the vast hall in which her majesty was seated, Isabella's escort halted at the lower end, and she herself advanced alone in all her inconceivable beauty, producing an effect like that of a brilliant meteor shooting through the sky on a calm clear night, or of a sunbeam darting at the first dawn of day through a mountain gorge. A comet she seemed, portending a fiery doom to the hearts of many in that presence hall. Full of meekness and courtesy, she advanced to the foot of the throne, knelt before the queen, and said to her in English, "May it please your Majesty to extend your royal hands to your servant's lips, who will henceforth esteem herself exalted, since she has been so fortunate as to behold your grandeur."

The queen remained a good while gazing on her without saying a word, figuring to herself, as she afterwards told her lady of the bed-chamber, that she had before her a starry heaven, the stars of which were the many pearls and diamonds worn by Isabella; her fair face and her eyes its sun and moon, and her whole person a new marvel of beauty. The queen's ladies would fain have been all eyes, that they might do nothing but gaze on Isabella; one praised her brilliant eyes, one her complexion, another her fine figure, another her sweet voice; and one there was who said in pure envy, "The Spaniard is good looking, but I do not like her dress."

At last the queen motioned to Isabella to rise, and said to her, "Speak to me in Spanish, maiden, for I understand it well, and shall like to hear it." Then turning to Clotald, "You have done me wrong, Clotald," she said, "in keeping this treasure so many years concealed from me; but it is such a one as may well have excited you to avarice. You are bound however to restore it to me, for by right it is mine."

"My liege," replied Clotald, "what your majesty says is quite true; I confess my fault, if it is one, to have kept this treasure until it arrived at the perfection suitable for appearing before your majesty's eyes. Now that it has done so, I had it in mind to enhance it still more, by asking your majesty's leave for Isabella to become the wife of my son Richard."

"I like her name, too," returned the queen. "Nothing was wanting to the fulness of her perfection but that she should be called Isabella the Spaniard. But, mark you, Clotald, I know that, without my leave, you have promised her to your son."

"That is true, my liege, but it was in the confident hope that the many eminent services which my ancestors and I have rendered to the crown, would obtain from your majesty favours still more difficult to grant than the leave in question, the more so as my son is not yet wedded."

"Nor shall he be wedded to Isabella," said the queen, "until he has merited it in his own person. I mean that I will not have him avail himself to that end of your services or those of his forefathers. He must himself prepare to serve me, and win by his own deserts this prize which I esteem as if she were my daughter."

The queen had no sooner uttered these last words than Isabella again fell on her knees before her, saying in Spanish, "Such thwartings as these, most gracious sovereign, are rather to be esteemed auspicious boons than misfortunes. Your majesty has given me the name of daughter; after that what can I have to fear, or what may I not hope?"

Isabella uttered this with so winning a grace, that the queen conceived an extreme affection for her, desired that she should remain in her service, and committed her to the care of a great lady, her keeper of the robes, who was to instruct her in the duties of her new position.

Richard, who saw himself thus, as it were, deprived of his life in losing Isabella, was almost at his wits' end. Agitated and discomfited, he knelt before the queen, and said, "I need no other rewards to induce me to serve your majesty than such as my ancestors have obtained in the service of your royal predecessors; but since it is your majesty's pleasure that I should have new motives and incentives for my zeal, I would crave to know in what way I may fulfil your majesty's behest?"

"There are two ships ready to set out on a cruise," said the queen, "of which I have made the Baron de Lansac general. I appoint you captain of one of them, being assured that the qualities you derive from those whose blood is in your veins will supply the defect of your years. Mark what a favour I confer upon you, since I give you an opportunity to signalise yourself in the service of your queen, to display your capacity and your valour, and to win the highest reward, methinks, which you yourself could desire. I myself will be Isabella's guardian, though she manifests that her own virtue will be her truest guardian. Go in God's name; for since you are in love, as I imagine, I expect great things from your prowess. Fortunate were the king who in time of war had in his army ten thousand soldiers in love, expecting to obtain their mistresses as the reward of their victories. Rise, Richard, and if you have anything to say to Isabella, say it now, for to-morrow you must sail."

Richard kissed the queen's hands, highly prizing the favour she had conferred upon him, and went and knelt before Isabella. He tried to speak to her, but could not, for he felt as if there was a knot in his throat that paralysed his tongue. He strove with all his might to keep down the tears that started into his eyes, but he could not conceal them from the queen. "Shame not to weep, Richard," said her majesty, "nor think less of yourself for allowing such evidence of a tender heart to escape you, for it is one thing to fight the enemy, and another to take leave of one who is dearly loved. Isabella, embrace Richard, and give him your blessing: his affection well deserves it."

Isabella's heart ached to see Richard so cast down. She could not understand what her majesty said. Conscious of nothing but her grief, motionless, and blinded by her tears, she looked like a weeping statue of alabaster. The anguish of the two lovers drew tears from most of the beholders. In fine, Richard and Isabella separated without exchanging a word; and Clotald and his friends, after saluting the queen, left the hall full of grief and pity. Isabella felt like an orphan whose parents have just been buried, and dreaded lest her new mistress should make her abandon the rule of life in which she had been brought up.

Two days afterwards, Richard put to sea, distracted among many other sources of incertitude by two reflections—one was that he had to perform exploits by which he might merit Isabella's hand; and the other, that he could perform none without violating his conscience as a catholic, which forbade him to draw his sword against those of his own faith, but unless he did so, he should be denounced as a catholic or as a coward, to the peril of his life and his hopes. But, in fine, he determined to postpone his inclinations as a lover to his duty as a catholic, and in his heart he prayed heaven to send him occasions in which he might show himself at once valiant and a true Christian,—might satisfy his queen and merit Isabella.

For six days the two vessels sailed with a prosperous wind, shaping their course for the Western Islands, for, in that direction they could not fail to fall in with Portuguese East India men, or vessels returning from the West Indies; but on the seventh day the wind became contrary and continued that way so long that they could not make the islands, but were forced to run for the coast of Spain. On nearing it at the entrance of the straits of Gibraltar, they discovered three vessels, one very large and two small. Richard steered towards his commander's ship to know if it was his intention they should attack the three vessels just discovered; but on nearing it, he saw them hoist a black flag, and presently he heard a mournful sound of trumpets, indicating that either the general or one of his chief officers was dead. When he came within hail, which had not before been the case since they put to sea, there was a call from the leading ship for Captain Richard to come on board, as their general had died of apoplexy the preceding night. Sad as this news was, Richard could not help being glad, not of his admiral's death, but at finding himself in command of both ships, according to the Queen's orders for the contingency which had occurred. He went on board the flag-ship where he found some lamenting the old commander, and some rejoicing over the new one; but all promised him obedience, yet proclaimed him general with short ceremony, not having time for longer, for two out of the three vessels they had discovered had quitted the third and were bearing down upon them.

They at once made them out by the crescents on their flags to be Turkish galleys, to the great delight of Richard, who believed that with the help of Heaven he should make an important capture without prejudice to his religion. The two galleys came up to reconnoitre the English ships, which had not shown their national colours but those of Spain, in order to baffle those who might overhaul them, and prevent their recognising them as war cruisers. The Turks mistook them for trading vessels from India, and made sure of capturing them with ease. Richard took care to let them approach till they were well within range of his guns, which he let fly at them so opportunely, that with a single broadside he disabled one of the galleys, sending five balls through her middle and nearly cutting her in two. She immediately heeled over and began to founder; the other galley made haste to take her in tow, in order to get her under the lee of the large ship; but Richard, whose ships manoeuvred as rapidly as if they were impelled by oars, having reloaded his guns, pursued the retreating galleys, pouring upon them an incessant shower of balls. The crew of the crippled galley having clambered on board the large ship, Richard poured such a cross fire from his two ships on her consort, that she could neither use sails nor oars, and the Turks on board her, following the example of their comrades, took refuge in the large ship, not with the intention of defending her, but for the momentary safety of their lives. The Christian galley-slaves broke their chains, and mingling with the Turks also boarded the large ship, but as they were in danger from the musquetry of Richard's two ships as they were swarming up the side, he gave orders to cease firing on Turks and Christians alike. The former, however, had already lost the great part of their numbers, and the rest were cut to pieces with their own weapons by the revolted slaves, who, thinking the two English ships were Spanish, did marvels for the recovery of their freedom.

At last, when nearly all the Turks were killed, some Spaniards shouted from the deck to their supposed countrymen to come on board and enjoy the fruits of their victory. Richard asked them in Spanish what ship was that? They replied that she was a Portuguese ship from the West Indies, freighted with spices, and with such a quantity of diamonds and pearls that she was worth a million. She had been driven into those latitudes by a storm, much damaged, with all her guns thrown overboard, and her crew almost perishing of hunger and thirst. In that condition, being unable to make any resistance, she had been captured the day before by these two galleys, which belonged to the corsair Arnaut Mami,[79] and

123

which not having stowage room for her great cargo, had taken her in tow to convey her to the river Larache. Richard apprised them, in return, that if they supposed his two vessels were Spanish, they were greatly mistaken, for they belonged to the Queen of England. This information astonished and alarmed them, making them fear that they had escaped from one rock to founder on another; but Richard told them they had nothing to fear, and that they might rely on obtaining their liberty, provided they did not make any defence. "It would be impossible for us to do so," they said, "for as we have told you, we have neither cannon nor other arms, and have no choice but to throw ourselves upon the generosity of your general. Since he has freed us from the intolerable yoke of the Turks, let him enhance his good work by an act which will exalt his fame all over the world wherever the news reaches of this memorable victory and his magnanimity."

Richard lent a favourable ear to this request, and immediately called a council of his officers to consider what might be the best means of sending all the Christians to Spain, without incurring any risk from them, should their numbers encourage them to rise and attempt to overpower his crews. There were some who suggested that they should be brought on board one by one, and put to death as they entered. "No," said Richard; "since by God's grace we have obtained so rich a prize, I will not betray my ingratitude by such an act of cruelty. It is never well to have recourse to the sword, when, with a little forethought, the end may be secured by other means. I will, therefore, not have any Catholic Christian put to death, not that I care so much for them, but for my own sake and for yours, for I would not have the honour of our victory tarnished by cruelty. My orders are, then, that the crew of one of our ships, with all her guns and arms and the greater part of her stores, be put on board the large Portuguese vessel, which we will then take to England, and leave the Spaniards to return home on ours."

No one ventured to contravene this proposal, which to some appeared equally magnanimous and judicious, while others in their hearts condemned it as showing an undue leaning towards the Catholics.

Taking with him fifty arquebusiers Richard went on board the Portuguese ship, in which he found about three hundred persons, who had escaped out of the galleys. He immediately had the vessel he intended to discharge brought alongside, and had its guns brought on board. Then making a short speech to the Christians, he ordered them to pass into the discharged vessel, where they found stores enough for more than a month and for a greater number of people; and as they embarked he gave each of them four Spanish crowns, which he sent for to his own ship, in order partly to relieve their wants when they reached land, which was not far off; for the lofty mountains of Abyla and Calpe were in sight. They all thanked him heartily for his generous behaviour, and when they were nearly all embarked, the same person who had first spoken to him from the deck of the ship, addressed him, "You would do me a greater service, valorous sir, in taking me with you to England than in sending me to Spain; for, though it is my country, and it is but six days since I left it, I have nothing to look for there but grief and desolation.

"You must know, señor, that at the sack of Cadiz which happened about fifteen years ago, I lost a daughter, whom the English carried away with them to England, and with her I lost the comfort of my age and the light of my eyes, which since she passed from their sight, have never seen anything to gladden them. Grief for this calamity and for the loss of my property, of which I was also despoiled, so overcame me that I was no longer able or willing to apply myself to commerce, in which I had been so successful that I was commonly reputed to be the richest merchant in our whole city; and so indeed I was, for, besides my credit, which was good for many hundred thousand dollars, my estate was worth more than fifty thousand ducats. I lost all; yet all my losses would have been nothing had I not lost my daughter. After the general calamity and my own, want pressed me so hard, that not being able to bear up against it, myself and my wife—that woe-begone creature sitting yonder—determined to emigrate to the Indies, the common refuge of the well-born poor. We embarked six days ago in a packet-ship, but just outside the harbour of Cadiz we were captured by those two corsairs. This was a new addition to our affliction; but it would have been greater had not the corsair taken this Portuguese ship, which fortunately detained them until you came to our rescue."

In reply to Richard's question what was his daughter's name, the Spaniard said it was Isabella. This confirmed the suspicion which Richard had all along entertained, that the person before him was the father of his beloved mistress. Keeping this fact to himself, he told the Spaniard that he would willingly take him and his wife to London, where possibly they might obtain some intelligence about their child.

Taking them both on board his flag-ship, and having sufficiently armed and manned the Portuguese galleon, he set sail that night, avoiding the coast of Spain as much as possible, lest he should be intercepted in consequence of! information given by the liberated captives. Among the latter there were some twenty Turks, to whom also Richard granted freedom, to show that his conduct had been the result simply of his generous disposition, and not of any secret leaning to the Catholics: and he asked the Spaniards to set the Turks at liberty upon the first opportunity. The wind, which had blown fresh and fair at first, died away into a calm, to the dismay of the English, who murmured against Richard's unseasonable generosity, saying, that the liberated captives might give information of what had happened, and that if there chanced to be armed galleons in port, they might sally out and intercept them.

Richard knew that this was quite true, but strove to allay their fears in the best way he could. But what availed with them more than all his arguments, was that the wind sprang up again, so that they crowded all sail, and in nine days reached London, from which they had been only a month absent on their cruise. Richard would not enter the port with only joyous demonstrations, on account of the death of his late commander, but mingled signs of grief with them. At one moment bugles rang out cheerily, at the next they were answered by melancholy trumpet notes, and the wailing fife was heard at intervals between the lively rattle of the drum and the clash of arms. From one mast-head hung a Turkish banner reversed, and from another a long black streamer, the ends of which dipped in the water. In this manner he entered the river of London in his English ship, leaving the Portuguese ship at sea, for want of depth of water in the river to float it.

These conflicting demonstrations puzzled the vast multitudes, who observed them from the shore. They easily recognised the smaller vessel as the flag-ship of Baron Lansac; but they could not make out how it was that his second vessel had been exchanged for the large and powerful ship which lay out at sea. But the problem was solved when they saw the valorous Richard jump into his boat, fully equipped in rich and splendid armour. Without waiting for any other escort than that of a vast multitude of the people who followed him, he proceeded on foot to the palace, where the queen was standing in a balcony, waiting for news of the ships, and surrounded by her ladies, among whom was Isabella, dressed in the English style, which became her as well as the Castilian. A messenger, who had anticipated Richard's arrival, had startled her by the announcement of his coming, and she stood watching for him with feelings that fluttered between hope and fear, not knowing whether he had sped well or ill upon his expedition.

Richard was a young man of noble presence, tall and finely proportioned, and he looked to great advantage in a complete suit of Milanese armour all graven and gilded, and instead of a helmet, a wide-leafed fawn coloured hat with Walloon plumes. Thus equipped, and with his spirited bearing, to some he seemed like Mars the god of battles; others, struck by the beauty of his face, compared him to Venus sportively disguised in the armour of that god. When he came before the Queen he knelt, and gave a brief account of his expedition.

"After the sudden death of general de Lansac," he said, "I took his place in pursuance of your Majesty's gracious orders. Shortly afterwards we discovered two Turkish galleys towing a large ship, which we have brought home with us. We attacked them; your Majesty's soldiers fought with great spirit, as they always do, and the corsair galleys went to the bottom. I liberated in your Majesty's royal name the Christians who had escaped out of the hands of the Turks, and sent them away in one of our vessels; and have only brought with me one Spaniard and his wife, who desired of their own accord to come and behold your Majesty's greatness. The great ship we took, is one of those which come from the Portuguese possessions in India; being damaged by a storm, it fell into the power of the Turks, who took it without any difficulty. According to the account given by some of the Portuguese on board the ship, her cargo of spices, and the pearls and diamonds she carries, are worth more than a million. All is untouched, the Turks not having had time to lay hands on anything, and I have given orders that the whole should be presented to your Majesty. There is one jewel alone which, if your Majesty will bestow it upon me, will leave me your debtor for ten other ships. That jewel your Majesty has promised me: it is my Isabella, in obtaining whom I shall be richly rewarded, not only for this service, such as it is, which I have rendered your Majesty, but for many others which I intend to perform in order to repay some part of the incalculable amount which your Majesty will bestow upon me in that jewel."

"Rise, Richard," replied the queen, "and believe me that were I to deliver Isabella to you in the way of bargain at the price at which I value her, you could not pay for her with all the wealth of your prize-ship, nor with what remains in the Indies. I give her to you because I promised to do so, and because she is worthy of you, and you of her; your valour alone entitles you to have her. If you have kept the jewels in the ship for me, I have kept your jewel for you; and though it may seem to you that I do not do much for you in returning to you what is your own, I know that I confer upon you a boon the worth of which is beyond all human computation. Isabella is yours; there she stands; you may claim her when you will, and I believe that it will be with her own consent, for she has the good sense to prize your affection as it deserves. I shall expect you again to-morrow to give me a more detailed account of your exploits, and bring me those two Spaniards who wish to see me, that I may gratify their desire." Richard kissed the queen's hand, and her majesty retired.

The ladies now gathered round Richard, and one of them, the lady Tansi, who had taken a great liking to Isabella, and who was the liveliest and most facetious lady of the court, said to him, "What is all this, sir? Why these arms? Did you, perchance, imagine that you were coming here to fight your enemies? Believe me, you have none but friends here, unless it be the lady Isabella, who, as a Spaniard, is bound to bear you no good will."

"Let her only vouchsafe, Lady Tansi, to have me a little in her thoughts, and I am sure she will not think of me with ill will; for ingratitude can have no place in the heart of one so good, so wise, and so exquisitely fair."

"Since I am to be yours, señor Richard," said Isabella, "claim from me what you will in recompense for the praises you bestow upon me."

Whilst Isabella and the other ladies were thus conversing with Richard, there was a little girl present who did nothing but gaze at him, lift up his cuishes to see what was beneath them, touch his sword, and, with childlike simplicity, peep at her own image reflected in his bright armour. When Richard was gone away, she said, turning to the ladies, "Now I see what a fine thing war must be, since armed men look to such advantage even among ladies." "Look to advantage!" exclaimed Lady Tansi; "one might take Richard for the sun, come down from Heaven, to walk the streets in that garb." Every one laughed at the little girl's remark, and at Lady Tansi's hyperbole; and there lacked not back-biters, who thought his appearing in arms at the palace was an act of great impropriety; but others excused him, saying that it was a very natural and pardonable act of vanity on the part of a gallant young soldier.

Richard was most cordially welcomed by his parents, relations, and friends, and that night there were general rejoicings in London. On his return home, he found Isabella's parents already there, and told his father and mother who they were, but begged they would give no hint of the matter to Isabella till he should make it known to her himself. His desire was punctually observed. That night they began with a great number of boats and barges, and in presence of a multitude of admiring spectators, to unload the great galleon, but eight days were consumed in the work before they had disembowelled it of its aromatic and precious freight. On the following day, Richard went again to the palace, taking with him Isabella's father and mother, dressed in the English style, telling them that the queen wished to see them. They found the queen surrounded by her ladies, with Isabella by her side, wearing, by the queen's desire, for Richard's special gratification, the same dress in which she had made her first appearance at court. Isabella's parents were filled with admiration and astonishment at such a display of grandeur and gaiety combined. They looked at Isabella, but did not recognise her, though their hearts, prophetic of the happiness so near at hand, began to throb, not anxiously, but with an emotion of joy for which they could not account.

The queen would not allow Richard to kneel before her, but made him rise and be seated on a chair which was placed for him alone, an unusual favour, which provoked many envious comments. "It is not on a chair he sits," said one, "but on the pepper he has brought." "It is a true saying," remarked another, "that gifts can soften rocks, since they have mollified the hard heart of our queen." "He sits at his ease," said a third, "but there are those who will make bold to push him from his seat." In fact, that new mark of honour which the queen bestowed on Richard gave occasion to many to regard him with envy and malice; for there is no favour which the sovereign bestows on a subject but pierces the heart of the envious like a lance. In obedience to the queen's command, Richard narrated more minutely the details of his conflict with the corsairs, attributing the victory to God, and to the arms of her valiant soldiers. He extolled them all collectively, and made special mention of some who had particularly distinguished themselves, in order that the queen might reward them all and singly. When he came to speak of his having, in her majesty's name, set the Turks and Christians at liberty, he said, pointing to Isabella's parents, "These are the persons of whom I spoke yesterday to your majesty, who, desiring to behold your greatness, earnestly besought me to bring them away with me. They are from Cadiz, and from what they have told me, and from what I have myself observed, I am assured that they are persons of worth and quality."

The queen commanded them to approach her. Isabella raised her eyes to look at persons who she heard were Spaniards, and, above all, from Cadiz, longing to know if perchance they were acquainted with her parents. Her mother first encountered her gaze, and as she looked attentively at her, there rose on her mind some shadowy confused reminiscences that seemed to intimate she had seen that face before. Her father was in the same wavering state of mind, not daring to believe the evidence of his eyes, whilst Richard watched intently the workings of their perplexed and dubious souls. The queen too noticed the emotion of the two strangers, and also Isabella's uneasiness, for she saw her often raise her hand to her forehead, which was bedewed with perspiration. Whilst Isabella was longing that the person she imagined to be her mother would speak, thinking that the sound of her voice would resolve her doubts, the queen commanded her to ask the strangers in Spanish what had induced them voluntarily to forego the freedom which Richard had offered them, since freedom was the thing most prized, not only by reasonable creatures, but even by irrational animals. Isabella put this question to her mother, who, without answering a word, rushed abruptly and almost totteringly to Isabella, and forgetting all respect of place or circumstances, put her hand to her daughter's right ear, and discovered a dark mole behind it. Assured now beyond all doubt that Isabella was her daughter, she cried out, "Child of my heart! treasure of my soul!" and swooned in her arms. The father, no less tender hearted but with more self-command, gave no other token of his feelings than the tears that streamed down his venerable face and beard. With her lips pressed upon her mother's, Isabella bent her eyes upon her father, with looks that spoke the gladness of her soul.

The queen was greatly affected by this touching scene, and said to Richard, "I know not whether you have done wisely in contriving this meeting, for sudden joy, it is known, can kill as well as grief." Then, turning to Isabella, she withdrew her from her mother, who, after her face had been sprinkled with water, came to her senses, and recollecting herself a little better, fell on her knees before the queen, entreating her majesty's pardon. Elizabeth graciously replied, and commanded that the two strangers should take up their abode in the palace, that they might have the more opportunity of rejoicing in their daughter's society. Richard then renewed his request that the queen would fulfil her promise, and bestow Isabella upon him, if so it were that he had deserved her, but if not, he begged to be sent where he might find opportunities of doing so.

The queen was well aware that Richard was well satisfied with himself, and that there was no need of putting him to further proof; she told him, therefore, that in four days he should obtain the object of his desires, and that she would honour their union with her royal countenance. Richard then took his leave of her majesty, his heart swelling with joy at the near prospect of Isabella becoming his own for ever. Time sped, but not with the nimbleness he desired; for those who live on the hopes of pleasure to come, always imagine that time does not fly, but hobbles on the feet of sloth itself. At last the day came on which Richard expected, not to end his desires, but to find in Isabella new graces which should make him love her more, if more was possible. But in that brief space of time, in which he thought the bark of his fortunes was running with a prosperous gale towards the desired haven, it encountered such a fearful tempest, as a thousand times threatened it with wreck.

The queen's keeper of the robes, who had charge of Isabella, had a son aged two-and-twenty, named Count Ernest, whom his great wealth, his high blood, and his mother's great favour with the queen, made too arrogant and overbearing. He fell most violently in love with Isabella, and, during Richard's absence, he had made some overtures to her which she had coldly disregarded. Although repugnance and disdain manifested at the outset usually make the enamoured desist from their suit, yet Isabella's notorious disdain had the contrary effect on Ernest, for it fired his passion, and consumed his sense of honour. He was almost distracted when he found that the queen had adjudged Isabella to Richard, and that she was so soon to become his; but before he committed himself to the infamous and dastardly course which he ultimately adopted, he first besought his mother to use her influence with the queen on his behalf, declaring that his death was at hand unless he obtained Isabella for his wife.

The countess, well knowing her son's violent and arrogant disposition, and the obstinacy with which he pursued his desires, had reason to fear that his passion would lead to some unhappy result. With a mother's natural anxiety to gratify her son's wishes, she promised to speak to the queen, not with the hope of succeeding in the impossible attempt to make her majesty break her word, but in order not to sit down in despair, while any remedy remained to be tried. That morning Isabella was dressed by the queen's orders with a magnificence which defies description. With her own hands her majesty put on her neck a string of the largest pearls found in the galleon, valued at twenty thousand ducats, and a diamond ring on her finger worth six thousand crowns. But whilst the ladies were in great glee anticipating the glad time so near at hand, the keeper of the robes presented herself before the queen, and implored her on her knees to postpone Isabella's wedding for two days longer, declaring that if her majesty would only do so, it would more than reward her for all her past services. The queen desired to know, in the first instance, why she made that request, so directly at variance with the royal promise given to Richard; but the countess would not explain until the queen, urged by curiosity to discover the cause of this strange request, promised that she would grant it. Having thus succeeded in her immediate object, the lady keeper made the queen acquainted with her son's passion, and how, fearing that unless he obtained Isabella he would commit some desperate deed against himself or others, she had asked for that delay of two days in order that her majesty might devise the best means of saving the life of her son. The queen replied that had she not pledged her royal word, she would have found a way to smooth over that difficulty, but that, for no consideration, could she retract her promise or defraud Richard of the hope she had given him.

The lady keeper reported the queen's answer to her son, but nothing could overcome his headstrong presumption. Arming himself at all points he mounted a powerful charger, and presented himself before Clotald's house, and shouted for Richard to come to the window. Richard was dressed as a bridegroom, and was on the point of setting out for the palace with his friends, but hearing himself thus summoned, he went with some surprise and showed himself at an open window. "Hark you, Richard; I have something to say to you," said Count Ernest. "Our lady the queen ordered you to go forth on her service and perform exploits that should render you worthy of the peerless Isabella. You set out, and returned with ships laden with wealth, with which you think you have bought your title to Isabella. But though our lady the queen promised her to you, it was under the belief that there was no one at her court who could serve her better than you, or more justly aspire to the fair Spaniard's hand; but in this it may be that her majesty was mistaken. Being of that opinion, and holding it for very truth, I say that you have done no such deeds as can make you worthy of Isabella, nor can you ever perform any to raise you to that honour; and if you dare to maintain the contrary, I defy you to the death."

"I am in no wise called upon to take up your defial," replied Richard; "because I confess not only that I do not merit Isabella, but that no man living does so. Confessing, therefore, the truth of what you allege, I say again, that your defial touches not me; nevertheless, I accept it in order to chastise your insolence." So saying, he left the window and called for his arms.

Richard's family and the friends who had assembled to escort him to the palace were thrown into confusion by this untoward incident. The challenge having been so publicly given, it could not be but that some one should report it to the queen. This was done accordingly, and her majesty ordered the captain of her guard to arrest Count Ernest. The captain made such good speed that he arrived just as Richard was riding out from his father's house, mounted on a handsome steed, and equipped with the magnificent arms in which he had gone to pay his respects to the queen on his return from his expedition. The moment the count saw the captain of the queen's guard, he guessed his purpose, and resolving not to let himself be caught, he shouted out, "You see, Richard, how we are interrupted. If you are bent upon chastising me, you will look for me as I will look for you. Two people surely meet when they have a mind." "The sooner the better," said Richard. Meanwhile, the captain of the guards came up and, in the queen's name, arrested the count, who surrendered, requesting to be taken into the queen's presence. The captain complied, and carried Ernest before the queen, who, without entering into any discourse with him, ordered that he should surrender his sword and be committed to the Tower.

All these things were torture to the heart of Isabella and to her parents, who saw their new-found happiness so soon disturbed. The lady keeper advised the queen that to prevent the mischief which might break out between her own family and Richard's, the possible cause of it should be withdrawn, by sending Isabella to Spain. In support of this suggestion she added that Isabella was a Catholic, and so rooted in that faith, that all the arguments and persuasions she had used to withdraw her from it, and they were many, were of no avail. The queen replied that she esteemed her the more, since she was steadfast to the law taught her by her parents; and that as for sending her to Spain, it was not to be thought of, for she was charmed with her lovely presence and her many graces and virtues. In fine, the queen was resolved that Isabella should become Richard's wife, if not that day, on another, without fail. The lady keeper was so mortified by this reply that she withdrew without saying a word; and having already made up her mind that unless Isabella was removed there could be no hope of relief for her son or of peace between him and Richard, she determined to commit one of the most atrocious acts that could enter the mind of a lady of her exalted station.

Women being, for the most part, rash and sudden in the execution of their resolves, the lady keeper that evening gave Isabella poison in a conserve which she pressed her to take, under the pretence that it was good for the sinking and oppression of the heart which she complained of. A short while after Isabella had swallowed it her throat and tongue began to swell, her lips turned black, her voice became hoarse, her eyes fixed and glassy, and her breathing laboured and stertorous: in short, she exhibited all the symptoms of having been poisoned. The queen's ladies hastened to inform her majesty, assuring her that the lady keeper had been the author of the nefarious deed.

The queen had no great difficulty in coming to the same conclusion, and went at once to see Isabella, who seemed to be almost at the last gasp. Sending with all speed for her physicians, she, meanwhile, ordered that the sufferer should be given a quantity of powdered unicorn's horn and several other antidotes, with which great princes are usually provided against such casualties. The physicians arrived and begged the queen to make the lady keeper declare what kind of poison she had used (for no one doubted that she was the poisoner). This information having been obtained from the criminal, the physician applied the proper remedies with such good effect that, with God's help, Isabella's life was saved, or at least there was a hope that it would be so.

The queen ordered that the lady keeper should be arrested and confined in a chamber of the palace, intending to punish her as her crime deserved; whilst the guilty woman thought to excuse herself by saying that in killing Isabella she offered an acceptable sacrifice to heaven by ridding the world of a

Catholic, and removing with her the cause of affliction to her son. Finally, Isabella did not die; but she escaped only with the loss of her hair, eyebrows, and eyelashes, her face swollen, her bloom gone, her skin blotched and blistered, and her eyes red and humid. In a word, she was now become an object as loathsome to look at as she had before been surpassingly beautiful. The change was so frightful that those who knew her thought it would have been better had the poison killed her. But notwithstanding all this, Richard supplicated the queen to let him take her home with him, for the great love he bore her comprehended not only her body but her soul, and if Isabella had lost her beauty, she could not have lost her infinite virtues. "Be it so," said the queen. "Take her, Richard, and reckon that you take in her a most precious jewel, in a rough wooden casket. God knows how gladly I would give her to you as I received her; but since that is impossible, perhaps the punishment I will inflict on the perpetrator of the crime will be some satisfaction to your feelings."

Richard spoke earnestly in the culprit's behalf, and besought her majesty to pardon her. Finally, Isabella and her parents were consigned to his care, and he took them home to his father's house, the queen having added to the fine pearls and the diamonds she had bestowed on Isabella other jewels and rich dresses, such as manifested the great affection she felt for her. Isabella remained for two months in the same state, without the least sign appearing that her beauty would ever return; but at the end of that time her skin began to peel off, and she gradually recovered the natural bloom of her lovely complexion. Meanwhile, Richard's parents, thinking it impossible that Isabella should ever again be what she had been, determined to send for the Scotch lady, to whom they had at first intended to unite him. They did not doubt that the actual beauty of the new bride would make their son forget the lost beauty of her rival, whom they intended to send to Spain with her parents, giving them so much wealth as would compensate them for their past losses. All this was settled between them without Richard's knowledge, and soon after the new bride entered their doors, duly accompanied, and so beautiful that none could compare with her in London, now that Isabella's charms were gone.

Richard was astounded at this unexpected arrival, and fearing that it would have a fatal effect upon Isabella, he went to her bedside, and said to her, in presence of her parents, "Beloved of my soul, my parents, in their great love for me, but ill conceiving how great is mine for you, have brought hither a Scotch lady, to whom they arranged to marry me before I knew your worth. They have done so, I believe, upon the supposition that her great beauty will efface from my soul the image of yours, which is deeply impressed upon it. But from the moment I first loved you, Isabella, it was with a different love from that which finds its end attained in the gratification of the sensual appetite: for though your great beauty captivated my senses, your infinite virtues enthralled my soul, so that if I loved you in your beauty, I adore you in your plainness. That I may confirm that truth, put your hand in mine."

She held out her right hand; he took it in his, and continued:

"By the Catholic faith which my Christian parents have taught me; or, if that is not as pure and perfect as it ought, then, by that held by the Roman pontiff, and which in my heart I confess, believe, and hold, do I swear, and by the true God who hears us, I promise you, Isabella, soul of my soul! to be your husband; and your husband I am from this moment, if you will raise me up so high."

Isabella could only kiss Richard's hand again and again, and tell him in a voice broken by her tears, that she accepted him as hers, and gave herself to him as his slave. Richard kissed her disfigured face, which he had never ventured to kiss in its beauty; and her parents, with tears of affection, ratified their solemn betrothal. Richard told them that he would find a way to postpone his marriage with the Scotch lady, and that when his father proposed to send them to Spain they were not to refuse, but were to go to Cadiz and wait for him there or in Seville for two years, within which time he gave them his word he would be with them, if God spared his life. Should he not appear within that time, they might be assured that he was prevented by some insuperable impediment, and most probably by death. Isabella replied that she would wait for him not only two years, but all the years of her life, until she knew that he was no longer alive; for the moment that brought her that news would be her last.

Richard having at length quitted Isabella, went and told his parents that on no account would he marry the Scotch lady until he had first been to Rome for the satisfaction of his conscience; and he represented the matter in such a light to them and to the relations of Clesterna (that was the name of the Scotch lady), that as they were all Catholics, they easily assented, and Clesterna was content to remain in her father-in-law's house until the return of Richard, who proposed to be away a year. This being settled, Clotald told his son of his intention to send Isabella and her parents to Spain, if the queen gave them leave; perhaps her native air would confirm and expedite her incipient recovery. Richard, to avoid betraying his secret intentions, desired his father, with seeming indifference, to do as he thought best; only he begged him not to take away from Isabella any of the presents which the queen had given her. Clotald promised this, and the same day he went and asked the queen's leave both to marry his son to Clesterna, and to send Isabella and her parents to Spain. The queen granted both requests, and without having recourse to lawyers or judges, she forthwith passed sentence on the lady keeper, condemning her to lose her office, and to pay down ten thousand crowns for Isabella. As for Count Ernest, she banished him from England for six years.

Four days afterwards Richard set out on his exile, and the money had been already paid. The queen, sending for a rich merchant, resident in London, who was a Frenchman, and had correspondents in France, Italy, and Spain, put the ten thousand crowns into his hands, and desired him to let Isabella's father have bills for the amount on Seville or some other place in Spain. The merchant having deducted his profit, told the queen he would give good and safe bills on another French merchant, his correspondent in Seville, in the following manner:—He would write to Paris that the bills might be drawn there by another correspondent of his, in order that they should be dated from France and not from England, because of the interdicted communication between that country and Spain. It would only be necessary to have a letter of advice from him, with his signature and without date, in sight of which the merchant of Seville would immediately pay the money, according to previous advice from the merchant of Paris.

In fine, the queen took such securities from the merchant as made the payment certain; and not content with this, she sent for the master of a Flemish vessel who was about to sail for France, only to obtain a manifest from some French port, in order to be allowed to land in Spain; and she begged him to take Isabella and her parents, treat them well, and land them safely at the first Spanish port he reached. The master, who desired to please the queen, said he would do so, and would land them at Lisbon, Cadiz, or Seville. After this the queen sent word to Clotald not to take from Isabella any of the presents she had given her, whether jewels or clothes.

The next day Isabella and her parents came to take leave of the queen, who received them with great affection. The queen gave them the merchant's bills, besides many other presents, both in money and in things suitable for their voyage. Isabella expressed her gratitude in such terms as to increase the queen's gracious disposition towards her. She took leave of the ladies of the court, who, now that she had become plain, would rather have had her remain among them, having no longer reason to envy her beauty, and being willing to enjoy her society for the sake of her good qualities of mind and disposition. The queen embraced the three, and took leave of them, commending them to good fortune and to the master of the vessel, and asking Isabella to inform her of her arrival in Spain, and of her health at all times through the French merchant. That evening they embarked, not without tears on the part of Clotald, his wife, and his whole household, by whom Isabella was exceedingly beloved. Richard was not present at the departure, for, in order to avoid betraying his feelings, he had gone with some of his friends to the chase.

Many were the dainties which the lady Catherine gave Isabella for use on the voyage; endless were her embraces, her tears, and her injunctions that she should write to her; for all which Isabella and her parents returned suitable thanks. That night the vessel set sail, and having reached France with a fair wind, and obtained the necessary papers to enable them to enter Spain, they crossed the bar of Cadiz thirty days afterwards, and there Isabella and her parents disembarked. Being known to the whole city, they were joyfully welcomed, and warmly congratulated on their recovery of Isabella, and on their liberation, from their Turkish captors (for that fact had been made known by the captives whom Richard generously released), and also from detention in England. By this time Isabella began to give great hopes that she would quite recover her original beauty.

For more than a month they remained in Cadiz, recruiting themselves after the toils of their voyage; and then they went to Seville, to see if they should obtain payment of the ten thousand crowns upon the French merchant's bill. Two days after their arrival they called upon the person on whom it was drawn. He acknowledged it, but said that, until the arrival of advices from Paris, he could not pay the money. Isabella's father hired a large house facing St. Paul's, because there was in that holy convent a nun who was remarkable for rare musical talents, and who was his own niece. They chose the house to be near her for that reason, and because Isabella had told Richard that if he came to look for her he would find her in Seville, and her cousin, the nun of St. Paula's, would tell him where: he had only to ask for the nun who had the best voice in the convent; every one would know her by that description.

It was forty days more before the advices came from Paris, and two days after their arrival the French merchant paid Isabella the ten thousand crowns, which she handed over to her parents. With that sum, and something more made by the sale of part of Isabella's numerous jewels, her father again began business as a merchant, to the surprise of those who were cognisant of his great losses. After a few months his lost credit began to return; so, too, did his daughter's good looks, so that, whenever female beauty was the subject of discourse, the palm was universally conceded to the Spanish-English lady; for by that name, as well as for her great beauty, she was known throughout the city. Through the French merchant of Seville, Isabella and her parents wrote to the queen of England, announcing their

130

arrival in such grateful and dutiful terms as the many favours received at her Majesty's hands required. They also wrote to Clotald and Catherine, whom Isabella addressed as her revered parents.

Their letters to the queen remained unanswered, but from Clotald and his wife they received a reply, congratulating them on their safe arrival, and informing them that their son Richard had set out from France the day after their departure, and thence to other countries, which it behoved him to visit for the tranquillity of his conscience. Isabella immediately concluded that Richard had left England for no other purpose than to seek her; and cheered by this hope, she was as happy as she could be, and strove to live in such a manner that, when Richard arrived in Seville, the fame of her virtues should reach his ears before he learned where she lived.

She seldom or never quitted the house, except to go to the convent, and attended no other church services than those performed there. She never went near the river, or to Triana, or witnessed the general rejoicings at the Campo de Tablada, or the Puerta de Xeres on Sari Sebastian's day, celebrated by an almost innumerable multitude; in short, she never went abroad for any kind of amusement in Seville; her whole time was spent in her devotions, and in praying and hoping for Richard's arrival. The consequence of this strict retirement was a great increase of the general interest about her; thence came serenades in her street by night, and promenades by day. The desire which so many felt to see her, and the difficulty of accomplishing it, was a great source of gain to the professional go-betweens, who severally professed that they alone had the ear of Isabella, and some there were who had recourse to what are called charms, which are nothing but deceits and follies; but in spite of all this, Isabella was like a rock in the ocean, which the winds and waves assail in vain. A year and a half had now passed, and her heart began to yearn more and more as the end of the period assigned by Richard drew near. Already, in imagination, she looked upon him as arrived; he stood before her eyes; she asked him what had caused his long delay; she heard his excuses, of she forgave him, embraced and welcomed him as the half of her soul; and then there was put into her hands a letter from the lady Catherine, dated from London fifty days before. It was as follows:—

"Daughter of my heart,—You doubtless recollect Richard's page, Guillart. He accompanied Richard on his journey the day after you sailed, to France and other parts, whereof I informed you in a former letter. This said Guillart, after we had been sixteen months without hearing news of my son, yesterday entered our house with news that Count Ernest had basely murdered Richard in France. Imagine, my daughter, the effect upon his father, myself, and his intended wife, of such news as this, coming to us in such wise as left no doubt of our misfortune. What Clotald and myself beg of you once more, daughter of my soul, is that you will pray heartily to God for the soul of Richard, for well he deserves this service at your hands, he who loved you so much as you know. Pray also to our Lord to grant us patience, and that we may make a good end; as we will pray for long life for you and your parents."

This letter and the signature left no doubt in Isabella's mind of the death of her husband. She knew the page Guillart very well, and knew that he was a person of veracity, and that he could have had no motive for publishing false news in such a matter; still less could the lady Catharine have had any interest in deceiving her so painfully. In fine, in whatever way she considered the subject, the conclusion at which she invariably arrived was, that this dismal intelligence was unquestionably true. When she had finished reading the letter, without shedding tears or showing any outward tokens of grief, with a composed face and apparently tranquil breast, she rose from her seat, entered an oratory, and kneeling before a crucifix, made a vow to become a nun, thinking herself free to do so, as she was no longer a betrothed maiden, but a widow. Her parents studiously concealed the grief which this affecting news caused them, in order that they might the better console their bereaved daughter; whilst she, as if mistress over her sorrow, having subdued it by the holy Christian resolution she had made, became their comforter. She made her intention known to them, and they advised her to postpone its execution, until the two years were elapsed which Richard had assigned as the duration of his absence. That delay would suffice for confirming the news of his death, and then she might with more security change her condition. Isabella followed their advice; and the six months and a half which remained to complete the term of two years were spent by her in devotional exercises, and in arranging for her entrance into the convent of Santa Paula, in which her cousin was a nun.

The remainder of the two years elapsed, and the day arrived when she was to take the veil. The news having spread through the city, the convent, and the space between it and Isabella's abode, was thronged by those who knew her by sight, or by report only; and her father having invited her friends, and these having invited others, Isabella had for her escort one of the most imposing retinues ever seen in Seville on such occasions. It included the chief justice of Seville, the vicar-general, and all the titled personages of both sexes in the city, so great was the desire of all to behold the sun of Isabella's beauty, which had been for so many months eclipsed. And as it is customary for maidens about to take the veil to dress themselves in their very gayest attire on the day when they are to renounce for ever the pomps and vanities of the world, Isabella wore the same splendid dress in which she was presented to the queen of England, with her necklace and girdle of lustrous pearls, her diamond ring, and all her other sumptuous jewels. Thus gorgeously attired, Isabella set out from home on foot, for the short distance to the convent seemed to render carriages superfluous; but the concourse was so great that the procession could hardly advance, and its members regretted too late that they had not chosen to ride instead of walking. Some of the spectators blessed the father and mother of that lovely creature; others praised Heaven that had endowed her with so much beauty. Some strained forward to see her; others, having seen her once, ran forward to have a second view of her. Among those who were most eager to behold her, was a man who attracted the notice of many by his extraordinary efforts. He was dressed in the garb of a slave lately ransomed, and wore on his breast the emblem of the Holy Trinity, by which it was known that he had been redeemed by the charity of the Redemptorist fathers.

Already Isabella had set one foot on the threshold of the convent gate, where the prioress and the nuns stood ready to receive her with the cross, when this ransomed captive cried out, "Stop, Isabella, stop!" Isabella and her parents turned at this cry, and saw the man cleaving his way towards them through the crowd by main strength. The blue hat he wore having fallen oft through the violence of his exertions, disclosed a profusion of flaxen hair, and a clear red and white complexion, which showed him at once to be a foreigner.

Struggling, stumbling, and rising again, he at last reached the spot where Isabella stood, caught her hand in his, and said, "Do you know me, Isabella? I am Richard, your betrothed." "Well do I know you," said Isabella, "if indeed you are not a phantom come to trouble my repose." Her parents also examined his features attentively, and saw that this captive was indeed Richard. As for him, weeping at Isabella's feet, he implored her not to let the strange garb he wore prevent her recognising him, nor his low fortune impede the fulfilment of the pledges exchanged between them. In spite of the impression which the letter from Richard's mother had made on her memory, Isabella chose rather to believe the living evidence before her eyes; and embracing the captive, she said, "Without doubt, my lord and master, you are he who alone could hinder the fulfilment of my Christian determination; you are without doubt the half of my soul; my own betrothed! your image is stamped upon my memory, and treasured in my heart. The news of your death, sent me by your lady mother, not having killed me on the spot, I resolved to dedicate myself to religion, and I was just about to enter this convent for the rest of my days; but since God has shown us by so just an impediment that he wills otherwise, it is not for me to refuse obedience. Come, señor, to the house of my parents, which is yours, and there I will give myself to you in the way which our holy catholic faith prescribes."

This dialogue, overheard by the spectators, struck them all with amazement. The chief justice and the vicar-general immediately demanded what was all this ado, who was this stranger, and what marriage was this they talked about. Isabella's father replied, that what they had seen was the sequel of a story which required a different place for the telling of it; therefore, he begged that all who desired to hear it should turn back to his house, which was close by, and there he would fully satisfy their curiosity, and fill them with wonder at the strange things he should relate.

Just then one of the crowd cried out, "Señors, this young man is the great English corsair. It is not much more than two years since he took from the Algerine corsairs the great Portuguese galleon from the Indies. There is not the least doubt that he is the very man; I know him, because he set me at liberty, and gave me money to carry me to Spain, and not me only, but three hundred other captives likewise." These words increased the general excitement and the desire to see all these intricate matters cleared up. Finally, the principal persons of the city, with the chief justice and the vicar-general, went back with Isabella to her father's house, leaving the nuns sorely discomfited, and crying with vexation at the loss they had sustained in not having the beautiful Isabella to grace their nunnery. The company being arrived at the house of Isabella's father, she made them be seated in a long hall, and though Richard would willingly have taken it upon himself to tell his story, yet he thought it better to trust it to Isabella's tongue than to his own, which was not very expert in speaking Spanish. Accordingly she began her narration in the midst of profound silence and attention.

She related all that happened to her from the day when Clotald carried her off from Cadiz until her return thither; also Richard's engagement with the Turks; his liberality to the Christians; the promise they had given each other to be husband and wife; the two years' delay agreed on, and the news she had received of his death, which seemed to her so certain, as to have nearly occasioned her taking the veil! She extolled the liberality of the queen of England, the Christian faith of Richard and his parents, and she concluded by saying, that Richard would relate what had happened to him since he left London until that moment, when he stood before them in the dress of a captive, and with the mark of having been ransomed by charity. "I will do so," said Richard, "and briefly relate the hardships I have undergone.

"I quitted London to avoid marrying Clisterna, the Scottish Catholic lady, to whom Isabella has told you that my parents wished to unite me, and I took with me Guillart, my page, the same who carried the news of my death to London, as my mother stated in her letter. Passing through France, I arrived in Rome, where my soul was gladdened, and my faith fortified. I kissed the feet of the supreme pontiff, confessed my sins to the grand penitentiary, obtained absolution, and received the necessary certificates of my confession and penance, and of the submission I had paid to our holy mother, the church. This done, I visited the numberless holy places in that sacred city, and out of two thousand crowns I had with me in gold, I deposited one thousand six hundred with a money-changer, who gave me a letter of credit for them on one Roqui, a Florentine, in this city. With the four hundred that remained, I set out for Spain, by way of Genoa, where I had heard that there were two galleys of that signory bound for this country. I arrived with Guillart at a place called Aquapendente, which is the last town in the pope's dominions on the road to Florence, and in an inn at which I alighted, I met Count Ernest, my mortal enemy. He had four servants with him, he was disguised, and was going, as I understood, to Rome, not because he was a Catholic, but from motives of curiosity. I thought he had not recognised me, and shut myself up in a room with my servant Guillart, where I remained on my guard, intending to shift my quarters at nightfall. I did not do so, however, for the perfect indifference shown by the count and his servants made me confident that they had not recognised me. I supped in my room, locked the door, looked to my sword, commended myself to God, but would not lie down.

"My servant lay asleep, and I sat on a chair between asleep and awake; but a little after midnight, I was near put to sleep for eternity by four pistol shots fired at me, as I afterwards learned, by the count and his servants. They left me for dead, and their horses being in readiness, they rode off, telling the innkeeper to bury me suitably, for I was a man of quality. My servant, awaking in terror at the noise, leaped out of a window, and ran away in such mortal fear, that it seems he never stopped till he got to London, for it was he brought the news of my death.

"The people of the inn came up and found I had been struck by four balls and several slugs, but none of the wounds in any vital part. Calling for a confessor, I received all the sacraments as became a Catholic Christian; but I gradually recovered, though it was two months before I was able to continue my journey. I then proceeded to Genoa, but found no other means of passage than two feluccas, which were hired by myself and two Spanish gentlemen. One of them we employed to go before and pilot the way, and in the other we ourselves embarked. In this way we pursued our voyage, closely hugging the shore; but when we came to a spot on the coast of France, called the Three Marias, two Turkish galleys suddenly came out upon us from a creek, and one keeping to seaward of us, the other more in shore, they cut off our escape to the land and captured us. The corsairs stripped us to the skin, plundered the feluccas, and having completely emptied them, let them drift ashore, instead of sinking them, saying that they might serve to bring them more pickings another time.

"You may well believe how bitterly I felt my captivity, and above all, the loss of the certificates from Rome, which I carried in a tin case, with the bill for the sixteen hundred ducats; but, by good fortune, they fell into the hands of a Christian slave, a Spaniard, who kept them, for if the Turks had got hold of them, they would have required for my ransom at least the amount of the bill. They carried us to Algiers, where I found that the fathers of the Most Holy Trinity were redeeming Christian slaves. I spoke to them, told them who I was, and they, moved by charity, ransomed me, though I was a foreigner. The price set upon me was three hundred ducats; they paid down one hundred on the spot, and engaged to pay the remaining two hundred as soon as the ship should return with the contributions for the release of the Redemptorist father who remained in Algiers in pledge for four thousand ducats, which he had spent over and above the amount he had brought in hand; for so extreme is the charity of these compassionate fathers, that they give their liberty for another's, and remain in captivity that others may go free. In addition to the happiness of obtaining my liberty, I recovered the case with the certificates and the bill. I showed its contents to the good father, and promised him five hundred ducats, in addition to the amount of my ransom, as a contribution towards the payment of the sum for which he was a hostage.

"It was nearly a year before the ship returned with the redemption money. What befel me in that year would, of itself, furnish matter for another history too long to relate at present. I will only say, that I was recognised by one of the twenty Turks whom I liberated with the Christians on the occasion already mentioned; but he was so grateful and so honest, that he would not betray me, for had the Turks known me to be the person who had sunk two of their galleys, and despoiled them of the great Indian galleon, they would either have put me to death, or presented me to the Grand Turk, in which case I should never have recovered my liberty. Finally, the Redemptorist father came to Spain with me, and fifty other ransomed Christians. We made a general procession in Valentia, and from that place we dispersed and took each his own several way, wearing this garb in token of the means by which we had been released.

133

For myself, I arrived to-day in this city, burning with desire to see Isabella, my betrothed, and asked my way at once to the convent, where I was to hear of her. What happened there you all know. It now only remains for me to exhibit these certificates to satisfy you of the truth of my strange story."

So saying, he produced the documents from a tin case, and placed them in the hands of the vicar-general, who examined them along with the chief justice, and found nothing in them to make him doubt the truth of what Richard had stated. Moreover, for the fuller confirmation of his story, Heaven ordained that among the persons present should be that very Florentine merchant on whom the bill for sixteen hundred ducats was drawn. He asked to see it, found it genuine, and accepted it on the spot, for he had received advice of it several months before. Thereupon Richard confirmed the promise he had made of contributing five hundred ducats to the funds of the Redemptorist fathers. The chief justice embraced him, Isabella, and her parents, and complimented them all in the most courteous terms. So, too, did the vicar-general, who requested Isabella to commit this whole story to writing, that he might lay it before his superior, the archbishop, and this she promised to do.

The deep silence in which the audience had listened to this extraordinary narrative was broken by thanksgivings to God for his great marvels; and all present, from the highest to the lowest, congratulated Isabella, Richard, and their parents, and prayed for their happiness as they took leave of them. Eight days afterwards, Richard and Isabella were united before the altar, their marriage being honoured by the presence of the chief justice, and all the persons of distinction in Seville. Thus, after so many vicissitudes, Isabella's parents recovered their daughter, and re-established their fortune; and she, favoured by heaven, and aided by her many virtues, in spite of so many crosses and troubles, obtained for her husband a man so deserving as Richard, with whom it is believed that she lives to this day, in the house facing Santa Paula, which her father had hired, and which they subsequently bought of the heirs of a gentleman of Burgos, named Hernando Cifuentes.

This tale may teach us what virtue and what beauty can effect, since they are sufficient together, or either singly, to win the love even of enemies; and how Heaven is able to bring forth our greatest happiness even out of our heaviest misfortunes.

[78] In the year 1596, when the city was taken by Elizabeth's commanders, Admiral Howard and the Earl of Essex.

[79] Under whom Cervantes himself was for four years in slavery at Algiers.

THE FORCE OF BLOOD.

One night, after a sultry summer's day, an old hidalgo of Toledo walked out to take the air by the river's side, along with his wife, his little boy, his daughter aged sixteen, and a female servant. Eleven o'clock had struck: it was a fine clear night: they were the only persons on the road; and they sauntered leisurely along, to avoid paying the price of fatigue for the recreation provided for the Toledans in their valley or on the banks of their river. Secure as he thought in the careful administration of justice in that city, and the character of its well-disposed inhabitants, the good hidalgo was far from thinking that any disaster could befal his family. But as misfortunes commonly happen when they are least looked for, so it chanced with this family, who were that night visited, in the midst of their innocent enjoyment, by a calamity which gave them cause to weep for many a year.

There was in that city a young cavalier, about two-and-twenty years of age, whom wealth, high birth, a wayward disposition, inordinate indulgence, and profligate companions impelled to do things which disgraced his rank. This young cavalier—whose real name we shall, for good reasons, conceal under that of Rodolfo—was abroad that night with four of his companions, insolent young roisterers like himself, and happened to be coming down a hill as the old hidalgo and his family were ascending it. The two parties, the sheep and the wolves, met each other. Rodolfo and his companions, with their faces muffled in their cloaks, stared rudely and insolently at the mother, the daughter, and the servant-maid. The old hidalgo indignantly remonstrated; they answered him with mocks and jeers, and passed on. But Rodolfo had been struck by the great beauty of Leocadia, the hidalgo's daughter, and presently he began to entertain the idea of enjoying it at all hazards. In a moment he communicated his thoughts to his companions, and in the next moment they resolved to turn back and carry her off to please Rodolfo; for the rich who are open-handed always find parasites ready to encourage their bad propensities; and thus to conceive this wicked design, to communicate it, approve it, resolve on ravishing Leocadia, and to carry that design into effect was the work of a moment.

They drew their swords, hid their faces in the flaps of their cloaks, turned back, and soon came in front of the little party, who had not yet done giving thanks to God for their escape from those audacious men. Rodolfo laid hold on Leocadia, caught her up in his arms, and ran off with her, whilst she was so overcome with surprise and terror, that far from being able to defend herself or cry out, she had not even sense or sight left to see her ravisher, or know whither he was carrying her. Her father shouted, her mother shrieked, her little brother cried, the servant-maid tore her own face and hair; but

134

the shouts and shrieks were disregarded, the wailings moved no pity, the clawing and scratching was of no avail; for all was lost upon the loneliness of the spot, the silence of the night, and the cruel hearts of the ravishers. Finally, the one party went off exulting, and the other was left in desolation and woe.

Rodolfo arrived at his own house without any impediment, and Leocadia's parents reached theirs heart-broken and despairing. They were afraid to appeal for justice to the laws, lest thereby they should only publish their daughter's disgrace; besides, though well born they were poor, and had not the means of commanding influence and favour; and above all, they knew not the name of their injurer, or of whom or what to complain but their luckless stars. Meanwhile Rodolfo had Leocadia safe in his custody, and in his own apartment. It was in a wing of his father's house, of which he had the keys, a great imprudence on the part of any parent. When Leocadia fainted in his arms, he had bandaged her eyes, in order that she might not notice the streets through which she passed, or the house into which he took her; and before she recovered her senses, he effected his guilty purpose.

Apathy and disgust commonly follow satiated lust. Rodolfo was now impatient to get rid of Leocadia, and made up his mind to lay her in the street, insensible as she was. He had set to work with that intention, when she came to herself, saying, "Where am I? Woe is me! What darkness is this? Am I in the limbo of my innocence, or the hell of my sins? Who touches me? Am I in bed? Mother! dear father! do you hear me? Alas, too well I perceive that you cannot hear me, and that I am in the hands of enemies. Well would it be for me if this darkness were to last for ever, and my eyes were never more to see the light! Whoever thou art," She exclaimed, suddenly seizing Rodolfo's hand, "if thy soul is capable of pity, grant me one prayer: having deprived me of honour, now deprive me of life. Let me not survive my disgrace! In mercy kill me this moment! It is the only amends I ask of you for the wrong you have done me."

Confused by the vehemence of her reproaches, Rodolfo knew not what to say or do, and answered not a word. This silence so astonished Leocadia, that she began to fancy she was dreaming, or haunted by a phantom; but the hands she grasped were of flesh and blood. She remembered the violence with which she had been torn from her parents, and she became but too well aware of the real nature of her calamity. After a passionate burst of tears and groans, "Inhuman youth!" she continued, "for your deeds assure me that your years are few, I will forgive the outrage you have done me, on the sole condition that you promise and vow to conceal your crime in perpetual silence, as profound as this darkness in which you have perpetrated it. This is but a small recompense for so grievous a wrong; but it is the greatest which I can ask, or you can grant me. I have never seen your face, nor ever desire to see it. It is enough for me to remember the injury I have sustained, without having before my mind's eye the image of my ravisher. My complaints shall be addressed only to Heaven: I would not have them heard by the world, which judges not according to the circumstances of each case, but according to its own preconceived notions. You may wonder to hear me speak thus, being so young. I am surprised at it myself; and I perceive that if great sorrows are sometimes dumb, they are sometimes eloquent. Be this as it may, grant me the favour I implore: it will cost you little. Put me at once into the street, or at least near the great church; for I shall know my way thence to the house of my parents. But you must also swear not to follow me, or make any attempts to ascertain my name or that of my family, who if they were as wealthy as they are noble, would not have to bear patiently such insult in my person. Answer me, and if you are afraid of being known by your voice, know, that except my father and my confessor, I have never spoken with any man in my life, and that I should never be able to tell who you were, though you were to speak ever so long."

The only reply Rodolfo made to the unhappy Leocadia was to embrace her, and attempt a repetition of his offence; but she defended herself with hands, feet, and teeth, and with a strength he could not have supposed her capable of exerting. "Base villain," she cried, "you took an infamous advantage of me when I had no more power to resist than a stock or a stone; but now that I have recovered my senses, you shall kill me before you shall succeed. You shall not have reason to imagine, from my weak resistance, that I pretended only to faint when you effected my ruin." In fine, she defended herself with such spirit and vigour as completely damped Rodolfo's ardour. Without saying a word he left the room, locked the door behind him, and went in quest of his companions, to consult them as to what he should do.

Finding herself left alone, Leocadia got out of bed, and groped about the room, and along the walls, feeling for a door or window through which she might make her escape. She found the door, but it was locked outside. She succeeded in opening the window; and the moonlight shone in so brightly, that she could distinguish the colour of some damask hangings in the room. She saw that the bed was gilded, and so rich, that it seemed that of a prince rather than of a private gentleman. She counted the chairs and the cabinets, observed the position of the door, and also perceived some pictures hanging on the walls, but was not able to distinguish the subjects. The window was large, and protected by a stout iron grating: it looked out on a garden, surrounded by high walls, so that escape in that direction was as impossible as by the door.

Everything she observed in this sumptuous apartment showed her that its master was a person of quality, and of extraordinary wealth. Among other things on which she cast her eyes was a small crucifix of solid silver, standing on a cabinet near the window. She took it, and hid it in the sleeve of her gown, not out of devotion, nor yet with a felonious intention, but with a very proper and judicious design. Having done this, she shut the window as before, and returned to the bed, to see what would be the end of an affair which had begun so badly. In about half an hour, as it seemed to her, the door was opened; some one came in, blindfolded her, and taking her by the arm, without a word spoken, led her out of the room, which she heard him lock behind him.

This person was Rodolfo, who though he had gone to look for his friends, had changed his mind in that respect, not thinking it advisable to acquaint them with what had passed between him and the girl. On the contrary, he resolved to tell them, that repenting of his violence, and moved by her tears, he had only carried her half-way towards his house, and then let her go. Having come to this resolution, he hastened back to remove Leocadia before daylight appeared, which would compel him to keep her in his room all the following day. He led her then to the Plaza del Ayuntamiento, and there, in a feigned voice, speaking half Portuguese and half Spanish, he told her she might go home without fear, for she should not be followed; and he was already out of sight before she had taken the bandage from her eyes.

Leocadia looked all round her: she was quite alone: no one was in sight; but suspecting that she might be followed at a distance, she stopped every now and then on her way home, which was not far, and looked behind her. To baffle any spies that might perchance be watching her, she entered a house which she found open; and by and by she went from it to her own, where she found her parents stupefied with grief. They had not undressed, or thought of taking any rest. When they saw her, they ran to her with open arms, and welcomed her with tears. Choking with emotion, Leocadia made a sign to her parents that she wished to be alone with them. They retired with her, and she gave them a succinct account of all that had befallen her. She described the room in which she had been robbed of her honour, the window, the grating, the garden, the cabinets, the bed, the damask hangings, and, last of all, she showed them the crucifix which she had carried off, and before which the three innocent victims renewed their tears, imprecated Heaven's vengeance on the insolent ravisher, and prayed that he might be miraculously punished. She told her parents, that although she had no wish to know the name of him at whose hands she had received such cruel wrong, yet if they thought fit to make such a discovery, they might do so by means of the crucifix, by directing the sacristans of the several parishes in the city to announce from the pulpits that whoever had lost such an image would find it in the hands of a certain monk whom he should name. By this means, they would discover their enemy in the person of the owner of the crucifix.

"That would be very well, my child," replied her father, "if your plan were not liable to be frustrated by ordinary cunning; but no doubt this image has been already missed by its owner, and he will have set it down for certain that it was taken out of the room by the person he locked up there. To give him notice that the crucifix was in the hands of a certain monk would only serve to make known the person who deposited it in such keeping, but not to make the owner declare himself; for the latter might send another person for it, and furnish him with all the particulars by which he should identify it. Thus you see we should only damage ourselves without obtaining the information we sought; though to be sure we might employ the same artifice on our side, and deposit the image with the monk through a third hand. What you had best do, my child, is to keep it, and pray to it, that since it was a witness to your undoing, it will deign to vindicate your cause by its righteous judgment. Bear in mind, my child, that an ounce of public dishonour outweighs a quintal of secret infamy; and since, by the blessing of God, you can live in honour before the public eye, let it not distress you so much to be dishonoured in your ownself in secret. Real dishonour consists in sin, and real honour in virtue. There are three ways of offending God; by thought, word, and deed; but since neither in thought, nor in word, nor in deed have you offended, look upon yourself as a person of unsullied honour, as I shall always do, who will never cease to regard you with the affection of a father."

Thus did this humane and right-minded father comfort his unhappy daughter; and her mother embracing her again did all she could to soothe her feelings. In spite of all their tenderness her anguish was too poignant to be soon allayed; and from that fatal night, she continued to live the life of a recluse under the protection of her parents.

Rodolfo meanwhile having returned home, and having missed the crucifix, guessed who had taken it, but gave himself no concern about it. To a person of his wealth such a loss was of no importance; nor did his parents make any inquiry about it, when three days afterwards, on his departure for Italy, one of his mother's women took an inventory of all the effects he left in his apartment. Rodolfo had long contemplated a visit to Italy; and his father, who himself had been there, encouraged him in that design, telling him that no one could be a finished gentleman without seeing foreign countries. For this and other reasons, Rodolfo readily complied with the wishes of his father, who gave him ample letters of credit on Barcelona, Genoa, Rome, and Naples. Taking with him two of his companions, he set out on his travels, with expectations raised to a high pitch, by what he had been told by some soldiers of his acquaintance, concerning the good cheer in the hostelries of Italy and France, and the free and easy life enjoyed by the Spaniards in their quarters. His ears were tickled with the sound of such phrases as these: ecco li buoni polastri, picioni, presuto, salcicie, and all the other fine things of the sort, which soldiers are fond of calling to mind when they return from those parts to Spain. In fine, he went away with as little thought or concern about what had passed between him and the beautiful Leocadia as though it had never happened. She meanwhile passed her life with her parents in the strictest retirement, never letting herself be seen, but shunning every eye lest it should read her misfortune in her face. What she had thus done voluntarily at first, she found herself, in a few months, constrained to do by necessity; for she discovered that she was pregnant, to the grievous renewal of her affliction.

Time rolled on: the hour of her delivery arrived: it took place in the utmost secrecy, her mother taking upon her the office of midwife: and she gave birth to a son, one of the most beautiful ever seen. The babe was conveyed, with the same secrecy, to a village, where he remained till he was four years old, when his grandfather brought him, under the name of nephew, to his own house, where he was reared, if not in affluence, at least most virtuously. The boy, who was named Luis after his grandfather, was remarkably handsome, of a sweet docile disposition; and his manners and deportment, even at that tender age, were such as showed him to be the son of some noble father. His grandfather and grandmother were so delighted with his grace, beauty, and good behaviour, that they came at last to regard their daughter's mischance as a happy event, since it had given them such a grandson. When the boy walked through the streets, blessings were showered upon him by all who saw him—blessings upon his beauty, upon the mother that bore him, upon the father that begot him, upon those who brought him up so well. Thus admired by strangers, as well as by all who knew him, he grew up to the age of seven, by which time he could already read Latin and his mother tongue, and write a good round hand; for it was the intention of his grandparents to make him learned and virtuous, since they could not make him rich, learning and virtue being such wealth as thieves cannot steal, or fortune destroy.

One day, when the boy was sent by his grandfather with a message to a relation, he passed along a street in which there was a great concourse of horsemen. He stopped to look at them; and to see them the better, he moved from his position, and crossed the street. In doing so, he was not rapid enough to avoid a fiery horse, which its rider could not pull up in time, and which knocked Luis down, and trampled upon him. The poor child lay senseless on the ground, bleeding profusely from his head. A moment after the accident had happened, an elderly gentleman threw himself from his horse with surprising agility, took the boy out of the arms of a person who had raised him from the ground, and carried him to his own house, bidding his servants go fetch a surgeon.

Many gentlemen followed him, greatly distressed at the sad accident which had befallen the general favourite; for it was soon on everybody's lips that the sufferer was little Luis. The news speedily reached the ears of his grandparents and his supposed cousin, who all hurried in wild dismay to look for their darling. The gentleman who had humanely taken charge of him being of eminent rank, and well known, they easily found their way to his house, and arrived there just as Luis was under the surgeon's hands. The master and mistress begged them not to cry, or raise their voices in lamentation; for it would do the little patient no good. The surgeon, who was an able man, having dressed the wound with great care and skill, saw that it was not so deadly as he had at first supposed. In the midst of the dressing, Luis came to his senses, and was glad to see his relations, who asked him how he felt. "Pretty well," he said, only his head and his body pained him a good deal. The surgeon desired them not to talk to him, but leave him to repose. They did so, and the grandfather then addressed himself to the master of the house, thanking him for the kindness he had shown to his nephew. The gentleman replied that there was nothing to thank him for; the fact being, that when he saw the boy knocked down, his first thought was that he saw under the horses' heels the face of a son of his own, whom he tenderly loved. It was this that impelled him to take the boy up, and carry him to his own house, where he should remain all the time he was in the surgeon's hands, and be treated with all possible care. The lady of the house spoke to the same effect, and with no less kindness and cordiality.

The grandfather and grandmother were surprised at meeting with so much sympathy on the part of strangers; but far greater was the surprise of their daughter, who, on looking round her, after the surgeon's report had somewhat allayed her agitation, plainly perceived that she was in the very room to which she had been carried by her ravisher. The damask hangings were no longer there; but she recognised it by other tokens. She saw the grated window that opened on the garden: it was then closed on account of the little patient; but she asked if there was a garden on the outside, and was answered in the affirmative. The bed she too well remembered was there; and, above all, the cabinet, on which had stood the image she had taken away, was still on the same spot. Finally, to corroborate all the other indications, and confirm the truth of her discovery beyond all question, she counted the steps of the staircase leading from the room to the street, and found the number exactly what she had expected; for she had had the presence of mind to count them on the former occasion, when she descended them blindfold. On her return home, she imparted her discovery to her mother, who immediately made inquiries as to whether the gentleman in whose house her grandson lay ever had a son. She found he had one son, Rodolfo—as we call him—who was then in Italy; and on comparing the time he was said to have been abroad with that which had elapsed since her daughter's ravishment, she found them to agree very closely. She made all this known to her husband; and it was finally settled between the three that they should not move in the matter for the present, but wait till the will of Heaven had declared itself respecting the little patient.

Luis was out of danger in a fortnight; in a month he rose from his bed; and during all that time he was visited daily by his mother and grandmother, and treated by the master and mistress of the house as if he was their own child. Doña Estafania, the kind gentleman's wife, often observed, in conversation with Leocadia, that the boy so strongly resembled a son of hers who was in Italy, she never could look at him without thinking her son was actually before her. One day, when Doña Estafania repeated this remark, no one being present but herself and Leocadia, the latter thought it a good opportunity to open her mind to the lady, in the manner previously concerted between herself and her parents.

"Señora," she said, "when my parents heard of the terrible accident that had befallen their nephew, they felt as if the sky had fallen upon their heads. For them it was losing the light of their eyes, and the staff of their age, to lose their nephew, their love for whom far surpasses that which parents commonly bear towards their sons. But, as the proverb says, with the disease God sends the remedy. The boy found his recovery in this house; and I found in it reminiscences of events I shall never forget as long as I live. I, señora, am noble, for so are my parents, and so were all my ancestors, who, though but moderately endowed with the gifts of fortune, always happily maintained their honour where-ever they lived."

Doña Estafania listened attentively to Leocadia, and was astonished to hear her speak with an intelligence beyond her years, for she did not think her more than twenty, and without interrupting her by a single word, she heard her relate her whole story, how she had been forcibly carried into that chamber, what had been done to her there, and by what tokens she had been able to recognise it again. In confirmation of all this, she drew forth from her bosom the crucifix she had taken away with her, and thus addressed it: "Lord, who wast witness of the violence done to me, be thou the judge of the amends which are my due. I took thee from off this cabinet, that I might continually remind thee of my wrong, not in order to pray to thee for vengeance, which I do not invoke, but to beseech thee to inspire me with some counsel which may enable me to bear it with patience." Then turning to Doña Estafania, "This boy, señora," she said, "towards whom you have manifested the extreme of your great kindness and compassion, is your own grandson. It was by the merciful providence of Heaven that he was run over, in order that being taken to your house, I should find him in it, as I hope to find there, if not the remedy most appropriate to my misfortune, at least the means of alleviating it." Thus saying, and pressing the crucifix to her breast, she fell fainting into the arms of Doña Estafania, who as a gentlewoman, to whose sex pity is as natural as cruelty is to man, instantly pressed her lips to those of the fainting girl, shedding over her so many tears that there needed no other sprinkling of water to recover Leocadia from her swoon.

Whilst the two were in this situation, Doña Estafania's husband entered the room, leading little Luis by the hand. On seeing his wife all in tears, and Leocadia fainting, he eagerly inquired the cause of so startling a spectacle. The boy having embraced his mother, calling her his cousin, and his grandmother, calling her his benefactress, repeated his grandfather's question. "I have great things to tell you, señor," said Doña Estafania to her husband, "the cream and substance of which is this: the fainting girl before you is your daughter, and that boy is your grandson. This truth which I have learned from her lips is confirmed by his face, in which we have both beheld that of our son."

"Unless you speak more fully, señora, I cannot understand you," replied her husband.

Just then Leocadia came to herself, and embracing the cross seemed changed into a sea of tears, and the gentleman remained in utter bewilderment, until his wife had repeated to him, from beginning to end, Leocadia's whole story; and he believed it, through the blessed dispensation of Heaven, which had confirmed it by so many convincing testimonies. He embraced and comforted Leocadia, kissed his grandson, and that same day he despatched a courier to Naples, with a letter to his son, requiring him to come home instantly, for his mother and he had concluded a suitable match for him with a very beautiful lady. They would not allow Leocadia and her son to return any more to the house of her parents, who, overjoyed at her good fortune, gave thanks for it to Heaven with all their hearts.

The courier arrived at Naples; and Rodolfo, eager to become possessed of so beautiful a wife as his father had described, took advantage of the opportunity offered by four galleys which were ready to sail for Spain; and two days after the receipt of the letter he embarked with his two comrades, who were still with him. After a prosperous run of twelve days, he reached Barcelona, whence he posted in seven to Toledo, and entered his father's house, dressed in the very extreme of fashionable bravery. His parents were beyond measure rejoiced at his safe arrival, after so long an absence; and Leocadia was filled with indescribable emotions, as she beheld him, herself unseen, from a secret place in which she had been stationed by Doña Estafania's contrivance. Rodolfo's two comrades proposed to take leave of him at once, and retire to their own homes; but Estafania would not suffer them to depart, for their presence was needful for the execution of a scheme she had in her head.

It was nearly night when Rodolfo arrived; and whilst preparations were making for supper, Estafania took her son's companions aside, believing that they were two of the three whom Leocadia mentioned as having been with Rodolfo on the night of her abduction. She earnestly entreated them to tell her, if they remembered that her son had carried off a young woman, on such a night, so many years ago; for the honour and the peace of mind of all his relations depended on their knowing the truth of that matter. So persuasive were her entreaties, and so strong her assurances that no harm whatever could result to them from the information she sought, they were induced to confess that one summer's night, the same she had mentioned, themselves and another friend being out on a stroll with Rodolfo, they had been concerned in the abduction of a girl whom Rodolfo carried off, whilst the rest of them detained her family, who made a great outcry, and would have defended her if they could. They added that Rodolfo told them, on the following day, that he had carried the girl to his own apartment; and this was all they knew of the matter.

All doubts which could possibly have remained on the case having been removed by this confession, Estafania determined to pursue her scheme. Shortly before supper she took her son in private into a room, where she put the portrait of a lady into his hands, saying, "Here is something to give you an appetite for your supper, Rodolfo; this is the portrait of your bride; but I must tell you that what she wants in beauty is more than made up for in virtue. She is of good family, and tolerably wealthy; and since your father and I have made choice of her, you may be assured she will suit you very well."

"Well," said Rodolfo, staring at the portrait, "if the painter of this portrait has flattered the original as much as painters usually do, then beyond all doubt the lady must be the very incarnation of ugliness. Truly, my lady mother, if it is just and right that sons should obey their parents in all things, it is no less proper that parents should have regard to the inclinations of their sons; and since matrimony is a bond not to be loosed till death, they ought to take care that it shall press as smoothly and equably as possible. Virtue, good birth, prudence, and the gifts of fortune, are all very good things, and may well gladden the heart of whoever may have the lot to obtain this lady for a wife; but that her ugliness can ever gladden the eyes of her spouse, appears to me an impossibility. I am a bachelor to be sure, but I perfectly comprehend the coincidence there should be between the sacrament of marriage and the just and due delight mutually enjoyed by the married pair, and that if that be wanting, the object of marriage is frustrated; for to imagine that an ugly face which one must have before his eyes at all hours, in the hall, at table, and in bed, I say once more that is impossible. For God's sake, my lady mother, give me a wife who would be an agreeable companion, not one who will disgust me, so that we may both bear evenly, and with mutual good-will, the yoke imposed on us by Heaven, instead of pulling this way and that way, and fretting each other to death. If this lady is well-born, discreet, and rich as you say, she will easily find a husband of a different humour from mine. Some look for noble blood in a wife, some for understanding, others for money, and others again for beauty, and of the latter class I am one. As for high birth, thank Heaven and my ancestors I am well enough off in that respect; as for understanding, provided a woman is neither a dolt nor a simpleton, there is no need of her having a very subtle wit; in point of wealth, I am amply provided by my parents; but beauty is what I covet, with no other addition than virtue and good breeding. If my wife brings me this, I will thank Heaven for the gift, and make my parents happy in their old age."

Estafania was delighted to hear Rodolfo speak thus, for the sentiments he expressed were just such as best accorded with the success of the scheme she had in hand. She told him that she would endeavour to marry him in conformity with his inclination, and that he need not make himself uneasy, for there would be no difficulty in breaking off the match which seemed so distasteful to him. Rodolfo thanked her, and supper being ready they went to join the rest of the party at table. The father and mother, Rodolfo and his two companions had already seated themselves, when Doña Estafania said, in an off-hand way, "Sinner that I am, how well I behave to my guest! Go," she said to a servant, "and ask the señora. Doña Leocadia to honour our table with her presence, and tell her she need not stand on any punctilio, for all here are my sons and her servants." All this was part of her scheme, with the whole of which Leocadia had been previously made acquainted.

The lady soon appeared, presenting a most charming spectacle of perfect beauty, set off by the most appropriate adornments. The season being winter, she was dressed in a robe and train of black velvet, with gold and pearl buttons; her girdle and necklace were of diamonds; her head was uncovered, and the shining braids and ringlets of her thick chestnut hair, spangled with diamonds, dazzled the eyes of the beholders. Her bearing was graceful and animated; she led her son by the hand, and before her walked two maids with wax-lights and silver candlesticks. All rose to do her reverence, as if something from heaven had miraculously appeared before them; but gazing on her, entranced with admiration, not one of them was able to address a single word to her. Leocadia bowed to them all with courteous dignity, and Estafania taking her by the hand led her to a seat next herself and opposite to Rodolfo, whilst the boy was seated beside his grandfather. "Ah," said Rodolfo to himself, as he gazed on the lovely being before him, "could I find but half that beauty in the wife my mother has chosen for me, I should think myself the happiest man in the world. Good God! what is it I behold? Is it some angel in human shape that sits before me?" Whilst his eyes were thus making his soul captive to the lovely image of Leocadia, she, on the other hand, finding herself so near to him who was dearer to her than the light of those eyes with which she furtively glanced at him from time to time, began to revolve in her mind what had passed between her and Rodolfo. The hopes her mother had given her of being his wife began to droop, and the fear came strong upon her that such bliss was not for one so luckless as herself. She reflected how near she stood to the crisis which was to determine whether she was to be blessed or unhappy for ever, and racked by the intensity of her emotions, she suddenly changed colour, her head dropped, and she fell forward in a swoon into the arms of the dismayed Estafania.

The whole party sprang up in alarm and hastened to her assistance, but no one showed more earnest sympathy than Rodolfo, who fell twice in his haste to reach her. They unlaced her, and sprinkled her face with cold water; but far from coming to her senses, the fulness of her congested bosom, her total insensibility, and the absence of all pulse gave such mortal indications, that the servants began imprudently to cry out that she was dead. This shocking news reached the ears of her parents, whom Doña Estafania had concealed in another room that they might make their appearance at the right moment. They now rushed into the supper room, and the parish priest, who was also with them, went up to the prostrate lady to see if she could by any signs make known that she repented of her sins in order that he might give her absolution; but instead of one fainting person he found two, for Rodolfo lay with his face on Leocadia's bosom. His mother had left her to him as being her destined protector; but when she saw that he too was insensible, she was near making a third, and would have done so had he not come to himself. He was greatly confused at finding that he had betrayed such emotion; but his mother, who guessed his thoughts, said to him, "Do not be ashamed, my son, at having been so overcome by your feelings; you would have been so still more had you known what I will no longer conceal from you, though I had intended to reserve it for a more joyful occasion. Know then, son of my heart, that this fainting lady is your real bride: I say real, because she is the one whom your father and I have chosen for you, and the portrait was a pretence."

When Rodolfo heard this, carried away by the vehemence of his passion, and on the strength of his title as a bridegroom disdaining all conventional proprieties, he clasped Leocadia in his arms, and with his lips pressed to hers, seemed as if he was waiting for her soul to issue forth that he might absorb and mingle it with his own. Just at the moment when the tears of the pitying beholders flowed fastest, and their ejaculations were most expressive of despair, Leocadia gave signs of recovery, and brought back gladness to the hearts of all. When she came to her senses, and, blushing to find herself in Rodolfo's arms, would have disengaged herself, "No, señora," he said, "that must not be; strive not to withdraw from the arms of him who holds you in his soul." There needed no more than these words to complete her revival; and Doña Estafania having no further need of stratagem, requested the priest to marry her son to Leocadia on the spot. This was done; for the event took place at a time when the consent of the parties was sufficient for the celebration of a marriage, without any of the preliminary formalities which are now so properly required. I leave it to a more ingenious pen than mine to describe the gladness of all present; the embraces bestowed on Rodolfo by Leocadia's parents; the thanks they offered to Heaven, and to his father and mother; the congratulations on both sides; the astonishment of Rodolfo's companions who saw him so unexpectedly married to so charming a bride on the very night of his arrival; and above all, when they learned from the statement openly made by Doña Estafania, that Leocadia was the very person whose abduction her son had effected with their aid. Nor was Rodolfo less surprised than they; and the better to assure himself of so wonderful a fact, he begged Leocadia to give him some token which should make perfectly clear to him that which indeed he did not doubt, since it was authenticated by his parents.

"Once when I recovered from a swoon," replied Leocadia, "I found myself, señor, in your arms without honour; but for that I have had full compensation, since on my recovery from my this day's swoon I found myself in the same arms, but honoured. If this is not enough for you, let it suffice to mention a crucifix which no one could have purloined from you but myself, if it be true that you missed it in the morning, and that it is the same that is now in the hands of your mother, my lady."

"You are mine, the lady of my soul, and shall be so as long as God grants me life," cried Rodolfo; embracing her again, amidst a fresh shower of benedictions and congratulations from the rest of the party.

At last they sat down to a merry supper to the sound of music, for the performers, who had been previously engaged, were now arrived. Rodolfo saw his own likeness in his son's face as in a mirror. The four grandparents wept for joy: there was not a corner of the house but was full of gladness; and though night was hurrying on with her swift black wings, it seemed to Rodolfo that she did not fly, but hobble on crutches, so great was his impatience to be alone with his beloved bride. The longed-for hour came at last: every one retired to rest: the whole house was buried in silence; but not so shall be the truth of this story, which will be kept alive in the memory of men by the many children and descendants of that illustrious house in Toledo, where that happy pair still live, and have, for many prosperous years, enjoyed the society of each other, their children, and their grandchildren, by the blessing of Heaven, and through the force of that blood which was seen shed on the ground by the valorous, illustrious, and Christian grandfather of the little Luis.

THE JEALOUS ESTRAMADURAN.

Not many years ago there issued from a town in Estramadura a hidalgo nobly born, who, like another prodigal son, went about various parts of Spain, Italy, and Flanders, squandering his years and his wealth. At last, after long peregrinations, his parents being dead and his fortune spent, he made his appearance in the great city of Seville, where he found abundant opportunity to get rid of the little he had left. Finding himself then so bare of money, and not better provided with friends, he adopted the remedy to which many a spendthrift in that city has recourse; that is, to betake themselves to the Indies, the refuge of the despairing sons of Spain, the church of the homeless, the asylum of homicides, the haven of gamblers and cheats, the general receptacle for loose women, the common centre of attraction for many, but effectual resource of very few. A fleet being about to sail for Tierrafirma, he agreed with the admiral for a passage, got ready his sea-stores and his shroud of Spanish grass cloth, and embarking at Cadiz, gave his benediction to Spain, intending never to see it again. The fleet slipped from its moorings, and, amidst the general glee of its living freight, the sails were spread to the soft and prosperous gale, which soon wafted them out of sight of land into the wide domains of the great father of waters, the ocean.

Our passenger now became very thoughtful, revolving in his memory the many and various dangers he had passed in the years of his peregrinations, and the thriftless conduct he had pursued all his life long. The result of the account to which he thus called himself was a firm resolution to change his way of life, to keep a much better hold of whatever wealth God might yet be pleased to bestow upon him, and to behave with more reserve towards women than he had hitherto done.

The fleet was nearly becalmed whilst the mind of Felipe de Carrizales was actuated by these reflections. The wind soon after rose and became so boisterous that Carrizales had enough to do to keep on his legs, and was obliged to leave off his meditations, and concern himself only with the affairs of his voyage. It was so prosperous that they arrived without check or accident at the port of Cartagena. To shorten the introduction of my narrative and avoid all irrelevant matter, I content myself with saying that Felipe was about eight-and-forty years of age when he went to the Indies, and that in the twenty years he remained there he succeeded, by dint of industry and thrift, in amassing more than a hundred and fifty thousand crowns. Seeing himself once more rich and prosperous, he was moved by the natural desire, which all men experience, to return to his native country. Rejecting therefore great opportunities for profit which presented themselves to him, he quitted Peru, where he had amassed his wealth, turned all his money into ingots, and putting it on board a registered ship, to avoid accidents, returned to Spain, landed at San Lucar, and arrived at Seville, loaded alike with years and riches.

Having placed his property in safety, he went in search of his friends, and found they were all dead. He then thought of retiring to his native place, and ending his days there, although he had ascertained that death had not left him one survivor of his kindred; and if, when he went to the Indies poor and needy, he had no rest from the thoughts that distracted him in the midst of the wide ocean, he was now no less assailed by care, but from a different cause. Formerly his poverty would not let him sleep, and now his wealth disturbed his rest; for riches are as heavy a burden to one who is not used to them, or knows not how to employ them, as indigence to one who is continually under its pressure. Money and the want of it alike bring care; but in the one case the acquisition of a moderate quantity affords a remedy; the other case grows worse by further acquisition. Carrizales contemplated his ingots with anxiety, not as a miser, for, during the few years he had been a soldier, he had learned to be liberal; but from not knowing what to do with them; for to hoard them was unprofitable, and keeping them in his house was offering a temptation to thieves. On the other hand, all inclination for resuming the anxious life of traffic had died out in him, and at his time of life his actual wealth was more than enough for the rest of his days. He would fain have spent them in his native place, put out his money there to interest, and passed his old age in peace and quiet, giving what he could to God, since he had given more than he ought to the world. He considered, however, that the penury of his native place was great, the inhabitants very needy, and that to go and live there would be to offer himself as a mark for all the importunities with which the poor usually harass a rich neighbour, especially when there is only one in the place to whom they can have recourse in their distress.

He wanted some one to whom he might leave his property after his death, and with that view, taking measure of the vigour of his constitution, he concluded that he was not yet too old to bear the burthen of matrimony. But immediately on conceiving this notion, he was seized with such a terrible fear as scattered it like a mist before the wind. He was naturally the most jealous man in the world, even without being married, and the mere thought of taking a wife called up such horrible spectres before his imagination that he resolved by all means to remain a bachelor.

That point was settled; but it was not yet settled what he should do with the rest of his life, when it chanced that, passing one day through a street, he looked up and saw at a window a young girl apparently about thirteen or fourteen, with a face so very handsome and so very pleasing in its expression, that poor old Carrizales was vanquished at once, and surrendered without an effort to the charms of the beautiful Leonora, for that was the girl's name. Without more ado, he began to string together a long train of arguments to the following effect:—"This girl is very handsome, and to judge from the appearance of the house, her parents cannot be rich. She is almost a child too; assuredly a wife of her age could not give a husband any uneasiness. Let me see: say that I marry her; I will keep her close at home, I will train her up to my own hand, and so fashion her to my wishes that she will never have a thought beyond them. I am not so old but that I may yet hope to have children to inherit my wealth. Whether she brings me any dower or not is a matter of no consideration, since Heaven has given me enough for both, and rich people should not look for money with a wife, but for enjoyment, for that prolongs life, whereas jarring discontent between married people makes it wear out faster than it would do otherwise. So be it then, the die is cast, and this is the wife whom heaven destines me to have."

Having thus soliloquised, not once but a hundred times on that day, and the two or three following, Carrizales had an interview with Leonora's parents, and found that, although poor, they were persons of good birth. He made known his intention to them, acquainted them with his condition and fortune, and begged them very earnestly to bestow their daughter upon him in marriage. They required time to consider his proposal, and to give him also an opportunity to satisfy himself that their birth and quality was such as they had stated.

The parties took leave of each other, made the necessary inquiries, found them satisfactory on both sides, and finally Leonora was betrothed to Carrizales, who settled upon her twenty thousand ducats, so hotly enamoured was the jealous old bridegroom. But no sooner had he pronounced the conjugal "yes," than he was all at once assailed by a host of rabid fancies; he began to tremble without cause and to find his cares and anxieties come thicker and faster upon him than ever. The first proof he gave of his jealous temper was, in resolving that no tailor should take measure of his betrothed for any of the many wedding garments he intended to present her. Accordingly, he went about looking for some other woman, who might be nearly of the same height and figure as Leonora. He found a poor woman, who seemed suitable for his purpose, and having had a gown made to her measure, he tried it on his betrothed, found that it fitted well, and gave orders that it should serve as a pattern for all the other dresses, which were so many and so rich that the bride's parents thought themselves fortunate beyond measure, in having obtained for themselves and their daughter a son-in-law and a husband so nobly munificent. As for Leonora, she was at her wit's end with amazement at the sight of such gorgeous finery, for the best she had ever worn in her life had been but a serge petticoat and a silk jacket.

The second proof of jealousy given by Felipe was, that he would not consummate his marriage until he had provided a house after his own fancy, which he arranged in this singular manner. He bought one for twelve thousand ducats, in one of the best wards of the city, with a fountain and pond, and a garden well stocked with orange trees. He put screens before all the windows that looked towards the street, leaving them no other prospect than the sky, and did much the same with all the others in the house. In the gateway next the street, he erected a stable for a mule, and over it a straw loft, and a room for an old black eunuch, who was to take care of the mule. He raised the parapets round the flat roof of the house so high, that nothing could be seen above them but the sky, and that only by turning one's face upwards. In the inner door, opening from the gateway upon the quadrangle, he fixed a turning box like that of a convent, by means of which articles were to be received from without. He furnished the house in a sumptuous style, such as would have become the mansion of a great lord; and he bought four white slave girls, whom he branded in the face, and two negresses. For the daily supplies of his establishment he engaged a purveyor, who was to make all the necessary purchases, but was not to sleep in the house or ever enter it further than to the second door, where he was to deposit what he had brought in the turning box. Having made these arrangements, Carrizales invested part of his money in sundry good securities; part he placed in the bank, and the rest he kept by him to meet any emergencies that might arise. He also had a master key made for his whole house; and he laid up a whole year's store of all such things as it is usual to purchase in bulk at their respective seasons; and everything being now ready to his mind, he went to his father-in-law's house and claimed his bride, whom her parents delivered up to him with no few tears, for it seemed to them as if they were giving her up for burial.

Leonora knew not, poor young creature, what was before her, but she shed tears because she saw her parents weep, and taking leave of them with their blessing, she went to her new home, her husband leading her by the hand, and her slaves and servants attending her. On their arrival Carrizales harangued all his domestics, enjoining them to keep careful watch over Leonora, and by no means, on any pretence whatsoever, to allow anybody to enter within the second gate, not even the black eunuch. But the person whom above all others he charged with the safe keeping and due entertainment of his wife was a dueña of much prudence and gravity, whom he had taken to be Leonora's monitress, and superintendent of the whole house, and to command the slaves and two other maidens of Leonora's age whom he had also added to his family, that his wife might not be without companions of her own years. He promised them all that he would treat them so well, and take such care for their comfort and gratification, that they should not feel their confinement, and that on holidays they should every one of them without exception be allowed to go to mass; but so early in the morning that daylight itself should scarcely have a chance of seeing them. The servant maids and the slaves promised to obey all his orders cheerfully and with prompt alacrity and the bride, with a timid shrinking of her shoulders, bowed her head, and said that she had no other will than that of her lord and spouse, to whom she always owed obedience.

Having thus laid down the law for the government of his household, the worthy Estramaduran began to enjoy, as well as he could, the fruits of matrimony, which, to Leonora's inexperienced taste, were neither sweet-flavoured nor insipid. Her days were spent with her dueña, her damsels, and her slaves, who, to make the time pass more agreeably, took to pampering their palates, and few days passed in which they did not make lots of things in which they consumed a great deal of honey and sugar. Their master gladly supplied them with all they could wish for in that way without stint, for by that means he expected to keep them occupied and amused, so that they should have no time to think of their confinement and seclusion. Leonora lived on a footing of equality with her domestics, amused herself as they did, and even in her simplicity took pleasure in dressing dolls and other childish pastime. All this afforded infinite satisfaction to the jealous husband; it seemed to him that he had chosen the best way of life imaginable, and that it was not within the compass of human art or malice to trouble his repose: accordingly his whole care was devoted to anticipating his wife's wishes by all sorts of presents, and encouraging her to ask for whatever came into her head, for in everything it should be his pleasure to gratify her.

On the days she went to mass, which as we have said was before daylight, her parents attended at church and talked with their daughter in presence of her husband, who made them such liberal gifts as mitigated the keenness of their compassion for the secluded life led by their daughter. Carrizales used to get up in the morning and watch for the arrival of the purveyor, who was always made aware of what was wanted for the day by means of a note placed over-night in the turning box. After the purveyor had come and gone, Carrizales used to go abroad, generally on foot, locking both entrance doors behind him—that next the street, and that which opened on the quadrangle,—and leaving the negro shut up between them. Having despatched his business, which was not much, he speedily returned, shut himself up in his house, and occupied himself in making much of his wife and her handmaids, who all liked him for his placid and agreeable humour, and above all for his great liberality towards them. In this way they passed a year of novitiate, and made profession of that manner of life, resolved every one of them to continue in it to the end of their days; and so it would have been, if the crafty perturber of the human race had not brought their chaste purposes to nought, as you shall presently hear.

Now, I ask the most long-headed and wary of my readers, what more could old Felipe have done in the way of taking precautions for his security, since he would not even allow that there should be any male animal within his dwelling? No tom-cat ever persecuted its rats, nor was the barking of a dog ever heard within its walls; all creatures belonging to it were of the feminine gender. He took thought by day, and by night he did not sleep; he was himself the patrol and sentinel of his house, and the Argus of what he held dear. Never did a man set foot within the quadrangle; he transacted his business with his friends in the street; the pictures that adorned his rooms were all female figures, flowers, or landscapes; his whole dwelling breathed an odour of propriety, seclusion, and circumspection; the very tales which the maid servants told by the fireside in the long winter nights, being told in his presence, were perfectly free from the least tinge of wantonness. Her aged spouse's silver hairs seemed in Leonora's eyes locks of pure gold; for the first love known by maidens imprints itself on their hearts like a seal on melted wax. His inordinate watchfulness seemed to her no more than the due caution of an experienced and judicious man. She was fully persuaded that the life she led was the same as that led by all married women. Her thoughts never wandered beyond the walls of her dwelling, nor had she a wish that was not the same as her husband's. It was only on the days she went to mass that she set eyes on the streets, and that was so early in the morning, that except on the way home she had not light to look about her. Never was there seen a convent more closely barred and bolted; never were nuns kept more recluse, or golden apples better guarded; and yet for all his precautions poor Felipe could not help falling into the pit he dreaded,—or at least believing that he had so fallen.

There is in Seville an idle pleasure-seeking class of people who are commonly called men on town,[80] a sauntering, sprucely dressed, mellifluous race, always finding means to make, themselves welcome at rich men's feasts. Of these people, their manners and customs, and the laws they observe among themselves, I should have much to say, but abstain from it for good reasons. One of these gallants, a bachelor,—or a virote, as such persons are called in their jargon, the newly married being styled matones,—took notice of the house of Carrizales, and seeing it always shut close, he was curious to know who lived there. He set about this inquiry with such ardour and ingenuity, that he failed not to obtain all the information he desired. He learned the character and habits of the old man, the beauty of Leonora, and the singular method adopted by her husband in order to keep her safe. All this inflamed him with desire to see if it would not be possible, by force or stratagem, to effect the reduction of so well-guarded a fortress. He imparted his thoughts to three of his friends, and they all agreed that he should go to work, for in such an enterprise no one lacks counsellors to aid and abet him. At first they were at a loss how to set about so difficult an exploit; but after many consultations they agreed upon the following plan:—Loaysa (so the virote was named) disappeared from among his friends, giving out that he was leaving Seville for some time. Then drawing on a pair of linen drawers and a clean shirt, he put over them a suit of clothes so torn and patched, that the poorest beggar in the city would have disdained to wear such rags. He shaved off the little beard he had, covered one of his eyes with a plaster, tied up one of his legs, and hobbling along on two crutches, appeared so completely metamorphosed into a lame beggar, that no real cripple could have looked less of a counterfeit than he.

In this guise he posted himself closely at the hour of evening prayer before the door of Carrizales' house, which was fast shut, and Luis the negro locked up between the two doors. Having taken up his position there, Loaysa produced a greasy guitar, wanting some of its strings, and as he was something of a musician, he began to play a few lovely airs, and to sing Moorish ballads in a feigned voice, with so much expression that all who were passing through the street stopped to listen. The boys all made a ring round him when he sang, and Luis the negro, enchanted by the virote's music, would have given one of his hands to be able to open the door, and listen to him more at his ease, such is the fondness for music inherent in the negro race. When Loaysa wanted to get rid of his audience, he had only to cease singing, put up his guitar, and hobble away on his crutches.

Loaysa four or five times repeated this serenade to the negro, for whose sake alone he played and sang, thinking that the way to succeed in his sap and siege was to begin by making sure of old Luis; nor was his expectation disappointed. One night when he had taken his place as usual before the door, and had begun to time his guitar, perceiving that the negro was already on the alert, he put his lips to the key-hole and whispered, "Can you give me a drop of water, Luis? I am dying with thirst, and can't sing."

"No," said the negro, "for I have not the key of this door, and there is no hole through which I can give you drink."

"Who keeps the key, then?"

"My master, who is the most jealous man in the world; and if he knew that I was now talking here with any one, it were pity of my life. But who are you who ask me for water?"

"I am a poor cripple, who get my bread by asking alms of all good people in God's name; besides which I teach the guitar to some moriscoes, and other poor people. Among my pupils I have three negroes, slaves to three aldermen, whom I have taught so well that they are fit to sing and play at dance or in any tavern, and they have paid me for it very well indeed."

"A deal better would I pay you to have the opportunity of taking lessons; but it is not possible, for when my master goes out in the morning he locks the door behind him, and he does the same when he comes in, leaving me shut up between two doors."

"I vow to God, Luis, if you would only contrive to let me in a few nights to give you lessons, in less than a fortnight I would make you such a dabster at the guitar, that you need not be ashamed to play at any street corner; for I would have you to know that I have an extraordinary knack in teaching; moreover, I have heard tell that you have a very promising capacity, and from what I can judge from the tone of your voice, you must sing very well."

"I don't sing; badly; but what good is that since I don't know any tunes, except the 'Star of Venus,' or, 'In the green meadow,' or the tune that is now so much in vogue, 'Clinging to her grated window, with a trembling hand?'"

"All these are moonshine to what I could teach you, for I know all the ballads of the Moor Abendaraez, with those of his lady Xarifa, and all those comprising the history of the grand sofi Tomunibeyo, and the divine sarabands which enchant the souls of the Portuguese themselves, among whom they are most in vogue; and all these I teach by such methods and with such facility, that almost before you have swallowed three or four bushels of salt, you will find yourself an out-and-out performer in every kind of guitar music."

"What's the good of all that," (here the negro sighed heavily,) "since I can't get you into the house?"

"There's a remedy for all things: contrive to take the keys from your master, and I will give you a piece of wax, with which you may take an impression of the wards, for I have taken such a liking to you, I will get a locksmith, a friend of mine, to make new keys, and then I can come in at night and teach you to play better than Prester John in the Indies. It is a thousand pities that a voice like yours should be lost for want of the accompaniment of the guitar; for I would have you to know, brother Luis, that the finest voice in the world loses its perfection when it is not accompanied by some instrument, be it guitar or harpsichord, organ or harp; but the instrument that will suit your voice best is the guitar, because it is the handiest and the least costly of all."

"All that is very good; but the thing can't be done, for I never get hold of the keys, nor does my master ever let them out of his keeping; day and night they sleep under his pillow."

"Well, then, there's another thing you may do, if so be you have made up a mind to be a first-rate musician; if you haven't, I need not bother myself with advising you."

"Have a mind, do you say? Ay, and to that degree that there is nothing I wouldn't do, if it were possible anyhow, for sake of being able to play music."

"Well, if that's the case, you have only to scrape away a little mortar from the gate-post near the hinge, and I will give you, through that opening, a pair of pincers and a hammer, with which you may by night draw out the nails of the staple, and we can easily put that to rights again, so that no one will ever suspect that the lock was opened. Once shut up with you in your loft, or wherever you sleep, I will go to work in such style that you will turn out even better than I said, to my own personal advantage, and to the increase of your accomplishments. You need not give yourself any concern about what we shall have to eat. I will bring enough to last us both for more than a week, for I have pupils who will not let me be pinched."

"As for that matter we are all right; for with what my master allows me, and the leavings brought me by the slave-girls, we should have enough for two more besides ourselves. Only bring the hammer and pincers, and I will make an opening close to the hinge, through which you may pass them in, and I will stop it up again with mud. I will take the fastenings out of the lock, and even should it be necessary to give some loud knocks, my master sleeps so far off from this gate, that it must be either a miracle or our extraordinary ill luck if he hears them."

"Well, then, with the blessing of God, friend Luis, in two days from this time you shall have everything necessary for the execution of your laudable purpose. Meanwhile, take care not to eat such things as are apt to make phlegm, for they do the voice no good, but a deal of harm."

"Nothing makes me so hoarse so much as wine, but I would not give it up for all the voices above ground."

"Don't think I would have you do so; God forbid! Drink, Luis my boy, drink; and much good may it do you, for wine drunk in measure never did any one harm."

"I always drink in measure. I have a jug here that holds exactly three pints and a half. The girls fill this for me unknown to my master, and the purveyor brings me on the sly a bottle holding a good gallon, which makes up for the deficiency of the jug."

"That's the way to live, my boy, for a dry throat can neither grunt nor sing."

"Well, go your ways now, and God be with you; but don't forget to come and sing here every night until such time as you bring the tools for getting you within doors. My fingers itch to be at the guitar."

"I'll come, never fear, and I'll bring some new tunes too."

"Ay, do; but before you go away now, sing me something that I may go to sleep pleasantly; and for the matter of payment, be it known to the señor pobre that I will be more liberal than many a rich man."

"Oh, I ain't uneasy on that score. If you think I teach you well, I will leave it to yourself to pay me accordingly. And now I'll just sing you one song, but when I am inside you will see wonders."

Here ended this long dialogue, and Loaysa sang a sprightly ditty with such good effect, that the negro was in ecstacies, and felt as if the time for opening the door would never arrive.

Having finished his song, Loaysa took his departure, and set off at a rounder pace than might have been expected of a man on crutches, to report to his friends what a good beginning he had made. He told them what he had concerted with the negro, and the following day they procured tools of the right sort, fit to break any fastening as if it was made of straw. The virote failed not to serenade the negro, nor the latter to scrape at the gate-post till he had made a sufficiently wide hole, which he plastered up so well, that no one could perceive it unless he searched for it on purpose. On the second night Loaysa passed in the tools, Luis went to work with them, whipped off the staple in a trice, opened the door, and let in his Orpheus. Great was his surprise to see him on his two crutches, with such a distorted leg, and in such a tattered plight. Loaysa did not wear the patch over his eye, for it was not necessary, and as soon as he entered he embraced his pupil, kissed him on the cheek, and immediately put into his hand a big jar of wine, a box of preserves, and other sweet things, with which his wallet was well stored. Then throwing aside his crutches, he began to cut capers, as if nothing ailed him, to the still greater amazement of the negro.

"You must know, brother Luis," said Loaysa, "that my lameness does not come of natural infirmity, but from my own ingenious contrivance, whereby I get my bread, asking alms for the love of God. In this way, and with the help of my music, I lead the merriest life in the world, where others, with less cleverness and good management, would be starved to death. Of this you will be convinced in the course of our friendship."

"We shall see," said the negro; "but now let us put this staple back in its place, so that it may not appear that it has been moved."

"Very good," said Loaysa, and taking out some nails from his wallet, he soon made the lock seem as secure as ever, to the great satisfaction of the negro, who, taking him at once to his loft, made him as comfortable there as he could. Luis lighted a lamp; Loaysa took up his guitar, and began to strike the chords softly and sweetly, so that the poor negro was transported with delight. After he had played awhile, he drew forth a fresh supply of good things for a collation, which they partook of together, and the pupil applied himself so earnestly to the bottle that it took away his senses still more than the music had done. Supper over, Loaysa proposed that Luis should take his first lesson at once; and though the poor negro was too much fuddled to distinguish one string from another, Loaysa made him believe that he had already learnt at least two notes. So persuaded was the poor fellow of this, that he did nothing all night but jangle and strum away. They had but a short sleep that night. In the morning, just on the strike of six, Carrizales came down, opened both entrance doors, and stood waiting for the purveyor, who came soon afterwards; and after depositing the day's supplies in the turning-box, called the negro down to receive his ration and oats for the mule. After the purveyor was gone, old Carrizales went out, locking both doors after him, without having seen what had been done to the lock of one of them, whereat both master and pupil rejoiced not a little.

No sooner was the master of the house gone, than the negro laid hold on the guitar, and began to scrape it in such a manner, that all the servant maids came to the second door, and asked him, through the turning-box, "What is this, Luis? How long have you had a guitar? Who gave it you?"

"Who gave it me? The best musician in the world, and one who is to teach me in six days more than six thousand tunes!"

"Where is he, this musician?" said the dueña.

"He is not far off," replied the negro; "and if it were not for fear of my master, perhaps I would tell you where at once, and I warrant you would be glad to see him."

"But where can he be for us to see him," returned the dueña, "since no one but our master ever enters this house?"

"I will not tell you any more about the matter till you have heard what I can do, and how much he has taught me in this short time."

"By my troth, unless he is a demon who has taught you, I don't know how you can have become a musician all at once."

"Stop a bit and you shall hear him, and mayhap you will see him too some day."

"That can't be," said another of the women, "for there are no windows on the street through which we could hear or see anybody."

"Never mind" said the negro; "there's a remedy for everything but death. If you only could or would keep silence—"

"Keep silence! Ay that we will, brother Luis, as if we were born dumb. I give you my word, friend, I am dying to hear a good voice, for ever since we have been shut up here we have not even heard the birds sing."

Loaysa listened with great inward glee to this conversation, which showed how readily the women were taking the very bent he would have given them. The negro was afraid lest his master should return and catch him talking with them; but they would not go away until he had promised that, when they least expected it, he would call them to hear a capital voice. He then retreated to his loft, where he would gladly have resumed his lessons, but durst not do so by day for fear of detection. His master returned soon after and went into the house, locking both doors behind him as usual. When Luis went that day to the turning-box for his victuals, he told the negress, who brought them, to let her fellow-servants know that when their master was asleep that night, they should all of them come down to the turning-box, when he would be sure to give them the treat he had promised. He was enabled to say so much, having previously entreated his music-master to condescend to sing and play that night before the inner door for the amusement of the women. The maestro suffered himself to be pressed very hard to do the thing he most desired, but after much seeming reluctance he at last yielded to the solicitations of his esteemed pupil, and said he would be happy to oblige him. The negro embraced him cordially, in testimony of his grateful sense of the promised favour, and treated him that day to as good cheer as he could possibly have had at home, or perhaps better.

Towards midnight Luis knew, by the signals cautiously given at the turning-box, that the women were all there; whereupon he and Loaysa went down from the loft with the guitar, complete in all its strings and well tuned. The maestro asked how many were there to hear him, and was told that all the women in the house were there, except their lady, who was in bed with her husband. This was not what Loaysa wished for, nevertheless, by way of making a beginning and obliging his pupil, he touched the guitar softly, and drew from it such tones as ravished the ears of his audience. But who could describe the delight of the women when he sang Pesame de ello, and followed it up with the magic strains of the saraband, then new in Spain? There was not one of them that did not keep time to the music as if she were dancing like mad, but all noiselessly and with extreme caution, keeping scouts on the watch to warn them if the old man awoke. Loaysa finally played them several seguidillas, and so put the climax to his success, that they all eagerly begged the negro to tell them who was this marvellous musician. Luis replied that he was a poor beggar, but the most gallant and genteel man in all the back slums of Seville. They conjured the negro to contrive some means that they might see him, and not to let him quit the house for a fortnight, for they would take care to supply him with the best of good cheer, and plenty of it. They were curious to know how Luis had managed to get him into the house; but to this the negro made no reply. For the rest he told them that if they wanted to see the maestro, they might bore a small hole in the turning-box and afterwards stop it up with wax; and that as for keeping him in the house, he would do his best.

Loaysa then addressed them, and offered them his services in such obliging and polite terms, that they were sure such fine language never came out of the head of a poor beggar. They entreated he would come the next night, and they would prevail on their lady to come down and hear him, in spite of the light sleep of her lord and master—the result not so much of his age as of his extreme jealousy. Loaysa replied that if they wished to hear him without fear of being surprised by the old man, he would give them a powder to put in his wine, which would make him sleep more soundly. "Good heaven!" cried one of the damsels, "if that were true, what a blessing would have come home to us without our knowing or deserving it! It would not be a sleeping powder for him so much as it would be a powder of life for all of us, and for my poor dear lady, Leonora his wife, to whom he sticks as close as her shadow, never losing sight of her for a moment. Ah, señor of my soul! bring that powder, and may God reward you with all the good you can desire. Go! don't lose a moment—bring it, señor mio; I will take it upon me to put it in his wine and to be his cupbearer. Oh, that it might please God that the old man should sleep three days and nights! Three glorious days and nights they would be for us."

"Well, I'll bring it then," said Loaysa. "It is of such a nature that it does no harm to the person who takes it; the only effect of it being to cause a most profound sleep."

They all entreated him to bring it without delay, and then they took their leave of him, after agreeing that on the following night they would make a hole in the turning-box with a gimlet, and that they would try and persuade their mistress to come down. By this time it was nearly daylight, yet the negro wished to take a lesson. Loaysa complied with his desire, and assured him that among all the pupils he had ever taught, he had not known one with a finer ear; and yet the poor negro could never, to the end of his days, have learned the gamut.

Loaysa's friends took care to come at night to Carrizales' door to see if their friend had any instructions to give them, or wanted anything. On the second night, when they had made him aware of their presence by a preconcerted signal, he gave them, through the key-hole, a brief account of the prosperous beginning he had made, and begged they would try and get him something to be given to Carrizales to make him sleep. He had heard, he said, that there were powders which produced that effect. They told him they had a friend, a physician, who would give them the best drug for that purpose if he happened to have it; and after encouraging him to persist in the enterprise, and promising to return on the following night, they left him.

Presently the whole flock of doves came to the lure of the guitar, and among them was the simple Leonora, trembling for fear her husband should awake. So great was her dread of his discovering her absence, that her women had great difficulty in persuading her to make the hazardous venture. But they all, especially the dueña, told her such wonderful things of the sweetness of the music, and the engaging manners of the poor musician, whom, without having seen him, they extolled above Absalom and Orpheus, that they persuaded her to do what she would never have done of her own accord. Their first act was to bore a hole in the turning-box through which they might peep at the musician, who was no longer clad in rags, but in wide breeches of buff silk, cut sailor fashion, a jacket of the same material, a satin cap to match, and a starched double-pointed ruff, all which he had brought in his wallet, expecting that he would have to show himself on an occasion which would require him to change his costume. Loaysa was young, good-looking, and of pleasing deportment; and as the eyes of all the women had been so long accustomed only to the sight of old Carrizales, they fancied as they looked at Loaysa that they beheld an angel.

Each of them took her turn at the peephole, and that they might see him the better, the negro stood by him with a lighted flambeau, which he moved up and down before the maestro's body. After all the women, from the lady of the house down to the two negresses, had thus gratified their eyes, Loaysa took his guitar, and played and sang more bewitchingly than ever. Leonora's women were bewildered with delight, and all besought Luis to contrive so that the señor maestro should come in through the inner door, so that they might hear and see him better, instead of squinting at him through a gimlet-hole, and without the risk they ran of being caught in the fact by their master, which would not be so great if they had the musician concealed inside. Their lady strenuously opposed this proposition, declaring she would not permit any such thing. She was shocked to hear them mention it, for they could hear and see him well enough as it was, without danger to their honour. "Honour," exclaimed the dueña; "the king has plenty. Your ladyship may shut yourself up with your Methusalem, if you have a mind, but leave us to amuse ourselves as well as we can; the more so since this señor appears to be too much the gentleman to ask anything of us but what would be pleasing to ourselves."

"Never!" interposed Loaysa. "I came hither, ladies, with no other intention than to offer you my humble services, with all my heart and soul, moved by commiseration for the unparalleled rigour of your confinement, and for the precious moments that are lost to you through this recluse way of life. By the life of my father, I am a man so artless, so meek, so tractable and obedient, that I will never do more than I am bidden. If any one of you should please to say, 'Maestro, sit down here; Maestro, step this way, step that way, go yonder,' I will do just as you bid me, like the tamest and best trained dog that jumps for the king of France."

"Well, if that be so," said the inexperienced Leonora, "what is to be done, so that the señor maestro may come in?"

"Nothing can be easier," said Loaysa. "So please you, ladies, just take the trouble to make an impression on wax with the key of this door; and I will take care that by to-morrow night another shall be made exactly like it, which will answer our purpose."

"With that key," one of the women remarked, "we shall have those of the whole house, for it is a master-key."

"So much the better," said Loaysa.

"That is true," said Leonora; "but this señor must first of all swear, that when he is inside here he will not attempt to do anything but sing and play when he is asked, and that he will keep close and quiet wherever we may put him."

"I swear to this," said Loaysa.

"That oath is good for nothing," replied Leonora: "the señor must swear by the life of his father, and by the cross, which he must kiss in sight of us all."

"I swear by the life of my father," said Loaysa, "and by this sign of the cross, which I kiss with my unworthy mouth;" and crossing two of his fingers, he kissed them three times.

"That will do," said one of the women; "and now, señor, be sure you don't forget the powder, for that is the main thing of all."

Here the conversation ended for that night, and all parties retired highly satisfied with the interview. Good luck had evidently declared in favour of Loaysa; and just then, about two o'clock in the morning, it brought his friends to the door. On their giving the usual signal by blowing a French horn, he went to the door, told them what progress he had made, and asked had they brought the powder or other drug to put Carrizales to sleep. At the same time, he spoke to them respecting the master-key. They told him that on the following night they would bring the powder, or else an ointment of such virtue that one had only to rub the patient's wrists and temples with it to throw him into such a profound sleep, that he would not wake for two days, unless the anointed parts were well washed with vinegar. As to the key, he had only to give them the impression in wax, and they would have a false one made forthwith. Having said this, the friends retired, and Loaysa and his pupil went to rest for the short remainder of the night. The next day hung heavily on hand, as always happens to those who are filled with eager expectation; but the longest day must have an end, and Loaysa's impatient desire was at last gratified.

The appointed hour having arrived, all the domestics, great and small, black and white, repaired to the turning-box, longing to see the señor musico fairly within their seraglio; but no Leonora was there. When Loaysa inquired for her, they said she was in bed with her good man, who had locked the bedroom door, and put the key under his pillow; and that their lady had told them, that when the old man had fallen asleep she would take the key, and they were to go to her by and by for the wax impression she would take from it, and pass to them through a trap-hole in the door. Loaysa was astonished at the old man's extreme wariness, in spite of which he by no means despaired of baffling his precautions. Just then the French horn was heard: Loaysa hastened to the door, and received from his friends a pot containing the promised ointment. Bidding them wait awhile, and he would bring them the mould of the key, he went back to the turning-box, and told the dueña, who seemed the most eager of all the women for his admission, to give the ointment to her lady, bid her anoint her husband with it so cautiously that he should not be aware of what she was doing, and she would soon see wonders. The dueña took the pot, stole up to her mistress's door, and found her waiting on the inside, stretched full length on the floor, with her face to the trap-hole. The dueña laid herself down in the same manner, and putting her mouth to her mistress's ear, whispered that she had brought the ointment, telling her at the same time how to apply it. Leonora took the ointment, but told the dueña that she could by no means get the key, for her husband had not put it under the pillow as usual, but between the mattresses, just under where he lay. However, she was to tell the maestro, that if the ointment operated as he said, she could easily get the key as often as she pleased, and so there would be no need of copying it in wax. Having delivered this message at once, the dueña was to come back, and see how the ointment worked, for she intended to apply it forthwith. The dueña having reported all this to Loaysa, he sent away his friends who were waiting without for the mould of the key.

Trembling in every limb, and scarcely daring to breathe, Leonora began to rub the wrists of her jealous husband. Next she smeared his nostrils; but as she did so, the old man jerked his head, and Leonora was petrified with terror, believing that he was awake, and had caught her in the fact. It was a false alarm, however, and she went on with her task the best way she could, till she had completed it according to her instructions. It was not long before its effects manifested themselves; for presently the old man began to snore loud enough to be heard in the street. This was music more delightful to Leonora's ears than the maestro's voice or guitar; but still hardly trusting what she saw, she ventured to shake him, a very little at first, to see if he would wake; and then a wee bit more and more, till finding that he still snored on, she made bold to turn him over from one side to the other, without his showing any signs of waking. Seeing this, she stepped joyfully to the door; and in a voice not so low as before, called out to the dueña, who was waiting with her ear to the trap-hole. "Good news, sister; Carrizales is sleeping more soundly than the dead."

"What stops you then from taking the key, señora?" said the dueña. "The musico has been waiting for it this hour and more."

"Stay a moment, sister; I am going for it," said Leonora; and stepping back to the bed, she put her hand between the mattresses, and drew out the key without the old man's perceiving it. No sooner was the key in her hands, than dancing with delight she unlocked the door, and gave it to the exulting dueña, bidding her let in the maestro, and bring him into the gallery; but as for herself, she durst not stir from that spot, for fear of what might happen. But before all things she insisted that the maestro should ratify anew the oath he had taken not to do more than they should order him; and if he would not give this renewed pledge, he was not to be let in on any consideration.

"Never fear," said the dueña; "not a bit shall he come in until he has sworn, and sworn again, and kissed the cross at least six times."

"Don't bind him to any fixed number," said Leonora; "but let him kiss the cross as many times as he pleases; but be sure that he swears by the life of his father, and by all he holds dear; for then we shall be safe and sure, and we may take our fill of hearing him sing and play; and exquisitely he does so, upon my word. There now, get you gone without more delay, and let us not waste the night in words."

The good dueña caught up her petticoats, and ran with all her speed to the turning-box, where the whole party was impatiently awaiting her; and no sooner had she shown them the key in her hand, than they hoisted her upon their shoulders, and paraded up and down with her, crying "Viva! viva!" But still greater was their joy when she told them there was no need to have a false key made; for so soundly did the old man sleep after being anointed, that they might have the house-key as often as they required it.

"Quick then, good friend," said one of the troop, "open the door, and let in this gentleman who has been waiting so long, and let us have a jolly bout of music, for that is all we have now to do."

"Nay, but there is more to be done," replied the dueña; "for we must exact another oath of him; the same as last night."

"He is so good," said one of the slave girls, "that he won't grudge taking as many oaths as we like."

The dueña now unlocked the door, and holding it ajar called to Loaysa, who had been listening at the aperture to all that had passed. He was for springing in at a bound; but the dueña stopped him, laying her hand on his breast, and said, "Fair and softly, señor; I would have you to know, as God is my judge, we are all of us virgins here as truly as the mothers that bore us, except my lady; and I am one too, the Lord forgive me, though you would take me for forty years old; but I am not thirty all out, wanting two months and a fortnight of my thirtieth birthday; and if I look older, it is that cares, and troubles, and vexations tell upon one more than years. Now this being so, it does not stand to reason, that for the sake of hearing two or three songs we should risk the loss of so much virginity as is here collected together. And so you see, my sweet sir, before you enter our domain, you must first take a very solemn oath, that you will do nothing beyond our orders. If you think it is much we ask of you, do but consider how much more it is we risk; and if your intentions are good and proper, you will not be loth to swear; for a good paymaster does not mind giving security."

"Well said, Marialonso," cried one of the damsels; "spoken like a person of sense, and who knows what's what. If the señor won't swear, then let him not come in here."

"Tell you what," said Guiomar, the negress, in her broken jargon, "s'ppose him no swear, let him in all the same, in devil's name; for s'ppose him swear, once him in, him forget eberyting."

Loaysa listened very demurely to the Señora Marialonso's harangue, and replied with great gravity, "Be assured, ladies, my charming sisters and companions, my intention never was, is, or shall be other than to gratify and content you to the utmost of my powers; and therefore I make no difficulty with regard to this oath which is required of me, though I could have wished that some confidence had been reposed in my simple word, which, given by such a person as I am, would have been as good as a bond signed and sealed; for I would have you to know, ladies, that under a bad cloak there is often a good drinker. But to the end that you may all be assured of my upright intentions, I will take the oath as a catholic and a man of parts. I swear then by the immaculate efficacy, wherever it abides in greatest sanctity and fulness, by all the entrances and exits of the holy mount Libanus, and by all that is contained in the preface to the true history of Charlemagne, with the death of the giant Fierabras, not to swerve or depart from the oath I have taken, or from the commands which may be laid upon me by the least of these ladies, under penalty, should I do otherwise, or attempt to do otherwise, that from this time forth till then, and from thenceforth till now, the same shall be null and void and of no effect whatsoever."

When honest Loaysa had got so far in his oath, one of the young maidens, who had listened to him with wrapt attention, cried out, "Well, if that is not what you may call an oath! it is enough to melt the heart of a stone. Plague take me if you shall swear any more for me; for after such an oath as that you might enter the very cave of Cabra." So saying, she caught hold of him by the breeches, and drew him within the door, where the rest immediately gathered close round him. One of them ran off with the news to her mistress, who stood watching her husband; and who, when she heard that the musico was actually within doors, was moved almost at the same moment by joy and fear, and hurriedly asked if he had sworn. The girl told her he had done so, and with the most singular form of oath she had ever heard in her life.

"Well, since he has sworn, we have him fast," said Leonora. "Oh, what a good thought it was of mine to make him swear!"

They were now met by the whole party advancing in procession, with the musico in the midst of them, and the negro and Guiomar lighting the way. As soon as Loaysa saw Leonora, he threw himself at her feet to kiss her hands; but without saying a word, she made signs to him to rise, and he obeyed. Observing then that they all remained as mute as if they had lost their tongues, Loaysa told them they might talk, and talk aloud too; for there was no fear that their lord-master would wake and hear them, such being the virtue of the ointment, that without endangering life it made a man lie like one dead.

"That I fully believe," said Leonora; "for were it not so, he would have been awake twenty times before this, such a light sleeper he is, in consequence of his frequent indispositions; but ever since I anointed him, he has been snoring like a pig."

"That being the case," said the dueña, "let us go into the saloon, where we may hear the gentleman sing, and amuse ourselves a little."

"Let us go," said Leonora; "but let Guiomar remain here on the watch, to warn vis if Carrizales wakes."

"Ay," said Guiomar, "black woman stay, white woman go: God pardon all."

Leaving the negress behind, the rest all went to the saloon, where they seated themselves on a rich carpet, with Loaysa in the centre of the group. Marialonso took a candle, and began to examine the figure of the musician from bead to foot. Every one had something to say in his commendation: "Oh, what a nice curly head of hair he has!" said one. "What nice teeth!" cried another; "blanched almonds are nothing to them." "What eyes!" exclaimed a third; "so large and full, and so green! By the life of my mother, they look for all the world like emeralds." Leonora alone said not a word; but as she looked at the maestro, she could not help thinking that he was better looking than her good man. Presently the dueña took the guitar out of the negro's hands, and putting it into Loaysa's, begged he would sing to it a villanetta then in high fashion at Seville. He complied; the women all jumped up, and began to dance; whilst the dueña sang the words of the song with more good will than good voice.

Close you watch me, mother mine,
Watch me, and immure me:
Don't you know without my help
You can not secure me?
Appetite, 'tis said with truth,
By privation groweth;
Thwarted love, like flame confined,
All the fiercer gloweth.
Better therefore 'twere, methinks,
You should not immure me:
Don't you know without my help
You can not secure me?
Close you watch me, &c.
Moths will to the taper fly,
Bees on flowers will cluster;
Keep a loving maid who can
From love's golden lustre!
Fear you lest that beacon light
From your arms should lure me?
Well I know without my help
You can not secure me.
Close you watch me, &c.
There's a way where there's a will:
Keep the will from straying.
Wayward hearts will have their fling,
Spite of all gainsaying.
If you'd have me very good,
Don't be hard on poor me;
Sure I am without, my help
You can not secure me.
Close you watch me, &c.

The song and the dance were just ended, when in rushed Guiomar in wild affright, gesticulating as if she was in a fit, and in a voice between a croak and a whisper, she stammered out, "Master wake, señora; señora, master wake: him getting up, and coming." Whoever has seen a flock of pigeons feeding tranquilly in the field, and has marked the fear and confusion with which they take flight at the terrible sound of the gun, may picture to himself the fluttering dismay of the dancers at the unexpected news blurted out by Guiomar. Off they ran in all directions, leaving the musico in the lurch, and in a pitiable state of perplexity. Leonora wrung her beautiful hands; and the Señora Marialonso beat her face, and tore her hair, but not with great violence. In short, all was panic and confusion; but the dueña, who had more cunning and presence of mind than the rest, directed that Loaysa should go into her own room, whilst she and her mistress remained where they were, never doubting but they should find some excuse or another to put off upon Carrizales.

Loaysa hid himself, and the dueña bent her ear to listen for her master's footsteps; but hearing nothing, she took courage by degrees, and stealing on tip-toe to his bed-room, she found him snoring there as soundly as ever. Back she ran, at her best speed, to gladden her mistress's heart with the joyful intelligence; and then discreetly resolving not to lose so lucky an opportunity of being the first to enjoy the good graces of the musico, she told Leonora to wait there whilst she went and called him. Hastily entering the room where he was concealed, she found him sorely discomfited by the untoward issue of his adventure, cursing the inefficiency of the ointment, the credulity of his friends, and his own want of forethought in not making an experiment with the ointment on some other person before he tried its effect on Carrizales. But when the dueña assured him that the old man was sleeping as soundly as ever, there was an end to all his uneasiness, and he lent a complacent ear to the very liquorish language in which Marialonso addressed him. "Oho," said he to himself, "that's what you would be at, is it? Well, you will do capitally as a bait to fish with for your lady."

Whilst this tête-à-tête was pending, the rest of the women had one by one crept out of their several hiding-places, to see if it was true that their master was awake; and finding all still in the house, they returned to the saloon where they had left their mistress. Having learnt from her that the alarm had been a false one, they asked what had become of the musico and the dueña. Leonora told them that Marialonso had gone to fetch the maestro, whereupon they all stole out of the room as noiselessly as they had entered it, and set themselves to listen at the door to what was passing between the pair. Guiomar was one of the party, but the negro was not among them; for upon the first alarm he had run off, hugging his guitar, and hid himself in his loft, where he lay huddled up under the bed-clothes, sweating with terror; in spite of which he could not forbear from tinkling the guitar from time to time, so inordinate—may Satanas confound him!—was his love of music. The soft speeches of the amorous dueña were distinctly heard by the group outside the door; and there was not one of them but bestowed a blessing upon her from the wrong side of the mouth, with the addition of sundry epithets which I had rather not repeat. The result of the confabulation between the pair was that Loaysa would comply with the dueña's desires, provided that first of all she brought her mistress to consent to his. It cost the dueña something to subscribe to these conditions; but, after all, there was nothing she would not have done to compass the gratification of the desires that had laid hold on her soul and body, and were undermining her very bones and marrow. The bargain was struck; and quitting the room to go and speak to her mistress, she found all the rest of the women assembled round the door. Putting a bold face on the matter, she bade them all go to bed, and next night they should be able to enjoy themselves without any such false alarm as had spoiled their sport for that time. The women all knew well that the old dueña only wanted to be left alone; but they could not help obeying her, for she had command over them all.

Having got rid of the servants, the dueña went back to the saloon, and began to exercise her powers of persuasion upon Leonora. She made her a long and plausible harangue, so well put together that one might have supposed she had composed it beforehand. She extolled the good looks of the gentle musico, the elegance of his manners, his wondrous suavity, and his countless other good qualities; represented how infinitely more agreeable must be the caresses of such a charming young gallant than those of the old husband; assured her the affair would never be discovered, and plied her with a thousand other arguments which the devil put into her mouth, all so specious and so artfully coloured, that they might have beguiled the firmest mind, much more that of a being so artless and unwary as poor Leonora. O dueñas, born and used for the perdition of thousands of modest, virtuous beings! O ye long plaited coifs, chosen to impart an air of grave decorum to the salas of noble ladies, how do you reverse the functions of your perhaps needful office! In fine, the dueña talked with such effect, that Leonora consented to her own undoing, and to that of all the precautions of the wary Carrizales, whose sleep was the death of his honour. Marialonso took her mistress by the hand, led the weeping lady almost by force to Loaysa, and wishing them much joy with a diabolical leer, she left them both shut in together, and laid herself down in the saloon to sleep, or rather to await the reward she had earned. Overcome, however, by the loss of rest on two successive nights, she could not keep her eyes open, but fell fast asleep on the carpet.

And now, if we did not know that Carrizales was asleep, it would not be amiss to ask him, where now were all his jealous cares and precautions? What now availed the lofty walls of his house, and the exclusion from it of every male creature? What had he gained by his turning-box, his thick walls, his stopped up windows, the enormously strict seclusion to which he had doomed his family, the large jointure he had settled on Leonora, the presents he was continually making her, his liberal treatment of her attendants, and his unfailing alacrity in supplying them with everything he imagined they could want or wish for? But as we have said, he was asleep. Had he been awake, and disposed to reply, he could not have given a better answer than by saying, as he shrugged his shoulders and arched his eyebrows, that all this had been brought to nought by the craft of an idle and vicious young man, and the wickedness of a faithless dueña, working upon the weakness of an artless and inexperienced girl. Heaven save us all from such enemies as these, against whom the shield of prudence and the sword of vigilance are alike impotent to defend us!

Such, nevertheless, was Leonora's rectitude, and so opportunely did she manifest it, that all the villanous arts of the crafty seducer were of no avail; till both of them, wearied by the contest, the baffled tempter and the victorious defender of her own chastity, fell asleep almost at the moment when it pleased Heaven that Carrizales should awake in spite of the ointment. As usual he felt all about the bed, and not finding his dear wife in it, he jumped up in the utmost consternation, and with strange agility for a man of his years. He looked all over the room for her, and when he found the door open, and the key gone from between the mattresses, he was nearly distracted. Recovering himself a little, he went out into the gallery, stole softly thence to the saloon, where the dueña was asleep, and seeing no Leonora there, he went to the dueña's own room, opened the door gently, and beheld Leonora in Loaysa's arms, and both of them looking as if the soporific ointment was exerting its influence over themselves instead of upon the jealous husband.

Carrizales was petrified with horror; his voice stuck in his throat; his arms fell powerless by his sides, and his feet seemed rooted to the ground; and though the fierce revulsion of his wrath presently aroused his torpid senses, he yet could scarcely breathe, so intense was his anguish. Thirsting for vengeance as terrible as his monstrous wrong, but having no weapon at hand, he returned to his chamber as stealthily as he had quitted it, in search of a dagger, with which he would wash out the stain cast upon his honour in the blood of the guilty pair, and then massacre his whole household; but he had no sooner reached his room than his grief again overpowered him, and he fell senseless on the bed.

Day broke now, and found Leonora still in the arms of Loaysa. Marialonso awoke, and thinking it time to receive what she counted was due to her, she awoke Leonora, who was shocked to find it so late, and bitterly accused her own imprudence and the dueña's negligence. With trembling steps the two women crept up to Felipe's bedroom, praying inwardly to Heaven that they might find him still snoring; and when they saw him lying on the bed, apparently asleep, they made no doubt that he was still under the effect of the opiate, and embraced each other in a transport of joy. Leonora went up to her husband, and taking him by the arm, turned him over on his side to see if he would wake without their being obliged to wash him with vinegar according to the directions given with the ointment; but the movement roused Carrizales from his swoon, and heaving a deep sigh, he ejaculated in a faint and piteous tone, "Miserable man that I am! to what a woeful pass I am come!"

Leonora did not distinctly hear what her husband said; but seeing with surprise that the effect of the opiate was not so lasting as she had been led to expect, she bent over him, put her cheek to his, and pressing him closely in her arms, said, "What ails you, dear señor? You seem to be complaining?"

Carrizales opened his eyes to their utmost width, and turning them full upon her, stared at her a long while with a look of profound amazement. At last he said, "Do me the pleasure, señora, to send instantly for your parents in my name, and ask them to come hither, for I feel something at my heart which distresses me exceedingly. I fear I have but a short time to live, and I should like to see them before I die."

Leonora immediately despatched the negro with this message to her parents. She fully believed what her husband had told her, and attributing his danger to the violence of the opiate instead of to its real cause, she put her arms round his neck, caressed him more fondly than ever she had done before, and inquired how he felt, with such tender solicitude, as if she loved him above everything in the world; while he, on the other hand, continued to gaze upon her with the same unvarying look of astonishment, every endearing word or caress of hers being like a dagger to his heart. The dueña had, by this time, acquainted Loaysa and the domestics with her master's illness, which, she remarked, was evidently very serious, since he had forgotten to give orders that the street door should be locked after the negro's departure to summon her lady's parents. The message was itself a portentous occurrence, for neither father nor mother had ever set foot within that house since their daughter's marriage. In short, the whole household was in anxiety, though no one divined the true cause of the old man's illness. He lay sighing at intervals, so heavily that every sigh seemed like the parting of soul and body. Leonora wept to see him in such a state, whilst he beheld her feigned tears, as he deemed them, with a bitter smile, that looked like the grin of insanity.

Leonora's parents now arrived, and were struck with no little misgivings when they found both entrance doors open and the house all lonely and silent. They went up to their son-in-law's room, and found him in the posture he had all along maintained, with his eyes immovably fixed on his wife, whom he held by the hands, whilst both were in tears; she, because she saw his flow, and he at seeing how deceitfully she wept. As soon as they entered the room, Carrizales begged them to be seated, ordered all the domestics to withdraw except Marialonso, then wiped his eyes, and with a calm voice and an air of perfect composure addressed them thus:—

"I am sure, my respected father and mother-in-law, I need no other witnesses than yourselves to the truth of what I have now to say to you in the first place. You must well remember with how much love and what tender affection I received your daughter when you bestowed her upon me one year, one month, five days, and nine hours ago, as my lawful wife. You know, also, with what liberality I behaved to her, for the settlement I made upon her would have been more than enough to furnish three young ladies of her quality with handsome marriage portions. You must remember the pains I took to dress and adorn her with everything she could desire or I could think of as suitable to her. It is known to you likewise how, prompted by my natural disposition, fearful of the evil to which I shall surely owe my death, and taught by the experience of a long life to be on my guard against the many strange chances that occur in life, I sought to guard this jewel which I had chosen and you had bestowed upon me, with all possible care and caution. I raised the walls of this house higher, blocked up all the windows that looked on the street, doubled the locks of the doors, set up a turning-box as in a nunnery, and perpetually banished from my dwelling every vestige of the male sex. I gave my wife female servants and slaves to wait upon her: I denied neither her nor them anything they chose to ask of me. I made her my equal, communicated my most secret thoughts to her, and put my whole property at her disposal. Having done all this, I thought I might fairly expect to enjoy securely what had cost me so much, and that it would be her care not to afford me cause for conceiving any kind of jealous fear whatever. But it is not within the power of human efforts to prevent the chastisement which Heaven is pleased to inflict on those who do not rest their whole hopes and desires upon it alone. No wonder then if mine have been deceived, and I have myself prepared the poison of which I am now dying. But I see how anxiously you hang upon the words of my mouth. I will therefore keep you no longer in suspense, but conclude this long preamble by telling you, in one word, what no words were adequate to describe, were I to speak for ever. This morning I found this woman," (here he pointed to his wife,) "who was born for the ruin of my peace and the destruction of my life, in the arms of a young gallant, who is now shut up in the bed-chamber of this pestilent dueña."

Carrizales had no sooner uttered these words than Leonora swooned, and fell with her head upon his lap. Marialonso turned as white as ashes, and Leonora's parents were so astounded that they could not utter a word. After a short pause, Carrizales continued thus:—

"The vengeance I intend to take for this outrage shall be no common one. As I have been singular in all my other actions, so will I be in this. My vengeance shall fall upon myself, as the person most culpable of all, for I ought to have considered how ill this girl's fifteen years could assort with my threescore and ten. I have been like the silkworm, which builds itself a house in which it must die. I do not reproach you, misguided girl"—here he bent down and kissed his still insensible wife—"for the persuasions of a wicked old woman, and the wheedling tongue of an amorous youth, easily prevail over the little wit of a green girl; but that all the world may see how strong and how true was the love I bore you, I shall give such a proof of it here on my death-bed, as the world has never seen or heard of;—one that shall remain an unparalleled example, if not of goodness, at least of singleness of heart. I desire that a notary be immediately sent for to make my will, wherein I will double Leonora's jointure, and recommend her, after my death, which will not be long delayed, to marry that young man whom these gray hairs have never offended. Thus she will see that, as in life I never departed in the slightest particular from what I thought could please her, so I wish her to be happy when I am no more, and to be united to him whom she must love so much. The rest of my fortune I will bequeath to pious uses, after leaving to you both wherewith to live honourably for the rest of your days. Let the notary come instantly, for the anguish I am now suffering is such that, if it continues, my time here will be very short."

Here Carrizales was seized with a terrible swoon, and sank down so close to Leonora that their faces touched. During this scene the dueña stole out of the room, and went to apprize Loaysa of all that had happened. She advised him to quit the house immediately, and she would take care to keep him informed of all that was going on, for there were no locked doors now to hinder her from sending the negro to him whenever it was necessary. Astounded at this news, Loaysa took her advice, put on his beggar's rags again, and went away to make known to his friends the strange issue of his amour.

Leonora's father, meanwhile, sent for a notary, who arrived soon after both husband and wife had recovered their senses. Carrizales made his will in the manner he had stated, without saying anything of his wife's transgressions; he only declared that, for good reasons, he advised, and begged her to marry, should he die, that young man of whom he had spoken to her in private. When Leonora heard this, she threw herself at her husband's feet, and cried, while her heart throbbed as if it would burst, "Long may you live, my lord and my only joy; for though you may not believe a word I say, indeed, indeed I have not offended you, except in thought."

More she would have said, but when she attempted to exculpate herself by a full statement of what had really occurred, her tongue failed her, and she fainted away a second time. The poor old man embraced her as she lay; so, too, did her parents—all three weeping bitterly; and even the notary could not refrain from tears. Carrizales gave the negro and the other slaves their liberty, and left all the servants enough to maintain them; the perfidious Marialonso alone was to have nothing beyond the arrears of her wages. Seven days afterwards Carrizales was laid in his grave.

Leonora remained a mourning though wealthy widow; and whilst Loaysa expected that she would fulfil the desire which he knew her husband had expressed in his will, he learned that within a week she had become a nun in one of the most austere and rigid convents in all Seville. Mortified by this disappointment, he left the country and went to the Indies. Leonora's father and mother were deeply grieved, but found consolation in the wealth which their son-in-law had bequeathed them. The two damsels likewise consoled themselves, as did the negro and the female slaves, the former being well provided for, and the latter having obtained their freedom; the wicked dueña alone was left to digest, in poverty, the frustration of her base schemes. For my part I was long possessed with the desire to complete this story, which so signally exemplifies the little reliance that can be put in locks, turning-boxes, and walls, whilst the will remains free; and the still less reason there is to trust the innocence and simplicity of youth, if its ear be exposed to the suggestions of your demure dueñas, whose virtue consists in their long black gowns and their formal white hoods. Only I know not why it was that Leonora did not persist in exculpating herself, and explaining to her jealous husband how guiltless she had been in the whole of that unhappy business. But her extreme agitation paralysed her tongue at the moment, and the haste which her husband made to die, left her without another opportunity to complete her justification.

[80] "Men on town," gente de barrio, literally, people of the ward or quarter.

THE ILLUSTRIOUS SCULLERY-MAID.

In the famous city of Burgos there lived two wealthy cavaliers, one of whom was called Don Diego de Carriazo, and the other Don Juan de Avendaño. Don Diego had a son called after himself, and Don Juan another, whose name was Don Tomas de Avendaño. These two young gentlemen being the principal persons of the following tale, we shall for the sake of brevity call them Carriazo and Avendaño.

Carriazo might be about thirteen or little more, when, prompted by a scampish disposition, without having had any cause to complain of bad treatment at home, he ran away from his father's house, and cast himself upon the wide world. So much did he enjoy a life of unrestricted freedom, that amidst all the wants and discomforts attendant upon it, he never missed the plenty of his father's house. He neither tired of trudging on foot, nor cared for cold or heat. For him all seasons of the year were genial spring. His sleep was as sound on a heap of straw as on soft mattresses, and he made himself as snug in a hayloft as between two Holland sheets. In short, he made such way in the profession he had chosen, that he could have given lessons to the famous Guzman de Alfarache.

During the three years he absented himself from home, he learned to play at sheepshanks in Madrid, at rentoy in the public-houses of Toledo, and at presa y pinta in the barbacans of Seville. In spite of the sordid penury of his way of life, Carriazo showed himself a prince in his actions. It was easy to see by a thousand tokens that he came of gentle blood. His generosity gained him the esteem of all his comrades. He seldom was present at drinking bouts; and though he drank wine, it was in moderation, and he carried it well. He was not one of those unlucky drinkers, who whenever they exceed a little, show it immediately in their faces, which look as if they were painted with vermilion or red ochre. In short, the world beheld in Carriazo a virtuous, honourable, well-bred, rogue, of more than common ability. He passed through all the degrees of roguery till he graduated as a master in the tunny fisheries of Zahara, the chief school of the art. O kitchen-walloping rogues, fat and shining with grease; feigned cripples; cutpurses of Zocodober and of the Plaza of Madrid; sanctimonious patterers of prayers; Seville porters; bullies of the Hampa, and all the countless host comprised under the denomination of rogues! never presume to call yourself by that name if you have not gone through two courses, at least, in the academy of the tunny fisheries. There it is that you may see converging as it were in one grand focus, toil and idleness, filth and spruceness, sharp set hunger and lavish plenty, vice without disguise, incessant gambling, brawls and quarrels every hour in the day, murders every now and then, ribaldry and obscenity, singing, dancing, laughing, swearing, cheating, and thieving without end. There many a man of quality seeks for his truant son, nor seeks in vain; and the youth feels as acutely the pain of being torn from that life of licence as though he were going to meet his death. But this joyous life has its bitters as well as its sweets. No one can lie down to sleep securely in Zahara, but must always have the dread hanging over him of being carried off to Barbary at any moment. For this reason, they all withdraw at night into some fortified places on the coast, and place scouts and sentinels to watch whilst they sleep; but in spite of all precautions, it has sometimes happened that scouts, sentinels, rogues, overseers, boats, nets, and all the posse comitatus of the place have begun the night in Spain and have seen the dawn in Tetuan. No apprehensions of this kind, however, could deter Carriazo from spending three successive summers at the fisheries for his pastime; and such was his luck during his third season, that he won at cards about seven hundred reals, with which he resolved to buy himself good clothes, return to Burgos, and gladden the heart of his sorrowing mother.

He took a most affectionate leave of his many dear friends, assuring them that nothing but sickness or death should prevent his being with them in the following summer; for his heart was in Zahara, and to his eyes its parched sands were fresher than all the verdure of the Elysian fields. Ambling merrily along on shanks' mare, he arrived at Valladolid, where he stopped a fortnight to get rid of the mahogany hue of his complexion, and to change his rogue's costume for that of a gentleman. Having equipped himself properly, he had still a hundred reals left, which he spent on the hire of a mule and a servant, that he might make a good figure when he presented himself to his parents. They received him with the utmost joy, and all the friends and relations of the family came to congratulate them on the safe arrival of their son Don Diego de Carriazo. I had forgotten to mention that, during his peregrination, Don Diego had taken the name of Vidiales, and by that name alone he was known to his new acquaintances.

Among those who came to see the new arrival were Don Juan de Avendaño and his son Don Tomas, with the latter of whom, as they were both of the same age and neighbours, Carriazo contracted a very close friendship. Carriazo gave his parents a long and circumstantial account of all the fine things he had seen and done during the three years he had been from home, in all which there was not one word of truth; but he never so much as hinted at the tunny fisheries, though they were constantly in his thoughts, more especially as the time approached in which he had promised his friends he would return to them. He took no pleasure in the chase, with which his father sought often to divert him, nor in any of the convivial meetings of that hospitable city. All kinds of amusements wearied him, and the best enjoyments that could be offered to him were not to be compared, he thought, with those he had known at the tunny fisheries. His friend Avendaño, finding him often melancholy and musing, ventured to inquire after the cause, at the same time professing his readiness to assist his friend in any way that might be requisite, and to the utmost of his power, even at the cost of his blood. Carriazo felt that it would be wronging the great friendship subsisting between him and Avendaño if he concealed from the latter the cause of his present sadness; and therefore he described to him in detail the life he had led at Zahara and declared that all his gloom arose from his strong desire to be there once more. So attractive was the picture he drew, that Avendaño, far from blaming his taste, expressed his entire sympathy with it. The end of the matter was that Avendaño determined to go off with Carriazo, and enjoy for one summer that delicious life of which he had just heard such a glowing description; and in this determination he was strongly encouraged to persist by Carriazo, who was glad to be so countenanced in his own low propensities. They set their wits to work to see how they could scrape together as much money as possible, and the best means that occurred to them was that suggested by Avendaño's approaching departure for Salamanca, where he had already studied for three years, and where his father wished him to complete his education, and take a degree in whatever faculty he pleased. Carriazo now made known to his father that he had a strong desire to go with Avendaño and study at Salamanca. Don Diego gladly fell in with his son's proposal; he talked with his friend Don Juan on the subject, and it was agreed between them that the two young men should reside together at Salamanca, and be sent thither well supplied with all requisites, and in a manner suitable to the sons of men of quality.

The time for their departure being arrived, they were furnished with money, and with a tutor who was more remarkable for integrity than for mother wit. Their fathers talked much and impressively to their sons about what they should do, and how they should govern themselves, in order that they might become fraught with virtue and knowledge, for that is the fruit which every student should aspire to reap from his labours and his vigils, especially such as are of good family. The sons were all humility and obedience; their mothers cried; both parents gave them their blessing, and away they went, mounted on their own mules, and attended by two servants of their respective households, besides the tutor, who had let his beard grow, to give him a more imposing air of gravity, as became his charge.

When they arrived at Valladolid, they told their tutor they should like to remain there a couple of days to see the city, having never been in it before. The tutor severely reprimanded them for entertaining any such idle notion, telling them they had no time to lose in silly diversions; that their business was to get as fast as possible to the place where they were to pursue their studies; that he should be doing extreme violence to his conscience if he allowed them to stop for one hour, not to speak of two days; that they should continue their journey forthwith, or, if not, then brown bread should be their portion.

Such was the extent of the ability in his office possessed by this tutor, or major-domo, as we should rather call him. The lads, who had already gathered in their harvest, since they had laid hands upon four hundred gold crowns which were in the major-domo's keeping, begged that he would let them remain in Valladolid for that day only, that they might see the grand aqueducts, which were then in course of construction, for the purpose of conveying the waters of Argales to that city. He consented at last, but with extreme reluctance, for he wished to avoid the expense of an additional day on the road, and to spend the night at Valdiastellas, whence he could easily reach Salamanca in two days. But the bay horse thinks one thing, and the man on his back another thing, and so it proved in the major-domo's case. The lads, mounted on two excellent mules, and attended by only one servant, rode out to see the fountain of Argales, famous for its antiquity and the abundance of its water. On their arrival there, Avendaño gave the servant a sealed paper, bidding him return forthwith to the city, and deliver it to his tutor, after which the servant was to wait for them at the Puerta del Campo. The servant did as he was bid, and went back to the city with the letter; and they, turning their mules' heads another way, slept that night in Mojados, and arrived two days afterwards in Madrid, where they sold their mules.

They dressed themselves like peasants in short jerkins, loose breeches, and gray stockings. An old clothes dealer, to whom they sold their handsome apparel in the morning, transformed them by night in such a manner that their own mothers would not have known them. Lightly equipped, as suited their purpose, and without swords, for they had sold them to the old clothes dealer, they took to the road to Toledo. There let us leave them for the present, stepping out briskly with merry hearts, while we return to the tutor, and see him open the letter delivered to him by the servant, which he read as follows:—

"Your worship, señor Pedro Alonso, will be pleased to have patience and go back to Burgos, where you will say to our parents that we, their sons, having with mature deliberation considered how much more arms befit cavaliers than do letters, have determined to exchange Salamanca for Brussels, and Spain for Flanders. We have got the four hundred crowns; the mules we intend to sell. The course we have chosen, which is so worthy of persons of our quality, and the length of the journey before us, are sufficient to excuse our fault, though a fault it will not be deemed by any one but a coward. Our departure takes place now; our return will be when it shall please God, to whose keeping, we, your humble pupils, heartily commend you. Given from the fountain of Argales, with one foot in the stirrup for Flanders.

"CARRIAZO,
"AVENDANO."

Aghast at the contents of this letter, Pedro Alonso hurried to his valise, and found that the paper spoke but too truly, for the money was gone. Instantly mounting the remaining mule, he returned to Burgos to carry these tidings to his patrons, in order that they might take measures to recover possession of their sons' persons. But as to how he was received, the author of this tale says not a word, for the moment he has put Pedro Alonso into the saddle, he leaves him to give the following account of what occurred to Avendaño and Carriazo at the entrance of Illescas.

Just by the town gate they met two muleteers, Andalusians apparently, one of whom was coming from Seville, and the other going thither. Said the latter to the former, "If my masters were not so far ahead, I should like to stop a little longer to ask you a thousand things I want to know, for I am quite astonished at what you have told me about the conde's having hanged Alonzo Gines and Ribera without giving them leave to appeal."

"As I'm a sinner," replied the Sevillian, "the conde laid a trap for them, got them under his jurisdiction—for they were soldiers, and once having them in his gripe, the court of appeal could never get them out of it. I tell you what it is, friend, he has a devil within him, that same conde de Puñonrostro. Seville, and the whole country round it for ten leagues, is swept clear of swash-bucklers; not a thief ventures within his limits; they all fear him like fire. It is whispered, however, that he will soon give up his place as corregidor, for he is tired of being at loggerheads at every hand's turn with the señores of the court of appeal."

"May they live a thousand years!" exclaimed he who was going to Seville; "for they are the fathers of the miserable, and a refuge for the unfortunate. How many poor fellows must eat dirt, for no other reason than the anger of an arbitrary judge of a corregidor, either ill-informed or wrong-headed! Many eyes see more than two; the venom of injustice cannot so soon lay hold on many hearts as on one alone."

"You have turned preacher!" said he of Seville; "but I am afraid I can't stop to hear the end of your sermon. Don't put up to night at your usual place, but go to the Posada del Sevillano, for there you will see the prettiest scullery-wench I know. Marinilla at the Venta Tejada is a dishclout in comparison with her. I will only tell you that it is said the son of the corregidor is very sweet upon her. One of my masters gone on ahead there, swears, that on his way back to Andalusia, he will stop two months in Toledo, and in that same inn, only to have his fill of looking at her. I myself ventured once to give her a little bit of a squeeze, and all I got for it was a swinging box on the ear. She is as hard as a flint, as savage as a kestrel, and as touch-me-not as a nettle; but she has a face that does a body's eyes good to look at. She has the sun in one cheek, and the moon in the other; the one is made of roses and the other of carnations, and between them both are lilies and jessamine. I say no more, only see her for yourself, and you will see that all I have told you is nothing to what I might say of her beauty. I'd freely settle upon her those two silver gray mules of mine that you know, if they would let me have her for my wife; but I know they won't, for she is a morsel for an archbishop or a conde. Once more I say, go and see her; and so, good-bye to you, for I must be off."

The two muleteers went their several ways, leaving the two friends much struck by what they had overheard of the conversation, especially Avendaño, in whom the mere relation which the muleteer had given of the scullery-maid's beauty awoke an intense desire to see her. It had the same effect on Carriazo, but not to an equal degree, nor so as to extinguish his desire to reach his beloved tunny fisheries, from which he would not willingly be delayed to behold the pyramids of Egypt, or any or all of the other seven wonders of the world.

Repeating the dialogue between the muleteers, and mimicking their tones and gestures, served as pastime to beguile the way until they reached Toledo. Carriazo, who had been there before, led the way at once to the Posada del Sevillano; but they did not venture to ask for accommodation there, their dress and appearance not being such as would have gained them a ready welcome. Night was coming on, and though Carriazo importuned Avendaño to go with him in search of lodgings elsewhere, he could not prevail on him to quit the doors of the Sevillano, or cease from hanging about them, upon the chance that the celebrated scullery-maid might perhaps make her appearance. When it was pitch dark Carriazo was in despair, but still Avendaño stuck to the spot; and, at last, he went into the courtyard of the inn, under pretence of inquiring after some gentlemen of Burgos who were on their way to Seville. He had but just entered the courtyard, when a girl, who seemed to be about fifteen, and was dressed in working clothes, came out of one of the side doors with a lighted candle. Avendaño's eyes did not rest on the girl's dress, but on her face, which seemed to him such as a painter would give to the angels; and so overcome was he by her beauty, that he could only gaze at it in speechless admiration, without being able to say one word for himself.

"What may you please to want, brother?" said the girl. "Are you servant to one of the gentlemen in the house?"

"I am no one's servant but yours," replied Avendaño, trembling with emotion.

"Go to, brother," returned the girl disdainfully, "we who are servants ourselves have no need of others to wait on us;" and calling her master, she said, "Please to see, sir, what this lad wants."

The master came out, and, in reply to his question, Avendaño said that he was looking for some gentlemen of Burgos who were on their way to Seville. One of them was his master, and had sent him on before them to Alcalá de Henares upon business of importance, bidding him, when that was done, to proceed to Toledo, and wait for him at the Sevillano; and he believed that his master would arrive there that night or the following day at farthest.

So plausibly did Avendaño tell this fib that the landlord was quite taken in by it. "Very well, friend," said he, "you may stop here till your master comes."

"Many thanks, señor landlord," replied Avendaño; "and will your worship bid them give me a room for myself, and a comrade of mine who is outside? We have got money to pay for it, as well as another."

"Certainly," said the host, and turning to the girl he said, "Costanza, bid la Argüello take these two gallants to the corner room, and give them clean sheets."

"I will do so, señor," and curtsying to her master she went away, leaving Avendaño by her departure in a state of feeling like that of the tired wayfarer when the sun sets and he finds himself wrapt in cheerless darkness. He went, however, to give an account of what he had seen and done to Carriazo, who very soon perceived that his friend had been smitten in the heart; but he would not say a word about the matter then, until he should see whether there was a fair excuse for the hyperbolical praises with which Avendaño exalted the beauty of Costanza above the stars.

At last they went in doors, and la Argüello, the chamber maid, a woman of some five-and-forty years of age, showed them a room which was neither a gentleman's nor a servant's, but something between the two. On their asking for supper, la Argüello told them they did not provide meals in that inn; they only cooked and served up such food as the guests bought and fetched for themselves; but there were eating-houses in the neighbourhood, where they might without scruple of conscience go and sup as they pleased. The two friends took la Argüello's advice, and went to an eating-house, where Carriazo supped on what they set before him, and Avendaño on what he had brought with him, to wit, thoughts and fancies. Carriazo noticed that his friend ate little or nothing, and, by way of sounding him, he said on their way back to the inn, "We must be up betimes to-morrow morning, so that we may reach

Orgez before the heat of the day."

"I am not disposed for that," replied Avendaño, "for I intend, before I leave this city, to see all that is worth seeing in it, such as the cathedral, the waterworks of Juanelo, the view from the top of St. Augustine's, the King's garden, and the promenade by the river."

"Very well, we can see all that in two days."

"What need of such haste? We are not posting to Rome to ask for a vacant benefice."

"Ha! ha! friend, I see how it is, I'll be hanged if you are not more inclined to stay in Toledo than to continue our journey."

"That's true, I confess; it is as impossible for me to forego the sight of that girl's face, as it is to get into heaven without good works."

"Gallantly spoken, and as becomes a generous breast like yours! Here's a pretty story! Don Tomas de Avendaño, son of the wealthy and noble cavalier, Don Juan de Avendaño, over head and ears in love with the scullery-maid at the Posada del Sevillano!"

"It strikes me, I may answer you in the same strain. Here's Don Diego de Carriazo, son and sole heir of the noble knight of Alcántara of the same name, a youth finely gifted alike in body and mind, and behold him in love—with whom, do you suppose? With queen Ginevra? No such thing, but with the tunny fisheries of Zahara, and all its rogues and rascals,—a more loathsome crew, I suspect, than ever beset St. Anthony in his temptations."

"You have given me tit for tat, friend, and slain me with my own weapon. Let us say no more now, but go to bed, and to-morrow who knows but we come to our senses?"

"Look ye, Carriazo, you have not yet seen Costanza; when you have seen her, I will give you leave to say what you like to me."

"Well, I know beforehand what will be the upshot of the matter."

"And that is?"

"That I shall be off to my tunny fisheries, and you will remain with your scullery-maid."

"I shall not be so happy."

"Nor I such a fool as to give up my own good purpose for the sake of your bad one."

By this time they reached the inn, where the conversation was prolonged in the same tone, half the night long. After they had slept, as it seemed to them, little more than an hour, they were awakened by the loud sound of clarions in the street. They sat up in bed, and after they had listened awhile, "I'll lay a wager," said Carriazo, "that it is already day, and that there is some feast or other in the convent of Nostra Señora del Carmen, in this neighbourhood, and that is why the clarions are pealing."

"That can't be," said Avendaño; "we have not been long asleep. It must be some time yet till dawn."

While they were talking, some one knocked at the door, and called out, "Young men, if you want to hear some fine music, go to the window of the next room, which looks on the street; it is not occupied."

They got up and opened the door, but the person who had spoken was gone. The music still continuing, however, they went in their shirts, just as they were, into the front room, where they found three or four other lodgers, who made place for them at the window; and soon afterwards an excellent voice sang a sonnet to the accompaniment of the harp. There was no need of any one to tell Carriazo and Avendaño that this music was intended for Costanza, for this was very clear from the words of the sonnet, which grated so horribly on Avendaño's ears, that he could have wished himself deaf rather than have heard it. The pangs of jealousy laid hold on him, and the worst of all was, that he knew not who was his rival. But this was soon made known to him when one of the persons at the window exclaimed, "What a simpleton is the corregidor's son, to make a practice of serenading a scullery-maid. It is true, she is one of the most beautiful girls I have ever seen, and I have seen a great many; but that is no reason why he should court her so publicly."

"After all," said another, "I have been told for certain that she makes no more account of him than if he never existed. I warrant she is this moment fast asleep behind her mistress's bed, without ever thinking of all this music."

"I can well believe it," said the first speaker, "for she is the most virtuous girl I know; and it is marvellous that though she lives in a house like this, where there is so much traffic, and where there are new comers every day, and though she goes about all the rooms, not the least thing in the world is known to her disparagement."

Avendaño began to breathe more freely after hearing this, and was able to listen to many fine things which were sung to the accompaniment of various instruments, all being addressed to Costanza, who, as the stranger said, was fast asleep all the while.

The musicians departed at the approach of dawn. Avendaño and Carriazo returned to their room, where one of them slept till morning. They then rose, both of them eager to see Costanza, but the one only from curiosity, the other from love. Both were gratified; for Costanza came out of her master's room looking so lovely, that they both felt that all the praises bestowed on her by the muleteer, fell immeasurably short of her deserts. She was dressed in a green bodice and petticoat, trimmed with the same colour. A collar embroidered with black silk set off the alabaster whiteness of her neck. The thick tresses of her bright chestnut hair were bound up with white ribbon; she had pendents in her ears which seemed to be pearls, but were only glass; her girdle was a St. Francis cord, and a large bunch of keys hung at her side. When she came out of the room she crossed herself, and made a profound reverence with great devotion to an image of our Lady, that hung on one of the walls of the quadrangle. Then looking up and seeing the two young men intently gazing on her, she immediately retired again into the room, and called thence to Argüello to get up.

Carriazo, it must be owned, was much struck by Costanza's beauty; he admired it as much as his companion, only he did not fall in love with her; on the contrary, he had no desire to spend another night in the inn, but to set out at once for the fisheries.

La Argüello presently appeared in the gallery with two young women, natives of Gallicia, who were also servants in the inn; for the number employed in the Sevillano was considerable, that being one of the best and most frequented houses of its kind in Toledo. At the same time the servants of the persons lodging in the inn began to assemble to receive oats for their masters' beasts; and the host dealt them out, all the while grumbling and swearing at his maid-servants who had been the cause of his losing the services of a capital hostler, who did the work so well and kept such good reckoning, that he did not think he had ever lost the price of a grain of oats by him. Avendaño, who heard all this, seized the opportunity at once. "Don't fatigue yourself, señor host," he said; "give me the account-book, and whilst I remain here I will give out the oats, and keep such an exact account of it that you will not miss the hostler who you say has left you."

"Truly I thank you for the offer, my lad," said the host, "for I have no time to attend to this business; I have too much to do, both indoors and out of doors. Come down and I will give you the book; and mind ye, these muleteers are the very devil, and will do you out of a peck of oats under your very nose, with no more conscience than if it was so much chaff."

Avendaño went down to the quadrangle, took the book, and began to serve out pecks of oats like water, and to note them down with such exactness that the landlord, who stood watching him, was greatly pleased with his performance. "I wish to God," he said, "your master would not come, and that you would make up your mind to stop with me; you would lose nothing by the change, believe me. The hostler who has just quitted me came here eight months ago all in tatters, and as lean as a shotten herring, and now he has two very good suits of clothes, and is as fat as a dormouse; for you must know, my son, that in this house there are excellent vails to be got over and above the wages."

"If I should stop," replied Avendaño, "I should not stand out much for the matter of what I should gain, but should be content with very little for sake of being in this city, which, they tell me, is the best in Spain."

"At least it is one of the best and most plentiful," said the host. "But we are in want of another thing, too, and that is a man to fetch water, for the lad that used to attend to that job has also left me. He was a smart fellow, and with the help of a famous ass of mine he used to keep all the tanks overflowing, and make a lake of the house. One of the reasons why the muleteers like to bring their employers to my house is, that they always find plenty of water in it for their beasts, instead of having to drive them down to the river."

Carriazo, who had been listening to this dialogue, and who saw Avendaño already installed in office, thought he would follow his example, well knowing how much it would gratify him. "Out with the ass, señor host," he said; "I'm your man, and will do your work as much to your satisfaction as my comrade."

"Aye, indeed," said Avendaño, "my comrade, Lope Asturiano will fetch water like a prince, I'll go bail for him."

La Argüello, who had been all the while within earshot, here put in her word. "And pray, my gentleman," said she to Avendaño, "who is to go bail for you? By my faith, you look to me as if you wanted some one to answer for you instead of your answering for another."

"Hold your tongue, Argüello," said her master; "don't put yourself forward where you're not wanted. I'll go bail for them, both of them. And mind, I tell you, that none of you women meddle or make with the men-servants, for it is through you they all leave me."

"So these two chaps are engaged, are they?" said another of the servant-women; "by my soul, if I had to keep them company I would never trust them with the wine-bag."

"None of your gibes, señora Gallega," cried her master; "do your work, and don't meddle with the men-servants, or I'll baste you with a stick."

"Oh, to be sure!" replied the Gallician damsel; "a'nt they dainty dears to make a body's mouth water? I'm sure master has never known me so frolicksome with the chaps in the house, nor yet out of it, that he should have such an opinion of me. The blackguards go away when they take it into their heads, without our giving them any occasion. Very like indeed they're the right sort to be in need of any one's putting them to bidding their masters an early good morning, when they least expect it."

"You've a deal to say for yourself, my friend," said the landlord; "shut your mouth and mind your business."

While this colloquy was going on Carriazo had harnessed the ass, jumped on his back, and set off to the river, leaving Avendaño highly delighted at witnessing his jovial resolution.

Here then, we have Avendaño and Carriazo changed, God save the mark! into Tomas Pedro, a hostler, and Lope Asturiano, a water-carrier: transformations surpassing those of the long-nosed poet. No sooner had la Argüello heard that they were hired, than she formed a design upon Asturiano, and marked him for her own, resolving to regale him in such a manner, that, if he was ever so shy, she would make him as pliant as a glove. The prudish Gallegan formed a similar design upon Avendaño, and, as the two women were great friends, being much together in their business by day, and bed-fellows at night, they at once confided their amorous purposes to each other; and that night they determined to begin the conquest of their two unimpassioned swains. Moreover they agreed that they must, in the first place, beg them not to be jealous about anything they might see them do with their persons; for girls could hardly regale their friends within doors, unless they put those without under contribution. "Hold your tongues, lads," said they, apostrophising their absent lovers, "hold your tongues and shut your eyes; leave the timbrel in the hands that can play it, and let those lead the dance that know how, and no pair of canons in this city will be better regaled than you will be by our two selves."

While the Gallegan and la Argüello were settling matters in this way, our good friend, Lope Asturiano, was on his way to the river, musing upon his beloved tunny fisheries and on his sudden change of condition. Whether it was for this reason, or that fate ordained it so, it happened that as he was riding down a steep and narrow lane, he ran against another water-carrier's ass, which was coming, laden, up-hill; and, as his own was fresh and lively and in good condition, the poor, half-starved, jaded brute that was toiling up hill, was knocked down, the pitchers were broken, and the water spilled. The driver of the fallen ass, enraged by this disaster, immediately flew upon the offender, and pommelled him soundly before poor Lope well knew where he was. At last, his senses were roused with a vengeance, and seizing his antagonist with both hands by the throat, he dashed him to the ground. That was not all, for, unluckily, the man's head struck violently against a stone; the wound was frightful, and bled so profusely, that Lope thought he had killed him. Several other water-carriers who were on their way to and from the river, seeing their comrade so maltreated, seized Lope and held him fast, shouting, "Justice! justice! this water-carrier has murdered a man." And all the while they beat and thumped him lustily. Others ran to the fallen man, and found that his skull was cracked, and that he was almost at the last gasp. The outcry spread all up the hill, and to the Plaza del Carmen, where it reached the ears of an alguazil, who flew to the spot with two police-runners. They did not arrive a moment too soon, for they found Lope surrounded by more than a score of water-carriers, who were basting his ribs at such a rate that there was almost as much reason to fear for his life as that of the wounded man. The alguazil took him out of their hands, delivered him and his ass into those of his followers, had the wounded man laid like a sack upon his own ass, and marched them all off to prison attended by such a crowd that they could hardly make way through the streets. The noise drew Tomas Pedro and his master to the door, and, to their great surprise, they saw Asturiano led by in the gripe of two police-runners, with his face all bloody. The landlord immediately looked about for his ass, and saw it in the hands of another catchpoll, who had joined the alguazil's party. He inquired the cause of these captures, was told what had happened, and was sorely distressed on account of his ass, fearing that he should lose it, or have to pay more for it than it was worth.

Tomas followed his comrade, but could not speak a single word to him, such was the throng round the prisoner, and the strictness of the catchpolls. Lope was thrust into a narrow cell in the prison, with a doubly grated window, and the wounded man was taken to the infirmary, where the surgeon pronounced his case extremely dangerous.

The alguazil took home the two asses with him, besides five pieces of eight which had been found on Lope. Tomas returned greatly disconcerted to the inn, where he found the landlord in no better spirits than himself, and gave him an account of the condition in which he had left his comrade, the danger of the wounded man, and the fate of the ass. "To add to the misfortune," said he, "I have just met a gentleman of Burgos, who tells me that my master will not now come this way. In order to make more speed and shorten his journey by two leagues, he has crossed the ferry at Aceca; he will sleep to-night at Orgaz, and has sent me twelve crowns, with orders to meet him at Seville. But that cannot be, for it is not in reason that I should leave my friend and comrade in prison and in such peril. My master must excuse me for the present, and I know he will, for he is so good-natured that he will put up with a little inconvenience rather than that I should forsake my comrade. Will you do me the favour, señor, to take this money, and see what you can do in this business. While you are spending this, I will write to my master for more, telling him all that has happened, and I am sure he will send us enough to get us out of any scrape."

The host opened his eyes a palm wide in glad surprise to find himself indemnified for the loss of his ass. He took the money and comforted Tomas, telling him that he could make interest with persons of great influence in Toledo, especially a nun, a relation of the corregidor's, who could do anything she pleased with him. Now the washerwoman of the convent in which the nun lived had a daughter, who was very thick indeed with the sister of a friar, who was hand and glove with the said nun's confessor. All he had to do, then, was to get the washerwoman to ask her daughter to get the monk's sister to speak to her brother to say a good word to the confessor, who would prevail on the nun to write a note to the corregidor begging him to look into Lope's business, and then, beyond a doubt, they might expect to come off with flying colours; that is provided the water-carrier did not die of his wound, and provided also there was no lack of stuff to grease the palms of all the officers of justice, for unless they are well greased they creak worse than the wheels of a bullock cart.

Whatever Tomas thought of this roundabout way of making interest, he failed not to thank the innkeeper, and to assure him that he was confident his master would readily send the requisite money.

Argüello, who had seen her new flame in the hands of the officers, ran directly to the prison with some dinner for him; but she was not permitted to see him. This was a great grief to her, but she did not lose her hopes for all that. After the lapse of a fortnight the wounded man was out of danger, and in a week more, the surgeon pronounced him cured. During this time, Tomas Pedro pretended to have had fifty crowns sent to him from Seville, and taking them out of his pocket, he presented them to the innkeeper, along with a fictitious letter from his master. It was nothing to the landlord whether the letter was genuine or not, so he gave himself no trouble to authenticate it; but he received the fifty good gold crowns with great glee. The end of the matter was, that the wounded man was quieted with six ducats, and Asturiano was sentenced to the forfeiture of his ass, and a fine of ten ducats with costs, on the payment of which he was liberated.

On his release from prison, Asturiano had no mind to go back to the Sevillano, but excused himself to his comrade on the ground that during his confinement he had been visited by Argüello, who had pestered him with her fulsome advances, which were to him so sickening and insufferable, that he would rather be hanged than comply with the desires of so odious a jade. His intention was to buy an ass, and to do business as a water carrier on his own account as long as they remained in Toledo. This would protect him from the risk of being arrested as a vagabond; besides, it was a business he could carry on with great ease and satisfaction to himself, since with only one load of water, he could saunter about the city all day long, looking at silly wenches.

"Looking at beautiful women, you mean," said his friend, "for of all the cities in Spain, Toledo has the reputation of being that in which the women surpass all others, whether in beauty or conduct. If you doubt it, only look at Costanza, who could spare from her superfluity of loveliness charms enough to beautify the rest of the women, not only of Toledo, but of the whole world."

"Gently, señor Tomas; not so fast with your praises of the señora scullion, unless you wish that, besides thinking you a fool, I take you for a heretic into the bargain."

"Do you call Costanza a scullion, brother Lope? God forgive you, and bring you to a true sense of your error."

"And is not she a scullion?"

"I have yet to see her wash the first plate."

"What does that matter, if you have seen her wash the second, or the fiftieth?"

"I tell you brother she does not wash dishes, or do anything but look after the business of the house, and take care of the plate, of which there is a great deal."

"How is it, then, that throughout the whole city they call her the illustrious scullery-maid, if so be she does not wash dishes? Perhaps it is because she washes silver and not crockery that they give her that name. But to drop this subject, tell me, Tomas, how stand your hopes?"

"In a state of perdition; for during the whole time you were in gaol, I never have been able to say one word to her. It is true, that to all that is said to her by the guests in the house, she makes no other reply than to cast down her eyes and keep her lips closed; such is her virtue and modesty; so that her modesty excites my love, no less than her beauty. But it is almost too much for my patience, to think that the corregidor's son, who is an impetuous and somewhat licentious youth, is dying for her; a night seldom passes but he serenades her, and that so openly, that she is actually named in the songs sung in her praise. She never hears them to be sure, nor ever quits her mistress's room from the time she retires until morning; but in spite of all that, my heart cannot escape being pierced by the keen shaft of jealousy."

"What do you intend to do, then, with this Portia, this Minerva, this new Penelope, who, under the form of a scullery-maid, has vanquished your heart?"

"Her name is Costanza, not Portia, Minerva, or Penelope. That she is a servant in an inn, I cannot deny; but what can I do, if, as it seems, the occult force of destiny, and the deliberate choice of reason, both impel me to adore her? Look you, friend, I cannot find words to tell you how love exalts and glorifies in my eyes this humble scullery-maid, as you call her, so that, though seeing her low condition, I am blind to it, and knowing it, I ignore it. Try as I may, it is impossible for me to keep it long before my eyes; for that thought is at once obliterated by her beauty, her grace, her virtue, and modesty, which tell me that, beneath that plebeian husk, must be concealed some kernel of extraordinary worth. In short, be it what it may, I love her, and not with that common-place love I have felt for others, but with a passion so pure that it knows no wish beyond that of serving her, and prevailing on her to love me, and return in the like kind what is due to my honourable affection."

Here Lope gave a shout, and cried out in a declamatory tone, "O Platonic love! O illustrious scullery-maid! O thrice-blessed age of ours, wherein we see love renewing the marvels of the age of gold! O my poor tunnies, you must pass this year without a visit from your impassioned admirer, but next year be sure I will make amends, and you shall no longer find me a truant."

"I see, Asturiano," said Tomas, "how openly you mock me. Why don't you go to your fisheries? There is nothing to hinder you. I will remain where I am, and you will find me here on your return. If you wish to take your share of the money with you, take it at once; go your ways in peace, and let each of us follow the course prescribed to him by his own destiny."

"I thought you had more sense," said Lope. "Don't you know that I was only joking? But now that I perceive you are in earnest, I will serve you in earnest in everything I can do to please you. Only one thing I entreat in return for the many I intend to do for you: do not expose me to Argüello's persecution, for I would rather lose your friendship than have to endure hers. Good God, friend! her tongue goes like the clapper of a mill; you can smell her breath a league off; all her front teeth are false, and it is my private opinion that she does not wear her own hair, but a wig. To crown all, since she began to make overtures to me, she has taken to painting white, till her face looks like nothing but a mask of plaster."

"True, indeed, my poor comrade; she is worse even than the Gallegan who makes me suffer martyrdom. I'll tell you what you shall do; only stay this night in the inn, and to-morrow you shall buy yourself an ass, find a lodging, and so secure yourself from the importunities of Argüello, whilst I remain exposed to those of the Gallegan, and to the fire of my Costanza's eyes."

This being agreed on, the two friends returned to the inn, where Asturiano was received with great demonstrations of love by Argüello. That night a great number of muleteers stopping in the house, and those near it, got up a dance before the door of the Sevillano. Asturiano played the guitar: the female dancers were the two Gallegans and Argüello, and three girls from another inn. Many persons stood by as spectators, with their faces muffled, prompted more by a desire to see Costanza than the dance; but they were disappointed, for she did not make her appearance. Asturiano played for the dancers with such spirit and precision of touch that they all vowed he made the guitar speak; but just as he was doing his best, accompanying the instrument with his voice, and the dancers were capering like mad, one of the muffled spectators cried out, "Stop, you drunken sot! hold your noise, wineskin, piperly poet, miserable catgut scraper!" Several others followed up this insulting speech with such a torrent of abuse that Lope thought it best to cease playing and singing; but the muleteers took the interruption so much amiss, that had it not been for the earnest endeavours of the landlord to appease them, there would have been a terrible row. In spite indeed of all he could do, the muleteers would not have kept their hands quiet, had not the watch happened just then to come up and clear the ground. A moment afterwards the ears of all who were awake in the quarter were greeted by an admirable voice proceeding from a man who had seated himself on a stone opposite the door of the Sevillano. Everybody listened with rapt attention to his song, but none more so than Tomas Pedro, to whom every word sounded like a sentence of excommunication, for the romance ran thus:

In what celestial realms of space
Is hid that beauteous, witching face?
Where shines that star, which, boding ills,
My trembling heart with torment fills?
Why in its wrath should Heaven decree
That we no more its light should see?
Why bid that sun no longer cheer

With glorious beams our drooping sphere?"
Yes, second sun! 'tis true you shine,
But not for us, with light divine!
Yet gracious come from ocean's bed;
Why hide from us your radiant head?
Constance! a faithful, dying swain
Adores your beauty, though in vain;
For when his love he would impart,
You fly and scorn his proffered heart!
O let his tears your pity sway,
And quick he'll bear you hence away;
For shame it is this sordid place,
Should do your charms such foul disgrace
Here you're submissive to control,
Sweet mistress of my doating soul!
But altars youths to you should raise,
And passion'd vot'ries sound your praise!
Quit then a scene which must consume
Unworthily your early bloom!
To my soft vows your ear incline,
Nor frown, but be for ever mine!
His gladsome torch let Hymen light,
And let the god our hearts unite!
This day would then before its end,
See me your husband, lover, friend.

The last line was immediately followed by the flight of two brick-bats, which fell close to the singer's feet; but had they come in contact with his head, they would certainly have knocked all the music and poetry out of it. The poor frightened musician took to his heels with such speed that a greyhound could not have caught him. Unhappy fate of night-birds, to be always subject to such showers! All who had heard the voice of the fugitive admired it, but most of all, Tomas Pedro, only he would rather the words had not been addressed to Costanza, although she had not heard one of them. The only person who found fault with the romance was a muleteer, nicknamed Barrabas. As soon as this man saw the singer run off, he bawled after him; "There you go, you Judas of a troubadour! May the fleas eat your eyes out! Who the devil taught you to sing to a scullery-maid about celestial realms, and spheres, and ocean-beds, and to call her stars and suns and all the rest of it? If you had told her she was as straight as asparagus, as white as milk, as modest as a lay-brother in his novitiate, more full of humours and unmanageable than a hired mule, and harder than a lump of dry mortar, why then she would have understood you and been pleased; but your fine words are fitter for a scholar than for a scullery-maid. Truly, there are poets in the world who write songs that the devil himself could not understand; for my part, at least, Barrabas though I am, I cannot make head or tail of what this fellow has been singing. What did he suppose Costanza could make of them? But she knows better than to listen to such stuff, for she is snug in bed, and cares no more for all these caterwaulers than she does for Prester John. This fellow at least, is not one of the singers belonging to the corregidor's son, for they are out and out good ones, and a body can generally understand them; but, by the Lord, this fellow sets me mad."

The bystanders coincided in opinion with Barrabas, and thought his criticism very judicious. Everybody now went to bed, but no sooner was the house all still, than Lope heard some one calling very softly at his bed-room door. "Who's there?" said he. "It is we," whispered a voice, "Argüello and the Gallegan. Open the door and let us in, for we are dying of cold."

"Dying of cold indeed," said Lope, "and we are in the middle of the dog days."

"Oh, leave off now, friend Lope," said the Gallegan; "get up and open the door; for here we are as fine as archduchesses."

"Archduchesses, and at this hour? I don't believe a word of it, but rather think you must be witches or something worse. Get out of that this moment, or, by all that's damnable, if you make me get up I'll leather you with my belt till your hinder parts are as red as poppies."

Finding that he answered them so roughly, and in a manner so contrary to their expectations, the two disappointed damsels returned sadly to their beds; but before they left the door, Argüello put her lips to the key-hole, and hissed through it, "Honey was not made for the mouth of the ass;" and with that, as if she had said something very bitter indeed, and taken adequate revenge on the scorner, she went off to her cheerless bed.

"Look you, Tomas," said Lope to his companion, as soon as they were gone, "set me to fight two giants, or to break the jaws of half a dozen, or a whole dozen of lions, if it be requisite for your service, and I shall do it as readily as I would drink a glass of wine; but that you should put me under the necessity of encountering Argüello, this is what I would never submit to, no, not if I were to be flayed alive. Only think, what damsels of Denmark[81] fate has thrown upon us this night. Well, patience! To-morrow will come, thank God, and then we shall see."

"I have already told you, friend," replied Tomas, "that you may do as you please—either go on your pilgrimage, or buy an ass and turn water-carrier as you proposed."

"I stick to the water-carrying business," said Lope. "My mind is made up not to quit you at present."

They then went to sleep till daylight, when they rose; Tomas Pedro went to give out oats, and Lope set off to the cattle-market to buy an ass. Now it happened that Tomas had spent his leisure on holidays in composing some amorous verses, and had jotted them down in the book in which he kept the account of the oats, intending to copy them out fairly, and then blot them out of the book, or tear out the page. But, before he had done so, he happened to go out one day and leave the book on the top of the oat-bin. His master found it there, and looking into it to see how the account of the oats stood, he lighted upon the verses. Surprised and annoyed, he went off with them to his wife, but before he read them to her, he called Costanza into the room, and peremptorily commanded her to declare whether Tomas Pedro, the hostler, had ever made love to her, or addressed any improper language to her, or any that gave token of his being partial to her. Costanza vowed that Tomas had never yet spoken to her in any such way, nor ever given her reason to suppose that he had any bad thoughts towards her.

Her master and mistress believed her, because they had always found her to speak the truth. Having dismissed her, the host turned to his wife and said, "I know not what to say of the matter. You must know, señora, that Tomas has written in this book, in which he keeps the account of the oats, verses that give me an ugly suspicion that he is in love with Costanza."

"Let me see the verses," said the wife, "and I'll tell you what we are to conclude."

"Oh, of course; as you are a poet you will at once see into his thoughts."

"I am not a poet, but you well know that I am a woman of understanding, and that I can say the four prayers in Latin."

"You would do better to say them in plain Spanish; you know your uncle the priest has told you that you make no end of blunders when you patter your Latin, and that what you say is good for nothing."

"That was an arrow from his niece's quiver. She is jealous of seeing me take the Latin hours in hand, and make my way through them as easily as through a vineyard after the vintage."

"Well, have it your own way. Listen now, here are the verses;" and he read some impassioned lines addressed to Costanza.

"Is there any more?" said the landlady.

"No. But what do you think of these verses?"

"In the first place, we must make sure that they are by Tomas."

"Of that there can be no manner of doubt, for the handwriting is most unquestionably the same as that in which the account of the oats is kept."

"Look ye, husband, it appears to me that although Costanza is named in the verses, whence it may be supposed that they were made for her, we ought not for that reason to set the fact down for certain, just as if we had seen them written, for there are other Costanzas in the world besides ours. But even supposing they were meant for her, there is not a word in them that could do her discredit. Let us be on the watch, and look sharply after the girl; for if he is in love with her, we may be sure he will make more verses, and try to give them to her."

"Would it not be better to get rid of all this bother by turning him out of doors?"

"That is for you to do if you think proper. But really, by your own account, the lad does his work so well that it would go against one's conscience to turn him off upon such slight grounds."

"Very well; let us be on the watch as you say, and time will tell us what we have to do." Here the conversation ended, and the landlord carried the book back to the place where he had found it.

Tomas returned in great anxiety to look for his book, found it, and that it might not occasion him another fright, he immediately copied out the verses, effaced the original, and made up his mind to hazard a declaration to Costanza upon the first opportunity that should present itself. Her extreme reserve, however, was such that there seemed little likelihood of his finding such an opportunity; besides, the great concourse of people in the house made it almost impossible that he should have any private conversation with her,—to the despair of her unfortunate lover. That day, however, it chanced that Costanza appeared with one cheek muffled, and told some one who asked her the reason, that she was suffering from a violent face ache. Tomas, whose wits were sharpened by his passion, instantly saw how he might avail himself of that circumstance. "Señora Costanza," he said, "I will give you a prayer in writing, which you have only to recite once or twice, and it will take away your pain forthwith."

"Give it me, if you please," said Costanza, "and I will recite it; for I know how to read."

"It must be on condition, however," said Tomas, "that you do not show it to anybody; for I value it highly, and I should not wish it to lose its charm by being made known to many."

"I promise you that no person shall see it; but let me have it at once, for I can hardly bear this pain."

"I will write it out from memory, and bring it you immediately."

This was the very first conversation that had ever taken place between Tomas and Costanza during all the time he had been in the house, which was nearly a month. Tomas withdrew, wrote out the prayer, and found means to deliver it, unseen by any one else, into Costanza's hand; and she, with great eagerness, and no less devotion, went with it into a room, where she shut herself up alone. Then, opening the paper, she read as follows:—

"Lady of my soul, I am a gentleman of Burgos; and if I survive my father, I shall inherit a property of six thousand ducats yearly income. Upon the fame of your beauty, which spreads far and wide, I left my native place, changed my dress, and came in the garb in which you see me, to serve your master. If you would consent to be mine in the way most accordant with your virtue, put me to any proof you please, to convince you of my truth and sincerity; and when you have fully satisfied yourself in this respect, I will, if you consent, become your husband, and the happiest of men. For the present, I only entreat you not to turn such loving and guileless feelings as mine into the street; for if your master, who has no conception of them, should come to know my aspirations, he would condemn me to exile from your presence, and that would be the same thing as sentencing me to death. Suffer me, señora, to see you until you believe me, considering that he does not deserve the rigorous punishment of being deprived of the sight of you, whose only fault has been that he adores you. You can reply to me with your eyes, unperceived by any of the numbers who are always gazing upon you; for your eyes are such that their anger kills, but their compassion gives new life."

When Tomas saw that Costanza had gone away to read his letter, he remained with a palpitating heart, fearing and hoping either his death-doom, or the one look that should bid him live. Presently Costanza returned, looking so beautiful in spite of her muffling, that if any extraneous cause could have heightened her loveliness, it might be supposed that her surprise at finding the contents of the paper so widely different from what she had expected, had produced that effect. In her hand she held the paper torn into small pieces, and returning, the fragments to Tomas, whose legs could hardly bear him up, "Brother Tomas," she said, "this prayer of yours seems to me to savour more of witchcraft and delusion than of piety, therefore I do not choose to put faith in it or to use it, and I have torn it up that it may not be seen by any one more credulous than myself. Learn other prayers, for it is impossible that this one can ever do you any good."

So saying, she returned to her mistress's room, leaving Tomas sorely distressed, but somewhat comforted at finding that his secret remained safe confined to Costanza's bosom; for as she had not divulged it to her master, he reckoned that at least he was in no danger of being turned out of doors. He considered also, that in having taken the first step, he had overcome mountains of difficulties, for in great and doubtful enterprises the chief difficulty is always in the beginning.

Whilst these things were happening in the posada, Asturiano was going about the market in search of an ass. He examined a great many, but did not find one to his mind; though a gipsy tried hard to force upon him one that moved briskly enough, but more from the effects of some quicksilver which the vendor had put into the animal's ears, than from its natural spirit and nimbleness. But though the pace was good enough, Lope was not satisfied with the size, for he wanted an ass big and strong enough to carry himself and the water vessels, whether they were full or empty. At last a young fellow came up, and whispered in his ear, "If you want a beast of the right sort for a water-carrier's business, I have one close by in a meadow; a bigger or a better you will not find in Toledo. Take my advice, and never buy a gipsy's beast, for though they may seem sound and good, they are all shams, and full of hidden defects. If you want to buy the real thing, come along with me, and shut your mouth."

Lope consented, and away went the pair shoulder to shoulder, till they arrived at the King's Gardens, where they found several water-carriers seated under the shade of a water wheel, whilst their asses were grazing in an adjoining meadow. The vendor pointed out his ass, which took Lope's fancy immediately, and was praised by all present, as a very strong animal, a good goer, and a capital feeder. The bargain was soon struck, and Lope gave sixteen ducats for the ass, with all its accoutrements. The bystanders congratulated him on his purchase, and on his entrance into the business, assuring him that he had bought an exceedingly lucky ass, for the man who had sold him had, in less than a year, without over-working himself, made enough to buy two suits of clothes, over and above his own keep, and that of the ass, and the sixteen ducats, with which he intended to return to his native place, where a marriage had been arranged with a half kinswoman of his. Besides the water-carriers who assisted at the sale of the ass, there was a group of four stretched on the ground, and playing at primera, the earth serving them for a table, and their cloaks for a table cloth. Lope went up to watch their game, and saw that they played more like archdeacons than like water-carriers, each of them having before him a pile of more than a hundred reals in cuartos and in silver. Presently two of the players, having lost all they had, got up; whereupon the seller of the ass said, that, if there was a fourth hand, he would play, but he did not like a three-handed game.

Lope, who never liked to spoil sport, said that he would make a fourth. They sat down at once, and went at it so roundly, that, in a few moments, Lope lost six crowns which he had about him, and finding himself without coin, said if they liked to play for the ass he would stake him. The proposal was agreed to, and he staked one quarter of the ass, saying they should play for him, quarter by quarter. His luck was so bad, that in four consecutive games he lost the four quarters of his ass, and they were won by the very man who had sold him. The winner got up to take possession, but Lope stopped him, observing that he had only played for and lost the four quarters of his ass, which the winner was welcome to take, but he must leave him the tail. This queer demand made all present shout with laughter; and some of them, who were knowing in the law, were of opinion that his claim was unreasonable, for when a sheep or any other beast is sold, the tail is never separated from the carcass, but goes as a matter of course with one of the hind quarters. To this Lope replied that in Barbary they always reckon five quarters to a sheep, the tail making the fifth, and being reckoned as valuable as any of the other quarters. He admitted that when a beast was sold alive, and not quartered, that the tail was included in the sale; but this was not to the point in question, for he had not sold his ass, but played it away, and it had never been his intention to stake the tail; therefore he required them forthwith to give him up the same, with everything thereto annexed, or pertaining, that is to say, the whole series of spinal bones, from the back of the skull to where they ended in the tail, and to the tips of the lowest hairs thereof.

"Well," said one, "suppose it be as you say, and that your claim is allowed; leave the tail sticking to the rest of the ass, and hold on by it."

"No," said Lope, "give me up the tail, or all the water-carriers in the world shall never make me give up the ass. Don't imagine because there are so many of you, that I will let you put any cheating tricks on me, for I am a man who can stand up to another man, and put two handbreadths of cold steel into his guts without his being able to tell how he came by them. Moreover, I won't be paid in money for the tail at so much a pound, but I will have it in substance, and cut off from the ass, as I have said."

The winner of the four quarters and the rest of the company began to think that it would not be advisable to resort to force in this business, for Lope seemed to them to be a man of such mettle, that he would not be vanquished without some trouble. Nor were they mistaken; for, as became a man who had spent three seasons at the tunny fisheries, where all sorts of rows and brawls are familiar things, he rattled out a few of the most out of the way oaths in vogue there, threw his cap into the air, whipped out a knife from beneath his cloak, and put himself into such a posture as struck the whole company with awe and respect. At last, one of them, who seemed the most rational, induced the rest to agree that Lope should be allowed to stake the tail against a quarter of the ass at a game of quinola. So said, so done. Lope won the first game; the loser was piqued and staked another quarter, which went the way of the first; and in two more games the whole ass was gone. He then proposed to play for money: Lope was unwilling, but was so importuned on all hands, that at last he consented; and such was his run of luck that he left his opponent without a maravedi. So intense was the loser's vexation, that he rolled and writhed upon the ground and knocked his head against it. Lope, however, like a good-natured, liberal gentleman, raised him up, returned all the money he had won, including the sixteen ducats the price of the ass, and even divided what he had left among the bystanders. Great was the surprise of them all at this extraordinary liberality; and had they lived in the time of the great Tamerlane, they would have made him king of the water-carriers.

Accompanied by a great retinue, Lope returned to the city, where he related his adventure to Tomas, who in turn recounted to him his own partial success. There was no tavern, or eating house, or rogues' gathering, in which the play for the ass was not known, the dispute about the tail, and the high spirit and liberality of the Asturian; but as the mob are for the most part unjust, and more prone to evil than to good, they thought nothing of the generosity and high mettle of the great Lope, but only of the tail; and he had scarcely been two days carrying water about the city, before he found himself pointed at by people who cried, "There goes the man of the tail!" The boys caught up the cry, and no sooner had Lope shown himself in any street, than it rang from one end to the other with shouts of "Asturiano, give up the tail! Give up the tail, Asturiano!" At first Lope said not a word, thinking that his silence would tire out his persecutors; but in this he was mistaken, for the more he held his tongue the more the boys wagged theirs, till at last he lost patience, and getting off his ass began to drub the boys; but this was only cutting off the heads of Hydra, and for every one he laid low by thrashing some boy, there sprang up on the instant, not seven but seven hundred more, that began to pester him more and more for the tail. At last he found it expedient to retire to the lodgings he had taken apart from his companion in order to avoid Argüello, and to keep close there until the influence of the malignant planet which then ruled the hours should have passed away, and the boys should have forgotten to ask him for the tail. For two days he never left the house except by night to go and see Tomas, and ask him how he got on. Tomas told him that since he had given the paper to Costanza he had never been able to speak a single word to her, and that she seemed to be more reserved than ever. Once he had found as he thought an opportunity to accost her, but before he could get out a word, she stopped him, saying, "Tomas, I am in no pain now, and therefore have no need of your words or of your prayers. Be content that I do not accuse you to the Inquisition, and give yourself no further trouble." But she made this declaration without any expression of anger in her countenance. Lope then related how the boys annoyed him, calling after him for the tail, and Tomas advised him not to go abroad, at least with his ass, or if he did that he should choose only the least frequented streets. If that was not enough, he had an unfailing remedy left, which was to get rid of his business and with it of the uncivil demand to which it subjected him. Lope asked him had the Gallegan come again to his room. He said she had not, but that she persisted in trying to ingratiate herself with him by means of dainties which she purloined out of what she cooked for the guests. After this conversation Lope went back to his lodgings, intending not to leave them again for another six days, at least in company with his ass.

It might be about eleven at night, when the corregidor most unexpectedly entered the Posado del Sevillano, at the head of a formidable posse. The host and even the guests were startled and agitated by his visit; for as comets, when they appear, always excite fears of disaster, just so the ministers of justice, when they suddenly enter a house, strike even guiltless consciences with alarm. The unwelcome visitor walked into a room, and called for the master of the house, who came tremblingly to know what might be the señor corregidor's pleasure. "Are you the landlord?" said the magistrate with great gravity. "Yes, señor, and your worship's humble servant to command," was the reply. The corregidor then ordered that every one else should quit the room, and leave him alone with the landlord. This being done, he resumed his questions.

"What servants have you in your inn, landlord?"

"Señor, I have two Gallegan wenches, a housekeeper, and a young man who gives out the oats and straw, and keeps the reckoning."

"No more?"

"No, señor."

"Then tell me, landlord, what is become of a girl who is said to be a servant in this house, and so beautiful that she is known all over this city as the illustrious scullery-maid? It has even reached my ears that my son Don Perequito is in love with her, and that not a night passes in which he does not serenade her."

"Señor, it is true that this illustrious scullery-maid, as they call her, is in my house, but she neither is my servant, nor ceases to be so."

"I do not understand you. What do you mean by saying that she is and is not your servant?"

"It is the real truth, and if your worship will allow me, I will explain the matter to you, and tell you what I have never told to any one."

"Before I hear what you have to say, I must first see this scullery-maid."

Upon this the landlord went to the door and called to his wife to send in Costanza, When the landlady heard that, she was in great dismay, and began to wring her hands, saying, "Lord, have mercy on me! What can the corregidor want with Costanza, and alone! Some terrible calamity must surely have happened, for this girl's beauty bewitches the men."

"Don't be alarmed, señora," said Costanza, "I will go and see what the señor corregidor wants, and if anything bad has happened, be assured the fault is not mine;" and without waiting to be called a second time, she took a lighted candle in a silver candlestick, and went into the room where the corregidor was. As soon as he saw her, he bade the landlord shut the door, and then taking the candle out of her hand; and holding it near her face, he stood gazing at her from head to foot. The blush which this called up into Costanza's cheeks, made her look so beautiful and so modest that it seemed to the corregidor he beheld an angel descended on earth. After a long scrutiny, "Landlord," he said, "an inn is not fit setting for a jewel like this, and I now declare that my son Don Perequito has shown his good sense in fixing his affections so worthily. I say, damsel, that they may well call you not only illustrious, but most illustrious: but it should not be with the addition of scullery-maid, but with that of duchess."

"She is no scullery-maid, señor," said the host; "her only service in the house is to keep the keys of the plate, of which, by God's bounty, I have some quantity for the service of the honourable guests who come to this inn."

"Be that as it may, landlord," returned the corregidor; "I say it is neither seemly nor proper that this damsel should live in an inn. Is she a relation of yours?"

"She is neither my relation nor my servant; and if your worship would like to know who she is, your worship shall hear, when she is not present, things that will both please and surprise you."

"I should like to know it. Let Costanza retire, and be assured she may count on me in all things, as she would upon her own father; for her great modesty and beauty oblige all who see her to offer themselves for her service."

Costanza replied not a word, but with great composure made a profound reverence to the corregidor. On leaving the room she found her mistress waiting in great agitation. She told her all that had passed, and how her master remained with the corregidor to tell some things, she knew not what, which he did not choose her to hear. All this did not quite tranquilise the landlady, nor did she entirely recover her equanimity until the corregidor went away, and she saw her husband safe and free. The latter meanwhile had told the corregidor the following tale:—

"It is now, by my reckoning, señor, fifteen years, one month, and four days, since there came to this house a lady dressed in the habit of a pilgrim, and carried in a litter. She was attended by four servant-men on horseback, and two dueñas and a damsel who rode in a coach. She had also two sumpter mules richly caparisoned, and carrying a fine bed and all the necessary implements for cooking. In short, the whole equipage was first rate, and the pilgrim had all the appearance of being some great lady; and though she seemed to be about forty years of age, she was nevertheless beautiful in the extreme. She was in bad health, looked pale, and was so weary, that she ordered her bed to be instantly made, and her servants made it in this very room. They asked me who was the most famous physician in this city. I said Doctor de la Fuente. They went for him instantly; he came without delay, saw his patient alone, and the result was that he ordered the bed to be made in some other part of the house, where the lady might not be disturbed by any noise, which was immediately done. None of the men-servants entered the lady's apartment, but only the two dueñas and the damsel. My wife and I asked the men-servants who was this lady, what was her name, whence she came, and whither she was going? Was she wife, widow, or maid, and why she wore that pilgrim's dress? To all these questions, which we repeated many and many a time, we got no other answer than that this pilgrim was a noble and wealthy lady of old Castile, that she was a widow, and had no children to inherit her wealth; and that having been for some months ill of the dropsy, she had made a vow to go on a pilgrimage to our Lady of Guadalupe, and that was the reason for the dress she wore. As for her name, they were under orders to call her nothing but the lady pilgrim.

"So much we learned then; but three days after one of the dueñas called myself and my wife into the lady's presence, and there, with the door locked, and before her women, she addressed us with tears in her eyes, I believe in these very words:—

"'Heaven is my witness, friends, that without any fault of mine, I find myself in the cruel predicament which I shall now declare to you. I am pregnant, and so near my time, that I already feel the pangs of travail. None of my men-servants are aware of my misfortune, but from my women here I have neither been able nor desirous to conceal it. To escape prying eyes in my own neighbourhood, and that this hour might not come upon me there, I made a vow to go to our Lady of Guadalupe; but it is plainly her will that my labour should befal me in your house. It is now for you to succour and aid me with the secrecy due to one who commits her honour to your hands. In this purse there are two hundred gold crowns, which I present to you as a first proof how grateful I shall be for the good offices I am sure you will render me;' and taking from under her pillow a green silk purse, embroidered with gold, she put it into the hands of my wife, who, like a simpleton, stood gaping at the lady, and did not say so much as a word in the way of thanks or acknowledgment. For my part I remember that I said there was no need at all of that, we were not persons to be moved more by interest than by humanity to do a good deed when the occasion offered. The lady then continued, 'You must immediately, my friends, look out for some place to which you may convey my child as soon as it is born, and also you must contrive some story to tell to the person in whose charge you will leave it. At first I wish the babe to remain in this city, and afterwards to be taken to a village. As for what is subsequently done, I will give you instructions on my return from Guadalupe, if it is God's will that I should live to complete my pilgrimage, for in the meantime I shall have had leisure to consider what may be my best course. I shall have no need of a midwife; for as I know from other confinements of mine, more honourable than this, I shall do well enough with the aid of my women only, and thus I shall avoid having an additional witness to my misfortune.'

"Here the poor distressed pilgrim ended what she had to say, and broke out into a flood of tears, but was partly composed by the soothing words spoken to her by my wife, who had recovered her wits. I immediately went in search of a woman to whom I might take the child when it was born; and, between twelve and one o'clock that night, when all the people in the house were fast asleep, the lady was delivered of the most beautiful little girl that eyes ever beheld, and the very same that your worship has just seen. But the wonder was that neither did the mother make any moan in her labour, nor did the baby cry; but all passed off quietly, and in all the silence that became this extraordinary case. The lady kept her bed for six days, during which the doctor was constant in his visits; not that she had informed him of the cause of her illness, or that she took any of the medicines he prescribed; but she thought to blind her men-servants by his visits, as she afterwards informed me when she was out of danger. On the eighth day she left her bed, apparently as big as she had been before her delivery, continued her pilgrimage, and returned in three weeks, looking almost quite well, for she had gradually reduced the bulk of her artificial dropsy. The little girl had been christened Costanza, in accordance with the order given me by her mother, and was already placed with a nurse in a village about two leagues hence, where she passed for my niece. The lady was pleased to express her satisfaction with all I had done, and gave me when she was going away a gold chain, which is now in my possession, from which she took off six links, telling me that they would be brought by the person who should come to claim the child. She also took a piece of white parchment, wrote upon it, and then cut zigzag through what she had written. Look, sir, here are my hands locked together with the fingers interwoven. Now suppose your honour were to write across my fingers, it is easy to imagine that one could read the writing whilst the fingers were joined, but that the meaning would be lost as soon as the hands were separated, and would appear again as soon as they were united as before. Just so with the parchment; one half serves as a key to the other; when they are put together the letters make sense, but separately they have no meaning. One-half of the parchment and the whole chain, short of the six links, were left with me, and I keep them still, always expecting the arrival of the person who is to produce the counterparts; for the lady told me that in two years she would send for her daughter, charging me that I should have her brought up not as became her mother's quality, but as a simple villager; and if by any chance she was not able to send for the child so soon, I was on no account to acquaint her with the secret of her birth, even should she have arrived at years of discretion. The lady moreover begged me to excuse her if she did not tell me who she was; having for the present important reasons to conceal her name. Finally, after giving us four hundred gold crowns more, and embracing my wife with tears, she departed, leaving us filled with admiration for her discretion, worth, beauty, and modesty.

"Costanza remained at nurse in the village for two years. At the end of that time I brought her home, and have kept her ever since constantly with me, in the dress of a girl who had to work for her bread, as her mother directed. Fifteen years, one month, and four days I have been looking for the person who should come and claim her, but the length of time that has elapsed makes me begin to lose all hope of his coming. If he does not make his appearance before this year is out, it is my determination to adopt her and bequeath her all I am worth, which is upwards of sixteen thousand ducats, thanks be to God. It now remains for me, señor Corregidor, to enumerate to you the virtues and good qualities of Costanza, if it be possible for me to express them. First and foremost, she is most piously devoted to our Lady; she confesses and communicates every month; she can read and write; there's not a better lace maker in all Toledo; she sings without accompaniment like an angel; in the matter of behaving with propriety she has not her equal; as for her beauty, your worship has seen it with your own eyes. Señor Don Pedro, your worship's son, has never exchanged a word with her in her life. It is true that from time to time he treats her to some music, which she never listens to. Many señors, and men of title too, have put up at this house, and have delayed their journey for several days solely to have their fill of looking at her; but I well know there is not one of them can boast with truth that she ever gave them opportunity to say one word to her either alone or before folk. This, señor, is the real history of the illustrious scullery-maid, who is no scullion, in which I have not departed one tittle from the truth."

The host had long ended his narrative before the corregidor broke silence, so much was he struck by the strange facts he had heard. At last he desired to see the parchment and the chain; the host produced them without delay, and they corresponded exactly to the description he had given of them. The chain was of curious workmanship, and on the parchment were written, one under the other, on the projecting portions of the zigzag, the letters, TIITEREOE which manifestly required to be joined with those of the counterpart to make sense. The corregidor admired the ingenuity of the contrivance, and judged from the costliness of the chain, that the pilgrim must have been a lady of great wealth. It was his intention to remove the lovely girl from the inn as soon as he had chosen a suitable convent for her abode; but for the present he contented himself with taking away the parchment only, desiring the innkeeper to inform him if any one came for Costanza, before he showed that person the chain, which he left in his custody. And with this parting injunction the corregidor left the house, much marvelling at what he had seen and heard.

Whilst all this affair was going on, Tomas was almost beside himself with agitation and alarm, and lost in a thousand conjectures, every one of which he dismissed as improbable the moment it was formed. But when he saw the corregidor go away, leaving Costanza behind him, his spirits revived and he began to recover his self-possession. He did not venture to question the landlord, nor did the latter say a word about what had passed between him and the corregidor to any body but his wife, who was greatly relieved thereby, and thanked God for her delivery out of a terrible fright.

About one o'clock on the following day, there came to the inn two elderly cavaliers of venerable presence, attended by four servants on horseback and two on foot. Having inquired if that was the Posada del Sevillano, and being answered in the affirmative, they entered the gateway, and the four mounted servants, dismounting, first helped their master's out of their saddles. Costanza came out to meet the new-comers with her wonted propriety of demeanour, and no sooner had one of the cavaliers set eyes on her, than, turning to his companion, he said, "I believe, señor Don Juan, we have already found the very thing we are come in quest of." Tomas, who had come as usual to take charge of the horses and mules, instantly recognised two of his father's servants; a moment after he saw his father himself, and found that his companion was no other than the father of Carriazo. He instantly conjectured that they were both on their way to the tunny fisheries to look for himself and his friend, some one having no doubt told them that it was there, and not in Flanders, they would find their sons. Not daring to appear before his father in the garb he wore, he made a bold venture, passed by the party with his hand before his face, and went to look for Costanza, whom, by great good luck, he found alone. Then hurriedly, and with a tremulous voice, dreading lest she would not give him time to say a word to her, "Costanza," he said, "one of those two elderly cavaliers is my father—that one whom you will hear called Don Juan de Avendaño. Inquire of his servants if he has a son, Don Tomas de Avendaño by name, and that is myself. Thence you may go on to make such other inquiries as will satisfy you that I have told you the truth respecting my quality, and that I will keep my word with regard to every offer I have made you. And now farewell, for I will not return to this house until they have left it."

Costanza made him no reply, nor did he wait for any, but hurrying out, with his face concealed as he had come in, he went to acquaint Carriazo that their fathers had arrived at the Sevillano. The landlord called for Tomas to give out oats, but no Tomas appearing, he had to do it himself.

Meanwhile, one of the two cavaliers called one of the Gallegan wenches aside, and asked her what was the name of the beautiful girl he had seen, and was she a relation of the landlord or the landlady. "The girl's name is Costanza," replied the Gallegan; "she is no relation either to the landlord or the landlady, nor do I know what she is. All I can say is, I wish the murrain had her, for I don't know what there is about her, that she does not leave one of us girls in the house a single chance, for all we have our own features too, such as God made them. Nobody enters these doors but the first thing he does is to ask, Who is that beautiful girl? and the next is to say all sorts of flattering things of her, while nobody condescends to say a word to the rest of us, not so much as 'What are you doing here, devils, or women, or whatever you are?'"

"From your account, then," said the gentleman, "I suppose she has a fine time of it with the strangers who put up at this house."

"You think so. Well, just you hold her foot for the shoeing, and see how you'll like the job. By the Lord, señor, if she would only give her admirers leave to look at her, she might roll in gold; but she's more touch-me-not than a hedgehog; she's a devourer of Ave Marias, and spends the whole day at her needle and her prayers. I wish I was as sure of a good legacy as she is of working miracles some day. Bless you, she's a downright saint; my mistress says she wears hair-cloth next her skin."

Highly delighted with what he had heard from the Gallegan, the gentleman did not wait till they had taken off his spurs, but called for the landlord, and withdrew with him into a private room. "Señor host," said he, "I am come to redeem a pledge of mine which has been in your hands for some years, and I bring you for it a thousand gold crowns, these links of a chain, and this parchment."

The host instantly recognised the links and the parchment, and highly delighted with the promise of the thousand crowns, replied, "Señor, the pledge you wish to redeem is in this house, but not the chain or the parchment which is to prove the truth of your claim; I pray you therefore to have patience, and I will return immediately." So saying, he ran off to inform the corregidor of what was happening.

The corregidor, who had just done dinner, mounted his horse without delay, and rode to the Posada del Sevillano, taking with him the tally parchment. No sooner had he entered the room where the two cavaliers sat, than hastening with open arms to embrace one of them, "Bless my soul! my good cousin Don Juan de Avendaño! This is indeed a welcome surprise."

"I am delighted to see you, my good cousin," said Don Juan, "and to find you as well as I always wish you. Embrace this gentleman, cousin; this is Don Diego de Carriazo, a great señor and my friend."

"I am already acquainted with the señor Don Diego," replied the corregidor, "and am his most obedient servant."

After a further interchange of civilities they passed into another room, where they remained alone with the innkeeper, who said as he produced the chain, "The señor corregidor knows what you are come for, Don Diego de Carriazo. Be pleased to produce the links that are wanting to this chain; his worship will show the parchment which he holds, and let us come to the proof for which I have been so long waiting."

"It appears, then," said Don Diego, "that it will not be necessary to explain to the señor corregidor the reason of our coming, since you have done so already, señor landlord."

"He told me something," said the corregidor, "but he has left much untold which I long to know. Here is the parchment."

Don Diego produced that which he had brought; the two were put together and found to fit accurately into each other; and between every two letters of the innkeeper's portion, which as we have said were TIITEREOE there now appeared one of the following series HSSHTUTKN, the whole making together the words, This is the true token. The six links of the chain brought by Don Diego were then compared with the larger fragment, and found to correspond exactly.

"So far all is clear," said the corregidor; "it now remains for us to discover, if it be possible, who are the parents of this very beautiful lady."

"Her father," said Don Diego, "you see in me; her mother is not living, and you must be content with knowing that she was a lady of such rank that I might have been her servant. But though I conceal her name, I would not have you suppose that she was in any wise culpable, however manifest and avowed her fault may appear to have been. The story I will now briefly relate to you will completely exonerate her memory.

"You must know, then, that Costanza's mother, being left a widow by a man of high rank, retired to an estate of hers, where she lived a calm sequestered life among her servants and vassals. It chanced one day when I was hunting, that I found myself very near her house and determined to pay her a visit. It was siesta time when I arrived at her palace (for I can call it nothing else): giving my horse to one of my servants, I entered, and saw no one till I was in the very room in which she lay asleep on a black ottoman. She was extremely handsome; the silence, the loneliness of the place, and the opportunity, awakened my guilty desires, and without pausing to reflect, I locked the door, woke her, and holding her firmly in my grasp said, 'No cries, señora! they would only serve to proclaim your dishonour; no one has seen me enter this room, for by good fortune all your servants are fast asleep, and should your cries bring them hither, they can do no more than kill me in your very arms; and if they do, your reputation will not be the less blighted for all that.' In fine, I effected my purpose against her will and by main force, and left her so stupefied by the calamity that had befallen her, that she either could not or would not utter one word to me. Quitting the place as I had entered it, I rode to the house of one of my friends, who resided within two leagues of my victim's abode. The lady subsequently removed to another residence, and two years passed without my seeing her, or making any attempt to do so. At the end, of that time I heard that she was dead.

"About three weeks since I received a letter from a man who had been the deceased lady's steward, earnestly entreating me to come to him, as he had something to communicate to me which deeply concerned my happiness and honour. I went to him, very far from dreaming of any such thing as I was about to hear from him, and found him at the point of death. He told me in brief terms that his lady on her deathbed had made known to him what had happened between her and me, how she had become pregnant, had made a pilgrimage to our Lady of Guadalupe to conceal her misfortune, and had been delivered in this inn of a daughter named Costanza. The man gave me the tokens upon which she was to be delivered to me, namely the piece of chain and the parchment, and with them thirty thousand gold crowns, which the lady had left as a marriage portion for her daughter. At the same time, he told me that it was the temptation to appropriate that money which had so long prevented him from obeying the dying behest of his mistress, but now that he was about to be called to the great account, he was eager to relieve his conscience by giving me up the money and putting me in the way to find my daughter. Returning home with the money and the tokens, I related the whole story to Don Juan de Avendaño, and he has been kind enough to accompany me to this city."

Don Diego had but just finished his narrative when some one was heard shouting at the street-door, "Tell Tomas Pedro, the hostler, that they are taking his friend the Asturiano to prison." On hearing this the corregidor immediately sent orders to the alguazil to bring in his prisoner, which was forthwith done. In came the Asturian with his mouth all bloody. He had evidently been very roughly handled, and was held with no tender grasp by the alguazil. The moment he entered the room he was thunderstruck at beholding his own father and Avendaño's, and to escape recognition he covered his face with a handkerchief, under pretence of wiping away the blood. The corregidor inquired what that young man had done who appeared to have been so roughly handed. The alguazil replied that he was a water-carrier, known by the name of the Asturian, and the boys in the street used to shout after him, "Give up the tail, Asturiano; give up the tail." The alguazil then related the story out of which that cry had grown, whereat all present laughed not a little. The alguazil further stated that as the Asturian was going out at the Puerta de Alcantara, the boys who followed him having redoubled their cries about the tail, he dismounted from his ass, laid about them all, and left one of them half dead with the beating he had given him. Thereupon the officer proceeded to arrest him; he resisted, and that was how he came to be in the state in which he then appeared. The corregidor ordered the prisoner to uncover his face, but as he delayed to do so the alguazil snatched away the handkerchief. "My son, Don Diego!" cried the astonished father. "What is the meaning of all this? How came you in that dress? What, you have not yet left off your scampish tricks?" Carriazo fell on his knees before his father, who, with tears in his eyes, held him long in his embrace. Don Juan de Avendaño, knowing that his son had accompanied Carriazo, asked the latter where he was, and received for answer the news that Don Tomas de Avendaño was the person who gave out the oats and straw in that inn.

This new revelation made by the Asturiano put the climax to the surprises of the day. The corregidor desired the innkeeper to bring in his hostler. "I believe he is not in the house, but I will go look for him," said he, and he left the room for that purpose. Don Diego asked Carriazo what was the meaning of these metamorphoses, and what had induced him to turn water-carrier, and Don Tomas hostler? Carriazo replied, that he could not answer these questions in public, but he would do so in private. Meanwhile Tomas Pedro lay hid in his room, in order to see thence, without being himself seen, what his father and Carriazo's were doing; but he was in great perplexity about the arrival of the corregidor, and the general commotion in the inn. At last some one having told the landlord where he was hidden, he went and tried half by fair means and half by force to bring him down; but he would not have succeeded had not the corregidor himself gone out into the yard, and called him by his own name, saying, "Come down, señor kinsman; you will find neither bears nor lions in your way." Tomas then left his hiding place, and went and knelt with downcast eyes and great submission at the feet of his father, who embraced him with a joy surpassing that of the Prodigal's father when the son who had been lost was found again.

The corregidor sent for Costanza, and taking her by the hand, presented her to her father, saying, "Receive, Señor Don Diego, this treasure, and esteem it the richest you could desire. And you, beautiful maiden, kiss your father's hand, and give thanks to heaven which has so happily exalted your low estate." Costanza, who till that moment had not even guessed at what was occurring, could only fall at her father's feet, all trembling with emotion, clasp his hands in hers, and cover them with kisses and tears.

Meanwhile the corregidor had been urgent with his cousin Don Juan that the whole party should come with him to his house; and though Don Juan would have declined the invitation, the corregidor was so pressing that he carried his point, and the whole party got into his coach, which he had previously sent for. But when the corregidor bade Costanza take her place in it, her heart sank within her; she threw herself into the landlady's arms, and wept so piteously, that the hearts of all the beholders were moved. "What is this, daughter of my soul?" said the hostess; "Going to leave me? Can you part from her who has reared you with the love of a mother?" Costanza was no less averse to the separation; but the tenderhearted corregidor declared that the hostess also should enter the coach, and that she should not be parted from her whom she regarded as a daughter, as long as she remained in Toledo. So the whole party, including the hostess, set out together for the corregidor's house, where they were well received by his noble lady.

After they had enjoyed a sumptuous repast, Carriazo related to his father how, for love of Costanza, Don Tomas had taken service as hostler in the inn, and how his devotion to her was such that, before he knew her to be a lady, and the daughter of a man of such quality, he would gladly have married her even as a scullery-maid. The wife of the corregidor immediately made Costanza put on clothes belonging to a daughter of hers of the same age and figure, and if she had been beautiful in the dress of a working girl, she seemed heavenly in that of a lady, and she wore it with such ease and grace that one would have supposed she had never been used to any other kind of costume from her birth. But among so many who rejoiced, there was one person who was full of sadness, and that was Don Pedro, the corregidor's son, who at once concluded that Costanza was not to be his; nor was he mistaken, for it was arranged between the corregidor, Don Diego de Carriazo, and Don Juan de Avendaño, that Don Tomas should marry Costanza, her father bestowing upon her the thirty thousand crowns left by her mother; that the water-carrier Don Diego de Carriazo should marry the daughter of the corregidor, and that Don Pedro the corregidor's son, should receive the hand of Don Juan de Avendaño's daughter, his father undertaking to obtain a dispensation with regard to their relationship. In this manner all were finally made happy. The news of the three marriages, and of the singular fortune of the illustrious scullery-maid, spread through the city, and multitudes flocked to see Costanza in her new garb as a lady, which became her so well. These persons saw the hostler Tomas Pedro changed into Don Tomas de Avendaño, and dressed as a man of quality. They observed, too, that Lope Asturiano looked very much the gentleman since he had changed his costume, and dismissed the ass and the water-vessels; nevertheless, there were not wanting some who, as he passed through the streets in all his pomp, still called out to him for the tail.

After remaining a month in Toledo most of the party went to Burgos, namely, Don Diego de Carriazo, his wife, and his father; Costanza, and her husband, Don Tomas, and the corregidor's son, who desired to visit his kinswoman and destined bride. The host was enriched by the present of the thousand crowns, and by the many jewels which Costanza bestowed upon her señora, as she persisted in calling her who had brought her up. The story of the illustrious scullery-maid afforded the poets of the golden Tagus a theme on which to exercise their pens in celebrating the incomparable beauty of Costanza, who still lives happily with her faithful hostler. Carriazo has three sons, who, without inheriting their father's tastes, or caring to know whether or not there are any such things as tunny fisheries in the world, are all pursuing their studies at Salamanca; whilst their father never sees a water-carrier's ass but he thinks of the one he drove in Toledo, and is not without apprehension that, when he least expects it, his ears shall be saluted with some squib having for its burden, "Give us the tail, Asturiano! Asturiano, give us the tail!"

[81] See the romance of Amadis of Gaul.

THE TWO DAMSELS.

Five leagues from the city of Seville there is a town called Castelblanco. At one of the many inns belonging to that town there arrived at nightfall a traveller, mounted on a handsome nag of foreign breed. He had no servant with him, and, without waiting for any one to hold his stirrup, he threw himself nimbly from the saddle. The host, who was a thrifty, active man, quickly presented himself, but not until the traveller had already seated himself on a bench under the gateway, where the host found him hastily unbuttoning his breast, after which he let his arms drop and fainted. The hostess, who was a good-natured soul, made haste to sprinkle his face with cold water, and presently he revived. Evidently ashamed of having been seen in such a state, he buttoned himself up again, and asked for a room to which he might retire, and, if possible, be alone. The hostess said they had only one in the house and that had two beds, in one of which she must accommodate any other guest that might arrive. The traveller replied that he would pay for both beds, guest or no guest; and taking out a gold crown he gave it to the hostess, on condition that no one should have the vacant bed. The hostess, well satisfied with such good payment, promised that she would do as he required, though the Dean of Seville himself should arrive that night at her house. She then asked him if he would sup. He declined, and only begged they would take great care of his nag. Then, taking the key of the chamber, and carrying with him a large pair of leathern saddle-bags, he went in, locked the door, and even, as it afterwards appeared, barricaded it with two chairs.

The moment he was gone, the host, the hostess, the hostler, and two neighbours who chanced to be there, held a council together, and all extolled the great comeliness and graceful deportment of the stranger, agreeing that they had never seen any one so handsome. They discussed his age, and came to the conclusion that it was between sixteen and seventeen. They speculated largely as to what might have been the cause of his fainting, but could make no plausible guess at it. The neighbours after a while went home, the host went to look after the nag, and the hostess to prepare supper in case any other guest should arrive; nor was it long before another entered, not much older than the first, and of no less engaging mien, so that the hostess no sooner saw him than she exclaimed, "God bless me! how is this? Are angels coming to stop here to-night?"

"Why does the lady hostess say that?" said the cavalier.

"It is not for nothing I say it. Only I must beg your honour not to dismount, for I have no bed to give you; for the two I had have been taken by a cavalier who has paid for both, though he has no need of more than one; but he does that because no one else may enter the room, being, I suppose, fond of solitude; though upon my conscience I can't tell why, for his face and appearance are not such that he need be ashamed of them or want to hide them, but quite the contrary."

"Is he so good-looking, señora hostess?"

"Good-looking? Ay, the best of good-looking."

"Here, my man, hold my stirrup," said the cavalier to a muleteer who accompanied him; "for though I have to sleep on the floor, I must see a man of whom I hear such high encomiums;" and then dismounting he called for supper, which was immediately placed before him. Presently an alguazil dropped in—as they commonly do at the inns in small towns—and taking a seat, entered into conversation with the cavalier while he supped; not forgetting at intervals to swallow three large glasses of wine, and the breast and leg of a partridge, which the cavalier gave him. He paid his scot meanwhile by asking news of the capital, of the wars in Flanders, and the decay of the Turk, not forgetting the exploits of the Transylvanian, whom God preserve. The cavalier supped and said nothing, not having come from a place which would have supplied him with the means of satisfying these inquiries. By and by, the innkeeper, having seen to the nag, came in and sat down to make a third in the conversation, and to taste his own wine no less copiously than the alguazil; and at every gulp he leaned his head back over his left shoulder, and praised the wine, which he exalted to the clouds, though he did not leave much of it there, for fear it should get watered.

From one subject to another, the host fell at last upon the praises of the first comer; told how he had fainted, how he had gone to bed without supper, and had locked himself in; and spoke of his well-filled saddle-bags, the goodness of his nag, and the handsome travelling-dress he wore, all which made it strange that he travelled without any attendant. The cavalier felt his curiosity piqued anew, and asked the landlord to contrive that he might sleep in the second bed, for which he would give him a gold crown. The landlord's fingers itched to take the money; but he said the thing was impossible, for the door was locked inside, and he durst not wake the sleeper, who had paid so well for both the beds. The alguazil, however, got over the difficulty. "I'll tell you what is to be done," said he. "I will knock at the door, and say that I am an officer of justice; that I have orders from the señor alcalde to see this cavalier accommodated in this inn; and that as there is no other bed, he must have one of those two. The landlord will cry out against this, and say it is not fair, for the second bed is already engaged and paid for; and so he will clear himself of all responsibility, while your honour will attain your object." This scheme of the alguazil's was unanimously approved, and the cavalier rewarded him for it with four reals. It was carried into effect at once; the first guest was compelled, with manifest reluctance, to open the door; the second entered the room with many apologies for the intrusion, to which the first made no reply, nor did he even show his face; for instantly hastening back into bed, he turned to the wall, and pretended to be asleep. The last comer also went to bed, hoping to have his curiosity satisfied in the morning when they both got up.

The night was one of the long and weary ones of December, when the cold and the fatigues of the day should naturally have disposed the two travellers to sleep; but they had not that effect on the first of the pair, who not long after midnight began to sigh and moan as if his heart would break. His lamentations awoke the occupant of the other bed, who distinctly overheard the following soliloquy, though uttered in a faint and tremulous voice, broken by sighs and sobs.

"Wretch that I am! Whither is the irresistible force of my destiny hurrying me? What a path is mine; and what issue can I hope for out of the labyrinth in which I am entangled? O my youth and inexperience! Honour disregarded! Love ungratefully repaid! Regard for honoured parents and kindred trampled under foot! Woe is me a thousand times to have thus given the reins to my inclinations! O false words which I have too trustingly responded to by deeds! But of whom do I complain? Did I not wilfully betray myself? Did not my own hands wield the knife that cut down my reputation, and destroyed the trust which my parents reposed in my rectitude? O perjured Marco Antonio! Is it possible that your honeyed words concealed so much of the gall of unkindness and disdain? Where art thou, ingrate? Whither hast thou fled, unthankful man? Answer her who calls upon thee! Wait for her who pursues thee; sustain me, for I droop; pay me what thou owest me; succour me since thou art in so many ways bound to me!"

Here the sorrowing stranger relapsed into silence, broken only by sobs. The other, who had been listening attentively, inferred from what he had heard that the speaker was a woman. The curiosity he had before felt was now excited to the highest degree: he was several times on the point of approaching the lady's bed; and he would have done so at last, but just then he heard her open the door, call to the landlord, and bid him saddle the nag, for she wanted to go. It was a pretty long time before she could make the landlord hear her; and finally, all the answer she could obtain was a recommendation to go to sleep again, for there was more than half the night yet to come, and it was so dark that it would be a very rash thing to venture upon the road. Upon this she said no more, but shut the door, and went back to bed, sighing dismally.

The other stranger now thought it would be well to address her, and offer her his aid in any way that might be serviceable, as a means of inducing her to say who she was, and relate her piteous story. "Assuredly, señor gentleman," said he, "I should think myself destitute of natural feeling—nay, that I had a heart of stone and a bosom of brass—if your sighs and the words you have uttered did not move me to sympathy. If the compassion I feel for you, and the earnest desire I have conceived to risk my life for your relief—if your misfortunes admit of any—may give me some claim upon your courtesy, I entreat you to manifest it in declaring to me the cause of your grief without reserve."

"If that grief had not deprived me of understanding," said the person addressed, "I ought to have remembered that I was not alone in this room, and have bridled my tongue and suppressed my sighs; but to punish myself for my imprudent forgetfulness, I will do what you ask; for it may be that the pangs it will cost me to relate the bitter story of my misfortunes will end at once my life and my woes. But first you must promise me solemnly, that whatever I may reveal, you will not quit your bed nor come to mine, nor ask more of me than I choose to disclose; for if you do, the very moment I hear you move I will run myself through with my sword, which lies ready to my hand."

The cavalier, who would have promised anything to obtain the information he so much desired, vowed that he would not depart a jot from the conditions so courteously imposed. "On that assurance, then," said the lady, "I will do what I have never done before, and relate to you the history of my life. Hearken then.

"You must know, señor, that although I entered this inn, as they have doubtless told you, in the dress of a man, I am an unhappy maiden, or at least I was one not eight days ago, and ceased to be so, because I had the folly to believe the delusive words of a perjured man. My name is Teodosia; my birth-place is one of the chief towns of the province of Andalusia, the name of which I suppress, because it does not import you so much to know it as me to conceal it. My parents, who are noble and wealthy, had a son and a daughter; the one for their joy and honour, the other for the reverse. They sent my brother to study at Salamanca, and me they kept at home, where they brought me up with all the scrupulous care becoming their own virtue and nobility; whilst on my part I always rendered them the most cheerful obedience, and punctually conformed to all their wishes, until my unhappy fate set before my eyes the son of a neighbour of ours, wealthier than my parents, and no less noble than they. The first time I saw him, I felt nothing more than the pleasure one feels at making an agreeable acquaintance; and this I might well feel, for his person, air, manners, disposition, and understanding were the admiration of all who knew him. But why dwell on the praises of my enemy, or make so long a preface to the confession of my infatuation and my ruin? Let me say at once that he saw me repeatedly from a window opposite to mine; whence, as it seemed to me, he shot forth his soul towards me from his eyes, whilst mine beheld him with a pleasure very different from that which I had experienced at our first interview, and one which constrained me to believe that everything I read in his face was the pure truth.

"Seeing each other in this way led to conversation; he declared his passion, and mine responded to it with no misgiving of his sincerity, for his suit was urged with promises, oaths, tears, sighs, and every accompaniment that could make me believe in the reality of his devoted attachment. Utterly inexperienced as I was, every word of his was a cannon shot that breached the fortress of my honour; every tear was a fire in which my virtue was consumed; every sigh was a rushing wind that fanned the destructive flame. In fine, upon his promise to marry me in spite of his parents, who had another wife in view for him, I forgot all my maidenly reserve, and without knowing how, put myself into his power, having no other witness of my folly than a page belonging to Marco Antonio—for that is the name of the destroyer of my peace—who two days afterwards disappeared from the neighbourhood, without any person, not even his parents, having the least idea whither he was gone. In what condition I was left, imagine if you can; it is beyond my power to describe it.

"I tore my hair as if it was to blame for my fault, and punished my face as thinking it the primary occasion of my ruin; I cursed my fate, and my own precipitation; I shed an infinity of tears, and was almost choked by them and by my sighs; I complained mutely to heaven, and pondered a thousand expedients to see if there was any which might afford me help or remedy, and that which I finally resolved on was to dress myself in male apparel, and go in quest of this perfidious Æneas, this cruel and perjured Bireno, this defrauder of my honest affections and my legitimate and well-founded hopes. Having once formed this resolution, I lost no time in putting it in execution. I put on a travelling suit belonging to my brother, saddled one of my father's horses with my own hand, and left home one very dark night, intending to go to Salamanca, whither it was conjectured that Marco Antonio might have gone; for he too is a student, and an intimate friend of my brother's. I did not omit to take at the same time a quantity of gold sufficient for all contingencies upon my journey. What most distresses me is the thought that my parents will send in pursuit of me, and that I shall be discovered by means of my dress and the horse; and even had I not this to fear, I must dread my brother's resentment; for he is in Salamanca, and should he discover me, I need not say how much my life would be in peril. Even should he listen to my excuses, the least scruple of his honour would outweigh them all.

"Happen what may, my fixed resolve is to seek out my heartless husband, who cannot deny that he is my husband without belying the pledge which he left in my possession—a diamond ring, with this legend: 'Marco Antonio is the husband of Teodosia.' If I find him, I will know from him what he discovered in me that prompted him so soon to leave me; and I will make him fulfil his plighted troth, or I will prove as prompt to vengeance as I was easy in suffering myself to be aggrieved, and will take his life; for the noble blood that runs in my veins is not to be insulted with impunity. This, señor cavalier, is the true and sad history you desired to hear, and which you will accept as a sufficient apology for the words and sighs that awoke you. What I would beseech of you is, that though you may not be able to remedy my misfortune, at least you may advise me how to escape the dangers that beset me, evade being caught, and accomplish what I so much desire and need."

The cavalier said not a syllable in reply, and remained so long silent that Teodosia supposed he was asleep and had not heard a word she had been saying. To satisfy herself of this, she said, "Are you asleep, señor? No wonder if you are; for a mournful tale poured into an unimpassioned ear is more likely to induce drowsiness than pity."

"I am not asleep," replied the cavalier; "on the contrary, I am so thoroughly awake, and feel so much for your calamity, that I know not if your own anguish exceeds mine. For this reason I will not only give you the advice you ask, but my personal aid to the utmost of my powers; for though the manner in which you have told your tale proves that you are gifted with no ordinary intelligence, and therefore that you have been your own betrayer, and owe your sorrow to a perverted will rather than to the seductions of Marco Antonio, nevertheless I would fain see your excuse in your youth and your inexperience of the wily arts of men. Compose yourself, señora, and sleep if you can during the short remainder of the night. When daylight comes we will consult together, and see what means may be devised for helping you out of your affliction."

Teodosia thanked him warmly, and tried to keep still for a while in order that the cavalier might sleep; but he could not close an eye; on the contrary he began to toss himself about in the bed, and to heave such deep sighs that Teodosia was constrained to ask him what was the matter? was he suffering in any way, and could she do anything for his relief?

"Though you are yourself the cause of my distress, señora," he replied, "you are not the person who can relieve it, for if you were I should not feel it."

Teodosia could not understand the drift of this perplexed reply; she suspected, however, that he was under the influence of some amorous passion, and even that she herself might be the object of it; for it might well be that the fact of his being alone with one he knew to be a woman, at that dead hour of the night, and in the same bed-room, should have awakened in him some bad thoughts. Alarmed at the idea, she hastily put on her clothes without noise, buckled on her sword and dagger, and sat down on the bed to wait for daylight, which did not long delay to appear through the many openings there were in the sides of the room, as usual in inn-chambers. The cavalier on his part, had made ready exactly as Teodosia had done; and he no sooner perceived the first rays of light, than he started up from his bed, saying, "Get up, señora Teodosia, and let us be gone; for I will accompany you on your journey, and never quit your side until I see Marco Antonio become your lawful husband, or until he or I shall be a dead man;" and so saying, he opened the windows and the doors of the room.

Teodosia had longed for daylight that she might see what manner of man he was with whom she had been conversing all night; but when she beheld him, she would have been glad that it had never dawned, but that her eyes had remained in perpetual darkness, for the cavalier who stood before her was her brother! At sight of him she was stupefied with emotion, her face was deadly pale, and she could not utter a word. At last, rallying her spirits, she drew her dagger, and presenting the handle to her brother, fell at his feet, and gasped out, "Take it, dear señor and brother, punish the fault I have committed, and satisfy your resentment, for my offence deserves no mercy, and I do not desire that my repentance should be accepted as an atonement. The only thing I entreat is that you will deprive me of life, but not of my honour; for though I have placed it in manifest danger by absenting myself from the house of my parents, yet its semblance may be preserved before the world if my death be secret."

Her brother regarded her fixedly, and although her wantonness excited him to vengeance, he could not withstand this affecting appeal. With a placable countenance he raised her from the ground, and consoled her as well as he could, telling her, among other things, that as he knew of no punishment adequate to the magnitude of her folly, he would suspend the consideration of that matter for the present; and as he thought that fortune had not yet made all remedy impossible, he thought it bettor to seek one than at once to take vengeance on her for her levity. These words restored Teodosia to life; the colour returned to her cheeks, and her despair gave way to revived hope. Don Rafael (that was the brother's name) would speak no more on the subject, but bade her change her name from Teodosia to Teodoro, and decided that they should both proceed at once to Salamanca in quest of Marco Antonio, though he hardly expected to find him there; for as they were intimate friends, they would have met had he been at the university, unless indeed Marco Antonio might have shunned him from a consciousness of the wrong he had done him. The new Teodoro acquiesced in everything proposed by her brother;

and the innkeeper coming in, they ordered breakfast, intending to depart immediately.

Before all was ready another traveller arrived. This was a gentleman who was known to Don Rafael and Teodoro, and the latter, to avoid being seen by him, remained in the chamber. Don Rafael, having embraced the newcomer, asked him what news he brought. His friend replied that he had just come from the port of Santa Maria, where he had left four galleys bound for Naples, and that he had seen Marco Antonio Adorno, the son of Don Leonardo Adorno, on board one of them. This intelligence rejoiced Don Rafael, to whom it appeared that since he had so unexpectedly learned what it was of such importance for him to know, he might regard this an omen of his future success. He asked his friend, who knew his father well, to exchange the hired mule he rode for his father's nag, giving him to understand, not that he was coming from Salamanca, but that he was going thither, and that he was unwilling to take so good an animal on so long a journey. The other obligingly consented, and promised to deliver the nag to its owner. Don Rafael and he breakfasted together, and Teodoro alone; and finally the friend pursued his journey to Cazallo, where he had an estate, whilst Don Rafael excused himself from accompanying him by saying that he had to return that day to Seville.

As soon as the friend was gone, and the reckoning paid, Don Rafael and Teodoro mounted and bade adieu to the people of the inn, leaving them all in admiration of the comeliness of the pair. Don Rafael told his sister what news he had received of Marco Antonio, and that he proposed they should make all haste to reach Barcelona; for vessels on their way to or fro between Italy and Spain usually put in at that port; and if Marco Antonio's ship had not yet arrived there, they would wait for it, and be sure of seeing him. His sister said he should do as he thought best, for his will was hers. Don Rafael then told the muleteer who accompanied him to have patience, for he intended to go to Barcelona, but would pay him accordingly. The muleteer, who was one of the merriest fellows of his trade, and who knew Don Rafael's liberality, declared that he was willing to go with him to the end of the world.

Don Rafael asked his sister what money she had. She told him she had not counted it; all she knew was that she had put her hand seven or eight times into her father's strong box, and had taken it out full of gold crowns. From this Don Rafael calculated that she might have something about five hundred crowns, which, with two hundred of his own, and a gold chain he wore, seemed to him no bad provision for the journey; the more so, as he felt confident of meeting Marco Antonio in Barcelona. They pursued their journey I rapidly without accident or impediment until they arrived within two leagues of a town called Igualada, which is nine leagues from Barcelona, and there they learned that a cavalier who was going as ambassador to Rome, was waiting at Barcelona for the galleys, which had not yet arrived. Greatly cheered by this news, they pushed on until they came to the verge of a small wood, from which they saw a man running, and looking back over his shoulder with every appearance of terror. "What is the matter with you, good man?" said Don Rafael, going up to him. "What has happened to you, that you seem so frightened and run so fast?"

"Have I not good cause to be frightened and to run fast," said the man, "since I have escaped by a miracle from a gang of robbers in that wood?"

"Malediction! Lord save us!" exclaimed the muleteer. "Robbers at this hour! By my halidom, they'll leave us as bare as we were born."

"Don't make yourself uneasy, brother," replied the man from the wood, "for the robbers have by this time gone away, after leaving more than thirty passengers stripped to their shirts and tied to trees, with the exception of one only, whom they have left to unbind the rest as soon as they should have passed a little hill they pointed out to him."

"If that be so," said Calvete, the muleteer, "we may proceed without fear, for where the robbers have made an attack, they do not show themselves again for some days. I say this with confidence, as a man who has been twice in their hands, and knows all their ways."

This fact being confirmed by the stranger, Don Rafael resolved to go on. They entered the wood, and had not advanced far, when they came upon the persons who had been robbed, and who were more than forty in number. The man who had been left free, had unbound some of them; but his work was not yet complete, and several of them were still tied to the trees. They presented a strange spectacle, some of them stripped naked, others dressed in the tattered garments of the robbers; some weeping over their disaster, some laughing at the strange figure the others made in their robber's costume; one dolorously reciting the list of the things he had lost, another declaring that the loss of a box of Agnus Dei he was bringing home from Rome afflicted him more than all besides. In short, the whole wood resounded with the moans and lamentations of the despoiled wretches. The brother and sister beheld them with deep compassion, and heartily thanked heaven for their own narrow escape from so great a peril. But what affected Teodoro more than anything else was the sight of a lad apparently about fifteen, tied to a tree, with no covering on him but a shirt and a pair of linen drawers, but with a face of such beauty that none could refrain from gazing on it. Teodoro dismounted and unbound him, a favour which he acknowledged in very courteous terms; and Teodoro, to make it the greater, begged Calvete to lend the gentle youth his cloak, until he could buy him another at the first town they came to. Calvete complied, and Teodoro threw the cloak over his shoulders, asking him in Don Rafael's presence to what part of the country he belonged, whence he was coming, and whither he was going. The youth replied that he was from Andalusia, and he named as his birthplace a town which was but two leagues distant from that of the brother and sister. He said he was on his way from Seville to Italy, to seek his fortune in arms like many another Spaniard; but that he had had the misfortune to fall in with a gang of thieves, who had taken from him a considerable sum of money and clothes, which he could not replace for three hundred crowns. Nevertheless he intended to pursue his journey, for he did not come of a race which was used to let the ardour of its zeal evaporate at the first check.

The manner in which the youth expressed himself, the fact that he was from their own neighbourhood, and above all, the letter of recommendation he carried in his face, inspired the brother and sister with a desire to befriend him as much as they could. After they had distributed some money among such of the rest as seemed in most need of it, especially among monks and priests, of whom there were eight, they made this youth mount Calvete's mule, and went on without more delay to Igualada. There they were informed that the galleys had arrived the day before at Barcelona, whence they would sail in two days, unless the insecurity of the roadstead compelled them to make an earlier departure. On account of this news, they rose next morning before the sun, although they had not slept all night in consequence of a circumstance which had occurred at supper, and which had more surprised and interested the brother and sister than they were themselves aware. As they sat at table, and the youth with them whom they had taken under their protection, Teodoro fixed her eyes intently on his face, and scrutinising his features somewhat curiously, perceived that his ears were bored. From this and from a certain bashfulness that appeared in his looks, she suspected that the supposed youth was a woman, and she longed for supper to be over that she might verify her suspicion. Meanwhile Don Rafael asked him whose son he was, for he knew all the principal people in the town he had named as his birth place. The youth said he was the son of Don Enrique de Cardenas. Don Rafael replied that he was well acquainted with Don Enrique, and knew for certain that he had no son; but that if he had given that answer because he did not choose to make known his family, it was of no consequence, and he should not be questioned again on that subject.

"It is true," said the youth, "that Don Enrique has no children, but his brother Don Sancho has."

"He has no son either," replied Don Rafael, "but an only daughter, who, by the bye, they say is one of the handsomest damsels in Andalusia; but this I know only by report; for though I have been often in her town I have never seen her."

"It is quite true, as you say, señor, that Don Sancho has only a daughter, but not one so handsome as fame reports; and if I said that I was the son of Don Enrique it was only to give myself some importance in your eyes; for in fact, I am only the son of Don Sancho's steward, who has been many years in his service, and I was born in his house. Having displeased my father, I carried off a good sum of money from him, and resolved to go to Italy, as I have told you, and follow the career of arms, by which men even of obscure birth have been known to make themselves illustrious."

Teodoro, who listened attentively to all this conversation, was more and more confirmed in her suspicion, both by the manner and the substance of what the youth said. After the cloth was removed, and while Don Rafael was preparing for bed, she made known to him her surmise, and then, with his permission, took the youth aside, and, going out with him upon a balcony which looked on the street, addressed him thus:—

"Don Francisco," for that was the name he had given himself, "I would fain have done you so much service that you could not help granting me anything that I should ask of you; but the short time we have known you has not permitted this. Hereafter perhaps you may know how far I deserve that you should comply with my desires; but if you do not choose to satisfy that which I am now about to express, I will not the less continue to be your faithful servant. Furthermore, before I prefer my present request, I would impress upon you that although my age does exceed yours, I have more experience of the world than is usual at my years, as you will admit when I tell you that it has led me to suspect that you are not a man, as your garb imports, but a woman, and one as well-born as your beauty proclaims, and perhaps as unfortunate as your disguise implies, for such transformations are never made willingly, or except under the pressure of some painful necessity. If what I suspect is the case, tell me so, and I swear to you on the faith of a cavalier to aid and serve you in every way I can. That you are a woman you cannot make me doubt, for the holes in your ears make that fact very clear. It was thoughtless of you not to close them with a little flesh-coloured wax, for somebody else as inquisitive as myself, and not so fit to be trusted with a secret, might discover by means of them what you have so ill concealed. Believe me, you need not hesitate to tell me who you are, in full reliance on my inviolable secrecy."

The youth had listened with great attention to all Teodoro said, and, before answering her a word, he seized her hands, carried them by force to his lips, kissed them with great fervour, and even bedewed them copiously with tears. Teodoro could not help sympathising with the acute feelings of the youth, and shedding tears also. Although, when she had with difficulty withdrawn her hands from the youth's lips, he replied with a deep-drawn sigh, "I will not, and cannot deny, señora, that your suspicion is true; I am a woman, and the most unfortunate of my sex; and since the acts of kindness you have conferred upon me, and the offers you make me, oblige me to obey all your commands, listen and I will tell you who I am, if indeed it will not weary you to hear the tale of another's misfortunes."

"May I never know aught else myself," replied Teodoro, "if I shall not feel a pleasure in hearing of those misfortunes equal to the pain it will give me to know that they are yours, and that will be such as if they were my own." And again she embraced and encouraged the seeming youth, who, somewhat more tranquilised, continued thus:—

"I have spoken the truth with regard to my native place, but not with regard to my parents; for Don Enrique is not my father but my uncle, and his brother Don Sancho is my father. I am that unhappy daughter of his of whom your brother says that she is celebrated for her beauty, but how mistakenly you now perceive. My name is Leocadia; the occasion of my disguise you shall now hear.

"Two leagues from my native town there is another, one of the wealthiest and noblest of Andalusia, where lives a cavalier of quality, who derives his origin from the noble and ancient Adornos of Genoa. He has a son, who, unless fame exaggerates his praises as it does mine, is one of the most gallant gentlemen one would desire to see. Being so near a neighbour of ours, and being like my father strongly addicted to the chase, he often came on a visit of five or six days to our house, the greater part of that time, much of the night even included, being spent by my father and him in the field. From these visits of his, fortune, or love, or my own imprudence, took occasion to bring me down to my present state of degradation. Having observed, with more attention than became a modest and well-behaved maiden, the graceful person and manners of our visitor, and taking into consideration his distinguished lineage and the great wealth of his parents, I thought that to obtain him for my husband would be the highest felicity to which my wishes could aspire. With this thought in my head I began to gaze at him most intently, and also, no doubt, with too little caution, for he perceived it, and the traitor needed no other hint to discover the secret of my bosom and rob me of my peace. But why should I weary you by recapitulating every minute detail of my unfortunate attachment? Let me say at once that he won so far upon me by his ceaseless solicitations, having plighted his faith under the most solemn and, as I thought, the most Christian vows that he would become my husband, that I put myself wholly at his disposal. Nevertheless, not being quite satisfied with his vows alone, and in order that the wind might not bear them away, I made him commit them to writing, and give them to me in a paper signed with his own hand, and drawn up in terms so strong and unequivocal as to remove all my mistrust. Once in possession of this paper, I arranged that he should come to me one night, climb the garden-wall, and enter my chamber, where he might securely pluck the fruit destined for him alone. The night so longed for by me at last arrived—"

Up to this point Teodoro had listened with rapt attention, especially since she had heard the name of Adorno, but now she could contain herself no longer. "Well," she cried, suddenly interrupting the speaker, "and then, what did he do? Did he keep the assignation? Were you happy in his arms? Did he confirm his written pledge anew? Was he content when he had obtained from you what you say was his? Did your father know it? What was the end of this good and wise beginning?"

"The end was to bring me to what you see, for he never came."

Teodoro breathed again at these words, and partly recovered her self-possession, which had been almost destroyed by the frantic influence of jealousy. Even yet she was not so free from it but that she trembled inwardly as Leocadia continued her story.

"Not only did he fail to keep the assignation, but a week after I learned for certain that he had disappeared from home, and carried off from the house of her parents, persons of distinction in his own neighbourhood, a very beautiful and accomplished young lady named Teodosia. I was nearly mad with jealousy and mortification. I pictured Teodosia to myself in imagination, more beautiful than the sun, more perfect than perfection itself, and above all, more blissful than I was miserable. I read the written engagement over and over again; it was as binding as any form of words could be; but though my hopes would fain have clung to it as something sacred and inviolable, they all fell to the ground when I remembered in what company Marco Antonio had departed. I beat my face, tore my hair, and cursed my fate; but what was most irksome to me was that I could not practise these self-inflictions at all hours in consequence of my father's presence. In fine, that I might be free to indulge my woe without impediment, I resolved to quit my home. It would seem that the execution of a bad purpose never fails for want of opportunity. I boldly purloined a suit of clothes belonging to one of my father's pages, and from himself a considerable sum of money; then leaving the house by night I travelled some leagues on foot, and reached a town called Osuna, where I hired a car. Two days afterwards I entered Seville, where I was quite safe from all pursuit.

"There I bought other clothes, and a mule, and set out with some cavaliers who were travelling with all speed to Barcelona, that they might be in time for some galleys that were on their way to Italy. I continued my journey until yesterday, when the robbers took everything from me, and among the rest, that precious thing which sustained my soul and lightened my toils, the written engagement given me by Marco Antonio. I had intended to carry it with me to Italy, find Marco Antonio there, and present it to him as an evidence of his faithlessness and my constancy, and constrain him to fulfil his promise. At the same time I am conscious that he may readily deny the words written on this paper, since he has made nought of the obligations that should have been engraved on his soul; besides, it is plain that if he is accompanied by the incomparable Teodosia he will not deign to look upon the unfortunate Leocadia. But happen what may, I am resolved to die or present myself before the pair, that the sight of me may trouble their joy. This Teodosia, this enemy of my peace, shall not so cheaply enjoy what is mine. I will seek her out, I will find her, and will take her life if I can."

"But how is Teodosia in fault," said Teodoro, "if, as is very probably the case, she too has been deluded by Marco Antonio, as you, señora, have been?"

"How can that be so," returned Leocadia, "if he has her with him? Being with the man she loves, what question can there be of delusion? They are together, and therefore they are happy, and would be so, though they were in the burning deserts of Lybia, or the dreary wastes of Scythia. She is blest in his arms wherever she is, and therefore she shall pay for all I shall suffer till I find her."

"It is very likely you are mistaken," said Teodoro; "I am very well acquainted with this enemy of yours, as you call her, and I know her prudence and modesty to be such, that she never would venture to quit her father's house and go away with Marco Antonio. And even had she done so, not knowing you, nor being aware of any claim you had on him, she has not wronged you at all, and where there is no wrong, vengeance is out of place."

"Tell me not of her modesty, señor; for I was as modest and as virtuous as any maiden in the world, and yet I have done what I have told you. That he has carried her off there is no doubt. I acknowledge, looking on the matter dispassionately, that she has not wronged me; but the pangs of jealousy which she occasions me make me abhor her. If a sword were thrust through my vitals, should I not naturally strive to pluck it out and break it to pieces?"

"Well, well, señora Leocadia, since the passion that sways you makes you speak so wildly, I see it is not the fit time to offer you rational advice. I shall therefore content myself with repeating that I am ready and willing to render you every service in my power, and I know my brother's generous nature so well, that I can boldly make you the same promise on his part. We are going to Italy, and it rests only with yourself to accompany us. One thing only I entreat, that you will allow me to tell my brother what I know of your story, that he may treat you with the attention and respect which is your due. I think you had better continue to wear male attire, and if it is to be procured in this place, I will take care that you shall be suitably equipped to morrow. For the rest, trust to time, for it is a great provider of remedies even for the most desperate cases."

Leocadia gratefully thanked the generous Teodoro, saying he might tell his brother whatever he thought fit, and beseeching him not to forsake her, since he saw to what dangers she was exposed, if she was known to be a woman. Here the conversation ended, and they retired to rest, Teodosia in her brother's room, and Leocadia in another next it. Don Rafael was still awake, waiting for his sister to know what had passed between her and the suspected woman; and before she lay down, he made her relate the whole to him in detail. "Well, sister," he said when she had finished, "if she is the person she declares herself to be, she belongs to the best family in her native place, and is one of the noblest ladies of Andalusia. Her father is well known to ours, and the fame of her beauty perfectly corresponds with the evidence of our own eyes. My opinion is, that we must proceed with caution, lest she come to speak with Marco Antonio before us, for I feel some uneasiness about that written engagement she speaks of, even though he has lost it. But be of good cheer, sister, and go to rest, for all will come right at last."

Teodosia complied with her brother's advice so far as to go to bed, but it was impossible for her to rest, so racked was she by jealous fears. Oh, how she exaggerated the beauty of Leocadia, and the disloyalty of Marco Antonio! How often she read with the eyes of her imagination his written promise to her rival! What words and phrases she added to it, to make it more sure and binding! How often she refused to believe that it was lost! And how many a time she repeated to herself, that even though it were lost, Marco Antonio would not the less fulfil his promise to Leocadia, without thinking of that by which he was bound to herself! In such thoughts as these she passed the night without a wink of sleep; nor was her brother Don Rafael less wakeful; for no sooner had he heard who Leocadia was, than his heart was on fire for her. He beheld her in imagination, not tied to a tree, or in tattered male garments, but in her own rich apparel in her wealthy father's house. He would not suffer his mind to dwell on that which was the primary cause of his having become acquainted with her; and he longed for day that he might continue his journey and find out Marco Antonio, not so much that he might make him his brother-in-law, as that he might hinder him from becoming the husband of Leocadia. In fact, he was so possessed by love and jealousy, that he could have borne to see his sister comfortless, and Marco Antonio fairly buried, rather than be himself without hope of obtaining Leocadia.

Thus with different thoughts, they all quitted their beds at break of day, and Don Rafael sent for the host, and asked him if he could purchase a suit of clothes in that place for a page who had been stripped by robbers. The host said he happened to have one for sale which he would dispose of at a reasonable price. He produced it, Leocadia found that it fitted her very well, she put it on, and girt herself with sword and dagger with such sprightly grace that she enchanted Don Rafael, and redoubled Teodosia's jealousy. Calvete saddled the mules, and about eight in the morning, they started for Barcelona, not intending to take the famous monastery of Monserrate on their way, but to visit it on a future occasion, whenever it might please God to send them home again with hearts more at ease.

Words are not adequate to describe the feelings of the two brothers, or with what different eyes they severally regarded Leocadia; Teodosia wishing for her death, and Don Rafael for her life; Teodosia striving to find faults in her, in order that she might not despair of her own hopes; and Don Rafael finding out new perfections, that more and more obliged him to love her. All these thoughts, however, did not hinder their speed, for they reached Barcelona before sunset. They admired the magnificent situation of the city, and esteemed it to be the flower of the world, the honour of Spain, the terror of all enemies near and far, the delight of its inhabitants, the refuge of strangers, the school of chivalry, the model of loyalty, in a word, a union of all that a judicious curiosity could desire in a grand, famous, wealthy, and well-built city. Upon their entering it they heard a great uproar, and saw a multitude of people running with loud cries. They inquired the cause, and were told that the people of the galleys in the port had fallen upon those of the town. Don Rafael desired to see what was going on, though Calvete would have dissuaded him; for, as the muleteer said, he knew well what mischief came of interfering in such frays as this, which usually occurred in Barcelona when galleys put in there.

In spite of this good advice, Don Rafael and his fellow-travellers went down at once towards the beach, where they saw many swords drawn, and numbers of people slashing at each other without mercy, and they approached so near the scene without dismounting, that they could distinctly see the faces of the combatants, for the sun was still above the horizon. The number of townspeople engaged was immense, and great crowds issued from the galleys, although their commander, Don Pedro Vique, a gentleman of Valencia, stood on the prow of the flag-ship, threatening all who entered the boats to succour their comrades. Finding his commands disregarded, he ordered a gun to be fired without ball, as a warning that if the combatants did not separate, the next gun he fired would be shotted. Meanwhile, Don Rafael, who narrowly watched the fray, observed among those who took part with the seamen a young man of about two-and-twenty, dressed in green, with a hat of the same colour, adorned with a rich loop and buttons apparently of diamonds. The skill and courage with which he fought, and the elegance of his dress, drew upon him the attention of all the spectators, and Teodosia and Leocadia both cried out, as if with one voice, "Good heavens! either my eyes deceive me, or he in green is Marco Antonio." Then, with great nimbleness, they dismounted, drew their swords and daggers, cleared their way through the crowd, and placed themselves one on each side of Marco Antonio. "Fear nothing, Señor Marco Antonio," cried Leocadia, "for there is one by your side who will defend your life at the cost of his own." "Who doubts it," ejaculated Teodosia, on the other side, "since I am here?" Don Rafael, who had seen and heard all this, followed his two companions, and took sides as they did.

Marco Antonio was too busy smiting and defending himself to heed what his two seconds had said; he could think of nothing but fighting, and no man ever fought more bravely; but as the party of the town was every moment increasing in numbers, the people of the galleys were forced to retreat and take to the water. Marco Antonio retreated with the rest, much against his will, still attended on either side by his two valiant Amazons. By this time a Catalonian knight of the renowned House of Cardonas, made his appearance on a noble charger, and, throwing himself between the two parties, ordered the townspeople to retire. The majority obeyed, but some still continued to fling stones, one of which unluckily struck Marco Antonio on the breast with such force that he fell senseless into the water, in which he was wading up to his knees. Leocadia instantly raised and supported him in her arms, and Teodosia aided her.

Don Rafael, who had turned aside a little to avoid a shower of stones, saw the accident which had befallen Marco Antonio, and was hastening forward to his aid, when the Catalonian knight stopped him, saying, "Stay, señor, and do me the favour to put yourself by my side. I will secure you from the insolence of this unruly rabble."

"Ah, señor!" replied Rafael, "let me pass, for I see that in great danger which I most love in this world."

The knight let him pass, but before he could reach the spot, the crew of the flagship's boat had already taken on board Marco Antonio and Leocadia, who never let him out of her arms. As for Teodosia, whether it was that she was weary, or overcome with grief to see her lover wounded, or enraged with jealousy to see her rival with him, she had not strength to get into the boat, and would certainly have fallen in a fainting fit into the water, if her brother had not opportunely come to her aid, while he himself felt no less torment than his sister at seeing Leocadia go away with Marco Antonio.

The Catalonian knight being very much taken with the goodly presence of Don Rafael and his sister (whom he supposed to be a man), called them from the shore, and requested them to go with him, and they were constrained to accept his friendly offer, lest they should suffer some injury from the people, who were not yet pacified. Thereupon, the knight dismounted, and with his drawn sword in his hand, led them through the tumultuous throng, who made way at his command. Don Rafael looked round to see if he could discover Calvete with the mules; but he was not to be seen, for the moment his employers dismounted, he had gone off to an inn where he had lodged on previous occasions. On their arrival at the knight's abode, which was one of the principal houses in the city, he asked them in which of the galleys they had arrived. Don Rafael replied that they had not come in any, for they had arrived in the city just as the fray began; and it was because they had recognised the gentleman who was wounded with a stone that they had involved themselves in danger. Moreover, he entreated the knight would have the gentleman brought on shore, as he was one on whom his own dearest interests depended. "I will do so with great pleasure," replied the knight, "and I am sure the general will allow it, for he is a worthy gentleman and a relation of mine." Thereupon he went at once to the galley, where he found Marco Antonio under the hands of the surgeon, who pronounced his wound dangerous, being near the heart. With the general's consent he had him brought on shore with great care, accompanied by Leocadia, and carried to his own house in a litter, where he entertained the whole party with great hospitality.

A famous surgeon of the city was now sent for, but he would not touch the patient's wound until the following day, alleging that it had no doubt been properly treated already, army and navy surgeons being always men of skill, in consequence of their continual experience in cases of wounds. He only desired that the patient should be placed in a quiet room and left to rest. Presently the surgeon of the galley arrived, and had a conference with his colleague, who approved of what he had done, and agreed with him in thinking the case highly dangerous. Leocadia and Teodosia heard this with as much anguish of heart as if it had been a sentence of death upon themselves; but not wishing to betray their grief, they strove to conceal it in silence. Leocadia, however, determined to do what she thought requisite for her honour, and as soon as the surgeons were gone, she entered Marco Antonio's room, where, going up to his bed side, and taking his hand in presence of the master of the house, Don Rafael, Teodosia, and others, "Señor Marco Antonio Adorno," she said, "it is now no seasonable time, considering your condition, to utter many words; and therefore I shall only entreat you to lend your ear to some few which concern, if not the safety of your body, at least that of your soul. But I must have your permission to speak; for it would ill become me, who have striven never to disoblige you from the first moment I knew you, to disturb you now in what seems almost your last."

At these words Marco Antonio opened his eyes, looked steadfastly at Leocadia, and recognising her rather by the tone of her voice than by her face, said with a feeble voice, like one in pain, "Say on, señor, what you please, for I am not so far gone but that I can listen to you; nor is that voice of yours so harsh and unpleasing that I should dislike to hear it."

Teodosia hearkened most attentively, and every word that Leocadia spoke pierced her heart like an arrow, and at the same time harrowed the soul of Don Rafael. "If the blow you have received," continued Leocadia, "or rather that which has struck my heart, has not effaced from your memory, señor Marco Antonio, the image of her whom not long ago you called your glory and your heaven, you must surely call to mind who Leocadia was, and what was the promise you gave her in writing under your own hand; nor can you have forgotten the worth of her parents, her own modesty and virtue, and the obligation you are under to her for having always gratified you in everything you desired. If you have not forgotten all this, you may readily know, in spite of this disguise, that I am Leocadia. As soon as I heard of your departure from home, dreading lest new chances and opportunities should deprive me of what is so justly mine, I resolved, in defiance of the worst miseries, to follow you in this garb, and to search the wide world over till I found you. Nor need you wonder at this, if you have ever felt what the strength of true love is capable of, or know the frenzy of a deceived woman. I have suffered some hardships in my quest, all of which I regard as pastime since they have resulted in my seeing you; for, though you are in this condition, if it be God's will to remove you to a better world, I shall esteem myself more than happy if before your departure you do what becomes you, in which case I promise you to live in such a manner after your death that I shall soon follow you on that last inevitable journey. I beseech you then, for the love of heaven, for your own honour, and for my sake, to whom you owe more than to all the world, receive me at once as your lawful wife, not leaving it to the law to do what you have so many righteous motives for doing of your own accord."

Here Leocadia ceased speaking. All present had listened to her in profound silence, and in the same way they awaited the reply of Marco Antonio. "I cannot deny, señora," he said, "that I know you; your voice and your face will not suffer me to do that. Nor yet can I deny how much I owe to you, nor the great worth of your parents and your own incomparable modesty and virtue. I do not, and never shall, think lightly of you for what you have done in coming to seek me in such a disguise; on the contrary, I shall always esteem you for it in the highest degree. But since, as you say, I am so near my end, I desire to make known to you a truth, the knowledge of which, if it be unpleasant to you now, may hereafter be useful to you.

"I confess, fair Leocadia, that I loved you, and you loved me; and yet I confess also that my written promise was given more in compliance with your desire than my own; for before I had long signed it my heart was captivated by a lady named Teodosia, whom you know, and whose parentage is as noble as your own. If I gave you a promise signed with my hand, to her I gave that hand itself in so unequivocal a manner that it is impossible for me to bestow it on any other person in the world. My amour with you was but a pastime from which I culled only some flowers, leaving you nothing the worse; from her I obtained the consummate fruit of love upon my plighted faith to be her husband. That I afterwards deserted you both was the inconsiderate act of a young man who thought that all such things were of little importance, and might be done without scruple. My intention was to go to Italy, and after spending some of the years of my youth there, to return and see what had become of you and my real wife; but Heaven in its mercy, as I truly believe, has permitted me to be brought to the state in which you see me, in order that in thus confessing my great faults, I may fulfil my last duty in this world, by leaving you disabused and free, and ratifying on my deathbed the pledge I gave to Teodosia. If there is anything, señora Leocadia, in which I can serve you during the short time that remains to me, let me know it; so it be not to receive you as my wife, for that I cannot, there is nothing else which I will not do, if it be in my power, to please you."

Marco Antonio, who had raised himself on one arm while he spoke, now fell back senseless. Don Rafael then came forward. "Recover yourself, dear señor," he said, embracing him affectionately, "and embrace your friend and your brother, since such you desire him to be."

Marco Antonio opened his eyes, and recognising Don Rafael, embraced him with great warmth. "Dear brother and señor," he said, "the extreme joy I feel in seeing you must needs be followed by a proportionate affliction, since, as they say, after gladness comes sorrow; but whatever befals me now I will receive with pleasure in exchange for the happiness of beholding you."

"To make your happiness more complete," replied Don Rafael, "I present to you this jewel as your own." Then, turning to look for his sister, he found her behind the rest of the people in the room, bathed in tears, and divided between joy and grief at what she saw and what she had heard. Taking her by the hand, her brother led her passively to the bed-side, and presented her to Marco Antonio, who embraced her with loving tears.

The rest of those present stared in each others' faces in speechless amazement at these extraordinary occurrences; but the hapless Leocadia, seeing her whom she had mistaken for Don Rafael's brother locked in the arms of him she looked on as her own husband, and all her hopes mocked and ruined, stole out of the room unperceived by the others, whose attention was engrossed by the scene about the bed. She rushed wildly into the street, intending to wander over the world, no matter whither; but she was hardly out of doors before Don Rafael missed her, and, as if he had lost his soul, began to inquire anxiously after her; but nobody could tell what had become of her. He hastened in dismay to the inn where he was told Calvete lodged, thinking she might have gone thither to procure a mule; but, not finding her there, he ran like a madman through the streets, seeking her in every quarter, till the thought struck him that she might have made for the galleys, and he turned in that direction. As he approached the shore he heard some one calling from the land for the boat belonging to the general's galley, and soon recognised the voice as that of the beautiful Leocadia. Hearing his footsteps as he hastened towards her, she drew her sword and stood upon her guard; but perceiving it was Don Rafael, she was vexed and confused at his having found her, especially in so lonely a place; for she was aware, from many indications, that he was far from regarding her with indifference; on the contrary, she would have been delighted to know that Marco Antonio loved her as well. How shall I relate all that Don Rafael now said to Leocadia? I can give but a faint idea of the glowing language in which he poured out his soul.

184

"Were it my fate, beautiful Leocadia," he said, "along with the favours of fortune to lack also at this moment the courage to disclose to you the secret of my soul, then would there be doomed to perpetual oblivion the most ardent and genuine affection that ever was harboured in a lover's breast. But not to do it that wrong, I will make bold, señora, come of it what may, to beg you will observe, if your wounded feelings allow you, that in nothing has Marco Antonio the advantage of me, except the happiness of being loved by you. My lineage is as good as his, and in fortune he is not much superior to me. As for the gifts of nature, it becomes me not to laud myself, especially if in your eyes those which have fallen to my share are of no esteem. All this I say, adored señora, that you may seize the remedy for your disasters which fortune offers to your hand. You see that Marco Antonio cannot be yours, since Heaven has already made him my sister's; and the same Heaven which has taken him from you is now willing to compensate you with me, who desire no higher bliss in this life than that of being your husband. See how good fortune stands knocking at the door of the evil fortune you have hitherto known. And do not suppose that I shall ever think the worse of you for the boldness you have shown in seeking after Marco Antonio; for from the moment I determine to match myself with you, I am bound to forget all that is past. Well I know that the same power which has constrained me so irresistibly to adore you, has brought you also to your present pass, and therefore there will be no need to seek an excuse where there has been no fault."

Leocadia listened in silence to all Don Rafael said, only from time to time heaving a sigh from the bottom of her heart. Don Rafael ventured to take her hand; she did not withdraw it; and kissing it again and again, he said, "Tell me, lady of my soul, that you will be so wholly, in presence of these starry heavens, this calm listening sea, and these watery sands. Say that yes, which surely behoves your honour as well as my happiness. I repeat to you that I am a gentleman, as you know, and wealthy; that I love you, which you ought to esteem above every other consideration; and that whereas I find you alone, in a garb that derogates much from your honour, far from the home of your parents and your kindred, without any one to aid you at your need, and without the hope of obtaining what you were in quest of, you may return home in your own proper and seemly garb, accompanied by as good a husband as you had chosen for yourself, and be wealthy, happy, esteemed, and even applauded by all who may become acquainted with the events of your story. All this being so, I know not why you hesitate. Say the one word that shall raise me from the depth of wretchedness to the heaven of bliss, and in so doing, you will do what is best for yourself; you will comply with the demands of courtesy and good sense, and show yourself at once grateful and discreet."

"Well," said the doubting Leocadia, at last, "since Heaven has so ordained, and neither I nor any one living can oppose its will, be it as Heaven and you desire, señor. I take the same power to witness with what bashfulness I consent to your wishes, not because I am unconscious of what I gain by complying with them, but because I fear that when I am yours you will regard me with other eyes than those with which hitherto perhaps you have mistakingly beheld me. But be it as it may, to be the lawful wife of Don Rafael de Villavicencio is an honour I cannot lose, and with that alone I shall live contented. But if my conduct after I am your wife give me any claim to your esteem, I will thank Heaven for having brought me through such strange circumstances and such great misfortunes to the happiness of being yours. Give me your hand, Don Rafael, and take mine in exchange; and, as you say, let the witnesses of our mutual engagement be the sky, the sea, the sands, and this silence, interrupted only by my sighs and your entreaties."

So saying, she permitted Don Rafael to embrace her, and taking each other's hand they solemnised their betrothal with a few tears drawn from their eyes by the excess of joy succeeding to their past sorrows. They immediately returned to the knight's house, where their absence had occasioned great anxiety, and where the nuptials of Marco Antonio and Teodosia had already been celebrated by a priest, at the instance of Teodosia, who dreaded lest any untoward chance should rob her of her new-found hopes. The appearance of Don Rafael and Leocadia, and the account given by the former of what had passed between them, augmented the general joy, and the master of the house rejoiced as if they were his own near relations; for it is an innate characteristic of the Catalonian gentry to feel and act as friends towards such strangers as have any need of their services.

The priest, who was still present, desired that Leocadia should change her dress for one appropriate to her sex, and the knight at once supplied both the ladies with handsome apparel from the wardrobe of his wife, who was a lady of the ancient house of the Granolliques, famous in that kingdom. The surgeon was moved by charity to complain that the wounded man talked so much and was not left alone; but it pleased God that Marco Antonio's joy, and the little silence he observed, were the very means of his amendment, so that when they came to dress his wound next day, they found him out of danger, and in a fortnight more he was fit to travel. During the time he kept his bed he had made a vow that if he recovered he would go on a pilgrimage on foot to Santiago de Galicia, and in the fulfilment of that vow

185

he was accompanied by Don Rafael, Leocadia, Teodosia, and even by the muleteer Calvete, unusual as such pious practices are with men of his calling; but he had found Don Rafael so liberal and good-humoured that he would not quit him till he had returned home. The party having to travel on foot as pilgrims, the mules were sent on to Salamanca.

The day fixed for their departure arrived, and equipped in their dalmaticas and with all things requisite, they took leave of their generous and hospitable friend, the knight Don Sancho de Cardona, a man of most illustrious blood and personally famous; and they pledged themselves that they and their descendants, to whom they should bequeath it as a duty, should perpetually preserve the memory of the singular favours received from him, in order that they might not be wanting at least in grateful feeling, if they could not repay them in any other way. Don Sancho embraced them all, and said it was a matter of course with him to render such services or others to all whom he knew or supposed to be Castilian hidalgos. They repeated their embraces twice, and departed with gladness, mingled with some sorrow. Travelling by easy stages to suit the strength of the lady pilgrims, they reached Monserrate in three days, remained as many more there, fulfilling their duties as good Catholic Christians, and resuming their journey, arrived without accident at Santiago, where they accomplished their vows with all possible devotion. They determined not to quit their pilgrim garbs until they reached their homes. After travelling towards them leisurely, they came at last to a rising ground whence Leocadia and Teodosia looked down upon their respective birth-places, nor could they restrain their tears at the glad sight which brought back to their recollection all their past vicissitudes.

From the same spot they discovered a broad valley, which divided the two townships, and in it they saw under the shades of an olive a stalwart knight, mounted on a powerful charger, armed with a strong keen lance and a dazzlingly white shield. Presently they saw issuing from among some olive trees two other knights similarly armed, and of no less gallant appearance. These two rode up to the first, and after remaining awhile together they separated. The first knight and one of the two others set spurs to their horses, and charging each other like mortal enemies, began mutually to deal such vigorous thrusts, and to avoid or parry them with such dexterity, that it was plain they were masters in that exercise. The third knight remained a spectator of the fight without quitting his place. Don Rafael, who could not be content with a distant view of the gallant conflict, hurried down the hill, followed by the other three, and came up close to the two champions just as they had both been slightly wounded. The helmet of one of them had fallen off, and as he turned his face towards Don Rafael, the latter recognised his father, and Marco Antonio knew that the other was his own, whilst Leocadia discovered hers in the third knight who had not fought. Astounded at this spectacle, the two brothers instantly rushed between the champions, crying out "Stop, cavaliers! Stop! We who call on you to do so are your own sons! Father, I am Marco Antonio, for whose sake, as I guess, your honoured life is put to this peril. Allay your anger; cast away your weapons, or turn them against another enemy; for the one before you must henceforth be your brother."

The two knights instantly stopped; and looking round they observed that Don Sancho had dismounted and was embracing his daughter, who briefly narrated to him the occurrences at Barcelona. Don Sancho was proceeding to make peace between the combatants, but there was no need of that, for he found them already dismounted and embracing their sons with tears of joy. There now appeared at the entrance of the valley a great number of armed men on foot and on horseback: these were the vassals of the three knights, who had come to support the cause of their respective lords; but when they saw them embracing the pilgrims they halted, and knew not what to think until Don Sancho briefly recounted to them what he had learned from his daughter. The joy of all was unbounded. Five of the vassals immediately mounted the pilgrims on their own horses, and the whole party set out for the house of Marco Antonio's father, where it was arranged that the two weddings should be celebrated. On the way Don Rafael and Marco Antonio learned that the cause of the quarrel which had been so happily ended was a challenge sent to the father of the latter by the fathers of Teodosia and Leocadia, under the belief that he had been privy to the acts of seduction committed by his son. The two challengers having found him alone would not take any advantage of him, but agreed to fight him one after the other, like brave and generous knights. The combat, nevertheless, must have ended in the death of one or all of them but for the timely arrival of their children, who gave thanks to God for so happy a termination of the dispute.

The day after the arrival of the pilgrims, Marco Antonio's father celebrated the marriages of his son and Teodosia, Don Rafael and Leocadia, with extraordinary magnificence. The two wedded pairs lived long and happily together, leaving an illustrious progeny which still exists in their two towns, which are among the best in Andalusia. Their names, however, we suppress, in deference to the two ladies, whom malicious or prudish tongues might reproach with levity of conduct. But I would beg of all such to forbear their sentence, until they have examined themselves and seen whether they too have not been assailed some time or other by what are called the arrows of Cupid, weapons whose force is truly irresistible. Calvete was made happy with the gift of the mule which Don Rafael had left at Salamanca, and with many other presents; and the poets of the time took occasion to employ their pens in celebrating the beauty and the adventures of the two damsels, as bold as they were virtuous, the heroines of this strange story.

LONDON: PRINTED BY WILLIAM CLOWES AND SONS, LIMITED, STAMFORD STREET AND CHARING CROSS.

Made in United States
North Haven, CT
05 October 2024

58368105R00114